More Dreams
To Come

Max

More Dreams To Come

The unsaid part of me...

Max

Manish Pawar

PARTRIDGE

ISBN: Hardcover   978-1-4828-1150-6
             Softcover   978-1-4828-1151-3
             eBook   978-1-4828-1149-0

Print information available on the last page.

To order additional copies of this book, contact
Partridge India
000 800 10062 62
orders.india@partridgepublishing.com

www.partridgepublishing.com/india

Contents

DEDICATED TO

That sweet Bengali girl,
who, once happened to be a part of my life.
What I am today, it's all thanks to you.
To my Parents.
Someday you will be proud of me.
And the every other person,
who believed in me and to those who thought,
Manish could do nothing in life.

Acknowledgements

I always thought that someday I will write something. But, yes if it was not for these people I would have never been able to finish writing for maybe another, only God knows how many years. It was only because of these very few special crazy people around me that I continued to write even when I wanted to give up.

They aren't very intelligent or super-duper cool nerdy fellows. But yes they did help me at every point of time to make this book a descent readable material even without having read the actual manuscript. They never knew that I always took their silliest comments as a way to improve myself better.

So to begin with it was Reshmi, one of my sweetest friends, whom I miss a lot always. Well, the first person to read those very first few pages until I knew the word for it was manuscript. Her eyes were filled with tears and wanted me to write it from my heart. I have tried my best Reshmi.

The next were my so called editors Anuja, Aditi and Harshad. Their way of helping me edit the book, gave me a completely new direction and approach towards the book. Anupama, who had always been a great support at the times I needed one. While reading each chapter of the book she always made sure I stick to the storyline and not get carried away in my thoughts. Akshay who helped me correct my grammar so did Aasawari.

My college friends Abhishek, Harish, Rahul and all the others who were equally shocked about the book, well let me tell you we guys always rock the unplanned trips every year. Few of my guitar class friends Anand, Anup, Sameer, Prasad, Akshada and all the others were also the one who always gave some surprised expressions. I promise you would enjoy reading.

Rahul and Ritesh who were constantly behind me to finish writing, the wait is over guys. Maybe, I could get some more time (Just kidding.) If it was not for you two guys I would have almost given up many times. Thanks for never letting down my spirit. Not to forget my sister Poonam, the one who is always there for me.

My friends whom I should not forget to mention Parag, Namrata, Paresh, Pooja, Casmel and Naresh. I just enjoy to the fullest when you guys are around. Parag I hope everyone likes the cover page just like I did. Apart from this, if there are any names that I have missed would be, only because you guys know I forget things. You guys are still equally important. But before going any further let me not forget Praveen who helped me get connected with the publisher 'Partridge Publishing India'. My publisher, who has been very patient and has given me ample amount of time to complete the manuscript and a special thanks to Kathy, I am sorry I took a lot of your time. And yes, Sarthak Sharma my Facebook friend I owe you a special thanks too.

With this I hope you all would love my first novel and enjoy it a lot. Happy Reading!!!

Dear Radhika

'When I was Alone…
I thought
I need someone whom I could see forever.
I need someone who would believe in me.
Whom I would admire in my thoughts.
Who would be my Real Best friend…
I need someone who will be with me Forever…
Who would drive me crazy
And make me smile and giggle…
I wanted someone who would hold my hand in her's and walk along.
Could look into my eyes with lots of love…
Someone who would never leave when we both are holding each other closely.
Who just kisses me and takes my breath away.
And then, like a princess…
You came across one day in my world that changed everything.
I was happy, I was thrilled as my wishes were fulfilled
I wanted to propose you in a manner that you could feel
Like an Angel getting married…
I wanted to grow old with you.
But I woke up…
As my dream collapses,
And reality strikes… nobody's there…
But I really wanted that Love, back one day…"
"So now, I know what's best for me.
And that's to get over you, even though I can't.
My life still lingers over every drop of love you ever gave me.
Even though I may not have always felt that love,
I knew it was still there, and like a fool,
I let go off the thing so special to me, something I never knew I needed.
I had you then…
But, if this is love, I'll fall for it again…
Radhika…

                                        Love Dhruv.

Prologue

'EYEON FUSION' the final software, could end my 3D Animation course in MAAC, provided I attend lectures regularly. Well, terms and conditions always applied in my case, as everything around me had changed. No more mobile messages during the lectures, nobody to miss me, no more surprise kisses to wake me up, nobody to say you're the best, nobody left around to say you're not alone.

Life is sometimes so strange... I had the entire world around me, but when left alone, why was it so difficult to win it back...? These thoughts bugged my mind during the lecture. I had to concentrate, as this software could help me in my demo-reel. I jotted down everything in my notes, the things shown on the projector screen, but failed to understand the concepts. Things were never difficult for me, but I just couldn't make them simpler.

"Come-on Dhruv...! Don't be a bore and concentrate on what's being taught. Within the next few minutes everybody will know you had a terrible heart-break, with, wow! . . . . Should I take her name?" My mind started again.
"Oh! No need to take her name and please let me concentrate." I replied.
"Oh! Yes sure, concentrate dude, I guess he's waiting to ask you the next question."

Well that gesture was right. The talk within me vanished, as sir fired the next question upon me.
"Dhruv...!" He said as I looked towards him. "What is your specialization?"
"Character Animation... Sir!" I replied and prepared myself for the further questions.
"So Dhruv you must have animated a ball in the previous 3D software. Right?"
"Yes. I did... Sir."
"Help us animate this ball in FUSION." he said waiting for my reply.
I looked in my book, then at the screen as everybody seemed quiet. I made an attempt to answer which turned out to be perfect. Later, I stayed more alert and ignored my thoughts. The lecture got over by 11 o'clock. On my way downstairs I could hear every single wicked comment about him as nobody liked him.
"Will this happen to me too? Will I be able to teach properly?"
This thought struck my mind as I was the newly appointed faculty in NIIT.

Reaching there, I met the counselor in NIIT who always carried a smile on her face and had also helped me get this job.

"So Dhruv how does it feel? Everybody would call you SIR." she said.

"It's nice, let's see how it turns out to be. My brother is all set to call me 'MASTER-JEE'... A for Apple B for Ball." I said while she smiled.

"Your brother is crazy, but you seemed confident maybe that's how you got this job, you'll do well." She said and tried to boost up my low confidence. It was strange, people who hardly knew me believed in me than the people who have actually known me for years.

The Center Head came within an hour and informed me to take my first batch; she assured that she would put me through the faculty training the next week. My first lecture was at 7.00pm. I had entire day to prepare myself. I had to get rid of my fear, be confident, to give my best.

Dhruv! Best of Luck. Believe in yourself. Everything will be fine. And the most important thing, don't be afraid of anything or else you would mess up." I said to myself as I didn't want to lose.

The students arrived at 7 sharp; the center head came to me and said, "Dhruv, you have to impress these students as you would be teaching them for the next two years."

"Ok and how would I do that?" I replied a bit nervous and confused.

"It's simple! Be friendly, get to know them more and if you do well, I'll give you another batch tomorrow. And, I don't think you need any training, you seem confident."

That sounded weird but I had to do this. People around believed in me and I couldn't let them down. *"You have to do this Dhruv,"* I said to myself and went inside the classroom.

A bit of nervousness still lingered around me which disappeared as I began. Somehow, I managed to overcome my fear by asking few questions. Later, I taught the concepts precisely feeling as if I was a master in it and around 8.45pm called the day off.

Here I learnt the most important lesson which life had to offer me, *'Never let the person in front know that you are afraid in any situation. Be calm and confident.'*

On my way back home, my eyes got wet. I wanted to share my happiness with her. I missed her and was doing this for her. She was the one who had changed my life and whom I respected the most. It was her with whom I had gathered those beautiful moments and dreamt of spending my whole life with her. I truly loved Radhika, but today it was me, alone. I kept the thoughts aside and wiped off the tears as I reached home.

I went to bring candles from the grocery shop as there was a power cut in our area. On my way towards shop I wanted to narrate my first day experience to Radhika. I thought of calling her, instead called up a friend, he didn't pick up so it was Parth on the list. It was totally unbelievable how he made fun of my emotions by his wicked laughter. Finally I called up my sister who cleared up everything for me.

"What was so funny, if I say Radhika would have been very happy today and would have felt proud for me?" I asked her.
She waited for a second and said, "Dhruv I know how you feel but, if you behave like this, it will turn back to you. People will laugh and make fun. But keep in mind this is just the beginning."

*****

Part - 1

Dreams and Memories...

Chapter 1

The Beginning...

17th April 2007, the last day of my graduation exams. I was out of college, free from studies with new aims for the future. Well, let me first introduce myself to you. I am Dhruv. Dhruv Deshmukh, a person who dreams a lot. Yes, DREAMS that's the word, which can tell a lot about me. I wasn't a studious guy, but, I'd known the importance of my life and my dreams. I was an average guy and the very first image which is formed in your mind about me is not me. Try to create some more images.

I had lost two precious years in completing my graduation in BCS (Bachelor of Computer Science). So, I had decided something else than becoming a Software Engineer, thanks to all my college friends. One day when we were in the college canteen frustrated with BCS, someone came up with an idea of starting up a tea stall. The idea got us into a serious yet funny discussion that we started calculating the income we could make if this idea works. Strange! Isn't it? But yes, I had such friends in college with such amazing ideas. That moment, I thought about it but, I wanted something different. I knew BCS was tough for me, so I decided to choose animation and become an ANIMATOR. How would I make it? I had no clue.

Ours was a group of 10-15 guys. Girls were never invited; rather we never felt we need the company of any girl when we were together. College life was fun, bunking lectures and watching movies; every Friday was always enjoyable, where we would make fun of the couples seated in the corner seats of the movie hall. Sometimes, unplanned short trips would always be successful than those planned ones. Everyone was treated equally and teasing each other was always fun.

During exams we would gather for group studies and help each other as we would never miss our private coaching classes. So it wasn't like we always had fun, we were serious about our studies. Likewise, we also had some strange names for all our professors like 'Yeda Anna', 'I Robot' and some girls were also baptized by with some weird names. During Electronics practical if a circuit board was screwed, the blame would always be on the next person. So when caught by the professors we always had one or the other excuse. The best part was my innocent face and my favorite line 'I AM INNOCENT' would always keep me away from trouble.

But, the enjoyment couldn't last for long as I flunked in the first year due to continuous illness during exams. I had to struggle a lot, but thanks, to those wonderful friends I was never treated as a mediocre because of my failure. Things were still the same for me but, maybe, my life was planned in a different manner. I had to take a break from studies for another year due to some financial problems at home which unfortunately kept me away from completing the graduation for another year.

Somehow, I managed to overcome everything and here I was out of the college campus with a smile on my face. I didn't worry about the result much as I knew whatever the result would be my decision was firm, work in a BPO for some days and study animation simultaneously. I knew life had been tough. Although, I had always tried to struggle with a smile, never letting anybody know what I was going through.

The entire college life had flashed in front of my eyes as I walked down the streets, with a hope that everything will change and I will live an awesome life ahead. I called up a friend, who had arranged an interview for me while I was about to reach home. She asked me to reach her office as soon as possible. The interview was for the position of a Technical Support Officer for Microsoft part of Convergys BPO. I was sure that the previous work experience would certainly help me. As I reached the office, my friend asked me to brush up for the interview using the notes she handed over to me. After a long wait, the HR arrived and the interview began. Clearing the technical round I met the HR for the personal interview. Luckily I cleared it and was asked to reach their office the next day for the final round with the Operations Manager.

I came home with the new hope that if I clear the final round I might get this job and things would be simpler. I informed everybody and as usual mom was busy cooking food. My elder sister Diya was helping her. Krish my younger brother was out with his friends and my dad was busy watching television. Well, this was the daily routine of my family.

My mom is one of those typical mothers who scolded their children but loved them a lot. Many said I look like her and maybe that's why I'm so handsome you know (Just kidding). Mom worked in a marketing firm as well as ran a household mess where we had many pretty girls coming home from the hostel in the next lane. My father was approaching his sixties and was retired from bank; he looked more like the famous film-star Mr. Amitabh Bachhan in his young age. Well, I had two other uncles who resembled some famous personalities. About them, maybe some time later. People were always confused about me and Krish; they often consider us as twins. Well, he had looks similar to my father so was his nature. He was always considered to be elder and also more matured than me. And I had no clue why people thought that way. Diya was close to me and was always considered as the most decent girl of our family. But, these days she lived a life as if she was nobody in our family.

My house was located in the heart of Pune which made possible for me to be at any place within few minutes. My grandfather bought this house for 1000bucks during his young age and I loved it a lot. We were on the first floor whereas, my two other uncle stayed on the ground floor.

I got fresh and was up with my favorite computer game Max Payne. I was crazy for this game and always loved myself to be called as Max. Mom, even though was busy with her work never missed a chance to shout her lungs out whenever the volume increased on my computer.
"Dhruv, switch off the computer and stop playing games". That was all; I loved my family no matter how weird it was.

Next day, I woke-up a bit late with a fresh state of mind for the final round. I had to reach the office in Aundh by noon, so I took my time to get ready. While leaving home Diya wished me luck and I guess, she was the only person to do so. I shared a strong bond with her as she knew exactly what was going in my mind and I had no idea how she would do that.

The HR was waiting for me and as I reached the office he said the most astonishing thing.
"Hi Dhruv, how are you?"
"I am fine."
"So all set for the final round?"
"I guess so, do I have any option?"
"Well, not exactly, but Dhruv we have a small problem here."
Small problem always mean, you are in big trouble. I was right as he continued without a pause.

"The test you gave yesterday, somehow the paper got misplaced and we are not able to find it. So maybe you would have to give that test again".

I was surprised as he continued, "Dhruv, you would also have to clear the voice and accent round. Well, we never conducted it yesterday and then the telephonic round and finally the Operations Manager. The test would be easy, you already know the answers. We have discussed yesterday. Right?"

At that moment all I felt was I was stuck in a same kind of situation the one Saif was stuck in the movie-Dil Chahta Hai.

Haa mein Magar woh...

Suno toh

as before I could say anything he handed over the test papers to me.

I grabbed a chair feeling I was back in the examination hall of BCS, struggling for answers, thinking was this the single round of interview? Soon, I started biting my nails to recall the answers. And to my surprise I was able to recall everything and was successful to clear up every round without any snags. After that, few of us were asked to wait for the final round when I met a guy from Bangalore. His tall dark feature half-sleeves, properly tuck-in formals and specks of course explained a lot about him, his formal and confident attitude. His Mallu accent could let everyone know he was from South, Bangalore to be specific.

"You seem to be nervous." He guessed.

"Ah…Yes a little bit."

"Well don't be. He won't eat you, just be confident and look directly into his eyes while answering his questions as he would ask normal stuff about computers". He said and tried to encourage me. It helped me a lot and I gave my best. After sometime the HR came along with the offer letter.

"Congratulations Dhruv, YOU'VE BEEN SELECTED AS A TECHNICAL SUPPORT OFFICER. Come with me so that we could discuss the package you would receive." The HR person asked me to follow her.

"Kya baat hai Dhruv, so finally you are selected." I started my self-conversation again.

"I know…! Ab meri personality hi aisi hai that people select me immediately".

The thoughts continued with a smile while the HR explained me the details in the Offer-Letter. I thanked this guy who helped me overcome my fear and build up that confidence, at the last moment. I came home happily and informed everyone about this. I knew today nobody would stop me if I played Max Payne.

'Sometimes a job changes everything, most important, the perception of how people look at you…'

I informed all my college friends and later met Natasha my childhood friend and also my neighbor. She was special in her own unique way, as I loved the way she would stammer while talking. Apart from this her curly hair was her best feature. I always considered her my best friend.

She was very happy for my achievement and said, "I am proud of you Dhruv. Work hard and fulfill your goal and prove your mother wrong about the thing she once said to me".
"I will definitely". I replied.

My mother had once shown her uncertainty towards my success. That day I decided that I will make my parents feel proud about me. After talking with Natasha I came home and started playing Max Payne. During every move in the game I had a smile and a thought which did say I have got the key to fulfill my dreams but still a long way to go.

*****

Chapter 2

Microsoft, Animation and me...

I reached office the next day, to submit the required documents and complete the joining formalities. I met the guys who were selected along with me. A formal Hi-Hello was lined-up with a smile on my face. We were asked to be seated in one of the training rooms. I grabbed a chair for myself and later my eyes rolled in all the corners of the room to see who all were recruited. It clogged at this skinny guy named Ashwin who had a whitish complexion and pretty long hair that could cover his entire face. Very soon, the HR person walked in to collect our documents. This process didn't take much of the time and I was back home by afternoon. A strange but wicked truth made me rush home immediately to get the missing document.

"Your salary won't be credited in your account this month", was the statement made by one of the HR. I submitted the document before evening and completed the joining formalities. The joining date was next week so it was me again with my favorite computer game. Evenings I would be along with my childhood friends Vishal or Natasha when the hostel girls would be at home for dinner.

Within a flash the weekend was over and I was ready to go to office. The new job gave me a feel that an adventure had just begun. I knew this job would definitely make my life awesome. New dreams started to rise with new desires to fulfill. I planned many things, like never letting myself down for anything, enjoy life to the fullest and do everything that I always dreamt of, all my life long.

On the first day we were briefed about the Company and its policies, some rules to follow, the transport facilities that would be provided at our door-step sounded great. By the end of the day we got our salary accounts opened. I made many new friends in a few days- to begin with Ashwin, the skinny guy whom we nicknamed Chinki, Niraj, who was a mimicry artist, a great observer and an amazing person at heart. Just given him 10 minutes to observe your mannerisms and he would do a perfect impersonation of you. Not to forget Amar-the guy who helped me during the interview and Ranveer who was very well known as Major as he was an ex NDA cadet. Due to some leg injury he had to quit NDA and here he was with us. The next best thing to happen for me was the perfect trio, Ashwin, Niraj and me who loved to crack all-time hit dialogues of the movie 'Andaz Apna' throughout the training. We had a training period of two months, during our breaks Ashwin would be in the smoking zone with Amar whereas, Niraj and I would be in the Cafeteria standing in front of the vendor staring at the eatables and our discussion would begin.

"Niraj let's try something new. How about the chocolate-pie?" I'd say.

Immediately he would ask the vendor. The vendor would disclose the price and soon we would ask about the other eatables and the vendor would tell us the prices one after another and we would buy a "Dairy Milk Fruit n Nut' instead. Also, being late after a break during the training sessions one had to either dance, sing or get chocolates for the entire batch. So office was fun during the training sessions. I was enjoying my life at home as well, when my first salary doubled the excitement. It did create a cheerful environment at home.

Days passed with my fixed schedule, week-days were in office and weekends for movies with office friends or at times with family which included Krish, Diya and my other cousins Sana, Shivam and Pal. Krish had joined the Frankfinn institute to build up his career in the field of aviation. On the other hand, I was looking for good animation institutes when I found one. The counselor gave me a brief idea about animation. All I knew about it was that we have to draw cartoons and then animate them, but it was lot more than that. Animation was tough it needed patience and talent which I knew I had in me. I continued to search some more institutes. I wanted an institute which was the best and which won't affect my work timings. So by the time I could find one another month had passed. I got happy as I had received a decent amount of 12K. I gave 500 to Krish and Diya each and kept around 1000bucks for me. Rest I handed over to mom and as usual she gave it to Krish to pay his fees. Even though I did not like her decision much I never expressed it. Apart from this, I loved the happiness on mom's face when I contributed my salary every month at home. Also everyone in the house was happy considering the fact that I took responsibilities such as paying the monthly cable and newspaper bills. I got a new landline telephone and internet connection for the computer. I gave Krish the add-on credit card which came along the credit card offered by a bank. I made sure everyone's needs were fulfilled and they would never complaint about me being irresponsible. Moreover, I wanted to keep myself down to earth and not be carried away by the amount I would earn. About Krish, I felt that he was going for a course which had no future. But, the best part according to me was, 16girls in a batch of 20 students. Now that's what I call lucky Krish…! So the credit card and pocket money given to him was for this very same reason.

Watching movies on weekends became my passion and one such day I would never forget, 2nd June 2007. Krish, Pal, Diya and I had gone to watch 'Pirates of The Caribbean-3' which was an early morning show and was marvelous. Later, my colleague Ram called up for the same movie, which I couldn't refuse and enjoyed watching it again. In the later evening, I went along with Vishal to withdraw money from the ATM. There I saw a hoarding: 'MAAC (Maya Academy of Advanced Cinematics)'.

"Come let's go and find out what it's about." I said instantly, dragging him in the institute. As I entered the campus, I was thrilled and more excited by the pleasant environment. I found Asifa sitting in the counselor's cabin.

"Hey Asifa! How come you are here? I guess I had seen you in some institute. Remember, you had asked me to draw that cartoon character?" I said.

"Yes, I remember you and it's good to see you". She replied with a smile. She then explained me about the courses offered in MAAC. She showed me the campus when my eyes were stuck on a frame which had a cartoon image along with something written, which I began to read.

WHAT IS ANIMATION?
If You Have Ambition
Tickle Your Mind into Imagination
Come Out With A New Creation
Turn It Into Animation
Soar High And Reach The Destination
MAAC Helps You To Get A Unique Recognition.

It was inspiring. She showed us the Auditorium where some students were watching a movie. She had some good reasons to join MAAC and also persuaded me to get admitted. I had withdrawn 5000Rs so I thought for a while and then got myself registered.

A bit confused but still happy about the admission I came home, after withdrawing the entire 7000 from my account. I gave the money to mom and told her about my admission. She gave me a bizarre look but didn't say anything more as the hostel girls were already at home for dinner.

I went to share my excitement with Natasha but an unusual thing happened.

"Dhruv, what is going in your mind?" She asked.

"Nothing. Why? Anything serious?" I replied.

"Let me make you one thing very clear, I am observing this from many days so today I thought I should tell you." I couldn't understand her gestures until she said it.

"Dhruv, I have a boyfriend and I don't like the way you always keep loitering around me."

I was stunned for a moment! Her words hurt me a lot but as usual I smiled and said, "Wow Natasha you never told me."

"I won't tell you his name coz I don't trust you. And I want you to stop bothering me. I am happy that you found a path for yourself now focus on it." Her words were hurting me like a weapon pierced into a body. But, still I just tried to stay calm and replied.

"Are you crazy Nats, you are a good friend of mine I never thought about you in that way and if you feel I am creating problems in your life I would stay away."

I couldn't wait any longer still I stood with a smiley face. I decided not to snivel when I started walking back home. Everything seemed to be changed within a moment. The entire day of enjoyment had disappeared with the humiliation that crept upon me. What did I do wrong? I asked myself again and again. I found myself lost even while I tried to engage my mind in the computer games. It didn't help as her thoughts made me think more. She meant a lot to me and I never expected this to happen. After dinner, I was about to sleep when dad called me. Diya, Krish and mom were also present in the room.

"Dhruv you paid 5000Rs for that course of yours, did you consult your mom or anybody in the family?" he asked me.

"No" I replied immediately and continued, "I wanted to learn animation, I found this institute worth so I paid the fees." I said as was still struggling with the thoughts about Natasha.

"But do you know the consequences of it?"

"What would happen?" I tried to focus on what he was about to say.

"How can we manage Krish's fees? You just gave 7000 to your mom; do you think it can be possible to manage everything in that? And can't you wait till his course gets over? He would get a job and then you can start your career." He sounded a bit eerie to me.

"I can't wait for a year till he finishes his course and then start mine. I have already lost 2 years." I wanted to say this and be sturdy with my objection towards his statement but, I kept quiet.

"How will you manage it with your job?" He asked and I couldn't say anything as the mixed thoughts in my mind broke me into tears.

"What happened to you Dhruv? He is not shouting on you, he is just asking you." Mom added.

I wiped my tears and left the room. I got into my bed and pulled the blanket over my head not letting anybody know how I felt when my family didn't have faith in me. What was this all about? I find a class I had been searching past two months. My father expects me to pay Krish's class fees instead of thinking about my career. It makes no bloody sense. How could I wait for a year till his course is over, and then think about mine? Whereas Natasha, supposed to be my best friend ended up saying something I never expected. Maybe I was expecting too much from everyone. I didn't know how to tackle this situation, whether I should wait for another year or stand firm on my decision. People don't trust me, my father doubts me, rather being happy for me. Somehow these thoughts couldn't stop the rolling tear drops. I wanted a way out of this absurd situation as the thoughts weren't helping me, so all I thought at that moment was joining my hands and pray to GOD. I was still finding it difficult as what should I pray. I wanted God to be with me even if nobody trusts me and believes me. I asked him be with me, guide me throughout the path of success or maybe send someone who would believe in me and be there for me.

*****

Chapter 3

Riya and the Change...

Next day being Sunday, there were no plans. I just wanted to stay away from dad as I didn't want the same stuff again. It wasn't difficult as I got myself busy in the computer. Diya came in and asked me,

"Why did you cry Dhruv?" I stopped my work and stared at her as she continued, "Do you feel that people don't believe in you?"

"Is there any logic behind whatever he said? It's like wait, let Krish setup his career; if he is successful then you can start yours. Wow! I feel like a fool." I voice raised unknowingly as nobody was in the room except us.

"I know Dhruv how you feel. Now that you've already paid the money study hard. I am with you, even though I may not be of great help to you, I'll try to convince mom and let her know about this."

"Forget it, I'll go to MAAC tomorrow and will tell them I can't join right now. Maybe, I don't deserve to live my dreams."

"Are you crazy Dhruv, don't even think that way. I am with you, just think how you would collect the first installment fees for your course and study hard." Whatever she said had a point, it made me feel strong and maybe she was right. If I had made the decision I should stick to it.

In office, on the last day of our training we were informed about a process party at Soho's, my first party in a pub of Pune. I was ecstatic about the party and wanted to have fun. Free beer, loud music, some awards to be distributed gave a real unique feel to me. Maybe, BPO's work in this way, and I knew we would receive such awards in the days to come ahead. It was a great experience for me and my team-mates, as we all got to know many people who were the top performers on the floor.

For every BPO, the parameters of an employee's performance are AHT (Average Hold Time) on a call, which is nothing but the total amount to time taken to resolve a particular query of the customer over the phone. CSR (Customer Satisfaction Ratio) - how an agent is rated by the customers for the experience they had over the call. A performance chart is prepared for every employee as well as the team for a particular month based upon these parameters.

Within a week's time we all were ready for these parameters and gave a rocking performance on the floor. It made everyone proud and the floor became livelier due to this. We had another party to enjoy, the annual party of Convergys. I knew we would enjoy it as we were keen to know the new team-mates who would be joining our team. The dress-code for the party was RED & BLACK. Black was fine but RED, the color I would never buy, except for this theme party.

We had some great performances by many employees. Gaurav Shekhawat, our Operations Manager sung awesome and had set the stage on fire along with his friends and their band. Later, when we were on the dance floor, Amar pointed out to a girl dancing right next to us- our new team member. I was stunned by her beauty and on every move she made on the dance numbers. I would glance at her once a while. She was wearing a red and white stripes T-shirt and carbon black jeans. My eyes couldn't make a move away from her graceful step and the best feature was her curly hair.
"Is she really joining our team?" I asked him to confirm.
"Let's see I have heard there are two girls named Riya. She is one of them." He replied with a smile. That very moment I wished she's the one to join the team. I couldn't hide my excitement about this girl.

But some things are really strange, we moved away from the dance floor and I didn't recall looking at her again. Next day we were introduced to the new team and yes my wish was fulfilled as I saw Riya. She looked different than what she did in the party although I liked her formal attire. I continued to stare at her and I was sure everybody was fully aware of my behavior. In the beginning, we had some conflicts with the new members in our team; still I managed to get close to her. Things began to change; I got a new friend and was happy to be with her. Riya was friendly with everyone and I got to know her better through the messenger chats. She would share a lot of her secrets with me as she did with her best friend Abhi. Abhi had joined our team along with Riya; I hated him as his presence would make me feel ignored.

Well a movie always helps in such case, I convinced Riya to come along to watch 'Harry Potter and Order of Phoenix'. So it was Riya, Abhi, Amar and me for the movie. After the movie was over Abhi left immediately and it gave me a chance to know her better. Soon we exchanged our phone numbers and within few days our interaction with each other increased through frequent messages. Riya used to message me and we would often talk about our daily routine outside office. We began spending time with each other in coffee shops after office. I began to like her company. One day I expressed my feelings towards her. We were seated in the corner table while listening to the beats of the soft music. I looked towards her and smiled. She smiled back and then few minutes later I told her everything. That was the very first time I was trying to express my feelings to a girl. She wasn't surprised as she knew it was going to come up someday from me. She took everything in a friendly manner and shared her true feelings about me. She liked me as a friend and the way she expressed her feeling about me changed my approach towards her and I began to respect her a lot, she thus became my best friend. She had changed my approach towards life and maybe my lost smile was back again due to her.

31st July 2007 that year, I was eager to celebrate my birthday with the new friends. I had to get ready for the graveyard shift from 1.30am to 10.30am in the morning. All my office friends and team-mates waited for this day since they came to know just for the simple reason...Birthday Bumps! As I reached office I was greeted by everyone, after which they lifted me and started kicking one-after another on my ass. Well, let me tell you it hurts a lot even if you are wearing the thickest jeans of the world. That day, I cursed all the shoe manufacturers, as I was not able to sit properly the entire day.

Well there was another round, as Amar had missed the chance to hit me. So, I was lifted again in the smoking zone for few more kicks after the shift was over. Well, no matter how hard everybody kicked the smile and laughter that stayed on everyone's face mattered a lot to me. I could never forget the free kicks in the cafeteria and the smoking zone. Most important Riya's face continuously saying, "Guys it's enough, don't hit him so hard." Later she showed her concern asking "Are you Ok Dhruv?"

When I reached home everyone wished me in my family. I went off to bed and in the evening I was waiting for my relatives to come as mom had prepared my favorite Gulab-Jamun and Pav-Bhaji. But strange things are lined up when we least expect them to happen. My relatives came home around 7 in the evening. I was busy on my computer when my aunt called me downstairs. "Happy Birthday Dhruv." She said.
"Thanks." I replied as I sensed something was wrong.
"We are leaving can't come later, as your father said. It will be late and what will we do till 9pm." She said.

Well, my father had asked them to come after 9pm. Wow! That was strange but he did say so. A girl named Kavita was going back home and today was a kind of farewell to her, the Pav-Bhaji and stuff was planned for her and not me. I was speechless.

"Dhruv we'll celebrate your birthday sometime later, come home when you get your weekly off." She said.

"Ok!" I replied with a frown and came upstairs in anger and yelled on mom, "I had told you not to call those girls today then, why the hell you called them?"

"I told your father but he never listens, you know him. Anyways once everyone leaves we will celebrate your birthday", she said.

I got angry with her reply. Diya's eyes had an expression which said she could do nothing. The anger drove me crazy. Later, I could not believe myself, the way my father was happily chit-chatting with this girl with stupid talks like so what is your future plan?

Ask me I will answer to it. I want to kill her. I said to myself and ignored whatever she had replied. This girl was always the first one to be at home for dinner and I hated her more today. She was that one girl I never liked but had to bare her till the time she was enjoying her dinner and the free entertainment watching me crash many cars, on my PC. I tried to call Riya but she was sleeping and all my college friends were busy in their own world so I was left alone on my birthday to bare the nonsensical talk between the two, my father and her. I tried to convince myself and avoided all the weird thoughts running in my mind. The other girls were coming upstairs and their loud voices pissed me off. I turned off the computer and went off to sleep in the other room when my phone started ringing, it was Natasha.

"Now why the hell is she calling? I am not interested to talk with her." I said to myself but still picked up the phone.

"Hello!!" I said in a dull voice.

"Hi Dhruv… Happy Birthday!!!" She said.

"Thanks Natasha." I replied.

"Why are you sounding so dull?"

"I have a headache and am trying to sleep."

"Is everything normal Dhruv?" She guessed nothing was normal within a second

"Yes it is Natasha, now can I sleep?"

"Dhruv come to my place I want to meet you."

"Sorry I am not coming, please let me sleep."

"Ok fine! I am coming at your place. Come down." Before, I could say anything she hung up.

"What the hell? Why can't she leave me alone? It's all because I picked up her phone. I don't want to see her face."

I said and tried to sleep when Diya woke me up and said, "Dhruv, Natasha is standing downstairs go and meet her." So, with all the frustration within me I tried to smile and went downstairs to meet Natasha.

"Happy Birthday Dhruv. She said and we shook hands. "You are looking handsome today and it's a really nice shirt."

"Thanks Natasha I am glad you noticed it." I said.

"Ok, I knew something was wrong. Now, can you tell me?" She knew me from childhood. I tried hard to refrain from telling her as she was the one who didn't trust me. But then, I ended up saying everything that happened.

"Dhruv, I am sorry for whatever I said that day I know I was wrong, I shouldn't have said those things to you. I guess maybe that's the reason you were avoiding me." She said curiously waiting for my reaction.

"Natasha it's not like that I was busy." I replied.

"Let it be Dhruv, I know you very well. Although you never tell me I can understand what's in your mind."

We talked with each other for the next 5-10mins and then I came up. Somehow, the small talk with Natasha lit up a smile on my face, but I couldn't forget that my birthday was spoiled by my father. I ignored everyone once again and then I tried to sleep. Later my cousin and his wife came home, they tried to convince me and I finally had dinner with everyone. I can't forget to mention that the Gulab-Jamun made by mom were awesome, as they always are. I couldn't resist myself from eating at-least 8-10pieces at once. Yes I am crazy for Gulab-Jamun. With that the day ended for me, it was 10.30pm. My cousin left home wishing me again, I gave up my anger and that was another year gone for me, now I was officially one-year older and at that perfect age where people think guys of my age should get settled in a good job and so on. The best part was I had a job but I was single. I wanted to complete my course and get settled within the next 3years, was my resolution as I turned 24.

"Hello, is this Dhruv?" A voice said as I picked up the call.

"Yes I am." I replied.

"Hi Dhruv, I am Asifa calling from MAAC. I called to inform you that your classes for AD3D+ would begin next week at 2.00pm." She said and confirmed the timing, if it was suitable for me.
"It was indeed." I said as I would be able to manage everything properly with that class timing.

I informed mom as I had to arrange the first installment of 25,000Rs. I had not made any arrangements for it. I spoke with Ram in office to get a personal loan. So one Saturday after the shift he took me in the bank where his loan was approved quickly. I thought if everything goes well I won't have to go anywhere for money. But many times things do not work the way you want them to. The bank was ready to give me loan but it was not even half the amount I needed to pay the fees. So mom gave me the option to approach my aunt which I always wanted to avoid until I had no other option.

Finally, I went to attend the first day of my animation class. We were introduced to the various aspects of animation and were given the details about the course. The exact process of making an animated film consists of 3parts: Pre-production, Production and Post-production. So the course was designed to teach us from the basics, like sketching and drawing along with clay-modeling before moving to software learning. This included Adobe Photoshop, 3Ds Max, Autodesk Maya and many other post-production softwares. So a huge stuff was lined up for me to explore.

Many things were new to me in the class along with the classmates. I noticed that within few days' I got myself a hectic schedule to follow with the graveyard shift timing. But I had begun to like the schedule and couldn't give up so easily. With Ganesh Festival approaching I had completed 6months at work. A new change happened around me in office. Riya was avoiding me and I wasn't able to find any specific reasons behind it. My team-mates began to quit the job. I had no plans to quit the job; I enjoyed working here as I had these friends along with me. Every-day after 6am we would end up playing Counter-Strike making groups in the network as the call flow was low.

Everything was going well, but my friends were leaving one after other. I couldn't change their mind as they had some better opportunities waiting for them. I felt sad but at the same time Ashwin's filmy story I could never forget. His grandfather died so he first took leaves from work. Later, he had problems in his family, the typical fight which we see in many TV serials. Then his father decided that they have to shift back to home town so that Ashwin does farming instead of working here. Poor Ashwin had no other options. Our team manager

Nishant got very upset listening this stuff. On the other end we were not able to control our laughter in the parking zone.

"Dude you would be in deep shit if you get caught for this non-sense." I said

"It doesn't matter; I won't be coming back again." He replied.

"But I will miss you. What about our Andaz Apna Apna trio even Niraj is planning to leave next month." I said.

"We will stay in touch. I will be in Pune and by the way when you have Riya around why will you ever miss me? Enjoy with her." He said.

"She is not talking with me anymore; I don't know what happened to her." I said.

"Now you realize bugger that's how we felt when you were ignoring us when she was around." He replied and punched me in my stomach.

"Ladki ka chakkar Babu Bhaiya. Bahut kuch karwata hai, Dhruv he is leaving the job not dying." Niraj finally said something after observing us.

"Ok now don't be too much emotional or else I will have to bring a new twist in the story." Ashwin said and we all started laughing and hugged each other. Nishant was passing by. He gave a smile and went away and we busted in laughter again. Till today I still miss the fun I had with these two guys. But I had something new started for me an animation course which I had dreamt about but at the same time I wished Riya had told me the reason for ignoring me all of sudden. Did I do anything wrong?

*****

Chapter 4

Something New...

Every year, Ganesh Festival preparations are on full swing. This time I had decided to buy a Digital Camera somehow, got a Handy-Cam instead. During this time to get a hands on practice of what was being taught in the class I decided to sketch the Ganesh Idol. It turned out to be nice and earned me few compliments from the hostel girls, especially from Radhika. A new girl in Pune who come for her article-ship in CA (Chartered Accountant) along with her friend Shreya. She was impressed by my work and since then I began to observe her without being noticed by anyone.

24th September 2007, one of the best day for India and an amazing evening it was for me. India vs. Pakistan T-20 Final, Radhika came home running and shouted to turn on the TV. I was curious to check what happened to her all of sudden. She wanted to view the cricket match and had come home early from her office. I too got myself seated on the bed to watch the match quietly as my father was still in the room. The match was worth watching as the excitement for me increased as my father left for his work. The entire room was filled with girls who didn't want to move away from the TV screen. I asked Krish to remove the Handy-Cam and we started recording the excitement for the 2nd innings on everyone face when the Pakistani players were dismissed from the field. Also, the disappointed look they gave when these players hit a six or four. At that time my guess-work turned out to be amazing when I started.
"See he would hit a six." I said and soon the player hit a six.
"Now, we want a four", and there was a smashing boundary.
"Dhruv, please don't say anything whatever you say it's coming true". A girl named Jiya shouted back on me.
"Ok, no problem but see now he will get out." I replied.
And immediately one of the players got run-out.
"Say something nice like this." Shreya turned around and said. So the excitement continued till the last over and I was just not able to control my laughter when things I said were coming true.
"Ok now this one is a wide," I said and everyone turned back in anger towards me as it was the last crucial over.
The match had taken a complete twist as 12 runs were required in 6 balls.

"Come-on, we need a six." I said. Soon everyone shouted in one voice Dhruv please keep your mouth shut.

"Ok, fine but I know one thing India will win." I said and that was an end to Pakistan's innings as India won by 5runs. Everyone busted out shouting and dancing in excitement, Krish whistled out loud to join them. We went downstairs to burst fire crackers while I was talking with Jiya as the others were enjoying the crackers. I noticed Natasha looking at us from her balcony the way these girls were going crazy. Later, we all came upstairs and had dinner together.

After all the fun I went off to bed and woke up at around 11.30pm as had to get ready for office. I tried to narrate the entire story to Riya but she seemed less interested in it. I really didn't understand what had happened to her and why she was avoiding me. I tried to approach her but she just spoke few words and then avoided me. I used the online messenger to talk with her but no response, so I decided to ignore her.

The animation lectures began to speed up, and there was a shift change at work. Due to this, I wasn't able to complete the assignment on time. I decided to complete my work in office, after getting Nishant's permission. Whenever I was not on call I was busy sketching when I heard a voice.

"What's going on Dhruv?" It was Gaurav Shekhawat-our Operations Manager. He had that dashing personality and most of the employees were scared of him and I was worried if he would throw me out as he stood behind me. I looked at him and he seemed to be in a good mood.

"Nothing Sir, I'm completing my assignments as there isn't any work at the moment." I replied confidently looking into his eyes as I could still recall Amar's words during the interview.

"What are you learning?" He asked

"Animation Sir."

"Good, I liked your sketches." He said going through them. "Keep it up!" He patted my back with a smile and left. I turned around to see who was paying attention to the conversation when I found the entire team had eyes on me with curiosity. Riya gave a cute smile but I immediately turned back to work giving her a weird look. She came close and said, "Dhruv, what kind of guy you are? Is that a way you behave with your friend."

"What did I do?" I asked her.

"You are not talking with me."

"Wow! I am not talking, are you out of your mind Riya? I've been doing all sort of things to get your attention. Now, just because I ignored you 2-3times you felt bad, what about me? You've been ignoring me from past 2-3weeks." I said and immediately I could see some guilt in her eyes when she replied.

"I am sorry Dhruv; I didn't mean to hurt you. I was going through some issues and I didn't want to discuss with anyone. I wasn't talking with Abhi either."

"And I guess you didn't feel to share it with me coz you don't trust me right!" I said.

"Yes, you are absolutely right, coz at times you always behave like a kid."

"Oh! Come-on Riya I don't behave like kid, I like to enjoy my life. And I am trying really hard to prove myself so that you would stop calling me a kid. I am not a kid." I replied in anger.

"Look at you Dhruv, cute angry kid." She said to make me laugh.

"Dhruv and Riya can you please go out and discuss these things. Riya please give him a hug quickly or else he would trouble the entire floor." Mr. Gaurav Dubey the most senior member of our team interrupted and we started laughing as he had that perfect timing to crack such statements.

"Oye Gaurav it's our personal matter no need to interfere and now I will talk later Riya, got a call." I said as I picked up the call.

"Thank you for calling Microsoft, this is Dhruv, how may I help you today?" Everybody could sense the happiness and excitement within me, as Riya spoke with me.

Meanwhile even working at office didn't help much. I still had some missing sketches and I needed more time to complete my assignments, but something happened in MAAC. Many faculties left MAAC due to some unknown issues. There were mixed thoughts as I didn't have to worry about the assignments, but then who would conduct the further classes was a question in front of us. We were assured that it will be taken care by the new center head who was a very strict lady when it came to discipline and students. Well it did took few days for our classes to begin properly again. During those days I received a very good salary due to my performance which made me come up with many future plans. Some positive thoughts began to flow that maybe I would not have to struggle much now for my dreams to come true. Few days later mom-dad had kept a small Pooja at home and called up many relatives and friends for dinner. At home after that cricket match most of the girls began to share a smile once a while. So that day, I remember challenging Radhika for eating maximum Gulab-Jamun who loved them just like me. The best part was some girls were cheering both of us and it was fun. Things were moving fast, I could see a new change happening for me. But there was still something missing to make my dreams work. I had to give my graduation final exams again as I couldn't clear them. I got my leaves sanctioned from our team leader and then focused myself on the upcoming exams.

My exams were over Krish and I went for shopping. We bought new clothes for ourselves and then everyone for Diwali. My shift timings changed to 7.30pm till 4.30am with Thursday Friday as weekly off. The time was good, the fact that I would be able to manage my classes properly kept me happy although I had to work at the weekend, but it was fine with me. The animation classes began with few new faculties joining MAAC. We moved to the new section of learning the photo-editing software Adobe Photoshop - digital painting, matte paintings, vector images, magazine cover designs and many more was in the list. Photoshop gave a new creative vision whereas it was fun to learn. But I had not been able to give full time to class, so making new friends in class was a bit difficult although I managed to get one, Pramod a guy who seemed to be very keen and easy to get along with. The interaction with other guys was very formal.

One weekend after dinner, I was downstairs roaming with my pet Sweety talking to myself. Some thoughts flowed in my mind as I was walking when my cell phone rang. It was Natasha.
"Hey Dhruv what's up?" She said.
"Nothing special. How come you called me?" I asked.
"Well Dhruv I thought you were talking with Sweety?"
"Why would you think that way?"
"Dhruv, I've been watching you for the past 5-10mins. What the hell are you talking with yourself?" She said and started laughing.
"It's Ok Dhruv, I know you have that habit of talking to yourself but you seemed funny while talking so I called you."
"I know Natasha and listen, I'm keeping the phone your mom is calling me at your shop. Please come down." I said to her and went to meet her mom.
"What were you talking to yourself Dhruv?" Her mom asked the same question and Natasha joined her mom to tease me. I was speechless and tried to avoid the embracement and came home.

"I am not talking with you again" I said to myself.

"What happened Dhruv? With whom are you not going to talk?" Diya had a big question mark on her face as I had again spoke loudly to myself.

A day later, in office I was lost in my thoughts when Riya came close to me. "Dhruv, what's the matter. Why are you so quiet, any problem? Come-on you can tell me." She said.

"Nothing Riya, everything is fine, I am cool." I replied.

"Something is wrong Dhruv, I have never seen you serious like this before, and will you please tell me what's wrong with you? Is everything fine at home?" She asked again. Those questions tempted me and I decided to play a prank on her.

"Ok, fine if you don't want to share its ok, I won't ask you again." She said again and gave me those killing looks which I couldn't resist and called her to my desk.

"Riya, come here and why the hell you have to get angry for stupid things. I mean...What?"

Finally she came back and asked again.

"Will you tell me, what is the matter with you?" She asked again.

"Ok, one of my close friend, he is suffering from Brain Tumor. Doctor said it's the initial stage but..." I paused to check her reaction and from where did this come, I had no clue.

"Dhruv, don't worry everything will be fine. And are you sure this is the only issue and not something else."

I tried to remain serious and said, "Riya it's me who is suffering from Tumor." I still regret that moment when I said this to her but yes I did.

For a while she didn't uttered a single word and then she asked again.

"Are you serious Dhruv?"

"Have you ever seen me this serious in office?" I replied and I couldn't believe what could happen after that. I tried to talk with her but she ignored me again.

She didn't talk with me the entire shift, she kept quiet and while leaving office she asked again,

"Dhruv are you serious of whatever you said?" That moment I thought of telling her the truth but I couldn't with the fear that maybe she would get angrier. She didn't say anything after that, her eyes had turned red. Later, she didn't pick up my calls, but promised me to keep it between the two of us.

A day before her birthday after the Photoshop lecture was over; I went out with Pramod to get something for Riya. We were not able to figure out anything, when we were attracted towards a squeaky sound made by a fur toy.

It began to dance and sing when some girls touched it. We stared at it for a while and finally bought it without any hesitation.

"Dhruv let me know your girlfriend's expression when she opens it." He said.

"Pramod she is not my girlfriend." I said.

"She is a girl and a friend, so doesn't it make her your girlfriend?"

"What logic?" I said and came back home.

Anything that looks suspicious where I spend money, mom is all set with her never-ending questions.

"Dhruv, what's in it?" She said tried to open it.

"Mom, don't touch. It's a gift for Riya." I replied and kept the box elsewhere.

"Who got it and how much did you spend on it?" Now she came to the point, I wanted to say it's me who has spent the money but then, "All my colleagues from office have contributed." I said.

She didn't believe me and had a huge list of questions prepared at the very moment. The only way for me to escape the questions was to get involved in some other work, but Vishal helped me escape her questions when he came home.

1st December 2007, officially World AIDS day, I called up Riya to wish her, happy birthday. I asked her if she had any plans and if she was at home. She asked me to come home as she had a big surprise for me. Now I wondered what the surprise would be and got ready to meet her. On my way towards her home few thoughts started mingling in my mind.

"I guess she is planning for a candle-light dinner."

"Yes, candle-light dinner early in the morning, you are amazing Dhruv."

"Maybe, she would admit today that she loves me."

"Now, Dhruv! Stop fooling and come to the point. You said something two days back which was not expected from you."

"I know why the hell I say that."

"Now guess what the surprise is...It's no more a secret and she has told this to everyone in the office. Bravo Dhruv! This would be the most exciting experience of your life."

"Brain Tumor, you are right I should have thought 100 times before saying something like this."

The thoughts continued in my mind till I almost reached Aundh. I stopped my bike in front of a flower shop and asked him to prepare a nice bouquet of few yellow roses with two red roses in between, then bought a Cadbury's Temptation for her and called her as I reached her place.

"Riya where are you? Come quickly I am in the parking." I said. She came downstairs and was looking very beautiful.

"Riya Happy Birthday" I said to her as we shook hands.

"Aur kya baat hai aaj toh ekdum rapchik lag rahi hai bole toh ekdum dingchak." I said looking at her.

"Huh!!! What happened to you Dhruv?" Riya was surprised.

"Dear rapchik means sexy and dingchak bole toh it's my new word."

"Yes, you and your new words Dhruv but I like it. What does it mean?"

"Arre dingchak bole toh...let me think!!! I don't know. It just came out as I saw you. Anyways for your beauty I have something." I said as I removed the bouquet from my bag and gave her along with the chocolate.

"Wow Dhruv flowers and all."

"Ekdum dingchak, right?" Her eyes were filled with happiness as she saw the flowers and her favorite chocolate.

"These are lovely and my favorite chocolate." We stood in the parking while her mom came downstairs.

"Amma he's Dhruv." She said while she introduced me to her mom.

Her mom replied something in her native language which I couldn't understand but found something fishy in the way her mom looked at me.

"Riya I want to give you a good news but only if you promise to do something for me in favor." I said.

"Anything for you Dhruv", she said.

"What happened to you Riya all of sudden, that is supposed to be my line." I said.

"It's all because of you Dhruv." She said.

"Firstly, let me tell you your mom is very beautiful!" She smiled and I continued, "and I want you to promise me three things."

"What? Now, don't ask me to marry you." She had a quick response.

"Oh! No. I need you to promise me that first, you would never leave me no matter what happens you would be there for me."

"I will Dhruv you are my best buddy."

"Wow that's great, so can I get a hug?"

"Ok, now that's weird, don't tell me this is the second thing you want. Anyways I would have given you but, not here my mom could be back anytime."

"Riya I know, I was kidding. The second thing you have to quit smoking and the third I'll ask later when time comes." Well Riya used to smoke at times and I wanted her to quit smoking as soon as possible.

"Well Dhruv, I can assure you that I will always be there with you but the second thing it's difficult but I'll try." She said. While are talk continued her mom was back, they both spoke something in their local language something… something about coffee upstairs.

I could only get the coffee part when I said to myself aunty coffee only in CCD.

"It's ok aunty I have to leave soon for my classes." I said.

"Now Riya I would give you the good news but before that tell me what is happening here, why you and your mom giving that weird look. Did you tell her anything?" I asked Riya as her mom went upstairs.

"I am sorry Dhruv, I told everything to her about your illness." She said.

"Are you crazy Riya? I told you I was about to get it confirmed from another doctor."

"I know Dhruv, but I was worried for you and I had to tell someone and mom realized as I couldn't stop crying after whatever you told me."

"Riya" I paused for a moment as I could not guess how I should react after this. "I had been made fool by one of my friend I don't have any Tumor." I had another lie to hide my previous lie. Immediately I could see a smile on her face.

"Dhruv that is the best gift for my b'day I am very happy. But there's a slight problem."

"Now what happened?"

"I told Nishant."

"Congratulations Dhruv, tera toh band bajj gaya." I mumbled.

"Wow Riya! Today is my last day in the company. Cool."

"Relax Dhruv, nothing of such will happen I don't want to lose you either. I will talk to him. But you should kick that friend of yours."

"I did Riya but anyways here's something else for you." I said and finally removed the gift from my bag to give her.

"Dhruv, 3 gifts on a single day? What's in your mind?"

"Marry me Riya". I said holding her hand.

"Now it's not possible, I cannot. How will I tell my mom that it was a joke? I cried like hell you Dumbo." She said and had a cute smile on her face.

"Riya, now I will have to convince your mom. Forget it I'll search a new girlfriend."

"Kaminey. What about me then?" She said and punched me in my stomach.

"You will always be the best for me. Anyways I should get a hug now… See I gave you the best news today."

"Forget it you will never get it. You made me cry."

"Riya I should leave now go up open the gifts and let me know if you like it."
"Bye Dhruv and thanks for coming."
"Bye Riya and I love you."
"Chal Bhag aren't you getting late for your class." She said and I left her place.
I was in the middle of the road when Riya called me.
"Dhruv the gift is awesome, my mom liked it the most, love you Dhruv." That lit up a smile on my face and it did strengthen the bond we shared. Friendship that stays strong and a real good friend are always hard to find. I thanked God for sending Riya into my life as I reached home.

Whatever happened in the morning gave me a very positive feeling and the respect for Riya grew stronger in my mind. I didn't feel bad that she was not my girlfriend but I was happy she was my best friend I could ever have in my life. Yes, she was the night's wish that came true. A friend I've always dreamt of and wished to GOD. In the evening I reached office and thought Nishant would have forgotten about whatever Riya said. But Nishant called up Riya at his desk the very next moment. After a while he was looking at me with a smile and then called me up.
"Are you a fan of Rajesh Khanna by any chance?" He said and looked at me.
"Nice drama you setup Dhruv to seek her attention. You could have told her directly she would have never said no to you." He continued and later both of them began laughing. My lips were sealed with embarrassment but I had to speak.
"My friend fooled me Nishant it wasn't my fault. Riya I had told you not to tell anyone."
"It's ok Dhruv now accept it that you made up this story." Riya said as she left towards her desk.
"Nishant see what you are did, creating problems between the two of us, I told you that my friend fooled me and am going back to my desk." I replied. Nishant was the coolest manager of all and never took any action against me.
"What happened Dhruv?" Gaurav asked in curiosity.
Before I could reply anything Nishant replied "We have a big fan of Rajesh Khanna among us."
"Nishant no one is listening to you. Bye Nishant, you have lots of work to do." I said raising my voice. Everyone guessed something funny had happened, but it was between Riya, Nishant and me. They didn't let anybody know about this.
"Come on get back to work now." Nishant patted my back and went back towards his desk. Day ended as Riya cut the cake Abhi and I clicked some snaps with Riya in the cafeteria.

Few days passed, my cousin Pal, her mom, Diya, Krish and me decided to go for a short trip to Ganapati Pule during the weekend. I came home from work, it was 20th December 2007. Krish and Diya to woke up as we had to leave at 7. Krish was driving car for the first time, aunt was sitting next to him and I was busy sleeping, right in between Pal and Aisha. I always love to be in the center. Let be it any place also in group photographs with friends or family. I didn't drive as I didn't know how to drive. During my 12th, I had an opportunity to learn driving but mom stopped me, as studies were more important at that time. So till date I could never learn to drive a car and never felt a need to do so, as I never owned a car. I enjoyed sleeping as well as taking snaps at regular intervals on the highway whenever we halted. We reached Ganapati Pule late in the evening. We headed towards the beach after we found a suitable room to stay. I called up Riya to inform her about the trip. Next day, again we were on the beach early morning. After a bath we headed towards the temple. During this particular period we were walking around the mountain. That moment, I wished if I could get someone who wouldn't let my cell phone be silent. I guess my best friend (Bappa) had already started to plan things for me. On our way back home I caught cold and kept sneezing continuously. When we reached home, I went and meet my friends starting with Abhishek, Natasha and Vishal to share the fun of the trip instead of taking rest. Unfortunately, the next day I had to be on bed. I informed Nishant. He advised me to take care and granted me a sick leave.

Even though I had fever, I wasn't taking any rest, I hopped here and there in the house, while mom shouted," Dhruv take some rest you are not well."
"What happened to you Dhruv?" Well that was Mahi the girl from hostel. She stayed back after her lunch.
"Well I have fever." I said.
"It doesn't look so." She said with a smile.
"Well, that's the way I am." I replied to her as I was hypnotized by her smile for a while.

Mahi was one of the cutest girls who came home. She was from Ajmer and was learning Fashion Designing from one of the colleges in Pune. Once, when I was talking with Vishal, I saw her and was attracted towards her beauty. I had predicted she would be engaged with someone. That was a year ago. Since then I never remembered talking about her. After the 20-20 World Cup Finals, I had edited one of her pics and she admired it a lot. Being impressed by my work she often spoke with me but it was always a formal conversation. I always found her talking on the phone and wondered how she wasn't talking today. She wanted some songs transferred in her IPOD. Krish was helping her for a long time, but there was no progress. I figured out, the I-tunes software was missing. Mahi was clueless about it. So she asked me to transfer the songs in her mobile phone. Krish got a call so I helped her transfer songs.

After some time I went off to bed as Mahi left. She came back in the evening as she was alone in the hostel. The other girls had left for their respective homes to celebrate the new year.
"How are you Dhruv?" She said.
"Well, am fine but, still have some fever." I replied.
"Take care and stop roaming here and there." She said.
"Mahi, he will keep jumping and will never learn to take care of himself." I wondered why Diya said that.

Next day afternoon, Mahi stayed back to watch movie, along with Krish, Diya and me. At that moment, she asked if we could go out somewhere. Mom stopped us as I was not well. I informed Nishant I won't be coming to office for another day. He was annoyed at first but he granted me another leave. We didn't go anywhere, Mahi spent time with us and I liked it. Next day 24th December, I again convinced Nishant for another leave even though I was fine. We planned to go out to the newly opened Kakade Mall in camp. We all went there in the evening and enjoyed every moment in this mall. Later, we came near a cottage that was made right at the entrance of the mall. I suggested Mahi to click some snaps with us. So within the next few minutes we had almost clicked 10-15 pictures, which was amazing. Well, it was because I loved capturing those beautiful moments spent with every friend and Mahi was a new friend.

25th December 2007, Christmas, one of my favorite day. I liked celebrating all the festivals apart from those included in the Hindu calendar. I never went to the church on this day but it was always a special day for me. We decided to watch the movie 'Taare Zameen Par' in the morning and then enjoy the rest of the day together. I was excited as it would be the first movie with Mahi so I got ready early morning whereas Krish and Diya where just out of bed when Mahi came home. She was looking awesome in her blue jeans and the brown top. She was annoyed, that Diya and Krish were not ready. She asked them to hurry and we both started looking for the show timings in the newspaper.

"Dhruv the show is at 11.00am at Inox". Mahi said.

"Mahi I don't think that we would be able to make it and get the tickets as its already 10".

"I know. Krish and Dee get ready soon I want to see the movie." She said and pushed Krish to get ready.

Diya suggested we go ahead and buy the tickets, which I agreed immediately before she could give any other options. We both reached Inox but the tickets were sold out. We proceeded towards Gold Adlabs and got the tickets for the show at 12.00pm. I called up Krish and told him to come by 11.30am to Gold Adlabs. Now, I had ample amount of time to spend with Mahi till they came.

"So where shall we spend time now." I asked her.

"Well I don't know you decide." She said.

"Let's go in the Life-Style mall." I said after eyeing on every possible option around.

We spent a good time together, as I clicked few snaps of her through my cell phone and soon we exchanged our numbers by the time Krish and Diya arrived.

"Dee..., Dhruv is crazy, he just starts clicking photos anywhere he gets a chance." Mahi said to Diya.

"But I am the best Mahi you should accept that when you see the pictures." I said while I showed the photos to Krish.

"Ok, now don't be flattened by that I know you take good pictures but it's not the photographer it's the person in the photo that makes the photo look good." She said.

"Ha ha very funny now let's get inside." I said as we smiled at each other. Mahi sat next to me in the movie hall. The movie was nice and we all recalled our school days during the movie.

I wanted to spend more time with Mahi, as I began to like her company. I wanted to stay home and avoid office but I thought I could share this sweet experience with Riya so I went to work instead. I reached office at around 7.30pm, I was late so I logged in quickly into the Avaya and found that we were not receiving any calls due to Christmas. I met Nishant and asked him why Riya didn't turn up to office. He gave me a smile and said, "She is your girlfriend, didn't she tell you anything?"

"Oh come-on Nishant you very well know that we are just good friends so stop smiling and tell me where is she?"

"Go call her, even I don't know where she is." He had given her a leave as her mom was not well. When I was done with the call he couldn't stop teasing me

with his funny smile. There was no work and to chill we were playing cricket in office, when my Ops Manager said to me,
"Tu bimaar tha na, chal ab thik se fielding kar warna batting nahi milegi."
Well that was fun, life at office along with Riya my best friend. And now I guess Mahi as well, who was missing me back home.

*****

Chapter 5

CCD- A Lot Can Happen Over Coffee...

After a long weekend and enjoyment with Mahi, it was time for me to get back to work. I had missed a few lectures at MAAC. The Photoshop lectures were almost over and the class had begun with a completely new software 3Ds Max. Our third faculty Ajay was quite young, had good knowledge about the tool and was happy to see me back in class. He had given us some time to understand the software and then later began with the basic concepts as why this software was used in the industry. Ajay sir had begun to teach character modeling. Most of us found it difficult maybe it was because the software was new to us. He had informed us that if we are able to get our hands on female modeling then we can create any model efficiently. During the sketching lectures we were taught to draw human figures and now with the help of those references we had to create them in the 3-dimensional workspace.

He taught us the basic layout of the model and we began to try on our respective computers. During that time, I received a message from Mahi, asking me out for coffee.

I thought for a while then replied yes and went to meet her once the lecture was over.

"So how was your class?" Mahi asked me

"It was good." I replied struggling through the menu card what exactly I should order.

"Does an Irish coffee actually contain Whiskey in it?" I asked Mahi.

"Yes it does, have you never been to CCD before?" She replied.

"Well I have many times with Riya but usually she places the order, I am clueless as to which coffee we should try."

"Well, even I have never tried Irish coffee so let's go for it."

"Ok no problem, two Irish coffee please." I said and we began to talk, I noticed she was continuously messaging her boyfriend during our conversation which was quiet annoying. Yes, Mahi had a boyfriend in Ajmer and I believed she was in a serious relationship with him.

"So tell me something about your boyfriend, how you guys meet?" I said to avoid the silence between us. She told me everything and I just peeked through

33

the window when my bike was being lifted from the no parking zone. I couldn't leave the conversion so I told her about it later

The Irish coffee was nice so was the conversation between the two of us. After a while we went to get my bike in a rickshaw when Mahi said "I am feeling sleepy and my head is paining." I didn't realize when she kept her head on my shoulder. Wow!!! that feeling, of Mahi actually resting on my shoulder, was amazing. She had something stuck on her lips which I tried to remove with my fingers. As I touched her lips I could feel the softness of her lips and was the second best feeling in this world. For the first time I thanked the traffic department for lifting my bike. The worst part here was the bike was taken to a different location so we had to travel a lot. I asked her to return home as she had a headache but she stayed together. Somehow we managed to get the bike back and I thanked Mahi for being with me.
"It was my fault Dhruv I called you for the coffee so maybe your bike got picked up." Mahi said.
"Don't blame yourself Mahi. I parked my bike in the no parking zone. I am sorry but anyways we would meet again for a coffee next time and I promise this thing won't happen again." I said and dropped her to hostel and came home and started getting ready for office as it was already late. I was about to leave when she came home.
"Where are you going?" She asked.
"Office, its already late." I said.
"Ok bye." She said and went upstairs.

By the time I reached office I had a message in my inbox, *'Thanks for the time we spent together I really liked your company we'll definitely go for another cup of coffee tomorrow. Miss you, bye take care.'* I was surprised with the message 'Mahi' and 'Miss You' two unpredictable things that were put in front of me. Well it had happened for the first time so I was very excited and wanted to narrate the entire scene to Riya.

"Riya come fast and login quickly I need to tell you something." I shouted as I saw her coming in the lobby.
"I know Dhruv, just give me a minute." She said trying to grab her chair.
I had already setup a computer for her next to me on my right. Saurav was sitting on my left. She logged into the Avaya and the computer and then later turned towards me.
"Ok, come on tell me everything, I can see the happiness on your face." She said.
"He is in cloud nine Riya just look at him." Saurav spoke in between.

"Saurav, you've got a call concentrate on your work and give us some space." I said as I saw the light flashing on his Avaya.

"Ok lover-boy enjoy" he said as he poked his finger in my stomach side-ways and I jumped on my chair. I looked at him as he began with the call, "Thank you for calling Microsoft…." I turned back to Riya.

"So Riya where was I ah… yes, I had gone with this girl, she is awesome; she invited me for a coffee. You know what I actually drank Irish coffee. And, how is your mom?" I said when Saurav interrupted again putting his customer on mute.

"He was dancing all the way on the floor."

"Saurav concentrate on your work." I said and hit him on his back.

"My mom's fine and what is her name?" Riya asked in curiosity.

"Her name is Mahi."

"Well that's a nice name, where did you meet her?" She asked again.

"I didn't go anywhere she came home."

"Well that's cool. What else did you guys do?" She said and I ended up narrating the entire scene that happened. She was happy for me and I could see that through her cute smiling face.

"So what is your plan for the new year?" Mahi asked me while she sipped through the cup of cappuccino.

"Nothing, maybe I will take a leave if you cancel your plan to Mumbai." I said in order to stop her from going to Mumbai.

"What will we do if I stay?"

"We can do everything, maybe we'll go to a pub if you want. Later at night you can stay at my place. We can inform mom."

"No please you won't tell anybody at home. We are together because I treat you as my friend and like a dumb, you end up telling everything at your home the moments we spend together."

"Well, so what's the problem?"

"I don't want you to share our secrets with anybody. It's between you and me then why the hell you want to share it with anybody else. I don't like it."

"Ok, I am sorry Mahi. I didn't know you think in such a way."

"Its common sense Dhruv, friend's secrets should be with friends."

Within these 2-3days we had shared a lot of things together and I was pretty sure that she would stay back in Pune to celebrate the New Year with me, rather than her relatives. I was right she did agree to stay. Now at work this is the time when majority of the people plan their leaves, so getting a leave for this stupid reason, I wanted to celebrate New Year with Mahi was impossible. Nishant would have never agreed, so I never wanted to ask but I still tried.

"Nishant, how many leaves do I have left for this year?" I asked him when I found him free.

"Don't even think of taking leaves for New Year I will never approve it."

"I am coming to work don't worry I am not here to ask for leaves. Can't I come to your desk when I am bored."

"You can but you only come here when you need leaves or Riya is not talking with you."

"It's never like that Nishant see I am here right now." I tried to defend myself.

"But why do you both always keep on fighting?" His sarcastic smile continued.

"We never fight Nishant. We are good friends now don't start it again." I said when he stood up and called up Riya.

"Riya, see what Dhruv is talking about you."

"What are you saying Dhruv?"

"Nothing Riya he is trying to make us fight again." I said.

"Nishant stop smiling and we are good friends."

"Ok fine, come-on you guys get back to work and maybe from next year onwards you won't get so much of time as the call flow would increase."

The moment he said that, our talk changed into some serious stuff where he also said that he would tell more about it in the team-meeting.

Later, I thought what I would do if I won't get a leave, I will go crazy here and Mahi would kill me. She had cancelled her plan for me. So, my creative brain had to come up with a new idea.

"So where are we going today." Mahi asked me

"You tell me. Where exactly should we go?"

"I don't know you decide."

"I am not able to decide so I asked you."

"Don't ask me I am very bad at this." She said and finally after a long discussion we decided to spend time in camp and when we were about to leave I got a call from Nishant.

"Where are you Dhruv?" He said.

"Nishant I am not well I could not sleep the entire day as had problems at home. Please I won't be able to come." Somehow that was not at all convincing for Nishant so I tried to convince Mahi.

"Mahi, I have to go back to work." I said in a sad voice.

"But we were about to leave for camp right." She said.

"Yes I know Mahi but I am sorry, my manager called and wants me at work. I'll try to make some excuse." I tried to convince her that I would come back from office soon. I also promised her that we would start the New Year together early morning. As I reached office I squeezed orange peels in my eyes in order to show I was not well. I went upstairs and found none of the managers were present on the floor as they had gone to celebrate Gaurav Sir's b'day.

I ran to the washroom as my eyes were burning. I was jumping here and there as was not able to bare the pain. Finally after washing my eyes for the fifth time I decided, I would never use this trick ever. And, I was back to work talking calls in a dull voice "Thank You for calling…"

I wished I could have changed my decision of coming to office, I felt bad for the fact that Mahi could have enjoyed with her relatives but stayed here for me and I screwed up things. The clock struck 12, everyone was wishing each other I did the same. One best thing happened, when my customer (John Thompson) asked me," What is this noise all about?"

I told him it's the New Year.

"Oh! Happy New Year, then." He said.

"Well, same to you John." I sounded dull.

"Well, it seems I might be bugging, you should be celebrating with your friends."

"That's no problem John, I have to work."

"Well, you can put me on hold, go wish all your friends and come back. I'll grab a beer for myself as the windows updates are still installing on the computer."

"Oh! Thanks John." I said and put him on hold and went happily out. I took my cell phone from the locker and called Mahi.

"Hi Mahi, Happy New Year." I said.

"Same to you and you were supposed to come back." She replied.

"I am sorry, my manager is not is office so I couldn't talk with him."

"See I told you, but you were dying to go and celebrate it with Riya more than me."

"She is not in office. Anyways be ready in the morning at 7, we'll go to Dagdushet temple and then decide where to go later."

"Ok fine, now let me sleep now, bye, good night and I miss you." She said in drowsy tone and hung up.

Just a small talk with her bought a huge smile on my face and I was back on the call.

"So did you wish all your friends?" John asked.

"Yes I did as I had to call one of my friend." I replied.

"Well, that must be your girlfriend I guess."

"Well not exactly but maybe, anyways so John what's the status of the updates?" I replied with a smile.

"You are a smart man Dhruv, changed the topic within seconds." He said and laughed.

"If you say so, maybe, I am smart. Thanks John!" I joined him in his laugh and later we were back with the updates installation.

I left office at 4.30 in the morning and decided to sleep for some time and wake up at 7, so that I can go with Mahi. She used to come home by 7.30am take her Tiffin and then go to college, so I left home when she came, mom was surprised as what I was up to so early morning.

"Where are you going Dhruv in such a hurry?" Mom asked me.

"I am going to the temple." I replied while drinking water without making any eye contact with her.

"Wait then, even I will come with you." She said

"No..., I'll have to come back soon. You will take time." I said and left.

Mahi was watching everything but didn't say anything, she called me on my cell phone once she left home.

"Hey, where are you?" She said.

"I am standing near the small bridge down the lane", I said. That was the place where I always stood after that and later we named it as bridge spot.

"Ok wait, I am coming."

"Come fast." I said and then we went to the Dagdushet temple. As we reached early there was no rush in the temple and we were able to go peacefully in the temple. Later we also went to Saras Bagh temple. It was 8.30am so we had plenty of time as her college was at 10.

"So where should we go now." I asked

"Let's go someplace where we can eat. I am hungry." She said.

"Me too", I added while riding my bike.

The feel of Mahi seated behind me on the very first day of the year was surprisingly nice. We headed towards her college and decided to go to the Good Luck Café.

"So what should we order?" She asked.

"Don't ask me I am coming here for the first time." I said checking the menu cards.

"Mahi I think you should go ahead, do the honors. Order something I am very bad at this." I said.

"I want to eat boiled egg or wait let me see." She said.

"I looked at her, she was looking very cute while reading the menu card. The way she bit her finger deciding what to order made me smile when she finally said.

"Let's order scrambled egg with toast."

"Now what the hell is that? I've never heard this name before." I said.

"Well it's amazing you have never tried it."

"No". I said with a big question mark on my face.

So we ordered the scrambled egg with toast and I was busy staring at her.

"What are you looking at Dhruv?" She asked.

"Nothing, just looking at the pendant around your neck."

"Oh! This one, mummy gave me."

"It's nice, tell you something. Those rings in your fingers remind me of Riya." I tried to tell her everything that I do when I get a chance to hold Riya's hand and how I play with her ring in office. Mahi smiled and thought I was crazy.

"Your hands are so cute and small Mahi." I said

"Yes I know, maybe that's the reason Gaurav calls me Chotta Baby." She said

"Chotta Baby that's cool, the name suits your personality. Gaurav, your boyfriend right", I said.

"Yes", she said

"Oh! The EGG Scramble is here." I said as the waiter placed the order in front of us along with two cup of tea.

"Mahi you know something I won't be able to eat this thing."

"Why? What happened?"

"I don't know how to eat with a fork and knife."

"Ok, then just drink tea I will enjoy it." She said with a smile. She then cut a piece of egg and toast with the knife, with the fork she dipped it in the tomato ketchup and then she said holding the piece in front of my mouth.

"Here, taste this."

I looked at her for a moment then opened my mouth and gulped the piece crushing it into pieces.

"It's good." I said. Later every alternate piece was fed to me with her cute little hands added a smile every time she fed me. I was speechless. Later, I dropped her to college and came back home wishing everyone Happy New Year on my way.

Those few days Mahi and I started living for each other even though, we were busy in our respective schedule. She would wake me up every day early morning and she began to come home early after college in order to spend time together. Missing you messages continued to flash on my cell phone. My cell phone had got a new life always filled with messages and phone calls by Mahi. My breaks were fixed in order to talk with her. Sometimes she would avoid her boyfriend in order to talk with me. I felt happy and was attracted towards her especially after the day 6th January 2008.

She had decided to go to Mumbai to meet her relatives for a day. I had to drop her in the morning to the bus stand.
"Why are you in such a hurry today Dhruv." Riya said.
"Nothing Mahi is leaving for Mumbai, need to drop her."
"Oh! Someone is blushing ha." She said with a smile.
"Arre... it's not what you think, she has a boyfriend." I said to stop further discussions.
"Dhruv you never dropped me home on your bike."
"You are such a liar. I have dropped you many times" I said. She winked at me and then smiled.
"I was just kidding Dhruv. You go I still have some work." She replied.

I left office and then called up Mahi. Around 5.00am I reached her hostel it was very cold. I gave a miss call when she came down and sat behind me.
"Why the hell are you shouting Dhruv? Shut your mouth." She scolded on me as I greeted her when she came down. A bit angry, I kept quiet till we reached the bus stand.
"Come-on let's drink tea." She said, but I did not respond.
"You get angry so easily Dhruv."
"It's not me Mahi; it's you who gets angry quickly. I was not shouting I was happy to see you early morning so I said good morning and that was not that loud." I said trying to explain things.
"See even now you are shouting. Ok come-on it's very cold let's drink tea." She said making a cute face which made me smile. We drank tea in a hotel near Station and within the next 5-10mins we were back at the bus stand. We still had some time to talk with each other. Mahi was seated on the bike and I was standing very close to her. Due to the freezing temperature, we were holding each other's hands while we were talking. These few days we had come really close to each other and never wanted to be apart. So holding each other's hands

was just another part of affection towards each other. I wanted to hug her as she had become a part of my life. A girl who was driving me crazy. But how to approach her kept me quiet till the bus arrived.

"Chalo bye, take care and go to sleep." She said as she picked up her bag and got up from the bike. I was still confused whether I should hug her or not but I couldn't gather those guts in me so I said, "Bye, take care. I'll miss you." She started walking towards the bus. I waited there for a moment and when I lifted my hand to wave her good-bye, she turned back and came running towards me and hugged me. One more moment when she left me speechless. As soon as she wrapped her arms around me I gathered my courage and hugged her back. She smiled and went back in the bus and I waived my hand for the final good bye with a smile on my face.

10ᵗʰ January 2008, Mahi's birthday I had decided to make it the best for her. I called her at midnight and wished her from work. I bunked my animation class but left home normally at the same time. We had decided to meet in the afternoon. I got two cards a soft toy along with a nice bouquet of red flowers for her before I met her.

"Happy Birthday Mahi." I greeted her with a smile.
"Thanks Dhruv." She replied with a smile. She was wearing a light green colored top with black hearts shaped design on it along with blue jeans. She was looking pretty, never missing a chance to compliment her.
"Mahi you are looking beautiful today."
"Thanks Dhruv, so what's the plan where are we going?"
"You tell me. It's your birthday."
"Don't ask me we would end up going no-where, you only decide."
We were walking down the streets of FC road when we reached the CCD outlet.
"By the way, this is for you." I said and handed over the bag with all the cards and bouquet to her when we finally got place for us in CCD.
"Hey thanks, what's in it?"
"Actually I was confused which card to select so I got both, you would definitely like them I guess. And one more thing I just gave you this teddy and nothing else. Well mom would ask you at home today."
"Of Course Dhruv, I can't show her these cards where you have written love you bachha. Actually I liked it a lot and the flowers are amazing." We ordered two cappuccinos and by the time we received our order she was carefully reading the contents in the card and I was busy watching her.

"Dhruv it's really beautiful. I just loved them. Hey let's do one thing we'll go somewhere out and spend some time together as in the evening we won't be able to talk much." She said.

"Ok fine but where?" I said.

"That you decide don't ask me."

"Ok let's go for a movie."

"Ok fine no problem but before that I need to go to the hostel and keep my bag I can't carry this bag along with us, its too heavy." She said and within few minutes we left CCD.

"I'll check if I can get my bike." I said as we took a rickshaw. We reached home as my mom had the first question to ask, "Did you get the gift for Mahi?"

"Yes I did and I gave it to her."

My mom gave me and angry look and said, "We had decided to give it to her in the evening when she comes home. Why were you in such a hurry? And what did you give?" Her questions were all lined up one after another, I took the keys quickly and tried to escape saying, "I am going to my friend's place and will come late. I bought her a teddy."

Mahi was standing near Apollo theatre and as decided we went to Gold Adlabs. We occupied one of the corner tables near the fast food joints as we didn't find any movie exciting. We talked with each other and did order a pizza. During this time her boyfriend Gaurav kept calling Mahi every 30minuntes, which for the first time I didn't like at all. Later, we got involved in each other and clicking photos after small interval that we never noticed it was almost evening.

"Oh shit, its 6.30." Mahi said.

"Yes it is, anything serious about the time showing 6.30pm. Should I tell time not to show that time it brings a strange feeling on my Chotta baby."

"Very funny, come on lets go."

"Go...Where?" I asked.

"I have to go to hostel and then come to your place." She said as she stood up the chair.

"Ok, then you go I don't feel like coming."

"Ok fine you sit here I'll take your family for dinner."

"No... I am coming, wait." I jumped up my chair and started walking with her.

I reached home and got fresh and within an hour she was back home. She asked everyone to get ready for the party as they wished her.

"We can't come" Mom said as she had to look after the other girls, so Diya, Krish and I went along with her.

"Ok no problem you, me and uncle will go later." She replied.

"Only I am allowed that time right?" I interrupted.

"No ways, if you want to come later then sit home now." She said smiling.

"Oh no I am coming now."

"Then get ready quickly. Krish, even girls don't take so much time to get ready". She said shouting on Krish to get ready. We all went to the food court at the Central Mall as suggested by Krish and later after dinner we came home 9.30pm. Mahi waited home as we had another surprise for her- birthday cake. I told her to open the box slowly and then was waiting for her reaction after reading "Happy Birthday Chotta Baby."

I noticed her smile throughout and wanted her to be with us for some more time. But she was already late so I couldn't stop her. She reached her hostel and within few minutes she messaged me for making her birthday memorable. Soon we were up with our late night talks on phone.

Mahi got busy with her college exhibition held on 26th and 27th of January 2008. She wanted to buy new clothes. We had planned to go together but, something's never work with me. I was in the bank to get the credit cards balance transferred on the new card. It took a long time and I knew Mahi was about to kill me. She was waiting for me near pizza hut for an hour and I kept saying give me 10minutes whereas I was late, very late.

"Can you ever learn to be punctual Dhruv?" She began to yell at me to gather the entire attention of that flower vendor who seemed very interested in the argument.

"Mahi I am sorry, please sit back and let me explain." I said.

"I don't want to buy any clothes with you." Mahi vented her anger more which attracted even the people walking down the streets.

"Ok fine Mahi but please sit back I'll explain everything. It won't happen again". I tried hard to convince her but she decided to leave and started walking the opposite direction. I parked my bike and asked that flower vendor to look after it for a minute.

"It's not my responsibility". He was adamant. Now it was a tough situation for me should I go behind her or not. But, I parked my bike and ran towards her.

"Mahi last time won't happen again please, we'll go somewhere else, where you would feel better then maybe we'll go buy your clothes". I tried to convince her again which did work this time.

"I don't want to buy clothes and don't ask me where to go." She replied while she came with me and sat behind.

"Should we go to Central I am hunger maybe we can eat something." Now that was again a stupid question at the wrong time. Mahi was still angry for spoiling her plan. Well she did agree and we reached the food court. I was still trying to figure out how to make her smile and cool down her anger.

"So Mahi what should we order, let's try the same vegetable wonton. Or, maybe some ice-cream to cool you down." Well that didn't work, she was sitting in anger and I had no other option but to take her out. We came down and sat on the stairs where we could see all the vehicles chasing each other. I had to get her back to normal but I really couldn't understand why girls get angry so quickly.

"Mahi look, I'm sorry and it was not my fault was on my way but Krish took me and it was all spoilt." It took me some time to explain her everything and get her back to normal.

"Whatever the reason was at least now your expressions changed. Thank God and I know I will make you smile soon and you would definitely kiss me if not a hug." I said.

"Aap bahut kharab ho, I hate you." After a long time she smiled and gave me a hug, while later kissed me on my cheek. Well kiss on cheek is the symbol of true friendship don't take me wrong. We did spend time talking with each other for some time and I said.

"We'll definitely go tomorrow Mahi and I'll be there on time."

Never ever, well this is a piece of advice from me to everyone. Never ever, go shopping with a girl who is learning fashion designing and plans to look the best in her class. Well best part was, I got to know all the boutiques on MG road. Worst part, we were visiting each and every boutique and my legs had given up on me. Around 2-3hours later, finally we were able to find something that would match her personality. What a relief!

Saturday 26th January 2008, I got a call from my college friend Enosh to meet. Somehow I was least interested to talk with them as I was more focused on Mahi and her thoughts. I left early to meet her.

"Mahi, I need to say something. Well please don't take me in a wrong way." I was not able to decide whether I should say it or not when I finally said it.

"What is it Dhruv? Tell me quickly as we have to leave soon."

"Yes, Ok fine I'll say it." I gathered all my courage in order to let her know my feelings.

"Mahi do you remember the very first day we came to CCD I told you something about myself."

"What?"

"I get used to people very soon."

"Yes, I remember. So what about that?" She asked

"Don't take me wrong but I think I am falling in love with you."

"Shut up Dhruv. Don't just say anything."

"I am serious Mahi. I know you have a boyfriend and we are good friends but if you feel I am causing problem between you and Gaurav I will move out." She kept silent and didn't utter a word from her mouth. I kept staring at her while a song from 'Neil and Niki' was being played at the cafe...'Like a dream...' I knew that song might add some effect to our conversation and yes it did as Mahi finally spoke.

"Should I tell you something, even I feel the same. But I am confused."

"Confused then let's do it this way." I tried the movie 'RHTDM' trick.

"Close your eyes for the next 10seconds and let's see if you see me in front of you." I said.

She did accordingly but again kept quiet. We left CCD and I dropped her at her friend's place and came home. Later, Diya and I went to see her exhibition before leaving for office. I got ready in my favorite formals with the off-white jacket on. We reached her college and then I saw her walking towards us in black top and the cool off-white colored skirt. She was looking amazing in the new clothes. I was stunned looking at her beauty felt like I should grab her and kiss her. A sudden desperate thought that came in my mind but I took it off soon. She greeted us and began to show us her exhibition.

"How am I looking Dhruv?" Mahi asked.

"I feel like kissing you." I spoke softly in her ears.

"Shut up not here in my college and come I'll show you something." She replied with a smile and went near Diya.

"Dee, the work in which Dhruv helped me it's has been displayed at the start and everyone praised it a lot." She said as she pointing towards the image I helped her in Photoshop. She also introduced us with all her friends. After viewing the entire exhibition I dropped Diya at my aunt's place and went to office. As I reached office a message flashed on my mobile.

'What have you done to me Dhruv? I am not able to concentrate in anything and anyways I got a compliment for you. My friends say you are very handsome. Bye, miss you, take care.'

I smiled and was thinking about a reply and messaged her, *'I told the truth Mahi. And even you were looking awesome. Miss you too Sweetheart.'* My message had a sugar coated word in it 'SWEETHEART' something new for me.

Next day I planned a dinner with Mahi as she was to leave the next day for a wedding in Ajmer. I met her in her college after the exhibition was over and we went to a nearby restaurant. The people there continued to stare at us. Mahi asked me to ignore everyone and enjoy the food. She was wearing an off-white colored silk saree with silver lining on it and it looked wonderful. We enjoyed the dinner together and later headed towards the lane next to Central Mall. We sat outside the park holding each other's hand and were busy discussing our childhood memories. We were unaware of the time when it was already late. I dropped her back home but, our talk continued on the phone.

Next day, we were waiting for her bus to arrive. I was still waiting for her answer and finally decided to propose her officially with a rose and her favorite chocolate Cadbury's Fruit n Nut. I gave her the rose and the chocolate and said, "Mahi, I love you."
She smiled and said nothing.
"I mean say something. Smiling doesn't give me any answers." I said. She remained quiet so I sat next to her. Later, we were looking at a girl who was just about to cry, I guess her boyfriend was about to leave her. She asked me if I was really serious about her and I assured her holding her hand and giving her a nod.
"I'll let you know once I come back." She said.
"I can't wait till then, I'll die. Ok fine let's do it this way that boy doesn't go, he waits back for his girlfriend you would let me know." I said but this didn't work as he was the first one to get inside the bus. Mahi hugged me and went inside the bus and I crossed the street and was about to leave when I saw the bus stopped. The boy got down and my cell started ringing it was Mahi." I love you Dhruv and I'll miss you a lot." It bought up a big smile on my face as I finally got a girlfriend. Whereas, the boy who got down wiped off the tears of his girlfriend and they hugged each other.

*****

Chapter 6

Valentine and the others...

"So what did she say?" Riya asked.

"Well... ah! She said, she loves me." I said with a smile.

"I had told you she will say that." Riya said smiling more than me.

"Riya now I guess you are still hiding something. Come on you can trust me." I said to her.

"Promise me Dhruv nobody will know anything about this."

"Go on, I won't tell anybody."

"First promise me."

"Ok fine I promise won't tell anybody that you are trying to tell something about somebody."

"Can you ever be serious?"

"Yes, I am, Riya. Did you see me smiling?" I said trying to control my emotions and later said, "Come on tell me fast before I get a call."

"Ok, there's a guy I'm dating past few days."

"What?" I shouted.

"Dhruv don't shout, people are taking calls."

"What's going on between the two of you?" Gaurav interrupted.

"Nothing Gaurav, it's a top secret between Riya and me." I said holding her hand.

"That's it, you always some or the other reason to hold her hand." He said smiling and continued, "You got a girlfriend Dhruv at least now leave her."

"You will leave me Dhruv?" Riya said with a cute frown.

"I won't Riya. I love you first, Mahi comes later."

"Tu kabhi nahi sudhrega na?" Gaurav added.

"Woh sudhar gaya toh poore XP floor ka bhala ho jayega Gavdu." Well that was Parth who was keenly listening to our conversation. He was a guy who was best at making fun of people, new in our team. Nothing much to say about him you would get to know him later.

"What are you doing bachha?" Mahi called up after 2-3days.

"I am getting ready for class."

"Ok, so can we talk for some time?" She asked.

"Yes go ahead. I was about to call you, I had this amazing dream today. You need to make it come true."

"What? Is it like I was kissing you or something?"

"Yes it was, how did you guess?" I said.

"I know you and your crazy dreams very well. Anyways I am coming tomorrow, so please come to pick me at the station in the morning."

"What time?" I asked.

"Around 5.30am."

"Are you crazy? It's so early it's my week off I need to sleep."

"Ok then you sleep and forget the kiss."

"I am coming, I am coming… 5.30am sharp." I replied immediately.

Yes, my immediate reaction would definitely indicate that maybe, I was too desperate for a kiss or I really cared for her. But this was not the first time she was coming alone at that time from the Pune Station. A girl who can travel alone from Ajmer to Pune, why exactly would she need someone to pick her up. Then, why exactly was that need of insecurity in her mind that she wanted me to pick her from Station. Sometimes, we guys would always avoid such thoughts when we really care for someone. Her thoughts continued in my mind throughout the day. I was eagerly waiting to meet her. Yes, I was never so attached with anyone before maybe that was the reason I woke up early and went to the station. Her train was on time and seeing her I was very happy. I wanted to hug her but instead Mahi instructed me to pick up her luggage and quickly to drop her to hostel.

"Walk fast." She said. I wondered what happened to her all of sudden. I dropped her to her hostel and came back home. I was completely annoyed with her behavior, although she did ask me to meet at CCD outlet in the morning.

Around 10, she came home and her voice made me jump off the bed.

"Dhruv, if you are late I won't talk with you." She whispered in my ear.

I got ready quickly as she was busy talking with mom and the others. She had got some sweets from Ajmer. Later, we reached CCD and our conversation continued as Mahi kept it very formal. I was wondering what had happened to her. Why was she actually behaving like a stranger? Or maybe, she was upset with me, I really couldn't understand.

"Mahi I thought you would kiss me or at least hug me, when I came to pick you in the morning." I finally said what was in my mind.

"Are you crazy why the hell will I do that?" She replied in a rude way. I didn't bother to say anything to her. I finished the coffee and we were walking towards my bike.

"Where should I drop you?" I asked politely.

"Hostel, where else will I go? Not like you I have a hell lot of work to do." She shouted in anger.

"Ok! fine no problem don't shout." I replied while she smiled and made feel confused.

She asked me to look at her and then slowly she came close to me. I was tensed whether she would slap me. Instead, she put her hands around my neck and kissed me on my lips. It was amazing! The first ever kiss of my life.

"Haila... now what was that?" I said.

"I was missing you like hell Dhruv and I love you. Happy now?" She said.

"Yes,.... I am." I said with a smile.

"Mahi, then why were you behaving so rudely?"

"I was just testing you Dhruv. Now come-on drop me to hostel we'll meet later in the evening I really have lot of work."

For any relation to work successfully, what exactly is required? I guess lots and lots of kisses. A really bad thought this was. But does that really strengthen a relation. Strange thoughts peeked in my mind when I wanted to kiss Mahi again. Well, it did happen on 3rd February 2008 the most amazing and embarrassing day of my life.

That Sunday, we had planned to go for a movie named 'Sunday' in the afternoon after lunch. I left home before Mahi left and we met on our bridge spot and went for the movie. Later, we spent time in a restaurant and I came home. My father was watching TV with his unique style of holding a remote in the left hand and then counting the Rudraksh in his right hand. He never got up from his chair for next 2 hours if he had the Rudraksh in his hand.

Without any hesitation I called up Mahi and we were sitting in my room. My father was unaware she was with me. I put on a movie on my computer and Mahi sat next to me holding my hand. After a minute I checked if my father was still busy and came back in my room. Mahi moved closer and kissed on my lips. It felt good I hold her tight and for the next 10-20seconds we were kissing passionately. I never thought I would kiss Mahi in my room, but yes it was happening with me. After few minutes I again went out to check my father's status and came back in soon. The next 5-10 minutes got us into each other. I almost forgot everything else and was completely enjoying the moment. It was already 8, I had to leave for office. I went in the kitchen my father was still busy watching TV I informed him that I am leaving for office. I came inside my room and was wearing my shoes when Mahi kissed me for the last time. She stood in front of me and kept her hands on my shoulder, I hold her waist and didn't notice when my hand was inside her top touching her bare skin. We stood in that posture for the next 5seconds until my father entered the room. He turned back immediately and didn't say anything.

"Oh Shit! We are screwed Mahi I am dead." I said. I didn't know what I could do now so was sitting all tensed when Mahi said, "Dhruv, go to office I'll talk with him."

"Everything is going to be messed up now. I know you won't talk with me, you will leave me. I always screw things."

"I had warned you Dhruv, not to do this at home but you never listen to anyone. Don't worry, go to office and I won't leave you". She assured me holding my hand.

"You give me a call when you talk with him and let me know", I said and kissed her twice like a shameless guy not feeling anything been caught by my own father kissing a girl. I knew he won't say anything but all the way to office I continued to think about what to do next. Mahi called saying everything was normal and came up with a story if anybody asked what we were doing

Next day when I opened my eyes I could see mom's face full of anger and questions staring at me. I pretended to be sleepy and pulled up the blanket over my head. Later, mom accompanied me to the doctor to get a medical certificate. I had the left leg problem, it used to pain a lot I had no clue about. Doctor said it was due to lack of calcium intake. But that was not important the most important thing was mom's questions.

"What were you and Mahi doing in your room yesterday?" She asked.

"Nothing. Why? What happened?" I said trying to be innocent.

"Do you know what your father told me about you, tell me the truth what's going between you and Mahi?"

"Nothing she is just a friend."

"So do you sit alone with your friend so close that you are not aware of anything around." I knew my father would have explained in a real un-explanatory manner. I remained silent for a minute.

"Mahi is getting married soon with her boyfriend. I said I will miss you so she hugged me. That's it." I said.

Wow! That was the story Mahi had come up with last night but mom was not going to believe this her next question was amazing.

"So is your father lying about what he saw last night?"

"I don't know."

"I will talk with Mahi, let her come home. I am not going to leave her". Mom's harsh words were a signal that she was really up to something. Soon this became a big gossip for everyone in the family. I had to face everyone with one stupid question. Where you really kissing Mahi?

"Why didn't you go to village if you had to kiss her?" Krish said when I was discussing the things with him.

"I don't know."

"Mahi knows that restaurant. She has been a lot many times there."

"Well she never told me."

"But when did you guys started dating." He asked eagerly.

"Well it's a long story, to cut it short a lot can happen over a coffee."

Mahi and I soon planned to visit the restaurant secretly. For me it was office party and for her she was going to her friend's place. All we did was making out in village passionately kissing each other. After that incident mom's behavior totally changed with Mahi. Due to this Mahi came less frequently at home. Somehow we always came up with some fake reasons to be together. The day was coming for which I would say I am not single anymore. Valentines' Day, the day when many couples are eagerly searching gifts for each other. I was also lined up with them in the gift shops to find the best gift for Mahi. All I could find was a champagne glass filled with dark chocolates. We met each other and decided to spend some time together. Well, the reason I gave at home was unique I was meeting Riya today and the gift was for her. On the other hand Mahi was out of town. We met each other in the afternoon and I gifted the champagne glass to Mahi. Later we went to the movie Fool's Gold at E-Square. After the movie it was dinner at some high quality restaurant my responsibility. So overall the day cost me a lot but I was very happy all dipped in the valentine fever to say I have a valentine and I don't hate Valentine's Day any more.

With Mahi around it was very difficult for me to continue my work and I didn't want myself to lose focus on my career. Things became normal at home and Mahi began to come again. At times when I would be working on the 3Ds Max software, Mahi would come along with her college projects. Some graphic designs which she would find it difficult to work on Adobe Photoshop, I would help her with it. She always sat next to me rather not move until her work was done. So I had to give some more time for my work. MAAC was planning for an exhibition where students would get a chance to showcase their talents in various fields of Animation starting right from clay modeling to animation and VFX. I wanted to work on it but was not able to come up with any concept to work upon. I wasn't sure as what exactly I could make in regards to the theme of the exhibition. I didn't get any proper ideas to work for me so I would continue to help her finish her project and other work. I began to get serious about her never wondered why that would happen to me. On the other hand Mahi expectations were increasing for me as even she was in love with me

She had invited me for the inter-college fashion show in which she was participating. I took Vishal along with me. We saw her perform and later waited for her near Nucleus Mall. She came along with her friend and asked me to drop her as it was already late. Vishal stayed back and we both left. Mahi was happy and tired but I never realized it. I dropped her nearby rather going along till her hostel. She was annoyed but didn't utter a work. Later, she vented her anger on phone and I had a hard time bringing her back to normal.

A day later, Mahi and I were at CCD when Enosh came to meet. I introduced him to Mahi and soon Mahi noticed his passion for photography. He began to click pictures with his phone of every other object which he found to be attractive.
"Mahi you can ignore him that will always happen." I said when she was smiling looking at him.
"He is just like you; anywhere you begin to click pictures." She replied.
"Yes we both do. Our friends always try to keep us away as we don't stop clicking given a camera."

Later, I was eagerly waiting for Enosh's response about Mahi.
"She is a nice girl."
"That's it."
"Yes. I know you won't marry her." He said.
"What if?"
"Then God help you." I couldn't understand his weird comment, rather I just ignored it. I was happy when Mahi was along and I never needed anybody. Mahi and I would continue to spend time with each other like and watch every possible movie and enjoy it to the fullest. One such was 'Jodha Akbar' where she gave me the entire knowledge of her state as many scenes were shot in Rajasthan. It was awesome.

Our team again gave a good performance in terms of the scorecard prepared and we got a chance to celebrate. After a huge discussion in the team meeting we finally decided to go to Mahabaleshwar as a part of team outing. So it was all set 2nd March 2008 a day to spend with the team. Although I was missing Mahi this outing helped me a lot to understand first Parth and then Riya. So talking about Parth he had grayish brown eyes not so fat but a healthy personality. He was best at giving people nicknames like Ashwin became Tommy, Vishal in our team became Harry Potter and I became Dukkar(meaning pig) and later Duksey. Vishal a very quiet guy who was never noticed on the entire floor but because he had specks he was given the name Harry Potter by Parth. About me I had no idea from where did he find that name for me. On the way to Mahabaleshwar we halted for tea where everyone spoke with Mahi along with Ashwin whose instant reaction where, "It's feels like I was talking to a kid Parya."

"Yes she is I call her chotta baby." I said and immediately he took the phone and asked Mahi "why do people call you chotta baby. Ok fine don't answer talk with Dhruv and it was nice talking to you." He said and handed over my phone.

"Does everyone in your office know me?" Mahi asked.

"Yes they do except Gaurav he's missing here and you want to talk with Saurav." I said.

"No baba you enjoy with your friends you make so many friends I really don't understand how?"

"Well, that's the way I am."

"I know and that's why I love you."

"I love you too. Bye, take care." I said and kept the phone.

"Ashwin she said, bye Tommy." I said.

"This is all because of this Parth."

"Maine kya kiya. People tease you not my fault." Parth always ready with this explanation every time and we ended up laughing. As we reached Mahabaleshwar we took pictures on every spot and enjoyed the scenic beauty of this awesome hill station. As the evening approached we were in the Mapro garden. Parth and I decided to buy the highest priced item Hot Chocolate Brownie. Everyone ordered the same. Nishant had ordered pizza which we all finished in few seconds, as the chocolate brownie was too sweet to digest. But it was indeed a fun trip along with everyone.

Few days later Suresh Enosh and I went along the same road towards Wai near Mahabaleshwar to attend Ajit's elder brother wedding. So if it was Enosh and I together it had to be more and more pictures on the way. That's what we did. But Ajit would have definitely killed if we hadn't reached on time so we continued our photo session later on our way back home. By the time we reached home I was totally exhausted. Enosh and I reached home and were surprised seeing Diya, mom, Mahi, Devika and Mentos everybody in my room, all set enjoying their third movie I guess Enchanted it was. I wondered how my computer was hijacked by these girls, but as Mahi was seated along with them, I didn't say anything.

I never had to introduce Enosh to Mahi as they already knew each other, while we were checking our pics the girls began to comment on each of them. So to begin with Devika, her looks would give an impression about her studious nature. Well, she was one but, the very first impression I had about her, she can never be trusted. My face reading was never wrong at times. She had those huge numbered specs just like Radhika. I wonder how people can screw up their eyes reading novels. Next was Mentos. Her bubbly and joyful nature helped her get this particular name. Her friends always called her Mentos as she was something out of this world. Radhika and Shreya were missing. I guess they had left for their classes. These four were the ones I hated the most as many times I would wake up with their loud voices. But here I was today getting familiar with everyone. Enosh left after he got the photos copied for him. I went out along with Mahi and all I did was watch her fight on the phone with her boyfriend. She was very upset so I got her home. We were surprised as the Chinese food was waiting for us bought by Devika and Mentos.

Few days later, at Holi mom made Gulab-Jamun, I ate the first piece and it reminded me of the competition I had with Radhika. I messaged her and very soon got a reply. She was on leave for some wedding at her native place. That year was an unexpected year I celebrated Holi with the hostel girls. We enjoyed at the water park, had got each other colored with different colors. That time I got myself into a playful mood along with Jiya whom I got friendly very quickly. I was enjoying every ride with her without any bad intentions in my mind or a thought of avoiding Mahi. Later in the evening, we all danced along the music beats played by the DJ. Mahi was upset with my behavior, thanks to Krish her anger reached the highest peak. It had made very difficult to get her back to normal. Again it was that another feeling in love called jealousy I found it in her. I had begun to enjoy this beautiful world which I had created around me. But, reality is what keeps you awake.

*****

Chapter 7

The Hostel Girls and Radhika...

Life always seems beautiful when you are surrounded by people and if you are always in demand. Mostly, when the people around are happy and smiling. I always wanted to be the reason for their laughter and smiles. I could see this happening in every aspect. Let it be in office, class or at home. But somewhere it was leading me I could have never thought of. After Holi, the girls started spending a lot of time at home. Mostly Radhika, even though we hardly spoke I began to like this girl. She was from Jabalpur, had come along with her friend Shreya during September 2007. These two were a perfect example of the female version Sholay's Jai-Veru kind of friendship. They were always found together. Radhika was Bengali, bubbly, enthusiastic and a fun to be with person, but on the other hand I would say I had never seen such a studious and career oriented girl in my life. She always shared a smile when I passed by which I never knew how to respond so it had to stop after few days. After the 20-20 world cup final she used to talk with me in a while or maybe I used to initiate small talks and was able to know a lot about her.

My parents treated every girl nicely so they always felt our house to be their home at least Radhika did. She used to share a lot of stuff about her class and office. I always found her and Shreya busy and running sometimes I for their early morning classes or maybe work. Hardly had I found them free except for cricket matches. I always wondered how they managed to be so active and sporty. Well, as per I remember even I used to be hyper-active during my college days, but everything changed. These days, sometimes it was Mahi who helped me wake up with her morning kisses when nobody was around and sometime it was Radhika's loud voice. I began to like the change happening around. That time, I never realized when Radhika became a very good friend of mine. And I still remember my very first mistake which lead to a big misunderstanding between me and her, which I was never able to rectify.

I had given some documents to Radhika in order to file my income tax returns and this is what happened. As usual the leg pain was unavoidable and was getting worst day by day. I had decided not to go out anywhere but,
"What are you doing Dhruv?" Radhika called up.
"I am about to sleep as have to go to work in the evening." I said.

"Can you come to my office to sign your documents?" She asked and I avoided going as was sleeping whereas, the truth was I wasn't able to bare my leg pain. I called her home even though it was my work.

She came home with the documents but something else had to happen with me as Mahi called up.

"Dhruv get ready quickly we have to go and get my laptop from Hinjewadi my brother has sent me." She said rather ordered me.

"Mahi my legs are paining. I won't be able to come." I tried to convince her but it didn't work.

"You had promised me yesterday I don't know anything. You have to come or else don't show me your face again."

I couldn't say no at that time and had to go all the way to Hinjewadi. On the other hand it lead to a great disappointment for Radhika. She came home along with the documents for my signature, but I went out along with Mahi. She didn't say anything, she left the documents at home I signed them and she got the work done the next day. My leg pain increased and in office causing tears to roll down my eyes as I was not able to bare the pain. Radhika avoided me for the next few day, well it was obvious but the worst was I wasn't able to avoid my leg pain but could never tell her the truth.

15th April 2008 Tuesday, I took Krish as Devika joined us to see the exhibition held by MAAC. I wasn't able to submit my work which kept hammering my mind. Many students had participated in it and had created their marvelous master piece to make the exhibition a great success. Few of them got job offers by some animation studios which I missed.

"I would have done a lot if I knew we can present any work." I said.

"It's ok bhaiya, you can do it next time." Devika tried to convince me. "I believe in you that you can create wonders." She said and I was not sure whether she was saying the truth or just trying to keeping my confidence up at that moment. But like I said she was the last girl to trust on this earth. I decided to work hard for the next exhibition and gave up my disappointment while we were coming back home.

Mahi had gone to Ajmer and I had nothing to do on the weekends. So Radhika, Devika, Krish and I went to Kakade Mall which was now renamed to SGS Mall as it was sold to a businessman. I took some snaps with Radhika and Devika. The phone calls and talk with Mahi started decreasing day by day.

There was always a change in her behavior when she was at home. I ignored thinking maybe she was with her family. Whenever she came back the change in her would make me go crazy but, given her some time she would be back to normal.

But somewhere in this enjoyment I forgot I was completely avoiding my sister Diya. Something was in her mind I always wanted to ask but I never did. One day she had to be admitted in the hospital due to her continuous illness. Doctor diagnosed it as TB; the reasons behind her illness were many. But when you have people around you never have to worry. The girls visited her in the hospital and also helped to recover from her illness and Diya was discharged from the hospital within a month.

It had been quite a long time I had watched any movie so I planned it with Diya but mom didn't allow her to come as she was still on medicines. 'Chronicles of Narnia-Prince Caspian' the sequel of 'Chronicles of Narnia' I watched it with my college friends. I liked the movie and wanted to watch it again so Diya didn't come but then it was Mahi and Radhika to watch the movie at Inox. In the movie hall, like always I wanted to sit in between the two. But, Mahi sat in middle instead, giving me no chance at all to interact with Radhika. But that never stopped us from talking with each other.
"Why are you holding my hand like a girl?" I said walking downstairs after movie.
"What do you mean Dhruv? I am a girl." She replied.
"I know that but you holding my hands is making me feel uncomfortable." Ok I never replied, just smiled at her and continued walking, thinking about Radhika. The way she was holding my hand without any fear of someone watching us. I would have never left her hand if Mahi wouldn't have been with us. I was happy that I was with these two lovely girls and wanted to spend some more time, clicking more pictures together. But mom had warned us to reach home early after the movie or else she won't serve the lunch made us run home immediately. I loved one thing here that everything was going perfect for me. Mahi my girlfriend and an awesome friend Radhika with whom I shared a special bond called friendship.

Few days later I was back home from night shift. Mahi was eagerly waiting for her results. Well, leaving my work aside I was forced to do her work so even I wanted to know her final exam results. I called her as I reached home after office.

"So what's the result?" I asked her.

"I am still waiting don't know if I'll get good marks." She said

"Relax Mahi, you will get good marks I know you are the best." I tried to calm her down.

"I know but I want to score more than these girls of my college who always want to compete me."

"You will. Anyways I am sleeping now. Once you get the result come home." I said and went off to sleep.

Later in the evening, I heard loud noises, thought it would be another dream. But the sound was familiar, it was Mahi. She secured 86% and stood first in her college. She was jumping off joy I felt very inspired at that moment and said to myself. Dhruv if it's not for you it should be for this girl you will become an Animator. While checking her mark-sheets all I said in her ears, "Congrats Mahi I love you and want to hug you right away but maybe not here when we meet in the evening." It was that evening again on the Nucleus mall terrace we were again hugging and kissing each other after a long time as next day she left for Ajmer for her vacations.

Yet another Sunday afternoon ended after another movie session. The girls came up with a plan to go out together in the evening. I suggested camp but then, it was their regular hangout place. So we decided to visit Saras Baugh. So it was Krish and me along with these 8girls except for Diya as she was still on bed rest.

We visited Saras Baugh, everyone was still deciding about dinner I was staring at Radhika while talking with Mahi. Mahi was in the train to Ajmer.

"Dhruv as soon as I left you are all set to flirt with the other girls." She said.

"I am not flirting Mahi, I was getting bored so we made this plan."

"Oh ho! Good… then you enjoy. I am about to sleep."

"So early?"

"Yes everyone in this train is already fast asleep so am feeling sleepy. Chalo you enjoy will talk later Love you... Bye."

"Me too..." I said and smiled while Radhika stood in front of me with a smile on her face. Krish had suggested a restaurant which everyone agreed and we ordered some eatable stuff which included a spicy pav bhaji.

I had ordered a non-spicy Pav-Bhaji but felt it was very spicy. So I wondered what the spicy would taste like. I tasted a bite of the spicy one in order to impress everyone rather say Radhika. Should say I really hate spicy food as I couldn't stop myself from sweating. These girls watched me carefully as I gulped water after every bite.

"Dhruv bhaiya you just can't eat anything spicy. Isn't it?" Mentos question left me in the most embarrassing situation. During this time, I continuously stared at Radhika, though I was interacting with her I must say I couldn't take my eyes of her. She was looking nice with a white blue hair-belt setting her curly hair behind and the white t-shirt. As we got out of the restaurant, I took Devika's bike and somehow convinced her to go by rickshaw as Radhika wanted to ride her bike. It was the very first time I was sat behind a girl.

We stopped at Sujata Cold-Drinks to drink Mastani (flavored milk). After spending a nice time with these girls we were back home. Not to forget, seating behind Radhika was the best part. But, it wasn't over yet as there was something more to come.

I got call while I was downstairs for a walk with my pets.

"Hi! Is this Dhruv?" All I could guess was a girl's voice.

"Yes I am Dhruv" I replied.

"Hi! I saw you few days back and I am madly in love with you. Can you meet me?"

I was confused and didn't know how to react so I disconnected the call. But again from the same number it was another girl.

"Why did you cut the phone I wanted to talk with you." She said.

"Hey listen I don't know who you are and I don't talk to strangers."

"It's ok, you are not a stranger for me I've been watching you for quite a few days.

"But you are for me." I said all aggravated.

"Ok fine let's meet. I stay near your house and if possible come and meet me right now." She said.

"Ok, I need some time to think. Give me some time." I said.

"Ok I'll call back in 15minutes. Bye." I tried to recall if I had heard this voice before. It sounded familiar but it kept changing the very next minute.

"Whom were you talking with Dhruv? You seem worried." Natasha asked me as I was already near her shop.

"I don't know, got this strange phone call. Can you check if you know this number?" I said as I told the entire plot to her. She tried to help me, but I got a call back again.

"Dhruv, why did you get Natasha involved in this? I want to meet you, not her". She said and it confused me.

"She is my friend and I need to know who you are, at least tell me you name."
"You know me very well Dhruv." She made me more confused and I didn't know how to react finally I hang up my phone and didn't pick up her call when she tried to callback for the next 3-4times. I went home and checked my mom's record where she stored all the information about the girls. Finally, my doubt was cleared it was the girl from hostel. I called back on the number.
"You girls have no other work than to trouble me?" I said.
"What do you mean you girls? There's nobody here with me."
"I know, Pooja I can hear Shreya, Radhika, Devika Mentos and the others laughing and giggling in the background." I said. The sound increased as the phone was on loudspeaker mode. Later, I spoke with everyone when one after another everyone had the same thing to say.
"Really Dhruv, we never thought you would get trapped so easily." I was speechless.

I always loved to gather information about people around in my slam book whenever I found them interesting and sweet. Mahi had already filled in and now Radhika was one such person. So I gave the book to her. She hadn't filled anything in it from the last two days. I asked her to get it filled straightaway as I had to give the other girls. They use to come home around 6.00pm instead of 8.30pm for dinner and I started to like it. Radhika came around 8 and handed over me the book.
"Radhika how much time you need to fill this book?" I asked her as she was taking a long time and when she gave me the book I was speechless. She had given her best to make the slam book look the best. She pasted various stickers on it one had the name Max, one pointed towards a car saying *'Apni Swift'*, well we both dreamt to buy one someday. One rough sketch of McDonald's coke-float, everything was too good. I read everything twice till I gave it to Shreya. Obviously I couldn't expect the same from her. For some reason I always felt a strong connection between Radhika and me. A strong bond was thus created between me and her. One incident I remember which did increase the respect for her; it was when I had asked her.

"Radhika do you drink beer?"
"Not really but have tried it with my uncle." She said.
"So would you like to come with me, I really feel like I want to drink it." I was expecting a yes.
"Sure Dhruv we'll go I have no problem." She said happily.

"Ok then, we'll go tomorrow as I have a weekly off. But what will you tell mom?" I asked her.

"I'll tell her that I am going to my aunt's place."

"Cool then tomorrow I'll pick you from somewhere, near your office." I said and the plan was all set.

Later that day in office I told Riya, I'm going out.

"What's new in that you always go out every day with Mahi."

"It's not Mahi, she is out of town. It's Radhika."

"What...?" She was shocked.

"Now who the hell is she?" She asked.

"Well she is from Jabalpur and comes home and is a very good friend of mine." I said.

"Dhruv, you never asked me out and what about Mahi?"

"Riya with you I am ever ready, let's go tomorrow. I'll cancel it with her." I said holding her hand and left it quickly as never wanted to give others a chance to say anything else.

"Stop flirting Dhruv, I know you very well you won't do anything of such and I am going out with Nitin", she said.

"Nitin, who? Oh! Your boyfriend. Well enjoy then, but I'll have a great time with her we are going for couple of beers."

"Dhruv you can't handle sprite and you are going to drink beer, are you crazy?"

"No ways it's never like that let's see tomorrow."

"Make sure you don't fall on her or else she will never come with you again. But I think I should call up Mahi."

"Oye Riya, why do you want to kill me? You enjoy your date, I'll enjoy mine."

Next day, I was ready to meet Radhika in the evening. After my animation class I came home, got ready and on my way I bought a red rose and a Cadbury's Temptation(Rum N Raisin). I picked her from office and we went to Koregoan Park area. I wanted to be with her in the same place where I had been with Mahi, but it was closed forever. Maybe it was for some good cause. Now I had no other clue of any other hotel in the area. I called up a friend who guided me and we reached Carnival. I had heard a lot about the place so this was the chance to explore it. On the way I asked Radhika

"Tumhe phool jyada pasand hai ya chocolates." The famous lines from the movie 'Kuch Kuch Hota Hai'.

"What happened to you all of sudden?" She asked.

"No I have not got anything. I am just asking."

"Wow Dhruv red rose for me." She said as I gave her the rose and then the chocolate.

"Dhruv you know something I don't eat chocolates."

"What? Are you serious?" I asked as my voice raise a bit.

"Yes Dhruv. Didn't Shreya tell you the day you all had gone to eat CAD-B."

"Well I don't remember but I still recall how horrible the food was in that reception party we all had been to. Anyways you will like this one and let me know how it is." I said as we reached Carnival.

The place was not exactly what I had thought of, it was totally different. As we moved in, we were guided to one of the cottage. This place had many cubicles of different sizes where we saw many couples sitting in each other's arms. A group of friends who enjoyed the drinks together in full swing so was the loud music that played the most horrible song of the year, 'mein talli ho gayi'. I stared at Radhika for a while when we sat down close to each other reading the menu card. She had worn a white t-shirt and blue jeans and was looking beautiful. We ordered beer and then the most unexpected thing Radhika gave me a red rose which I didn't know how exactly I should react to. No girl ever gives a red rose to a guy and guys never take red roses from girls but this one was something different, I accepted it. In a while the waiter came with a huge bottle of beer and stood in front of me I had no clue. I touched the bottle and then said yes ok. Within a moment he should have understood that I was a dumb in his restaurant and he then directly started pouring it in those large mugs. "Are we actually drinking so much? Well, I had to or else I would land-up making a fool of myself." A thought ran in my mind.

"Cheers Radhika for our first official beer together. Hope we never come back again because I don't know how the hell I will drink this." She started laughing on hearing this.

"It's ok Dhruv; nobody has forced you to finish the entire mug. Drink till you feel you can." She said.

I was totally lost that day and wanted to do something with her. I could have crossed my limits when something coming from Radhika stopped me as well as encouraged me that moment.

"Dhruv I love you from the day I saw you I am in love with you." She said holding my hand more tightly. That moment I totally forgot I was going around with Mahi and put my hand around her waist and pulled her closer towards me.

"What are you doing Dhruv?" She asked softly.

"I want to kiss you." I said. So was it the beer so something else that pushed me into these things I had no clue but I knew somewhere this was wrong. This wasn't me.

"I don't know how to kiss." She replied and maybe to break the silence I said. "And I don't know how to finish this beer. Look at this, you finished half the mug and it's only a sip from my glass. We ordered Chinese food and that helped me to finish half the glass. I took my hand away from her and then started to think when we would move outside this place.

"What happened Dhruv?" Radhika asked again.

"Nothing, I am not liking this place with all this loud music feel like going out."

"It's ok Dhruv, everything happens for a reason and I like this place with you, come-on taste the Chinese its really good." She tried to convince me and then she kept her head on my shoulder. She wrapped her hand around me grabbing it more tightly. I didn't know how to respond. I did kiss her on her forehead and then later checked the beer mug again.

"Radhika I never thought you can drink so fast. You've almost finished your mug and mine is still half filled. Can you help me, finish mine?" I said.

"Sure Dhruv but I guess we came to drink beer right?" She had that weird smile on her face.

"I know but tell you the truth I had never tasted beer ever in my life. This is my first time."

"Mine too, Dhruv."

"What you saying? Nobody will say this is your first time." And we both laughed at each other.

For that first time I thanked God that the Village restaurant was closed forever. I knew I would have taken an advantage of her innocence but it made me fall in love with her. She wanted the time to stop forever at that moment so did I but never tried to express it to her. While driving bike she had her arms around me holding tightly and later she kissed me on my cheek. The time spent with her was the most wonderful time I was never able to forget. Moreover, I was introduced to an innocent part of Radhika I had never known. I knew she can be that girl with whom anyone would wish to marry without any hesitation.

I dropped her to the hostel and her happy and smiling face made me more nervous. I drove my bike to all places in order to find an end to the roads in Pune. But neither the road ended nor did my thoughts. What I did that was wrong. I was leading to a wrong path as I had come across a girl who loves me, I knew she would let me do anything with her and will never say no to it. But wouldn't that be cheating on Mahi. But I never thought of Mahi that moment when I was with her. So what is it for me Mahi or Radhika? I was confused but finally, I left it to God, maybe he will know what can be best for me.

"So, how was your date with what's her name." Riya asked me.

"Radhika, it was good." I said.

"That's good but why are sounding dull? Didn't you enjoy it?" She asked me with a smile.

"Radhika loves me." I said.

"Oh Dhruv that's great, someone is rocking. What about me Dhruv?"

"Riya marry me, there won't be any problems in my life."

"And what should I tell mom that your tumor disappeared all of sudden."

"I know can't help it now, but why did you tell your mom?"

"You made a fool out of me Dhruv."

"I am sorry but tell me what should I do?" I asked again and soon we got ourselves into serious discussion.

"Dhruv you decide who is more important Mahi or Radhika. If she is just a friend then treat her as a friend and not as a girlfriend please don't give her false hope."

"I know. I will try." I said and got back to work. Later, we took dinner break together. Just a short 15 minutes short break was enough for us to enjoy the Chicken Biryani in a single plate. Well, that would be our everyday schedule which I always enjoyed. So everything was going perfect except for the fact I didn't knew if I would be able to tell Radhika the truth. I didn't love her but I didn't want to lose a friend either. What was happening to me I couldn't understand. Sometime I felt she was like the best thing that happened to me the previous day. Although I tried I couldn't avoid her leading to more problems in my life.

8th July 2008, a short trip planned to Mahabaleshwar, suggested by Rahul one of my college friend. His only guess was it must be drizzling in Mahabaleshwar and would have created a cool atmosphere, so nobody could avoid it.

"Where are you going Dhruv?" Radhika asked. I wanted to ignore her but I couldn't.

"I am going to Mahabaleshwar coming?" I asked just to check her opinion.

"When?" She said.

"Tomorrow morning 5.30am, its Sunday so it shouldn't be a problem right."

"Sure I'll be ready."

"But I am going with my friends."

"It's ok you will be there?" She said and went to her hostel happily. I totally forgot about this when I went to Abhishek's place to check who all were going. I wasn't sure if I would be able to keep myself away from her even though one part of my mind was continuously trying to avoid her. I couldn't and was never aware that my joke would be taken so seriously by her that she was all set to go the next day. The other unobvious thing that happened was it was raining so heavily that we were not able to drive our bikes properly. As we reached near Wai we had to stop under the shelter of a tree and when Rahul arrived, "Rahul. Is this what you call drizzling? We are not able to see the street properly." Everyone shouted one after another while I was busy with Enosh taking photos of everyone's reactions. We did give Rahul nice birthday bumps so at one point everyone loved the rains except for me, I hate rains.

Around 2.00pm I called up Radhika.

"Hey what's up?" I said.

"I was all ready for your phone call early morning Dhruv." She said.

"What? I am so sorry Radhika I totally forgot. Anyways how will I take you with my college friends where no girls are allowed" I said.

"Yes you are right but I took you seriously my fault maybe that's why I was crying the entire morning waiting for your call." She said.

"I am sorry Radhika I didn't know. Maybe next time we'll go together." I said trying to convince her.

"I will never come, Dhruv." And she hung up the phone and didn't pick up my call the entire day.

"You are screwed up Dhruv." I said to myself.

It's a hell lot of work to convince a girl. Living up to someone's expectations is a real tough job as for me it was Radhika. But not everything is so tough if you know how to play the game, I mean I knew how to convince people quickly and that was how she could never stay angry with me for a long while. My family decided to visit our sacred temple a place near Wai so called Mandra Devi. Yes that's the name we visit this place every year but this year it was after a real long time. Krish brought our cousin's car and dad invited Radhika to come with us.

My shift timing changed to graveyard shift and something's are always unexpected especially my brother Krish. I always had a habit of taking a bath as soon as I wake up. So I got ready early before everyone and later when Krish woke up and had to make a scene as always. The car needed a wash.

"I am not a driver here, every time this happens with me I know to drive so I have to wash the car he will never do anything." He started shouting which drove me mad. Now, where the hell these things come from. I did make it simple for him if he would have told me earlier I would have done it alone I don't need help in every task like he does.

"Ok fine don't do it if it's a problem for you. Why does he always need people to work under him, can't he do it alone." I said trying to prove my point but mom asked me to help him, I ignored and somehow it raised my anger. Radhika came in and got the opportunity to see the angry me.

"I am not coming". I said.

"Now don't create a scene Dhruv, get ready quickly." Mom said.

I said nothing whereas Radhika was trying to convince me a lot.

"Krish, he gets angry quickly, what would have happened if he would have helped him?" Mom said this to Radhika.

"Why should I? Why should I always be under his command? Am I elder to him or he is elder to me." I said it again.

"Ok now it's all done your father has helped him wash the car get ready and come quickly after a long time we are going out." See how he always gets the benefit of being the younger kid, I said to myself at the moment.

"Get ready Dhruv. Please, this is the first I want to have fun with you." Radhika tried to convince but I was adamant for some time.

"Ok now will you go out or should I change my clothes in front of you?" I said and Radhika started laughing maybe she wanted to hug me at that moment. My anger seized that time only for Radhika. Later I came and sat in the car. Well mom, dad and Diya were sitting behind and I was sitting right in between Radhika and Krish.

"Dono pagal hai aur gussa toh naak pe rehta hai dono ke." My mom said as we all sat in the car I wanted to say something but considered myself to be quite. Like always I was considered to be at fault and being elder to Krish I had to understand things.

Anyways, we finally left for our journey. We first headed towards Wai to visit the Ganesh temple. I began taking as many as possible clicks along with everyone. Later, we headed towards Mandra Devi temple where the sudden change in the climate added glory to our trip. The foggy weather was simply amazing. After visiting the temple we stopped at the nearby bushy tree for some shade to have lunch. After the lunch it was Radhika and me along with Krish and Diya busy clicking pictures. It continued even in the car while returning back still

I fell asleep. We came back home in the evening and I must say trip was awesome as Radhika accompanied us. It could have never been better without her.

It was 2nd July 2008 midnight, in office we had a huge call-flow and it was difficult for us to get any breaks. The worst thing to happen was with the work load I totally forgot it was Radhika's birthday. The point is nobody remembered her birthday and wished her the way we had wished Shreya on her birthday. I messaged her as was very tired and went off to sleep when I came home; I also missed my class that day. Radhika came home from office, we all wished her. She had a very bad day in office and was badly missing her family. I got busy with my work and when I came back in the kitchen, I found Radhika was crying. I was shocked to see her that way. We all tried to convince her and get that smile back on her face. Shreya came and asked me to do something, so I made up a plan to take her out in McDonald's and celebrate her birthday. I called up Vishal and left the house with him.

Mom somehow convinced her and asked her to go out with everyone. Krish, Diya and Shreya got her to McDonalds. Vishal and I arranged the birthday cake and also got a bouquet with my favorite combination of the yellow flowers along with 2-3 red in it. He dropped me near McDonalds and left. She was surprised with all the stuff that we arranged for her maybe that's what she needed someone to celebrate her birthday to make her feel special.

I met Shreya and Krish and gave them the cake and flowers and asked them to grab a table for us. And then went towards Diya and Radhika who were about to order something.
"Hey Radhika what happened to you? Does anybody cry on a birthday?" I said.
"I was missing my parents". She said.
"So that doesn't mean you start crying."
"Anyways now treat us with a nice party. All I want is one happy meal one Mc-Chicken, one Mc-Veggie, one French Fries, one Coke Float, one Veg Pizza Mc-Puff and. . ." I continued which bought her smile back. I took her upstairs where Krish and Shreya were sitting on the table with the cake. She was surprised and happy to find a cake waiting for her and the flowers she liked the most. She sat next to me rather I did. We then had her cut the cake and like always I took photos on my cell. Somehow I managed to create an impression making her happy and smile throughout the time we were together. Later when we came home her message said it all.

"Thanks Dhruv, this was my best birthday ever."

*****

Chapter 8

Silver Jubilee...

July was the month for movies. Mahi was back from Ajmer and had started working in a boutique. She did fight with mom as for not making any plans while she was in Pune. As Mahi was busy Radhika became my new movie partner. 'Jaane Tu Ya Jaane Na' was the first one. Radhika's special birthday treat for me. The plan was to watch a movie and then spend the entire day together. Unfortunately, was not able to be with her as Krish called up and had to get some work done. Radhika although never liked any movies began to watch with me and loved them a lot. Sunday afternoons she had classes and somehow Mahi was free so Mahi planned up for a movie. So it was 'Sarkar Raj' with Mahi along with Diya. She sat in between me and Diya. I didn't know, whether I enjoyed movies more with Radhika or with Mahi. I loved being with both of them. One was my girlfriend and other my best friend. Both liked and loved me equally and I was confused. But that didn't stop me from watching the movies. Radhika joined me for 'The Dark Knight' an early morning show. The movie was a bit lengthy than we expected and then it was a hell ride to get her in office on time. We had to quit the end as she was late for work. I liked the movie and planned to go again.

26th July 2008, it was along with Devika, Mentos Diya me and 12 other friends from office.

"Oh my God did you book the entire theatre?" Devika said as I showed her the tickets.

"No... Just the entire row!!!" I said.

"Dhruv Bhaiya you are crazy." Now who exactly was crazy here me or this Devika who always wanted to sit behind my bike even though she could drive her own bike, not to forget she had a great record of guys proposing her and she rejecting them.

"Bhaiya do you know the count is 62 now." She said as we were about to reach E-Square.

"Wow! Devika, what are you up to? How many hearts will you break?"

"Bhaiya I love you. But you know what I am waiting for that perfect guy maybe it's difficult to find one. I wish I haven't made you my brother I would have purposed you."

"Ok, now stop bluffing." I said trying to change the topic. This one girl from the hostel was always unpredictable. Well, I believe every other girl is. She would always add up this line bhaiya I love you in between any conversation and I would always go blank for a second.

"You know bhaiya one thing I always wanted to tell you."

"What?" I said as I parked the bike.

"Let it be you will feel bad."

"Oye nautanki…Tell me quickly."

"I wanted to say that you will never help a girl if at all she is found in trouble." I was left with a surprised expression at that moment. I never thought that she could actually say this. I didn't try to defend myself at that moment, instead I said. "Yes one should never save you, I'll tell the people please take her. She really irritates a lot." I said and we went inside the movie hall but her words were still in my mind. Everyone enjoyed the movie except for my lovely team manager Nishant who was completely pissed off by the movie.

But leaving everyone aside, it was my birthday that was what I was waiting for. Being my 25th birthday and I had many plans. Though, the plan to buy Pulsar was totally messed up because of the animation fees. I had decided that I will take all my friends and family together for dinner it would be a grand treat. I called up Enosh and went along with him and gifted myself a brand new guitar. It bought up a smile on most of the girls but for my parents it was just another waste of money.

Finally, the day came. I was getting ready for work when Natasha called up.

"So Dhruv what's going on?" She said.

"Nothing. I'm getting ready for work." I said.

"So you must have bought new clothes."

"Yes, had gone with Mahi for shopping last week."

"Good your life is all rocking around girls."

"I guess yes and maybe I see the call on waiting, it's Mahi I guess."

"Ok don't pick up I want to talk with you."

"Remember I was always the first one to wish you on your birthday."

"I know but last time you didn't."

"Ok, I am sorry for that and wish you many many happy returns of the day may all your dreams come true and you always keep smiling."

"Thanks Natasha." I said and she kept the phone. My cab was waiting downstairs and I was still searching my new jeans. Finally, I found it and there it was Radhika, Mahi, Shreya, Devika, Mentos everyone calling me one after another not to forget the messages that were continuously flashing on my cell phone when mom shouted.

"Dhruv wear your clothes first and then talk."

"What… You are naked?" Radhika said on the phone.

"No ways. What you started imagining?" I said.

"Oh no please I better don't do that. Anyways, Happy Birthday."

"Thanks a lot and we'll talk later, my cab is waiting."

"Ok bye and enjoy." She hung up and then it was Mahi.

"Kya kar raha hai mera bachha?" She said.

"I am getting ready, my cab is waiting downstairs."

"So you are not going to talk with me? Anyways, Happy Birthday."

"Thanks Mahi and I am in a little hurry will talk later ok bye."

Mahi called up again and the phone calls continued one after another even in the cab. For the first time I was not sleeping in the cab, I was talking on the phone like others but today it was only me who was talking on the phone.

I reached office and first person to meet was Parth.

"Oh ho birthday boy many many happy returns of the day." He said.

"Thanks Parth." I said.

"Hey listen someone told the entire floor that you are going to throw a party I really don't know who did it."

"Wow! Thanks Parth and I am sure you might have got your carry bags along with you. By the way its you who spread the news asshole." I said staring at him and pushing him away.

"When did I? You very well know I never do such things. Anyways I have bought the carry bags and have not eaten anything since morning for the party, so you better give the party." He said but that was not enough, he called up everyone.

"Hey people the birthday boy is here, let's give him some birthday bumps." He shouted and soon everybody on the floor lifted me up including all the managers and they hit me so hard making it impossible for me to sit on the chair. All I did after that was went running behind Parth saying. "Parth I am going to kill you."

"What did I do?" He said when finally I stopped chasing him, he knew it very well I would do nothing but give him a punch in his stomach when he came near as he could not stay away for a long time.

"Happy Birthday Dhruv, someone is looking handsome today". Riya greeted as she met me.

"Thanks Riya now won't you give me a hug." Well I didn't say that instead didn't leave her hand.

"That's it you only need a reason to get close to Riya." Gaurav added.

"Please…Gaurav you people didn't even wish me and like always you will disturb me and Riya. Anyways she is sitting next to me so there won't be any problem." I said and later thanks to Parth everyone remembered my birthday and wished me one after another and entire day in office was awesome. I came home in the morning and then after attending all phone call I went off to bed. A smile continued throughout as I felt turning 25 was the best thing so far. In MAAC we were waiting for the next batch of Autodesk Maya to start so there were no classes. Around 3.00pm when I was still in bed when I saw with half opened eyes many gifts lying beside me. I checked them one after another, it contained a picture of me and Radhika framed in a nice wrapped card, then a pumpkin headed cup which had something written in it. 'You look like this when you avoid shaving'. A Donald duck pen stand which said 'stop copying Donald you are a better cartoon'. A fur-toy of a tiger with a tag that said 'Hello Sher-Khan'. I was thrilled by those gifts one thing that came up in my mind 'Radhika is crazy.' There was more. A pen-stand which had a bugs bunny character engraved on it. These girls had specially selected these stuff as they knew I was in to animation and these were some of my favorite cartoon characters especially Donald. After checking all the gifts I closed my eyes again as I had not totally woke up yet. So I didn't read the card but within 10-15 minutes I opened my eyes and started reading it.

To,
My Dearest, Sweetest, Wonderful and Brave Bhaiya,

You've always been so dear and
so warmly thought of, too,
That it really is a pleasure wishing
happiness for you,
Also wishing you the best of times
and hoping the year ahead will bring
Just what a special Bhaiya like you
always deserves--
The best of everything.

Have a Wonderful Birthday.

Well that was not all in that card on its right, Devika had filled up the entire page to make me feel special.

Dearest Bhaiya,

Feels like telling you a lots of things through this card. But unfortunately, every feeling cannot be put in to words.

I really never thought (when we first met) that we would end up so good friends, that you turn out to be so good.

Your birthday gives me the opportunity to tell you how important, is the position that you hold in my life. You are really a very "Special Bhaiya."

You are so considerate about everyone around you. You are the person who would not mind taking that one extra step to make your loved ones happy, even if it is at the cost of your happiness.

I am really lucky to have you as my brother. [This is NOT A JOKE].

Bhaiya, have a great day and a superb year. May God give you all the joy in this world. Really you deserve them all for being so good & wonderful.

HAPPY BIRTHDAY.

P.S:- That comment which I said in the parking at E-Square was just to get your reaction. I really didn't mean it. I know you are just the opposite of that... Keep Smiling.

What could I say after reading that? I was happy but most important very sleepy after stressing my eyes so much to read all the praises for me in that letter. I went off to sleep again and woke-up at 5.00pm.

"Dhruv was that a dream I getting those gifts, it was it was awesome." I said to myself when I got up.

"Wake up...Birthday boy. Did you check your gifts?" Diya said as she saw me awake.

I looked again besides my pillow and said, *"It was not a dream. This is all real, for the first time in my life. I am the best."* I said and started getting ready quickly. I took a bath and first went to Dagdushet temple and then spent some time with friends.

I came home soon as all the girls were waiting for me with a birthday cake. I had already decided that I will be taking all my friends and relatives together for dinner, so I was also waiting for all the others to come. Later around 7.30pm I cut the cake, Mahi took snaps while Radhika was feeding me the cake and it was a real fun to celebrate birthday among these girls. I asked everyone to come along with me to the hotel but they said no, there was a big reason behind it, not that they didn't wanted to come but they had decided not to come. Later,

Radhika and Mahi were busy with my nephew and Sweety's kids. She had given birth to seven puppies and maybe yet another reason why most of the girls were at home. Mom called me inside and then said,

"Don't ask anyone to come along with us your father won't like it as it is you are taking us out has already made him angry." I was shocked. It was my birthday and yet the second year for my father to act weird again. I had asked mom to give the girls a holiday. I had saved money for this day as it was my 25th birthday and I wanted to celebrate it with everyone. Maybe that was the reason, the girls already knew everything that was going in the family. Finally we left home and the girls were back to their hostel, we reached the hotel. It was crowded so the manager asked us to wait for 10-15minutes. My father didn't want to wait, I tried to stop him but he didn't. He just said, "You people carry on I won't wait I don't like this place."

"Why are you leaving? Should we go to another place?" Krish asked him but he didn't listen to anyone and started walking back home. I couldn't believe he was actually doing this. I tried to stop him but he didn't, later mom sent Krish to convince him but it was of no use. I didn't know how to react should I go behind my father back home and cancel the treat or should I wait with my relatives. Later I made up my mind not to think of him and just asked everyone to get inside as the manger called up my name within 5minutes. I tried to stop my tears I didn't cry or let anyone know how bad I felt at that moment for being treated in such a manner by my father. All I did was kept smiling in front of everyone. After we came out Krish shouted, "This is all because of her. Why don't you just get lost from our lives?" pointing towards Diya.

"I will even I don't want to be with you people." She said back and started crying. I didn't say anything at that moment was just watching everyone creating a scene outside the hotel, Diya kept crying out loud and I didn't do anything. I knew this would create some more problems but one thing I could never forget my birthday was ruined by my father again for the second time.

*****

Chapter 9

Diya Story

Some things happen unexpectedly and we can do nothing about it. There are chances we could work to get them working but before we know that could be done, it already gone.

6th August 2008, a year was complete with the animation course and with my ignorance towards the course I was just not able to understand how fast the time moved on so did the course. The second software of the production section was about to begin. Autodesk Maya, one of the best software used in the field of animation. Most of the animated movies are based on this software. So learning it was going to be fun and excitement. Within a year everything had changed in class, but the worst part with me was I was not able to get my hands on any of the software taught so far. I shouldn't blame anybody in this, it was entirely my fault. Anyways this was about the first day of the lecture for Autodesk Maya. Sarang sir was our new faculty, he was about to start when a discussion started within my batch-mates, I was just a listener at that moment. "He can't be our faculty I have heard that he can't teach properly." One of them said.

"Ajay sir was going to continue with the Maya software." I tried to speak.

"Yes, you are right we should talk to Swapnali madam about this". Sumeet said.

"Who will take the initiative?" Hrishikesh said.

"I'll go just one of you come with me. Sumeet you come we'll go." Swara said and left the classroom with him before sir entered with the attendance register. Within the next 15 minutes Swapnali madam was in the class.

"How many people are from Ajay sir's batch and have a problem here, raise their hands". She said.

She had a loud and firm voice which could set fear in the entire MAAC building, nobody was found in the lobby when she was around and after what she said I was in a confused state whether I should raise my hands or not.

"Come on, only these two people have problem?" She said and then within a second Hrishikesh raised his hand and so did the others. Finally I had to raise my hand even though I never had any problem. The reason was simple how can we judge a person whether he is not good enough if he has not taught us anything.

She called us outside the class and asked sir to continue teaching the others. "Ajay sir did you tell them to do such crazy things." Swapnali madam called Ajay sir as we all moved into her cabin. Now like fools we were all standing with our head down. For the first time I saw her talking very politely to all of us. She was trying to explain things to us that Sarang sir was send from the Andheri head-office to this branch and is one of the best faculties for Maya. Swara tried to defend that we wanted Ajay sir to continue teaching us and not the new faculty. The discussion continued for quite a long time with the final conclusion that we should attend a few lectures and then decide if he is not the correct faculty. So, it was Monday that we decided to sit for his lecture. The very first lecture we realized our mistake and came to know that he was actually one of the best faculties to teach this software.

At home everything was fine except the fact that Radhika always wanted to be with me and I was in a confused state of mind whether I should be with Mahi or Radhika. Obviously, I never needed anyone when I was with Mahi, the result was I broke up Radhika's heart and left her crying on many occasions. One of them was when we went to Tamhni Ghat along with Diya, Mahi, Devika, Mentos and Mahi's room-mate Pooja. It was a few hours' drive along with these girls and unfortunately the last day of enjoyment with Diya. We enjoyed a lot but on the other hand Radhika was attending her CA classes sitting all wet inside the class with her eyes all wet with tears. She would have bunked her class that day had I asked her to come. I was angry on her for some reason so I didn't ask her. She felt bad that I ignored her. The thing was I could never control my anger no matter how easy it was. I always used to be angry on her but somewhere I never wanted to hurt her. I felt bad when I came to know how she felt that day, but I never expressed it to her. She always enjoyed with me, but apart from this something big was coming for me and my family.

13th August 2008, I missed my class and had been sleepy the entire day whenever I opened my eyes I would find Diya doing something which I could not understand. She was continuously walking in the living room, maybe was thinking of something. Around 5, Mahi came home and asked.
"Didi kidhar hai?"
I just jumped out of bed when I heard this. She had gone and I began to search the entire house every room again and again. I looked out of the windows then again inside the house but was not able to find her. At that time it was only me and mom at home. Mom started crying out loud and Mahi didn't know how to react. She tried to console her saying kaku don't cry she might have gone out she will come back. I didn't know how to react later I went to my cousin's work

place and asked him to come with me. We tried to search her even though we didn't know where to find her. Mom asked Mahi not to let one else know about this. But things are always the opposite, every other girl was concerned about her and wanted to know where she was, but this time Mahi helped out a lot by telling everyone she has gone to her aunt's place. Around 9.30pm Radhika and Shreya returned home after their classes got over. Mom served them food and later stood in the window, her eyes still looking for her daughter. I came inside as soon as Shreya finished her food and left. Radhika ignored me; I didn't know how to talk with her as I had made her cry many times. I was sure she won't help me.

"Radhika. I need to talk with you"

"What Dhruv?" She said with all the anger in her eyes and avoided any eye contact with me.

"Didi has not gone to aunt's place she ran from the house in the evening." I said and immediately she looked up.

"What? Dhruv is this some kind of a joke in order to make me talk with you."

"No Radhika I am serious. Why do you think mom is standing near the window?" She didn't say anything after that but kept silent and before leaving she looked at me and came closer.

"Dhruv, if you need any kind of help call me any time I'll be there for you". She said and left I did know how to respond I tried to stop her but she didn't respond at that moment.

Later I messaged her and said, "I am sorry for being rude and ignoring you always but you are my best friend Radhika I never want to lose you". She didn't reply but I knew she will be with me. Later I asked mom to go to sleep, but around 1.30am I started hearing something which I didn't know how to react. Mom and dad were crying out loud I wanted to go inside and try to convince them not to cry but it was never possible for me. Maybe I never knew how I should do that. I thought for a while looked at Sweety, even her eyes seemed wet and while staring at her my eyes got wet and I began to sob. I wiped off my tears when mom came out.

"Dhruv don't you want to go to office." Mom asked.

"No, I'll go when Krish is back from work." I said. Krish had joined UBICS and was working from 6.00pm to 3.00am. He came home and I woke up again when it was these three crying all together.

"Why didn't you call me bhai?" Krish said wiping off his tears.

"I did but your cell was switched off."

"You should have left a message; I would have come home immediately." I didn't say anything as at that time I could feel the growing gap I was standing beside the door with Sweety besides me, whereas Krish was sitting in between mom and dad.

Diya left forever, leaving behind a huge gap between me and my parents which I am still not able to fill up. My family was split into two Krish mom and dad on one side and me on the other.

Diya is my elder sister, born on 15th October in Bhusawal. The first thing she gets from her father was negligence as she was a girl. My mom said that father never saw her face till the time she came back to Pune whereas, he came with a gold ring to see me when I was born. Now who can believe this the way he behaves with me I could never believe it. She was studying in Dastur I remember because of her brilliant performance I got the admission in that school. But she was ignored many times. So she failed in her 1st grade. My father sent her to his sister's place all the way to Satara. For the next 2-3years she was studying and doing all household work in Satara. Diya never uttered a word from her mouth, ignored the cruel behavior of my aunt. I never cared who she was to me but after Diya spoke about the way she was harassed by her she was only my father's sister and nothing else. Later when Diya came back home, I remember I was in fourth grade; Diya and I were playing with one of my younger cousin instead of studying during the exams. I used to score pretty decent marks always above 80% in class. Mom got angry and took a rod and hit me and Diya with it as we weren't studying. My anger was always uncontrollable I didn't talk with my mom for the next 2-3days whereas Diya began talking within the next 2-3hours as if nothing had ever happened. That was Diya, a cool person who never bothered in anyone's life, always known as the most descent girl of my family.

After we got her back from Satara she got admission in St. Anne's school where she somehow managed to pass fifth grade and a time came when I was in seventh and she was still in sixth. That moment she was again forced to take a huge jump in her academic career. She filled in the form for 10th externals which in the first attempt she cleared all the subjects with good marks except for algebra and geometry. She tried hard but she was never able to clear those subjects. In her long run she was never able to make any friends as most of the time she stayed home because she was a girl. Now how fair was that with her? I would have never thought about this as even I fought with her many times. About 5-6years back she finally got a job for herself in this small office of a

Vastu-Consultant. At that time our family was running through financial crises and she helped a lot to support the family. I can say even though she was not educated properly she had all the ethics and moral values for the family which nobody else did. She had no friends and no other life except for this office, so falling in love with her boss would be quiet obvious. But the only problem was he was already married apart from the caste. I always believe that all caste and religion doesn't matter, they give the same teaching to everyone, love and respect every individual. But many people always fail to understand this. Diya ran with her boss two years back to Bangalore and my family members did have him behind the bars for kidnapping their daughter which he didn't.

After that incident Diya started living with us but was tortured every day. She used to do everything which mom asked her to do and never uttered a word. She was always treated as if she had committed the biggest crime in this world. My father would abuse her and sometimes she would speak calmly to forget him. Nobody spoke with her properly neither did I. Maybe this could have been avoided by my dad, had he stayed back at the hotel on my birthday and Krish wouldn't have fought with her she wouldn't have left the house. But this was not only about the fight on my birthday. Diya had been living every day in humiliation. She never said to anyone and now she finally left. If at all I would have talked with her at least once this day would have never come.

Diya's entire life had flashed in front of my eyes while I kept driving towards office. The tears kept rolling down while I made one of the toughest decisions of my life that day, I would never talk with her again in my life. I didn't know if it was the right decision I took at that moment. It was 6.30am when I reached office, everyone kept staring at me while I was walking through the lobby towards Nishant's desk.

"Wow Dhruv that's so early to office." Gaurav said as he noticed me.

"Why did you come? As it is the office will get over after sometime." Saurav added.

They had more stuff to make fun of me at that moment but seeing my seriousness everyone became quiet after sometime. I met Nishant and his eyes had many questions lined up for me.

"Is this the time to come to office Dhruv? This is too much I should think of signing some warning letters to you now. You are utilizing too much of my freedom given to you."

"I am sorry Nishant."

"What sorry tomorrow everyone will start coming late if I don't take an action against you. Now come on login quickly we have a huge call-flow coming after 8.00am."

"Nishant I am not here to login in, instead I wanted your help." I said and his anger led into confusion of what I was up to. I told him everything that happened at home and he showed up his kindness as immediately he asked me to leave.

"Dhruv these things spread like fire and people would make fun of it, make sure you keep it for yourself and tell this to nobody in office. I will mark a sick leave for you if there are any."

"Oh Nishant", I paused and later said, "I don't have any sick leaves left I used all of them but I have two casual leaves".

"You would never change." He said.

"Yes Dhruv will never change Nishant." Saurav said as he came towards Nishant's desk.

"Get back to your desk Saurav I'll talk to you later." Nishant said and then asked me to leave and not to waste much time with the others.

Riya and Parth stopped me and I told them about Diya as I couldn't stop the tears for the moment. She hold my hand wiped off my tears and advised me to look after everyone in the family and myself. I knew those words of concern meant a lot to me and I knew I was never alone till the time I had friend like Riya.

Few days went, Ganesh Festival was about to start. Nobody showed interest in doing anything this year the decoration was not done and everything was all messed up at home. I was left alone and then only thing left for me was my same old routine, attend class and go to office. A day before the Ganesh festival Krish and I were struggling with the decoration as I was completely lost. Diya would always suggest ways to make it simple and we always fought on each other's view. I was missing her but never showed it to anyone. Radhika and Shreya came along with Devika and Mentos in the evening.

"Dhruv when will you put up everything?" Mentos said.

"I don't know." I replied.

"Need some help?" She asked.

"Sure." I said and these four helped us with the decoration and everything was setup on time which added a smile on my face.

Mentos wanted to come to get the Ganesh idol so I asked her to be on time. But, mom never told me that Radhika wanted to come and I forgot to ask her. Without any wrong intentions I was screwed up again as I didn't invite her. I totally forgot that Mahi and Radhika stayed in the same hostel so did Mentos. The next morning I called up Mahi and on the other hand Radhika was crying because I didn't inform her.

Radhika was upset and angry on me and didn't talk with me again for the next few days as I couldn't explain her it wasn't my fault I didn't mean to hurt her. During the entire time I felt the emptiness of Diya in the house. Had she been here I wouldn't have screwed up things so badly.

2-3 days later I was watching a movie on my computer as was alone at home. Krish mom and dad where again out in order to talk with Diya. They had found her and she was along with her boss. Later when Devika and Mentos came home I told them what exactly happened as finally my parents and Krish had found Diya. They went to her boss's home; he was sitting with his wife and Diya. They tried to convince her to come home but she didn't bother at all. My parents and Krish broke all the relation with Diya. Krish told me that she hit mom and later dad kicked her. The entire scene was horrible as Diya launched a police complaint against mom and dad for harassing her at her new home.
"Devika and Mentos I need a favor from you both."
"Yes bhaiya tell us."
"Will you come to the police station if at all you are asked to? You need to tell them that Diya was never in trouble when she was here."
"We will definitely, I am in." That was Devika's reaction and Mentos supporting her. Mahi joined us later but her response was totally different, maybe I expected too much from her.
"Dhruv, we are college students, we are here to study we can't spoil our career by getting into such things. I called up Gaurav and he had advised me to stay away from this matter, so I am sorry I won't be able to help." She said. I knew I was expecting too much from people as some times I was being neglected when mom and dad would discuss things only with Krish and I never knew what was going in their minds. I began eating dinner alone in my room watching a movie which became an everyday routine and till date I hardly remember if we all ate together.

Diya left the house and I felt as if I was detached from the family. A support she had always been to me I never knew I needed one until she was gone. Mahi was my girlfriend but every time she was back from her home town there was a change in her behavior. Radhika loved me but I was not sure if that would help me in anyway. Many things were messed up as Diya left and expecting from anyone would only leave me confused and worried. What was I expecting and what did Mahi and Radhika expect from me?

*****

Chapter 10

Unexpected Expectations...

With the changes happening around me I was certain there was much more for me. In office we were supporting only network-related calls so along with the operating system Windows-XP it was Windows Vista that we were being trained on. The training made me more tired and usually I ended up sleeping more and missed my animation classes on a regular basis. It was getting very difficult to stay awake till 4.00pm after I came home from work at 11.30am; also it was the exam that was making me take this particular decision to quit the job, but I wasn't sure if I would do it.

I still had to clear my graduation exams which I had screwed up twice. I made up my mind to quit the job and it was my last day everybody knew about it in the office except for my manager. That day I was sitting next to Riya when we were busy chatting through the online messenger.
"Dhruv, don't go. Whom will I fight with in office?" She replied and looked at me. We smiled and that chat continued till the day in office was over along with the last Chicken Biryani we ate together. Around 5.00am Riya, Abhi, Parth and I were near the tea-stall for break-fast. After the breakfast I asked Abhi to stay back as I went to drop Riya home.
"So that's it Dhruv the final day is over."
"I'll miss you Riya." I said.
"I will too Dhruv." She said and gave me a nice hug and a kiss on my cheek. After that she didn't wait for even a single second.
"Bye Dhruv. Take Care." She said and ran upstairs. Somehow that feeling of leaving Riya got my eyes wet and I returned back where Parth and Abhi were waiting.

2-3days later, Parth planned a dinner with Riya, me and Mahi. 26th September 2008, I guess that was the day he came home in his car, I got in and we picked up Mahi and then Riya. Riya was looking weird as she hadn't tied up her hair properly.
"Riya aaj kya ghar pe zhadoo lagaya kya?" Parth asked Riya.
"Why? What happened?" She asked
"Nothing Riya he is just trying to pull your legs, anyways Parth I should say that Riya has finally managed to take a bath after a long time. Yippee." I said.

"Oh! Shut up you guys, first of all you called up so early I couldn't get time to comb my hair properly. Anyways hi Mahi" She said waving off her hand to Mahi.

"By the way the ideal time to take a bath is in the morning and not in the evening Riya." I said as we all started laughing.

"Do these guys always trouble you Riya?" Mahi asked.

"Yes they do, especially Dhruv and today this Parth has started."

"What did I do? This is all because of this Dukkar." Parth said.

"Dukkar? You people call him that in office?" Mahi was surprised.

"I had warned him not to call me by that name in front of you." I gave an angry look to Parth and a punch on his hand.

"Maine kya kiya? Hey, Mahi control you boyfriend he's getting violent" Parth said.

"Why don't you hit him back?" She replied immediately.

"Oh no...no, we usually don't beat our pets; we take good care of them." He said again when I gave him another punch.

"Ok Dhruv, now tell me where to go I don't know the roads." Parth asked me for directions.

"I won't say anything."

"Riya don't blame me if we get late."

"Ok fine take a left from here."

"Why didn't you say that after we were in between the road. Riya people will kill me if I drive according to his instructions." He said trying to take that sharp turn as we had already reached in the middle of a square. We reached DP road where these two girls got down, Riya wanted to buy some chocolates for her boyfriend. While they were buying chocolates I bought flowers for these two. Later we moved on to a restaurant at Koregoan Park named 'Zafrani Zinc' suggested by Riya. We all liked the ambience of the restaurant. Also every bite of the food tasted real good. In short, everything seemed perfect after a real long time but to add more fun Parth was always ready.

After enjoying the meal, the waiter bought us a box which had the bill in it. "Bhaiya what dish is this we don't want it. Who ordered this? Riya, why do you order such dish?" Parth began as usual quiet loud to add a smile on the manager's face. I wondered what was that smile for. Then, suddenly it clicked me maybe that was a way to appreciate customers.

"Parth open the box it has fortune cards in it." Riya said which wiped out my thoughts and we picked up the cards and began reading.

Riya: You're guided to champion a cause, such as a social issue, a charitable group, or a person is distress. You can single handedly make a positive difference in the world.

Mahi: Although it may feel as if you're unsafe or in dark. You are completely safe, protected and guided. Don't be fooled by illusions of fear, instead, be courageous and shore up your personal strength. There's a blessing in this situation and by focusing on finding that benefit, you're sure to discover it.

Me: You need to play more music, because it will help you find the answers and solutions that you're seeking. This may involve playing an instrument perhaps by picking up one that you studied in the past or just taking lessons.

Parth: He didn't show up his card just tore it as soon as he read it.

We all didn't really believed in the fortune but mine made sense, so I was eager to read the others. Later Riya and Mahi were surprised as I gave them the flower bouquets.

"This is for spending a lovely evening with the smartest and the other not so smart bachelors, I mean me and Parth." I said while giving the flowers to Riya and Mahi.

"Why are you boring us Dhruv?" Parth said.

"I know, thanks guys for the surprise the flowers are nice." Riya added and we dropped her in the mid-way as she was about to meet Nitin, then later dropped Mahi.

"Dhruv, can we talk for some time?" Parth asked me.

"What happened Parth? Anything serious?" I said.

"Nothing, its ok if you are getting late I'll drop you back home."

"Let's go Parth I have plenty of time." I said and we went towards the Z-bridge. He light up a cigarette and started smoking.

"Do you have any friend who is good in Accounts I need someone to teach me?" He said.

"Is that what you wanted to say Parth?" I said. He stayed quiet and didn't say anything till his cigarette was over and he light up the second.

"There's this girl named Meera, I am in love with. For four years we were together." He said and paused for a moment. I could sense the seriousness in his tone. Maybe he wanted to say a lot but within moments I was able to see tears rolling down his eyes.

"I did everything for her whatever was possible to make her happy yet she broke up with me." He continued telling me each and every moment he spent with her and about his past life. I couldn't believe Parth actually had such a past which he had hidden from others. At that time every word he spoke felt as if he was lamenting his heart out. I was dazed but somehow I tried to convince him. He wiped off his tears and finished his cigarette.

"Hey Dhruv, please tell me if you find someone who could teach me accounts." He said and I knew if there's any person that could actually help him was Radhika.

"Parth I'll ask Radhika if she can help you with accounts. She is doing her CA." I said immediately. I knew Radhika would not hesitate to help him. She was always very helpful and I knew I was not wrong. Somehow I knew she would also help him get out of this as well. I had no clue why I thought so but I kept thinking about Parth the entire night after we came back home.

Next day Riya called me near Aundh CCD in the evening. As I was going through the menu when Riya handed over me a box saying, "Dhruv, I've bought you something."

"FAST-TRACK!" I shouted instantaneously, as I opened the box. "You liked it?" She said.

"Its awesome. I always wanted to buy one." I said.

"Come back Dhruv I'll miss you badly."

"I miss you too. I've decided that after my exams are over I will join the office again." I said.

"Are you serious Dhruv?" She said happily.

"Yes Riya, I am."

"I should have waited for some more time before giving you this gift." She said with a smile.

"Oh I know but I won't give it back to you now. What if I don't come back?" I said.

"Oh! Dhruv, keep it I won't take it but if you are serious please come back, I won't feel like working without you."

"Yes I will Riya and please can you do something for Parth."

"Did he tell you about Meera?"

"Yes he did and we should help him."

"Maybe try to get her number and we can talk with her."

"Yes, but Parth won't like it." She said and our discussion continued. Later she hugged me.

"I wished I would have left the office earlier maybe you would have hugged me n number of times till now then."

"Chal bhag Dhruv, I would have never done that." She said and we left, she went to office and I came back home. I started studying for my exams seriously and finally finished them with confidence. Later, Vishal and I joined a gym. I also joined a guitar class along with Riya. So I could meet her every alternate day.

"When are you planning to join office Dhruv?" Riya asked me.

"Next week, maybe. I don't know." I said.

"What do you mean I don't know?" Riya asked me.

"Mahi is not talking properly something has happened to her." I said.

"Call her up and talk with her Dhruv, everything will be fine."

"She is leaving Pune today." I said.

"So did you talk with her."

"No she is angry on me and I know once she returns back she would be total different person."

"Dhruv, if she is leaving today, go and meet her tell her what you feel for her. Everything will be fine." Riya said.

"Yes you are right Riya. Maybe I should leave right now. Her train is about to leave within the next half an hour. I'll meet her and sort it out." I said and left for station.

I called up Mahi when I reached the station. She was already getting inside the train so she hung up the phone before I could know where she was. I started checking each and every compartment as there was only one train on the platform.

"Mahi where are you?" I called up again.

"I left Pune you continue with Riya she is more important."

"Hey it not like that. Listen." I tried to stop her from hanging up the phone but was of no use. I stood there for a moment thinking what exactly had gone wrong. Riya was never a problem between me and her. Some questions I wasn't able to get answers from her. When I was about to return I saw a girl standing at the entrance of the compartment kissing her boyfriend. The smile looking at them just clicked a thought maybe I might have been wrong somewhere but where?

The exams were over, regular gym and guitar class had become a part of my routine along with the animation classes. Autodesk Maya was getting a bit tricky and interesting. One day after class I called up Radhika.

"Hey Radhika what are you doing?" I said.

"Nothing, I'm about to leave office."

"Come to pizza hut." I said.

"Fine I'll be there within 10-15minutes. Wait for me." She said and after which I called up Devika and Mentos. Radhika came within the next 10-15 minutes as she promised.

"Devika and Mentos are on the way they will reach here in 10-20 minutes." I said.

"Why did you call them Dhruv I thought it's only you and me."

"I thought we all can have fun instead of just you and me so I called them."

"When will you understand Dhruv?"

"What? Should I tell them not to come. I thought they were you're friends." I said.

"Not anymore Dhruv I don't like them and specially the way they talk about you behind your back in the hostel. I just hate that."

"Does it really matter Radhika I know who I am and I don't care what people talk behind my back."

"Ok fine now shut up they are here." Radhika said as Devika and Mentos entered the restaurant.

"Hi Bhaiya." Devika said whereas Mentos whispered in Radhika's ears. "Did we spoil your date?"

"She came first you drama queen." I said as I pulled Devika's hair a bit.

"Ah! bhaiya sorry, leave my hair. We were preparing for the exams so we didn't want to come. Anyways you should have told us that you are enjoying with Radhika we would have not come."

"Shut up you two and now order fast." I said giving a tap on her head.

We ordered two pizzas and a garlic bread along with coke and continued chit-chatting till it was 8.30pm. Later, Radhika and I left on my bike whereas the two went home walking once again. That day maybe I ignored but Radhika was right, people had changed I was able to see, the girls were leaving mess one after another. About Devika, she made my first opinion true about her she can never be trusted. She always said she will never leave even if all the girls left but was the first to leave. Maybe, I was expecting a lot from people who had started showing their true colors, or maybe it was because Diya left.

*****

Chapter 11

And the year ends with Radhika...

24th October 2008 Radhika came home and was busy with mom in the kitchen, the door was locked from inside. Few minutes later she came out and I was staggered at the moment. She was wearing Diya's maroon silk saree and was looking awesome but my sarcasm continued with laughter.

"Radhika! What are you wearing?"

"Why? Am I not looking good?" She said giving eccentric expressions.

"No it's ok, but when did you start behaving like a girl, it doesn't suit you. You are better in jeans and t-shirts."

"Stop laughing and come-on drop me till RTO."

"Please, like I don't have any other work left."

"Come-on Dhruv please drop me." She said as if she already thought I was never going to drop her.

"Dhruv, go and drop her, that area is not nice and come fast." Mom said and maybe that was all I was waiting for, mom should give the permission.

"Should I come like this in my shorts?"

"Dhruv come on, please wear trousers and not in these shorts. I am getting late."

"Ok fine wait." I said and changed my clothes.

"Radhika you are looking awesome. Let's elope." I said while driving the bike.

"Then what was all that at home?"

"You know mom, she would have never agreed me going to drop you so...You know, drama and all."

"But it was too much Dhruv."

"Ok now, I dropped you here as promised yesterday. But, I don't know if I would be able to come in the evening."

"Dhruv you have promised me."

"I know. What will I tell at home? Ok wait, I'll think of something and I'll let you know, you go your car is here." I said as I saw her company's car.

"Bye Dhruv, I'll call you later."

Later I came home with a thought in mind what if I marry Radhika, could life will be awesome. I had fought with her many time and made her cry, she was always there with me. This was never the reason for this particular thought.

I really admired Radhika a lot. But, it was difficult at times for me to choose between Radhika and Mahi. Radhika had got a couple invitation pass for the Hotel Central Park near Inox and we had planned to be together.

"So Radhika lets' do it this way." I said as I called her in the afternoon.

"What Dhruv?" She said.

"You will inform mom that you are going for the party and will be late. I'll leave the house saying I am going with my office friend Parth. And yes, you have to teach him accounts." I said.

"Dhruv, people should learn from you how to lie?"

"I know but I can't when it's actually required, you know how I am." I said.

"Yes, I know and maybe that why I am with you."

"Thanks Radhika." I said and hung up the phone and was eagerly waiting for evening fun.

I got ready in the evening in formals when Radhika came home in nice cool casuals.

"Kya baat hai Dhruv, where are you going?" Radhika said in front of mom.

"I am going on a date, any problems." I said.

"With Whom?"

"Top secret... Radhika."

"He is going out with a friend." Mom interrupted.

"Ok bye. Anyways where are you going Radhika?" I asked her.

"I am going for a party." She said.

"With whom?" I asked her.

"My new boyfriend."

"Sahi hai, I mean it's good." I said and started walking downstairs.

"Ruk tere ghar call karke mummy papa ko batati hoo." My mom said to Radhika.

"Mummy papa ko pata hai." She said and even she left the house.

I waited for her near the Apollo theatre when she came and sat on my bike.

"Let's go Dhruv. You are looking handsome today feel like giving you a kiss." She said.

"Don't hesitate Radhika I won't mind."

"But I am not planning to kiss you."

"By the way why are you dressed up in formals?" She asked.

"Oh, just like that, you know, I thought it's your office party so I should look descent maybe I can get a nice girl in the party."

"Oh really! You feel so." She said.

We reached Hotel Central Park. Now I should say this was my first time to visit such a big hotel was somewhat like a dream come true for me. I parked my bike in the parking and then while walking upstairs, I said, "Radhika I don't think this is a good idea to go in this hotel I have never been to such place. Let's go somewhere else."
"Shut up Dhruv, even I have not been to such place; let's see if we don't like it will leave immediately." She said.
"By the way, what about the Goa plans? I knew it will be cancelled."
"My friend is not well and the other broke-up with her boyfriend so maybe next year. Let's see if we like this hotel we'll come here on the new year's eve."
"Oh that would be fun." I said with a smile.

We were greeted by a manager of the hotel. Kimberly Clark was their important client as majority of the official meetings were held in such hotels. He first introduced himself with a smile.
"Hello, my name is Prashant and we have organized this small function to get to know our clients."
"Hi I am Radhika from Kimberley Clark and my friend Dhruv." With that formal hi-hello I concluded one more thing.
"Radhika I think he's gay." I whispered into her ears.
"Shut-up Dhruv, that was too loud."
"No it was not."
"Yes it was and please be quiet."
"What? Did you hear us?" I asked Prashant.
"I am sorry sir." He said.
"Oh no, forget it we were just discussing something. Can we get to see the hotel" I said in order to divert the topic.

He showed us some of the rooms which were amazing especially the bathrooms with the bath-tub and steam shower fittings. I started dreaming Radhika and me inside taking a small steam-bath.
"I think Dhruv we would enjoy more in the bath-tub." She said.
"Yes you are right first the steam-bath and then you and me alone in the bath-tub that would be amazing."
"Stop dreaming now get into reality." She said as we moved into the lift. He took us to view the roof-top restaurant. It was amazing as there was a small pool and a bar at one corner.

"Prashant your hotel is amazing. We liked it." I said as Radhika joined me, "Yes it is I'll definitely recommend this for all our client meeting and we'll definitely like to come here personally one day."

"Sure madam, it would be our pleasure to have you here."

Later we retuned back to the hall where the function was held.

"Radhika, will they give us a room to stay. It will be awesome just you and me."

"I won't stay here the entire report will go to office next morning."

"But seriously apart from the hotel there is nothing exiting in this party."

"I know Dhruv let's wait for some time and then we'll go. Anyways it's just 7.50pm now." She said while she checked her watch.

After sometime we moved on to have a glass of cocktail which Prashant had offered us. The function continued with some mimicry artist performing for us then felicitating the guests and later the best part which I was here for, FOOD.

"Let's dance first for some time Dhruv, and then we'll eat." Radhika suggested.

"Ok, but let him put some nice track. Ok fine let's go." I said as I could not handle those beseeching expressions on her face.

I continued dancing with her but at the same time my eyes moved on to the girl who was dancing right next to us. Radhika was feeling uncomfortable and jealous so I stopped looking at her for that moment and we went to have dinner.

After the dinner she went to the DJ and said something to him while I was drinking water. I saw all the couples were invited on the dance floor for the final dance when she took me again to dance.

"Radhika I can't dance and I am feel a bit awkward here."

"Nobody knows you Dhruv just enjoy the music and dance." She said as a song began 'Nothings Gonna Change My Love for You...' and the DJ announced "Come on all you people in love this song is a dedication was someone special out here."

Radhika always surprised me and I just said to myself.

"Dhruv this girl is crazy. I think there can't be anything better than this."

We left the place around 9.30pm and Radhika wanted to go out for a long drive with me at that moment. I showed her the place where I always drove my bicycle when I was in school and stopped the bike at one place. I kissed her and later we moved back home. She put her arms around my waist holding me tightly. At that moment along with the kiss I also wanted to thank her for making it the most beautiful evening for me, but I never said anything. Maybe

I should have told her how special that evening had been for me rather than assuming she might have understood everything.

When we reached home our story was ready we both met at Inox when I was with Parth she was allowed to bring a guest. She tried calling Krish he didn't pick up the call so it was me and her.

This year's Diwali Radhika was alone in her hostel as she didn't get leaves. Mom asked her to stay with us at home as she was scared to stay alone. She spoke with her family and they were very happy as she was staying with us, but not as much as I was. Well, for Radhika this was her second family but for me she was already a part of my family but I didn't let anybody know. Well many things were unsaid I always thought people would understand what they mean to me even if I don't let them know.

28th October 2008, we all went to mama's place and Radhika came along with us. The best part was even though we were together, nobody knew Radhika loved me or maybe I did the same. I actually was confused whether I really loved her. Everyone in the family liked her especially Sana and Pal. They asked me is Radhika your girlfriend bhai, when Radhika replied, "his girlfriend has gone back home to Ajmer." So there was no chance anybody would doubt on us. I had no trouble as long as all the cousins loved her.

In office on the occasion of Diwali I bought the rangoli colors and asked one of the senior manager's permission to decorate the entrance of the floor. It took around an hour to complete the rangoli and just a few seconds to get praised from everyone. I was happy that the two weeks rangoli course done with Vishal proved helpful many times for me. The best moment was when I received Sodexho gift coupons worth 1000Rs for the rangoli from our Operational Manager. Well, let me tell you the secret here, the idea of making a rangoli was just to make everyone forget I was on a one month leave for some stupid reason I was suffering from typhoid, well Riya and Parth helped me to make it believable in office.

Next day, as every year this year I tried to convince everyone for the movie but nobody seemed interested. So I didn't bother to ask anybody as I already had made up plans with Radhika for the movie 'Golmaal Returns'. She made up a plan to meet her aunt one-day prior so that she can accompany me for the movie.

Mahi returned from Ajmer, with many problems along with her. Firstly she wanted a job and the other problem was a guy named Mohit. He was her childhood friend whom she met after a long time in Ajmer. They both came along to Pune as he was pursuing his MBA. Uninvited trouble had just arrived for me which was about to change many things which I had least expected.

Few days later, I was talking with Natasha in her shop actually it was after a very long time.
"Hey Natasha you're looking fat." I said while going through the movie page in Pune Times.
"That's so mean Dhruv I have reduced a lot and what are you reading in the newspaper." She said.
"I am looking for the new released movies."
"Are you going with Mahi."
"No, she is busy with a new guy I'll go with Radhika."
"Dhruv you never ask me for a movie."
"Yes, because I know you will never come out with me."
"What if I come? Let's go for a movie together I want to see this movie 'Dostana' if you don't mind."
"Why would I? I know you would never come." I said and our discussion continued till the time Natasha became serious about watching a movie with me and Radhika. We reached Inox and as usual I sat in between the two as I always liked to be in the middle. Radhika was not able to see the movie properly, she did tell me but I couldn't understand. One mistake, which I did at that moment was to sit in between those two girls and the second was talking too much with Natasha which Radhika didn't like at that moment, but never said a word.

Few days later, I had asked Radhika to come along in order to buy a gift for Riya. That evening, Mahi, Radhika and I went out to eat pani-puri.
"Mahi can you come with me, I need to buy a gift for Riya". I said bluntly without even realizing I had already asked Radhika. She stood quiet without uttering a word.
Later, I told Mahi about this and even she was annoyed with my behavior. The only fact that I could spend some time with Mahi made me ask her.

We celebrated Riya's birthday the next day as Mahi came along with me to wish her. In the evening I gave her the photo album I had made for her. That was the last time maybe I saw Riya smile in office as the next day became very tough for her. She was asked to resign the company, no wonder how that happen but our team was closely monitored by the seniors as many calls were getting dropped and Riya was caught for a call drop which she was not aware of. One of the biggest offence in the call-center industry, result was she had to quit.

That day, I still remember, she was sitting in the parking zone alone on my bike waiting for me to come down. As soon as she saw me tears started rolling down her eyes. As I went close she hugged me and couldn't stop her tears.
"Oh Riya stop crying, you know you don't look ugly when you cry I mean you don't look beautiful when you cry, please don't cry." I said wiping off her tears.
"Dhruv, you are so mean, you don't even let people cry when they really want to." She said pushing me away.
"I know because crying is not good for health and kya ladki ki tarah roti hai." I said in order to make her smile.
"What? I am a girl Dhruv, don't you say that." She said with a smile on her face wiping off her tears.
"Riya I will quit the job soon, I came back for you. If you are not here what will I do in this office?"
"Don't be crazy Dhruv, serve a proper notice period and then quit this job." She said as I wipe off her tears. Later I was holding her hand and there was a silence when she spoke again.
"Everything changed all of sudden Dhruv. I feel like I am no more a part of this company which was mine."
"Riya get up from the bike please." I asked her to stand or rather just pulled her down.
"Give me a proper hug." I said and hugged her tightly.
"I'll miss you yaar, I'll really miss you a lot." That moment did made my eyes wet, giving that perfect reason for Riya to tease me.
"Thanks Dhruv and kya ab tu ladki ki tarah rota hai."
"I am not crying kachra gaya tha ankh mein." I said.
"Come on now go back to work I'll be here for some time after that I am going to Nitin's place. I won't tell my family or else all my planning to surprise him on his birthday will be ruined. And you know I didn't cry till the time I saw you."
"Riya his birthday is on the 19th and today its 4th. Don't you think they might understand everything? And if I make you cry I am the one who always makes you smile." I said.
"But first you make people cry, anyways I'll take care about that just somehow pray for me they never come to know. Now go don't exceed your break."
"Ok bye. Take care and don't you dare cry now." I said and started walking towards the stairs while I turned back to see her again.

"Go Dhruv I am fine, I won't cry." She said with a smile on her face.

A few days later, I made up a late-night movie plan at Inox with Radhika 'The Day the Earth Stood Still'. I never knew why exactly I selected this movie but I wanted to spend some time with her. Somehow I loved to spend time with her when Mahi was not around as Mahi often ignored me. We returned back home in a rickshaw as I had left my bike home. It was 11.30pm and unfortunately Radhika's hostel gates were closed and she didn't have the keys to enter back in the hostel.

"So, Radhika how will you go inside the hostel." I said in the rickshaw.

"I don't know Dhruv, I am very scared." She said holding my hands.

"Well, what will you do in that case, Radhika?" I said.

"Maybe, I'll have to stay at Deccan at Jiya's place."

"Whatever the case is, give me a call." I said as I left home and she went to her hostel.

A strange thought kept mingling in my mind as how I could leave her alone at this particular time. Somehow I was really worried about her so I called her as soon as I found everyone sleeping at home.

"Radhika where are you?" I said as I called her.

"I am Deccan. Dhruv I am very scared, I am not able to find her place." She replied.

"Where are you right now Radhika?"

"I don't know."

"I had told you to wait I would have checked if I am able to come out."

"But you told me that it won't be possible for you to come out, so I came here and these two boys are following me Dhruv." She said in a scared voice.

"Are you talking while you are riding the bike?" I asked.

"No Dhruv I am waiting for Jiya to come she has asked me to wait here. Please keep talking with me till she comes." She said and I had no clue how to react for my stupid ignorance had I been with her to drop her to Deccan this would have not happened.

"Dhruv, she is here will call you later once I reach her place."

Had I been with her, things would have been different. I thought for a while and wondered what if Jiya would have been late and those boys would have been seriously out to do something wrong. But thanks to God everything was alright but due to my fault Radhika had to sleep somewhere else instead of her hostel so I made up my mind that no late-night movies will be planned ever again when Radhika called back.

"Hello!" I said.

"Dhruv, I have reached here, safely will go to hostel in the morning."

"I am sorry Radhika, but next time no more late-night movie if at-all we go then I'll make sure I have a bike." I said.

"Ok Dhruv, it's very late now will talk to you tomorrow." She said and hung up.

My decision of avoiding the late-night movie with a girl didn't last for a long time. 18th December 2008, I went for a movie along with Riya. I don't know whether I should mention this but at that point of time I was never able to get my mind focused on anything. At times it was Radhika who used to make me feel happy by always being with me so was Riya, but on the other hand being ignored by Mahi was killing me from inside. Riya wanted to spend some time with me and I was a master in giving reasons at work, this time it was one of the cousins who met with an accident and there was nobody at home so I took leave. But, Nishant assumed it was true due to which I was never caught even if I lied. But, sometimes I could never lie in front of some people and was caught the very next moment if I tried to do.

"So, Dhruv what did you tell Nishant today?" Riya asked as we met.

"My cousin met with an accident." I said.

"This was the reason for last month right."

"Oh! That was my other cousin I told him when he asked me." I replied and we both started laughing.

"Dhruv, you would never change." She said.

"I know. Anyways what is the plan? Where are we going?" I said.

"Well, we have to get a cake from 11East-Street and then I have to do some shopping and we'll have dinner and then we'll go for a movie and then we'll go to Nitin's place." She said.

"Wow, that sounds like a plan. From Aundh to camp then back to E-Square and then…Ok, but I'm hungry can we eat something first." I said.

"Do you think anything else apart from food."

"Well, Radhika says the same thing every time we go anywhere out."

"Poor Radhika."

"Very Funny!! But, you know something she has started eating chocolates and watching movies with me, she is just awesome."

"You said the same about Mahi."

"But Radhika is the best."

"And what about me, Dhruv?"

"You are always the best."

"Are you serious about Mahi or in love with Radhika?"

"Well, I don't know but Radhika is my best friend. I like her a lot."

"Dhruv, be careful on what you are up to. If she is your friend don't treat her like your girlfriend and give her false hope."

"I am not doing such a thing, but whenever I am with her…
You know what, I never feel alone…I feel that I have someone who cares for me, someone who wants to be with me. I really don't want to get off that feeling when I am with her. So that fact is I am confused. What exactly should I do?"

"Dhruv, let there be some limit in your friendship. Don't treat her like you treat Mahi, or else you would mess up things."

"I know, I'll try to do as per you say." I said in a confused state of mind never could understand how our fun talks were rounded off with serious conversations.

"Come-on Dhruv now don't get so serious we are here to enjoy. I can't be with a guy who is carrying that stupid expressions on his face. So please change your expressions and chill mann." She said and bought up a smile on my face. We bought tickets for the movie 'Dil Kabaddi' another late night show at 11.15pm. We had around 2hours to spend whereas Riya had some shopping planned in camp.

"Dhruv, we would get the pastry after 45minutes". She said as I waited outside the pastry shop for her in camp.

"So what now, I am hungry, let's eat something."

"Why are you always hungry Dhruv?"

"Coz, I really am." I said.

"Ok well, first I have to collect some stuff then we'll go and eat." She said and we continued her shopping. After spending more than 30minutes we had some normal stuff along with coffee. Later we took the pastry and headed towards E-Square as we both didn't want to miss the beginning. As we went inside the movie hall all I could see was couples all around in the hall who wanted to make out with each other in the dark rather than watch the movie.

Riya hold my hand close to her and put her head on my shoulder. It felt good at that moment.

"Dhruv first it was Mahi then Radhika now its Riya, but be careful of what you are doing right now." A voice came from within me when we both were holding each other's hand. After sometime I freed my hands and we got busy watching the movie. The movie got over around 2am. We bought Chicken Biryani on our way from a restaurant as we reached Nitin's place. I wasn't feeling comfortable at that moment we entered his room. I might end up doing something which I shouldn't was the thought running at that moment but somehow had to focus myself.

"What happened Dhruv?" Riya asked me as I was staring at her while she served the Biryani.

"Nothing, it's very cold out here. Can't wait till you serve the Biryani." I tried to wipe out the thoughts running in my mind with that absurdity.

After finishing the Biryani we sat talking with each other about the days spend together and the memories we had collected so far. Later, around 3.00pm Riya hugged me while I was about to leave but after spending about more 10-15minutes I thanked her for spending such a wonderful time but maybe there were many things that we wanted to talk which Riya couldn't because of her shopping. I hugged her again and left. There's always a very thin line with friendship and love. I loved the bond of friendship between me and Riya. I never crossed my limits with Riya as it's very easy to get carried away at such times, especially if two people involved are close friends.

I fought with Radhika again and she went to Mumbai to meet her relatives on Christmas. Mahi being in Pune was busy with her friend Mohit than me as most of her time revolved around only two people Gaurav her boyfriend and then Mohit her supposed to be best friend. I never knew where I fitted in her criteria. I wasn't able to understand if she still loved me or was just playing with my emotions. Most important, we hardly met and the day we met we always ended up in a fight. Sometimes, I would only be listening to her gossip as how her day was made awesome by Mohit and how he was better than me. Obviously he was her best friend so I wasn't really supposed to oppose their kiss. I felt jealous the moment, I couldn't understand Mahi.

My life was getting tough in terms of my relation with Mahi as well as Radhika. Due to which I felt whether animation was the right path in my career. I failed to understand things being taught in class. Sometimes I felt everything was perfect but the other point of time I found everything was messed up and I was not able to clear the mess around me. That day, I reached office in the evening the entire floor was decorated and everyone was busy playing various games on the floor. I was blank as I could see everyone giggle and laugh and have fun around me but it couldn't change the expressions on my straight face. At one point of time Saurav tried a lot to get me out of my sickness, but it didn't help. I went into the washroom and wondered what was happening to me and why I was in this particular state of dilemma. I was able to see the two-sided coins properly but was not able to decide which side to choose. I enjoyed being with Radhika, but when I fought with her I used to think about Mahi. Although when Mahi was around I would ignore Radhika. Something was not correct with me. Finally I made-up my mind and came out, washed my face and went to meet Nishant.

"Nishant I wanted to talk something important". I said as he was offering me more coins to participate in the games.

"What happened Dhruv? Go play some games score some points for the team you won't get a chance to enjoy again on the floor." He said and handed over me the coins.

"I want to quiet the job Nishant." I said and within a fraction of seconds his facial expressions changed like a small baby crying for a toy, oh well that was a really horrible comparison but still one should have seen his face at that moment. He took me to his desk and asked me what the exact problem was and why I came to this sudden decision.

"Nishant I am not able to adjust my timings properly, everything is getting messed up with my animation studies. My exams are approaching and I am not able to study as half of the time is spent in office." I said.

"Well you were happy with the 8.30pm shift right."

"Yes, I was but it's not helping my much."

"What should I do then?"

"I want to quit."

"Maybe Dhruv you are taking this decision too fast think over it for a day or two and then we'll talk." He said and made me think again weather my decision was correct or was I getting too impulsive.

I came home in the morning and I messaged Mahi but her reply didn't help me. He was upset again as I didn't look at the time before I messaged her. I went off to bed and later woke up and went to class. I had already missed many classes so it was hard for me to cope with the course. Sir were about to finish the lighting concept in MAYA which I hardly knew what it was. It didn't bother much as he was about to start the new concept of rigging(adding bones and giving life to a character) in MAYA, I was very eager to learn it as this was the part I was always waiting for, it being the base of character animation. I decided to focus on the lectures and get rid of the other thoughts. Radhika was back from Mumbai and Mahi decided to leave for Ajmer again. My life was stuck between these two girls and was not able to find any direction to it. The only thought that was in my mind that maybe if I quit the job I'll get enough time to sort out the things properly and plan them accordingly in order to achieve excellence in my career. But life had much more for me to offer.

31st December 2008, the last day of the year, Radhika had planned to spend the year-end with her school friends and me in Goa, but it got cancelled. So we planned something else, during which Radhika told me about her friend Adeena who just had a breakup would soon be in Pune. Now I knew that was no good news for me as I knew things could change a lot if she comes to Pune. But I kept that topic away from my mind for some time as Parth had planned something for both of us.

"Radhika you are surely coming today?" I confirmed again as I called up Radhika after I woke up in the morning.

"Yes, but where are we going?" She asked

"I don't know Parth has planned and you have to teach him Accounts. I told you. Right?"

"Yes I know, you and your dumb friends." She said and started laughing in order to avoid any further discussion on it.

Our talk continued for the next few minutes, I wasn't sure what time she would come home, 31st being the crucial day for the finance people. I let her continue with her work and later got back with my routine. I was out with Vishal and when I came back in the evening I found my room was locked from inside. I wondered who could be inside, well it was Radhika.

"Dhruv don't bang the door Radhika is changing her clothes". Mom shouted before I would began to knock the door.

"Mottu coming just give me a minute." Oh yes I forgot to tell you I had put on weight so Radhika would often call me Mottu. I didn't like it before, but the way she added that extra sweet innocent accent to that word it would really sound cool. Few minutes passed and finally she opened the door. I went inside and was stunned to see her properly dressed up in a green top with nice matching ear-rings and a 3/4 jeans. She looked beautiful and this was the second time I couldn't take my eyes of her. But I continued to go with my sarcasm, first I started laughing out loud and then said,

"Oye Radhika what are you wearing."

"Why? What happened? Am I not looking good?" She said with a confused and worried face.

"Oh look at you what are you wearing and what's that on your lips, full-on shinning you're looking. Oh my GOD please help her." She then pushed me and came went out to ask mom.

"Kaku am I not looking good?" She asked mom.

"What are you wearing Radhika?" Radhika face was worth to watch when I busted into laughter and she went inside to change with a sad face, I went inside and hold her hand, pulled her close to me.

"Radhika you are looking awesome, feel like kissing you at this moment." I said.
"Don't you dare, your mom is out she can come inside anytime." She said and got herself free from me. I again hold her hand and pulled her and said.
"Hey Radhika will you marry me? You are looking just too good, if I had a ring with me now I would surely got engaged with you today." I said without thinking anything else.
"Ha ha very funny leave me and let me comb my hair properly."
"I am serious anyways now go out and let me change, even I can look nice, you know."
"You can change in front of me. I have no problem as it is I have seen you without your clothes many times right."
"Shut up Radhika and get out let me change." I said and pushed her out and within the next 5 minutes I was out in black.
"Kya baat hai Dhruv you're looking nice."
"You know my personality, its awesome right from childhood." I said and then called up Parth and we went to his place. The people in my area had all their eyes set on both of us as I drove my bike along with Radhika seated behind, I guess they were jealous.

We reached Parth's place and I introduced Radhika to Parth. We waited till 10, as Parth was still trying to arrange the passes for the pub along with his friends who were about to accompany us. Somewhere in my mind the confusion was still running, just the way Mahi was confused between me and Gaurav. But I decided to forget everything and simply enjoy. We reached the pub named Palazzo and Riya joined us within the next 10-15minutes to double the fun. We got ourselves inside and all I could see many couples enjoying to the fullest on the trance played by the DJ. We began to tap our feet on the music for some time.
"Kya hua Mottu?" Radhika asked.
"Nothing, I am not enjoying the music."
"Come-on hold my hand and dance with me just don't bother about the music." She put her hands around my neck and I put mine around her waist and was lost in her. It was 11.30pm when we came out as Riya had to leave. She wished new year to everyone and then left. We then went inside when the DJ stopped the music just 10seconds before the clock to strike 12 and the countdown began. When everyone in the crowd shouted out loud 'HAPPY NEW YEAR'. We wished each other and few minutes later, we all came out. Radhika stood close in my arms as she was feeling sleepy. The feel was amazing, though she was not my girlfriend that moment, I felt as if I had the entire world around me and should never let her go.

Parth's friend asked him about me and Radhika when he replied that we two are friends. Best Friends I stressed upon it immediately as Radhika turned back to support my reply. Later they all went inside to dance whereas Parth, Radhika and I waited outside the pub checking the other girls. We had our own unique funda about girls who wore shorts, our code word would be leg-piece and soon our eyes would move in all directions. Radhika soon got used to it and enjoyed the same along with us at various occasions as there were many girls around. We left the pub around 2, and went to a late-night restaurant where Parth and I ordered roasted chicken leg-piece.

"But I tell you that yellow skirt girl was amazing." Parth said as he took a bite of the chicken.

"Yes, Parth she was but the problem is we couldn't see her face." I said.

"It's good that you didn't see her face or else you would not be eating this chicken here." Radhika said and we began to guffaw. Radhika became friendly with Parth soon and had agreed to teach him Accounts. We finished the food and so did Parth's question," Are you sure you people weren't bored?" which he would ask every now and then. Radhika smiled and replied, "we enjoyed it a lot with your company and we'll meet soon. Send your syllabus along with Mottu so that I can understand what exactly I need to teach you." So somehow the new year brought a new wave of happiness for me that I was with the right girl. Radhika is awesome was continuously in my mind all the way till we reached home. I kissed Radhika before mom opened the door and Radhika went inside. I came down as Parth was waiting for me. We continued talking to each other where Parth acknowledged the fact that Radhika was much better than Mahi. I felt happy but got confused when he said Mahi.

*****

Chapter 12

The Confusion Cleared...

Radhika tried to wake me up in the morning before going to office around 7.00am but I woke up late when my phone rang. It was Mahi.

"Where were you last night?" She asked.

"I was in a pub. What happened?" I replied back in a rude tone.

"I had called you to wish you. All you could do was be nice and seems like Radhika is getting more important."

"How would I know Mahi? You never talk properly. There's nothing between me and Radhika."

"Happy New Year Dhruv. You would never understand my situation. I miss you, hence I had called." She said and hung up. I was confused again as I failed to understand these two girls, Mahi and Radhika.

Mahi's call confused me more. I wanted to be sure before I move further with Radhika. Mahi would talk with me whenever she had some work but this phone call Mahi seemed more concerned and it confused me. I tried to finish my morning chores but the thoughts still kept running in my mind. It was difficult to get them out of my mind even after talking with Radhika. She was angry as I woke up late; I assured her I would begin with my work soon. While I got myself busy with my work I received a call from my school friend Akash, always a topper in class and the only person who knew me well. He always knew Dhruv can do anything once he decides to work hard he can achieve it. He stayed in Bangalore and I was about to meet him after a long time.

Later, in the evening I met Natasha and later spent the evening with Radhika, so the New Year's start wasn't too bad for me. I understood all my confusion would be cleared the moment I meet Akash.

Next day I went to office and some unexpected things were waiting for me. "Where were you Dhruv for the last two days?" Nishant asked me before I could logon into a system. He called me towards his desk and I had to think of a new story that could help me to survive for some days.

"Nishant there was a small problem at my place."

"What happened?"

"I drank poison and I was hospitalized." Now that was one of the most unbelievable lie that came from me which no one on this earth would believe. Well I couldn't come up with anything else at that moment. I was asked to meet the Operations Manager who finally asked me to quiet the job, so 2nd January 2009 was officially my last working day in office.

I came back at my desk when my team-mates were all lined up for the gossip.
"What did you tell him?" Parth asked
"I had a small fight at home then I drank poison."
"So did he believe you?"
"I guess he had no other option, now stop laughing Parth let me be serious for some time or else he will understand". I said trying to stop Parth from laughing but his laughter continued to be loud enough for Abhi and the others to join him.
"Hey Nishant he is lying, he was with me on the 31st."
"Parth shut up as it is it's my last day in office now get back to work." I said and logged myself into the Avaya for the last time. Sometimes I was never able to understand Parth the way his mood would swing anytime from happy to sad, sometimes being caring and sometimes rude.

That day I decided that I won't take the calls properly which will screw up the team scores but I got the most descent and innocent customer whom I never wanted to be rude with. I helped them with their issues. Finally the day ended at work and I went to meet Nishant for the last time. He wished me luck for the future and I left office with Parth and Abhi. We headed towards our favorite tea-stall for our early morning break-fast. I knew this would be the last time and later I would sleep at night and work during the day, to achieve excellence in animation and fulfill my dream to become an Animator. Apart from this Krish was successful to get a housing loan approved on my salary pay-slips. My next target was to finish the course till April and then get a job till May. Whereas, Krish target was to get the new home constructed soon on the plot which my father bought few years back.

I reached home and slept peacefully after a long time. In the afternoon I went to class and got to know that the lectures would be conducted in the new building every morning 7am. I came home and the day ended normally after spending some time with Radhika as she came home from work. Being used to working in night-shifts it was difficult for me to sleep at night and wake up early in the morning. So I couldn't wake up for the class and I missed my first lecture on character animation. I managed to be on time the other day so I was able to learn the walk cycle of a human character. Within few days the syllabus was over in MAYA and I was only able to learn one concept of animation. Every-day, if I was late by 5-10minutes for class I was asked to go home. The new rules screwed up big time for me. During that time, Radhika helped me to create a photo album for Mahi for her birthday.

On her birthday I called Mahi at 12 midnight and wished her. My plans were to celebrate her birthday and make it special just like the previous year but she already had some plans with Mohit. She was completely ignoring me. She was at his place and then in the morning she went off with him. I waited till the evening to spend some time with her. Later, I went to Landmark and tried to read some books, but wasn't able to concentrate so I called up Radhika. "Hello." I said.
"Mottu where are you?" She said.
"I am in Landmark."
"What are you doing there? You didn't go for the party with Mahi?" I never expected Radhika would tease me and why was she really teasing me I had no clue. I wanted to be alone but she joined me at Landmark and so did Parth. I couldn't avoid these two, where Radhika was continuously blabbering about me.
"Parth let him go he doesn't like to be with us. Only Mahi is important for him we don't matter to him." She said when we three were seated in Parth's car. I wanted to be alone, but I couldn't express myself and kept listening quietly to whatever Parth and Radhika had to say which they had in their mind.
"Dhruv you know what your problem is? You need people around, only when you are in a good mood. Otherwise you don't need anyone." Parth said when I wanted to leave.
"It's not like that Parth, let it be, you won't understand." I left them as I couldn't handle their words anymore and went to Saras Baugh.

I went inside the Ganesh temple in Saras Baugh where I would always be whenever I needed peace of mind. I kept thinking where I was going wrong. Why Mahi was behaving with me like this? And why was it so difficult to forget her and get along with Radhika. Like always, my thoughts were interrupted, it was a phone call from Mahi.
"Where are you?" She asked.
"I am out with friends. Why? What happened?" I said.

"I am sitting in your house and the gift is amazing, come home soon I want to meet you." She sounded happy, while she turned the pages of the album.

"Sorry Mahi I can't come I am busy will be late."

"Ok fine then meet me tomorrow I can't wait its already late now but can't you try to come it's my birthday."

"I guess your birthday is over Mahi, its already 9.30pm you have to reach your hostel I waited the whole day for you but you were busy with Mohit."

"It's not like that, you should have come with us you would have enjoyed a lot."

"Did you ever ask me? I am no more in your priority list."

"It's not like that ok fine I am keeping the phone we'll meet tomorrow and go for a movie. Ok bye." She said and kept the phone. I waited for the next 5minutes and looked at the Ganesh idol with a smile and said she liked the gift. Later I called up Krish and confirmed if she had left and I messaged her for ruining my day. I came home and entered my room Mahi was sitting inside my room.

"You are late and it's already 10.30pm." She said and I was stunned with this girl's reaction, well girls are hard to understand.

"I did tell you I will be late." I said with anger which was about to disappear.

"Dhruv this is one of the best gift I have received ever in my life. Even Mohit's gift is nothing in front of this. This is the truth and not a lie." Krish left the room and I sat on the bed. I never wanted my gift to be compared with any other gifts. I made it for her and with true spirit to make her realize how much I cared for her. Radhika didn't ask for anything just wanted me to spend some time with her but I ended up spoiling her mood. I didn't know if I will be able to get her back to normal. I was thinking of Radhika that moment when Mahi was still in front of me.

"Dhruv plan for a movie, we'll go tomorrow and your message hurt me a lot. I am sorry." She said and left the room. Maybe Parth was right about the thing he said. I had spoilt three people's day because of my stupid behavior.

After dinner, I was down with my pets when Radhika called up. I wasn't sure if she was still angry on me.

"You shouldn't be roaming on the streets on your shorts like this Mottu. You look too sexy in it"

"What?" I was surprised with that comment of her. "How do you know what I am wearing to find me sexy in it? And I am not Mottu."

"I am looking at you from the window." She said and I immediately looked at her hostel building. She waved her hand but I wasn't able to see her properly. It was dark where she was sitting. "And you are Mottu, check your weight."

"Radhika. You would see I'll reduce within the next month."

"But I like you the way you are." She replied and our discussion continued. Next day, after the movie I came home and Mahi was back with Mohit. I couldn't ignore the fact we were watching the movie as strangers seated beside each other. That day I kept waiting for her at home but she never came home instead asked her roommates to get her tiffin at hostel. That was the last movie along with Mahi and I was lost in my own world until Radhika called up the next day.

"Dhruv I'll be waiting for you. You have to come in the evening to pick me from Parth's place." She said as called me from Parth's place. Her talk got me back to normal.

"I'll come anyways can you hand over the phone to Parth. I want to talk with him." I said and she gave the phone to Parth.

"Is she teaching you properly Parth?" I asked.

"Yes she is, with a ruler in her hand to hit me whenever I go wrong. She really hits me hard." Parth said sarcastically when Radhika kept shouting, "Liar. When did I hit you?" I kept laughing as the two were fighting on the phone.

"Give her the phone Parth."

"Hey why are you hitting my poor little innocent friend?" I said with those three adjectives specially for Parth.

"I am not hitting him, he is a liar."

"I know Radhika but still don't hit him. He's a poor little chap."

"Anyways jokes apart Parth are you guys studying seriously maybe that's one reason why she is there. Right!" I said as Parth kept the phone on speaker

"Yes we are studying and she is really good in accounts."

"Mottu when are you coming?"

"I'll come in the evening Radhika." I felt happy at that moment for Parth as Radhika had finally made it to teach him. By the time I kept the phone mom heard the last sentence.

"Where are you going Dhruv?" She said.

"To get Radhika, she is at Parth's place." I said.

"Is there any need. How did she go there?"

"She took a bus and she would be late so I have to go to get her back. Yes she also told me to inform you she won't be coming home for dinner."

"Why did she call you she can't call me instead to say so and you are not going anywhere to get her. She will manage on her own. Parth is your friend right?"

"Yes, what's with him?" I asked as found something fishy in her mind.

"You are mad Dhruv; I don't understand why you introduced Radhika to him." She said.

"He needs help in accounts and Radhika is good in it so I introduced her, what's wrong in it?"

"Does it make any sense he has no friends who can teach him accounts." I was not able to understand what was in her mind. Later I tried to convince her of going out to pick up Radhika but she was adamant.

She informed me that Krish needs bike as he was about to meet an architect in regards to the house construction. I stayed quiet as had no other option to convince her.

"Dhruv, come by 7.30pm and then we'll go out." Radhika called me again. I was totally upset as didn't know whether I should tell her the truth or not.

"Radhika, can you come on your own?" I asked.

"How can I Dhruv? You said you will come to pick me."

"I know but I am feeling bored. Don't want to go anywhere right now. Ask Parth to drop you." I lied in order to avoid my frustration.

"Dhruv you should have told me this before I would have left early. I waited for your call."

"I know but… Also my legs are paining I can't come."

"Ok fine." She said and hung up the phone in anger. Later Parth called up and I gave the same reason.

"Parth I won't find your home I don't remember how to come there."

"Dhruv come till Big Bazaar, give me a call I will guide you from there." He said again trying to convince me.

"Parth I can't, my legs are paining. You drop her."

"You were fine in the afternoon, what happened all of sudden. This is very disappointing Dhruv. I never expected this from you.".

"Parth I have a call on waiting, I'll call you later." I said and hung up the call to avoid further clashes. So one more incident added when I ended up screwing things between me and Radhika. Later she went out with Parth and got a chance to meet Parth's friends. The truth I never told her and she again lost the trust within me.

15th January 2009, Natasha's birthday, I wished her at midnight and in morning joined 'Dev's Music Academy' to continue learning guitar. Best part of this class was we get a free guitar within a month once we enroll our name. I was happy about it and strange thoughts flowed in my mind as I had made up plans along with the class to complete my animation showreel, but these two were always unpredictable.

"Dhruv, Parth and I are leaving for Mahabaleshwar are you coming with us?" Radhika called me up to confirm once again. I wasn't ready for this as I was pretty sure mom won't allow me. Also, I had to keep the enjoyment away for few days in order to work. The animation class timings had again changed to evening from 4.00pm to 6.00pm and we had already finished with the post production software Adobe After Effects. So it didn't make much a difference if Radhika was going anywhere with Parth.

"I won't be coming you guys enjoy." I replied back to her.

"Are you sure, you are not coming?" She asked again.

"Yes Radhika, you go and enjoy." I said and got back to work.

Next day, while returning from gym and I found Radhika and Parth waiting downstairs.

"I thought you guys left for Mahabaleshwar." I said.

"Yes we are leaving right now. Just came to meet you." Radhika replied, it sounded strange but I didn't feel bad about it I had already planned up my work for that day.

"Ok, have fun and enjoy." I said but somehow a fear within me, Radhika realized in seconds and said,

"Do you really feel I would go without you Dhruv?"

"I have no problems Radhika go and enjoy I trust you." I said when Parth started laughing.

"Dude go home get ready, we all are going for a movie and even I won't go without my pet Dukkar." He said and both of them burst into laughter.

"Get lost Parth you are pig, not me."

"Ok fine no more Dukkar how about Duksey." He said. "Doesn't this name sound cool and happening, Radhika?"

"Shut up Parth." I said immediately, as he would never miss a chance to tease me with such weird names.

"Anyways Duksey jokes apart. Go home quickly get ready and come soon we both are waiting. We won't go anywhere without you." He said.

"Parth I won't be able to come. What will I tell mom?" I said.

"Tell that you are going to Convergys to get your reliving letter." Radhika added.

"Ok fine let me see, I'll try."

"No try... You are coming." Parth forced me which I was not able to ignore. I had to keep my work aside as I felt these two are more important than my work. I convinced mom and we went to have breakfast and later for the most horrible movie 'Chandni Chowk to China'. The humor couldn't hold us till the end. Instead we came out with a question. Why did we see this movie?

I continued spending time with Radhika and Parth enjoying every day instead of working on the showreel. Day would begin when Radhika who would wake me up early morning around 7.30am and I used to get out of bed by 8.30 or 9.00am. By 10.30 or 11.00 I used to sit down in front of the computer and then later start working for an hour or two. Think on some concept for the showreel by the time I got any I was tired and I was off for a nap in the afternoon. Later in the evening spend time with Radhika and Parth. It was fun to be with these two but the only problem here was money. Every time it was either Parth or Radhika to spend. Few days later the construction of our new house started. It was far away from the city but I was least bothered as long as I had Radhika with me. I wasn't sure about Radhika whether she should be the next person of my life or not. Yes we did kiss each other many times but it was Mahi which was still in my mind. I had to choose one, either Mahi or Radhika which was the toughest decision to take.

"Where are you Dhruv?" Akash called as had reached on time and I was late.
"On my way, will reach there in next 5minutes." I said.
"Can you ever come on time?" He shouted on me.
"I'm coming I'm coming. Don't waste your time shouting or I'll be late." I said to cease down his anger.
"Come fast you asshole, I am getting bored or else I'll go inside." He said and kept the phone. We two always made plans to meet at the school and whenever we met, we would go and meet all our school-teachers.

"When will you learn to be punctual? Even in school you were never punctual." Akash said as we hugged each other then he punched me in my stomach for being late. We went inside and met all our teachers who always helped us lift up our spirits high. We met Mrs. Laxmi who motivated us as we talked with her for a long while. Later we came to know the changes that happened in our school. Oh! By the way I forgot to tell you I studied in Dastur Boys. In my entire 10years of school life, the only time I interacted with any girl was when Akash and I had gone to the Rotary Club Event. We had a formal Hi-Hello with girls from Rosary and the Mira's. I was always the most quiet and innocent child who teachers never knew existed in class except when somebody complaint me troubling them which would happen quiet often. Well, I am being sarcastic here; I was mischievous in school but much of an introvert at times.

"Akash. How things have changed here." I said as we walked back towards our bikes.

"Did you ever thought of this could happen to our school." He said.

"I would have never studied in this school we have been to right now."

"I mean how is it possible. Our school was known for all the extra-curricular activities and today the students are slogging with studies and no fun, poor chaps." Akash said with a disappointed look.

"Thank God we enjoyed our life in school to the fullest." I said.

"Yes we did, dude we always rock." Akash said giving me a hi-fi.

We headed towards SGS Mall after that and Akash ordered a Subway sandwiches.

"So, tell me. How is your girlfriend? She had a strange name. Right! That girl from Rajasthan." Akash asked after he took the first bite.

"Mahi…! She must be happy; I don't know where she is." I replied taking a smaller first bit to taste the sandwich. It was good.

"You guys broke-up. You said you wanted to marry her. Right?"

"When did I said that?"

"Yes you said you wanted to marry her."

"Shut-up! I never said that. Anyways I need your help in something." I said to stop his laughter.

"What's the new name now?"

"How did you know it's another girl?"

"Your expressions… It explains everything." He replied.

"Ok! her name is Radhika. She stays in the same hostel and she is awesome. A girl who is ready to do anything for me. She can actually do anything for me. Ok I said it twice but she can actually do anything for me."

"So what you slept with her? Cool mann Dhruv go ahead I am proud of you Dumbo." He said loud enough to attract the people sitting around us.

"Fuck-off Akash and don't be so excited I never did anything like that. I kissed her but that doesn't make her my girlfriend right."

"Does she love you?" He asked

"Yes I guess more than her." I replied.

"Dhruv. Let me make you one thing clear, no girl loves anyone more than she loves herself. But anyways what's the problem then."

"I am not able to get Mahi out of my mind, I still have feelings for her. But I don't want to lose Radhika either. So can you tell me what I should do?"

"If she loves you I would tell you go with her and forget Mahi. Give me one girl; you have so many around you."

"Get lost and you were supposed to be the most descent and innocent guy and now."

"What?? I am still the same but we have to change at one point of time as life fucks everybody."

We continued to talk with each other discussing many things about the past life and his present status with girls. Akash was the cutest guy in school and now he was more likely a dude. I came home in the evening around 6.00 when saw Mahi waiting for me.

"I was trying your phone for such a long time." She said.

"I was with Akash and how come you thought about me today." I replied being rude to her.

"I was missing you so I came to meet you." She said.

"What? Missing me? Are you serious? What happened to your friend?"

"He is always better than you at least he came to see my exhibition. You didn't even bother to come even when I called you."

"If you really wanted me to come you would have called me Radhika." I said.

"I was busy so I couldn't call you and my name is Mahi not Radhika. Maybe I got the answer for you not showing yourself on my exhibition." She said and left home. She came back again around 8.30pm along with her roommate Pooja. I tried to talk with her but her anger still rested on her little nose. She didn't utter a single word to me even though Pooja tried to encourage her to talk with me. Later I asked Pooja to meet me the next day early morning as Mahi left immediately after dinner.

It was 14th February, I met Pooja early morning as I gave her a bouquet and a chocolate for Mahi, whereas she bought something for me too.

"I really don't understand when you both can't live without each other why do you always fight." She said while she handed over me the card. To Dhruv it said as I opened it and began to read.

WE ARE BLENDED
    Together
        FOREVER AND EVER

*I didn't know how
real and special love could be
until you came
along one day and brought
it all to me...
I sensed a certain
something in my heart that felt so
true and I know I had
waited all my life to fall in love
with you... We have
come a long way in the caress
of our forever love and*

with you I fondly look forward to each beautiful tomorrow of

Our Special Togetherness'.

My eyes sparkled and expressions turned into a smile. Pooja was carefully studying every expression at that moment.

"Tell her this is really awesome and I want to meet her once." On my way back I started talking to myself.

"How am I supposed to....? I am screwed... And it's difficult to choose Radhika when Mahi is still... I don't know... Someone help me. Dhruv close your eyes once and check if it's still Mahi or Radhika." A reply from my lovely mind but I couldn't close my eyes as I had already reached home.

Later, I went out with Radhika around 11 am as she wanted to spend time with me till evening. I gave her a rose and we went to SGS Mall. Somehow I was falling short of words at the moment. I didn't know how I should talk with her or maybe tell her if I actually loved her. I was still confused. So I asked her if I could call Akash as he wanted to meet her. I heaved a sigh of relief when he came. I introduced him to Radhika and we had lunch together. We then enjoyed the day together clicked many photos and did make Radhika try various outfits at Westside.

"Dhruv go and propose her I think you shouldn't let her go." Akash said when Radhika was trying another outfit.

"I know she is the girl whom I can marry and trust blindly." I replied.

"Dhruv don't think of marriage right now first get to know each other spend some time together, marriage comes later." He said while Radhika came out and Akash gave me a t-shirt to try. I went inside the trail-room and came out when both were smiling at me.

"You are looking cool Mottu." Radhika said.

"Hey by the way, why do you call him Mottu? He has a pretty good name." Akash tried to put his point.

"I love calling him Mottu as he is getting fat day-by-day." She said when I was out back in my clothes.

"No I am not, Radhika." I said and put my hand around her waist and we started to walk.

"Mottu I want to ask you something. What did you tell Akash about me?"

"Nothing. Why? Did he say something to you?"

"Yes he was actually, let it be." She said and we came out of Westside. We left the mall and headed towards her class whereas Akash left to meet his girlfriend. When we reached to her class she got down and stood in front of me holding my hand maybe she wanted to spend some more time with me.

"Mottu I don't want to go, feel like spending some more time with you." She said.

"Ok then, we'll go somewhere else. Come sit." I said and waited for her reaction when I continued, "Go and attend your class, even I have to go for my guitar class. We'll meet at home after class." She went inside her class but didn't come home that day Shreya did something which screwed up things for Radhika and she had to stay there to support her friends.

22nd February 2009, it was Sunday the girls came home in the afternoon for lunch. Mahi came early and sat next to me in my room when I was working on my computer. While mom was frying pakoras, she got some in a bowl and said.

"Open your mouth Dhruv."

"I don't want." I said.

"I am feeding you. What's your problem? Come on eat it." She said and pushed it in my mouth.

Later when the taste melted in my mouth I asked her for more.

"Go to hell I won't give now." She said.

"Ok fine don't give." I said and turned back to the computer screen.

"Come on open your mouth and eat this quickly before someone comes." She said and fed me the last piece of the pakoras, kissed me on my cheek and ran outside. I was not sure what happened to her all of sudden.

"Dhruv! What's happening to her?" I said to myself smiled and forgot what I was up to with the next move of animation.

"Why are you smiling?" Mahi said as she entered the room again.

"Just like that." I replied.

"Ok then come to the kitchen fast your mom is calling." She said and went back to the kitchen.

I went to the kitchen and found that Mahi was serving the food today. It was strange the way she was behaving I couldn't understand. I took a glass of water and said.

"I'll eat after sometime I am not hungry." Immediately Mahi came close to me and said.

"Come and sit maybe this is the last time we would get a chance to eat together I don't know if we'll be able to sit like this again."

"Dhruv come and eat with everyone or else you will have to wash the utensils later." Mom said.

"Oh! No! I won't eat I'll wash... I mean... Mahi serve me I am coming." I said immediately.

After the lunch I came back on the computer as Mahi followed me. She stayed back as I wanted her help. By 2, everyone left and mom went out with dad and it was me Mahi and Krish in the house. Krish was watching the TV and we both were in my room. After a long time I had another chance to kiss her but not this time I controlled myself and did nothing.

"Dhruv you always wanted to know why I was with Mohit and not you." Mahi said.

"Yes but what's the use now. You are completely into him" I said when she started laughing.

"Do you really think that way Mohit is just a friend Dhruv. I wanted someone so that I can stay away from you. There are many reasons I can't tell you." She said. I hold her hand and tried to ask, when Radhika entered the room. Immediately I had to pull my hand back.

"Hi! What are you guys doing?" Radhika said.

"Nothing. Mahi is helping me in writing names on the DVD's. Anyways, where is my mobile? Just look at her. Isn't she looking beautiful?" I said to Mahi as she gave me my mobile. I clicked 2-3 photos of Radhika as she was really looking awesome. Radhika waited for some time and then went back to hostel.

She never stayed for a longtime whenever Mahi was around. I knew something was in her mind she never would say it to me, maybe she feared I would ignore her again because of Mahi. But that was really not possible I realized the most important thing after spending time with Mahi. I knew she would never come back maybe the relation between me and Mahi had to end here. She went back to her hostel and I knew I can never become a part of her life, the life which revolved around Gaurav, Mohit and her family. I must say Mahi was a beautiful part of my life she filled my life with joy but this had to end.

Radhika came in the evening she was wearing jeans and the blue t-shirt which I gifted her, she was looking pretty. I had to accept she was indeed looking sweet, cute and pretty altogether she was awesome.
"Why did you leave immediately Radhika?" I said.
"I didn't wanted to disturb you guys." She replied avoiding eye contact.
"Why do you still feel that I will go with her Radhika?"
"I don't feel Dhruv I have a strong believe in it."
"Come on Radhika its not the way you think it is."
"You think over it Dhruv you didn't even call me when she was with you. I felt ignored the moment I entered the room." She said.
"Are you crazy Radhika why will I ignore you? You're the best person I have in my life." I said and hugged her.
"Dhruv I had a fear that you would go back with her so I called up Parth and was talking with him for an hour in the afternoon." She said while I still hugged her.
"Don't you think in that way I am always with you." I said as I kissed on her cheek.
"Yes this is the only reason you want Radhika because she allows you to do everything." She said.
"Come-on Radhika, that's not true." I tried to cheer her.
"It's the truth Dhruv." She said and tried to be firm on her statement.

Our talk was interrupted as Parth called up, I asked him to come upstairs. We talked with each other for a while then took some snaps together as Radhika was really looking awesome and I didnt wanted to miss a chance to capture those moments. Later we went out for dinner when Parth informed about his new car he would get the next week.

1st March 2009, Sunday a day I hate the most but this one happened to be the best of all. I woke-up early and gave bath to my pets when Radhika came home around 10.00am. I had to get ready quickly as I was to meet Niraj after a long time. After he left Convergys he had started working in a KPO and was taking work seriously this time.

"Where are you going Mottu?" Radhika asked as she came inside while I was changing my clothes.

"Going to meet my friend from Convergys. Coming?" I said.

"Do I know him?"

"No but I'll introduce you as my girlfriend."

"No need. I am not coming with you, enjoy and come back soon."

"Yes I will now can you go out I have to wear my clothes."

"So you can wear it in front of me, I have seen you without clothes." She said with a smile.

"Ha ha very funny, now will you please?" I said and pushed her out of the room to change.

"By the way Mottu..." She again came inside

"Radhika wait go out." I said while she was laughing out loud."

"Can I come now?"

"Yes you can." I said with a bit of anger.

"Mottu you are looking smart are you sure you are meet your friend and not a girl right." She said.

"You don't trust me Radhika, so telling you something is pointless." I said wearing the shoes.

"I am leaving mom, will be late." I said while I drank a glass of water.

"Aren't you having your lunch." mom asked.

"No I will eat outside."

"He is going on a date kaku." Radhika said while she kept her hand on my shoulder.

"Ha ha he doesn't have any girlfriend he is going to meet his friend." My mom added.

"See my mom knows me very well." I said pushing her hand away and left home.

I reached FC road where Niraj was waiting for me. We greeted each other with a hug and then went to CCD. On the way he showed me his new bike and I was clueless about it. I didn't express any kind of expression till the time we sat inside CCD.

"Niraj you never owned a bike. Right!"

"Yeah! And that's what I showed you my new bike. But you didn't have any reaction on your face."

"Arre I am sorry I really didn't understand anything." I replied back immediately and congratulated him on his new bike. We spent some time talking and it felt nice to meet him after such a long time.

I came home around 5. I continued to work on the showreel till 7.30pm while I was waiting for Parth to show up with his new car. When he came everyone in my family went down to see his new car while Radhika entered my room while I was about to go downstairs. She kissed me and took my breath away. "Radhika someone would come inside." I said while I pushed her away. "Everyone's gone down to see the new car." She said on which I pulled her and we kissed each other twice. Parth gave the sweets to everyone, later Radhika and I went to camp along with him. Parth dropped us in camp as he had some work to do. So while coming back I was still struggling with my thoughts and my confusion was over. I decided that Radhika would be the one and nobody else after her. Mahi was totally out and thanks to her and Akash, things were pretty clear now. I knew what I wanted, I never said this to her until Mahi was in my mind. We were walking back home when I finally said it. "RADHIKA I LOVE YOU." I eagerly waited for her reply but instead she just gave a smile and continued to walk.
"Radhika say something. Don't just keep on smiling."
"Finally Dhruv, you said it. I had been waiting for this. We shared so much together I was wandering if you would ever say it to me." She said and I was speechless for a moment.
"Radhika it's not like that I always loved you but didn't know how to say it. Do you love me Radhika?"
"Dhruv then why the hell do you think I kissed you today." She said and it bought a smile and I jumped on the street.
"Yes... She loves me. I am the best."
"Ok Mottu control people was watching." She said and later we hold each other's hand while we continued walking.
"This is the best day Radhika." I said and we reached home.

Later she messaged me,' *Dhruv I have always loved you from the day I saw you. You are the only person in my life, never leave me love you bye.*' I smiled and replied,' *I will never leave you Radhika love you 2 3 4 bye good night.*'

*****

Chapter 13

Radhika, Me and the Exhibition...

8th March 2009 Women's day, I brought two bouquets of red roses for Radhika and for Riya on our way to Aundh. We had to wait for Riya as she was still busy with her mom, while I continued to click photos of Parth and Radhika. Radhika with the roses in her hand and the black top was looking wonderful. Parth was in formals and I always look awesome right from childhood.

"Look at him Parth. He is always used to praise himself if nobody does." Radhika said when I tried to praise myself after I showed them the pic.

"Radhika I am looking nice don't be jealous." I said.

"He is right Radhika, you should sometimes praise the pets I never disappoint them." Parth added as I ran behind him in order to hit him. In the meanwhile Riya came.

"Why are these guys running after each other?" She said

"Riya you should never take Parth anywhere. Anyways why are you always late? "I said.

"Look who is talking the person who is never on time." She replied.

"Hey Riya I was on time I got ready quickly."

"Riya he is lying I went home and he was still busy with his make-up." Radhika added.

"Anyways you are looking nice Dhruv."

"Thanks Riya, you are my only friend, see I bought flowers for you. Happy Birthday I mean Happy Women's Day." I said as I took one bunch of roses from Radhika.

"Liar, when did you get it? It was me who forced you to take it and I was holding it till here." Radhika said with a funny expression.

"Ok but I saw them first."

"Let it be Radhika I know Dhruv very well." Riya said as Parth came near and I got the chance to punch him in his stomach.

"Why are you hitting him Dhruv?" Riya asked as we moved in to Polka Dots a restaurant in Aundh suggested by Riya.

"Just like that." I replied.

"Riya do you know something or maybe Dhruv would have told you." Parth said as Riya was going through the menu list.

"What? Dhruv never said anything."

"I proposed Radhika."

"What????" Riya's shocked expressions were loud enough for people around to stare at us.

"So does that mean you guys have started to date each other."

"You can think it that way." I said.

"So tell me where have you been."

"Polka Dots." Radhika said and we all started to laugh.

"Hey Riya I've joined a new guitar class. I would be getting a free new guitar soon."

"Which class is this Dhruv a free guitar?" She asked all surprised.

"Yeah! It's this new class I found in Kothrud it's a nice class but it's not better than the class we went together."

"Our class is the best; anyways I don't think I will be able to continue any further because of my marriage."

"Riya when is your marriage?" Radhika asked in order to be a part of our conversation.

"It's on the 21st May." Riya replied.

"Ok now can we order something? I am hungry." I said.

"Like always..." Riya said while everyone laughed along with her. I kept the menu card on the table and drank water from the glass. We ordered the food and liked it a lot along with our talk. Riya was very happy for me as she knew I needed someone as Mahi wasn't with me. After the lunch was over we went to drop Riya, she had to leave soon with her mom so before she left we again had a photo session together. A new beginning to our new relationship ended with the Woman's day celebration at Riya's place.

Few days later, I was in MAAC to participate in clay modeling for the exhibition. MAAC's second exhibition I never wanted to miss the chance. This time it was big, the students from all MAAC centers in Pune would participate and I never wanted to miss this opportunity. My schedule was fixed everyday Radhika would wake me around 7.30am but I would get out of the bed an hour later, sometimes around 9, then get ready go to class to work with the clay models. I had decided to make model sets from the animated movies Shrek and Madagascar. I would work in MAAC till 4.00 or 4.30pm then later come home. At home I was trying to create the WALL-E character in Maya software. My work continued late night till 2 or 3.00am. During this period I met these 3 girls in class Palak, Neha and Anushka. Palak was a Gujju girl and the first thing one would notice about her was her skin color she was very fair. Neha was cute with her smile that would glow dimples on both side of her cheek. Anushka had a good height and she seemed to be sensible and studious among these three. Her hair was similar to Radhika and what else about them, I couldn't notice much. They were working on a giant Mickey Mouse and were best in order to distract anyone from work whenever they came for the clay modeling session. I always came early to start working on the model as sometimes these girls used to piss me off with their continuous chit-chatting and giggling. But it didn't take long for me to exchange phone numbers with Palak and when at home I tried to tease Radhika.

"I tell you she is so fair, haven't seen anybody like her. She is very beautiful, should I try?"

"What did you say?" She said and ran behind me while mom would be completely unaware of what was going between the two of us. I enjoyed my work and was very serious about the exhibition. I knew many students got placed in most of the reputed studios in the last exhibition. I wanted that thing to happen for me as well, so I was working hard on it that I even intended to ignore Radhika while I worked. Even during Holi when Radhika came home with colors I was working. Finally the WALL-E character was complete and I emailed it to Radhika. She replied as soon as she saw it.

Hi sweetheart, nice to see your Wall-e finally completed. You have done a great job. Tell you one thing. I saw your dedication for your work for the first time. Now I'm having a strong intuition that you will reach your desired goal very soon. Maybe we won't have to wait for a long time… ;-)

With lots of Love,
Radhika.

==

That certainly boosted my confidence and I was very happy with her reply. I told her about the fear I had of not getting selected through the exhibition. Immediately she replied back positively but it confused me, somehow as it had many contradictory things written by her. She told me that I need to work hard as our future depends on my work and I only had a year as even she would become a CA so as to talk with her father. I wasn't sure about it as she had also mentioned that I was playing with her heart, she tried to avoid me at times, but she could notice the way I had become ever since Mahi left. She had said this to me in the email, I ignored the part as I forwarded the next output file of WALL-E. Radhika was very happy about it which was reflecting in her mail.

It's looking great! But there's something wrong with Eva's dress. Check it if you can. The texture of Wall-E is look nice. Just too good!
I have a lot to say to you. You said that you don't trust anybody. Not even me? What did I do wrong? That day the very first thing which came into my mind was this question. I don't know the answer, but want to know what happened to you. What makes you feel so? If possible do tell me. Also I am a bit jealous with your work, you are so busy. When will your project get over?

It's like your work is becoming your girlfriend, and am becoming your ex.... (;-
(But I'm very happy to see your dedication towards your work. Hats off to you
Love you a lot

Plan out something, I want to spend time with you.
Love you... ☺

This reply confused me as I would often think if she really loved me but then I would wipe it off soon from my mind. I would consider only one thing, she loved me a lot and yes she was right I was working hard for the exhibition so the clay models were complete and we had to wait till we get any further instructions to paint the models. I submitted the Maya work and was relaxed after a long time.

After I was free from the exhibition work I asked Radhika to cook chicken for me at home. I had been asking her for a long time. So the very next day, she decided to cook it for me. I bought raw chicken from the market and then helped Radhika to cook. I mean... I helped her clean the chicken and taste the soup when it was ready. Around 2pm finally, the chicken was ready and it smelled really good. Radhika served 3 plates, two for us and one for my uncle who was busy with card games on my computer. The chicken news had spread till Jabalpur as Radhika's mom helped her with the ingredients and the preparation. Radhika and I were sitting in the kitchen about to take the first bite. As soon as I put the first bite in my mouth I started to taste the chicken and my tongue was rolling along when something funny came out of my mouth.
"Hey Radhika I guess chili powder is very cheap these days, or maybe you added a bit extra. Isn't it?" And then I shouted," I need water." I ran immediately and drank a glass of water. The chicken was very spicy but it was amazing I had never tasted such a wonderful chicken ever in my life.

"Sorry Mottu I couldn't understand how much chili powder I should add." She said with an innocent face, assuming it was her biggest mistake.
"So is that why you add so much. By the way how many spoons did you add."
"It was one and a half spoon."
"One and a half! Are you crazy? Even half a spoon would have been enough. Don't you know I never eat such spicy food."
"I am sorry Mottu won't happen again." She said.
"Its fine you are forgiven only for one reason, the chicken is amazing except for the fact that it's spicy." I said and meanwhile my uncle came inside and complimented her.

Again the thought struck my mind, if I marry Radhika I would definitely get to eat amazing chicken she cooks awesome except the fact that it could be spicy. I picked up one piece and tried to feed her when mom came in and immediately the piece went in my mouth instead of Radhika's mouth.
"What timing your mom has?" Radhika said and we both started to laugh when mom could not understand anything what we were talking about. After the lunch was over mom asked Radhika to wash all the utensils as she had already informed her to do so. I clicked her pics which was the most amazing part to be treasured in my memories.

Few days passed and I got a new routine when Radhika used to wake me up and then I used to go to the construction site along with Krish and in the evening sit down to work or spend time with Radhika, watch movies with her on the weekends, either on my computer or in multiplexes. 24th April, I remember it was the election day and she came early from office and we had no other work to do. I wanted to kiss her so the only option was a movie hall. We went to Inox for a movie. The movie hall was pretty empty and being on the corner seats we really enjoyed kissing each other. I wondered why many couple prefer watching such movies. There was no crowd and it was amazing to watch another couple going way ahead than just kisses. We came out and sat in Mc Donald's where for some stupid reason we had a fight. Now, why we fought I had really no clue but we fought and later didn't talk properly for few days with each other.

A month later, Radhika's informed me about her class party. She was waiting to celebrate it with her class friends. She came home all prepared to meet me before going to the party. She was looking amazing, blue jeans and blue t-shirt on top of which she wore a black shirt and a tie. Above all the best part was she had applied lipstick for the first time. I couldn't wait any longer and hold her close to me and kissed her. I should thank my family members that nobody entered my room while I kissed her which she loved a lot.

"Mottu my lipstick, I applied it for the first time. You spoilt everything."

"I know Radhika maybe that's why I couldn't control. It was amazing, I want one more."

"Forget it I will never kiss you now." She said and went out and came inside and before leaving the house she kissed me. Oh boy that was really amazing I tried to catch hold of her but she ran immediately as her friend Sahil was waiting for her downstairs and within a few seconds a message flashed on my screen I love you Mottu.

That day Radhika informed me that her friend Sahil proposed her. I knew this would come up some day as every time she spoke about him I was pretty sure he would say this to her. I was happy that she ignored him. Maybe she knew what would happen to me if she left me, that's why she was with me or maybe she really loved me. She made every day worth living for me by her presence. Sometimes it was the late night calls or the mails from office. Sometimes, a call from her office, every time I picked up she would say, "Hello! Radhika. Kya kar raha hai Mottu?" would bring a smile and our talks would continue. She wanted to spend an entire day with me watching movies and talking with me. Leaving these things apart she was a great support at that moment when I knew exhibition was cancelled due to some issues. I was frustrated as all the hard work had gone in vein. But Radhika hold my hand and said, "Mottu just think you were practicing for all these days." Her words kept my hope alive maybe, the exhibition would happen one day and I'll be successful.

*****

Chapter 14

Radhika and the new Friends….

The exhibition getting cancelled gathered negative vibes in my mind. I wanted to work but was not sure where to start from. On the other hand, there was a little insecurity in my mind for Radhika when she would be over-friendly with Parth. She would often compare me with stuff Parth would do and I would not. I was jobless and had left the job to begin the career into animation. I first step towards animation was getting recognized through the exhibition. It was cancelled and felt like a failure at times. Also many times I would only be a spectator to watch these two giggle and enjoy, Parth would bare the expenses or Radhika. Rarely did pay the bills, so I always felt I should get a job, as I hated being dependent on anyone. I thought I should begin with the showreel work and tried to gather some ideas. Within these few days I realized that I had started to complicate my life with these thoughts. As some time back I had a job a girlfriend and a best friend to be with, also a dream and desire to achieve a name into animation. But when you are lost there are ways through which you mind could be free from such thoughts.

There were times when it was only me and Radhika where I would do crazy stuff to build up memories with her. Did she really enjoy my craziness? I never thought about it but I could see she was happy with me. One such incident was when my cousin was out of town and had left the keys for his flat with us. That time I thought of taking Radhika to the flat in order to spend some time. I wanted to sit with her holding hands and discuss our future. But when you are alone in a flat very rarely you would discuss the future. We had decided to meet after my guitar class around 6.00pm. I was hungry so I got something to eat on our way.
"Why do you always think about eating Mottu?" Radhika asked while she sat behind my bike.
"I am hungry Radhika."
"You are always hungry Mottu."
"I know… This is the way I am." I said.

We reached and I unlocked the door. I kept the guitar in the living room and took her along to show the flat. Radhika was wearing formals, black shirt and off-white trousers with her cute specs. She always looked amazing in formals, but I never complimented her. On the other hand, I never missed a chance of being sarcastic to say Radhika you are looking horrible today and she would always say, "Do you ever find me nice?"

But this was not a point of discussion here, we both ate the samosas after she got fresh and I got the dumbest look from her. She was not at all hungry but still had to eat for me.

"Kuch meetha ho jaye Radhika." I said removing the dairy milk chocolate from my pocket.

"When did you get this?" She asked in surprise.

"Surprise!" I said as I opened the wrapper. I kept a piece in my mouth and went a bit closer to her. She cut a part of it with her teeth slowly with smile and later kissed me. I turned off the lights as we kissed and hugged each other. That moment when Radhika was in my arms I felt as if I had the entire world around me. We were totally lost in ourselves for a while when suddenly my mobile started ringing, it was mom. I picked up the phone and went out.

"Where are you?" She asked.

"I am in class. Why? What happened?" I lied.

"Nothing its 8.00pm you didn't come home so I called you come soon we are waiting for dinner."

"Ok will leave within few minutes." I said and had a narrow escape.

I came back and soon Radhika's phone rang, Krish had called her. She picked up the phone and convinced him that she was in the office but as soon as she kept the phone she began to cry.

"What happened Radhika?" I asked.

"Krish knows that we are together."

"How does he? I never told him anything."

"Then, why did he ask to tell you keep the house keys separate from the bike keys." She said and began to cry more loudly. It was getting difficult for me to persuade her. Finally, I hugged her and said,

"Radhika I am with you don't worry he will never know. I will take care of it don't worry. I love you." At that moment I was holding her tightly in my arms but never knew she would be so scared of being caught.

I wiped off her tears kissed her on her forehead and said, "Radhika we'll leave, I'll drop you at a bus station and then you reach home. I'll come home 10-15 min's later, as soon as you message me." I said. She agreed and got ready and I hugged her and tried to get a smile on her face, somehow I succeeded. We left the house within the next 10-15 min's and on the way back home Radhika said.

"You were supposed to show me what you have learnt till now in your guitar classes."

"I forgot anyways I love the way you kiss me. I love you Radhika."

"You are impossible Dhruv." She said.

"I know, I am the best." I replied back.

"I love you Mottu." She said and hugged me tightly while I drove the bike and later hold her left hand with close to my heart, one of the best moment while returning back home. I dropped her to the bus stop from where she left for home and I roamed around the city for the next 10-15 minutes waiting for her message. When I reached home everything seemed normal while Radhika was laughing and giggling with everyone, whereas my mom was lined up with many questions starting with," Why were you late? Where were you?" I answered the questions one after another and made up a story that I was with a new friend seeing his new electric guitar. On the other hand Radhika said, "Kaku he must be hanging on with a new girlfriend might have got a new one in his class."

"Yes Radhika I did get one and I did kiss her today should I tell you where exactly I kissed her." I whispered in her ears as she sat beside me, while mom asked me to stop talking and eat.

Next day I went late to class after Krish came home from the construction site. Radhika had gone to Parth's place to teach him Accounts after her office, so I had plenty of time in class. During this time I met some strange characters who I never thought would become my friends for life. I was practicing the chords when this guy introduced himself to me after being impressed by my notes. His name was Prasad, who was really good at playing all kind of lead songs on his guitar. Second was this guy named Harsh who kept running in and out of the classroom playing along his mobile. Most important he was running behind this girl named Preeti a cute little bubbly girl who reminded me of Mahi but within a moment I was irritated with these two. Right next to Prasad was seated Avni a skinny girl another member of this particular group. Opposite Avni was the grey eyed dude Sam whose long hair covered most of his face and next to him was this guy in formals- Aman who played his guitar and smiled every 5-10 seconds watching Harsh and Preeti.

"Do they always behave like this in class?" I asked Prasad.

"Yes dude Harsh is in love with her but she just knows how to tackle him on his fingers, so its great fun to watch them." He replied.

"Fun! No ways I am damn annoyed and I feel I should ask them to be quiet." I replied and we continued talking for some time. Moments, later there was an electricity cutout and we were standing in the parking where Preeti began to share some files through Bluetooth with me. That was it some new friends finally in this class adding me a reason to attend class regularly. When I came home it was time to let Radhika know about the fun, but she had something more to share. After the study session with Parth she met his friends and they had gone for dinner together. Sometimes I would envy her as she would easily get along with anyone and with Parth's friends it seemed she knew them for a long time. But I was happy that she would never feel alone as she felt after being ignored at hostel.

Next day, Preeti once again screaming and dancing in the class joined by Harsh. She was giving chocolates to everyone, I was not able to figure out the reason why she was doing so.
"What's the matter? Why is she distributing chocolates?" I asked Harsh.
"It's her 10th result today and she got 78% which is amazing." He replied exaggerating things.
"Oh! Ok! but 10th result is yet to be declared right."
"Yes, but she is from the CBSE board so her result is declared earlier."
"Hey congratulations Preeti and where's my chocolate?" I said.
"Oh! Max. I have brought one for you. Here's it and thank you." She replied and gave me the chocolate. Thanks to my Bluetooth device name Max Harsh and Preeti ended up calling me Max. Very soon Harsh shared a lot of stuff with me about him and Preeti how they first met in class. That time I told these guys about Radhika and they were eager to meet her.

13th June 2009, I left early from class as Parth and Radhika had planned to spend the entire night together. I reached home around 8.30pm, Radhika was having her dinner after which she came in my room and said," Dhruv get ready Parth would be coming by 9.30 we have to go."
"Do we really have to go Radhika?" I asked as I was in no mood for the night-out.
"Why are you saying like this? We had already decided that we would go today." She said.
"I know Radhika I was just kidding I'll be ready don't worry." I informed mom that there was a reunion of all the friends from Convergys and I had to go.
"When will you come back?" Mom asked.
"I don't know I might be late." I said.
"Is Radhika also coming with you?" She asked.

"Now, why the hell will she come? Its reunion of all my office friends and she hardly knows anybody except for Parth." I said but couldn't understand how she knew that Radhika would join. Maybe I never had an answer to this particular question but before I could get involved in her questionnaire Parth came. He was waiting across the street below my house. I walked towards his car and found that Radhika was already seated in the front seat, so without giving any chance to my thoughts I sat back.

We went to E-Square and bought the tickets for a movie. The show was at 10.45pm and we had plenty time to spend. Parth was driving his car in full speed. It was amazing but my silence was killing them.
"What happened to you Duksey? Why are you so quiet?" Parth asked me while driving the car.
"I am feeling sleepy." I said.
"I'll give one punch if you sleep we are not fools to come for you." He said in anger.
"I have not slept in the afternoon that's why I am feeling sleepy. You should have told me before." I said yawning.
"Do you think we have slept?"
"Come on Mottu don't sleep see we are going for a movie now." Radhika said holding my hands.
"I know. I won't sleep just give me some time I'll be fine." I said and later we went for the movie.

After the movie got over around we went to Mini Punjab in Hinjewadi. There we took three bottles of Canberry Breezer and a can of Beer. I had planned to start working upon the showreel and the thoughts were still in my mind as I was not able to do so. But, I decided to have fun with them and stop thinking. Later we went to Soho's and ordered something to eat. The atmosphere was very different instead of tables we had beds on the corners were we jumped onto one and I was ready to sleep. Later I took my mobile phone to capture some more moments, so did Radhika with her cell phone. By the time we finished eating it was 4.30am and Parth felt sleepy. We went and sat in his car, Radhika sat behind and I put my head on her lap.
"Let's sleep for some time." I said
"Duksey all the time you have only talked about sleeping next time we won't bring you, you such a lazy ass." Parth said while he was half asleep.
"Yes Parth you are right only we both will go." Radhika added.
"What we both will go? Look at him he's about to sleep." I said pointing towards Parth who had closed his eyes and was fast asleep in the front seat.

As soon as Radhika found Parth was sleeping she came closer and kissed me. I kissed her back and smiled at her.

"Kya hua Mottu?" Radhika asked me.

"Nothing. Good night." I said while I kissed her again and went off to sleep.

We woke up around 6.00am when we headed towards Pune Station for a cup of tea. I had to rush into bed before mom woke up but she was awake before I could enter my bed.

"Where were you Dhruv the whole night?" She asked.

"Was with friends we had gone for a movie then to Mini Punjab." I said and tried to explain that because of the rush at Mini Punjab I came late. It was pretty convincing but I had to close my eyes before any further questions. Mom, I tell you always there with her never ending questions. I woke up at 10. Radhika came home around 11.30am. Mom tried to explain her how I came late in the morning when we looked at each other and smiled. I think I really enjoyed with these two guys at that time but somewhere my work was being delayed. I wanted to avoid them but would never be able to avoid them.

18th June 2009, the most unexpected thing was waiting for me. The bonding with the guitar class friends had increased a lot; they almost shared everything with me. With Preeti completing her 10th it was Harsh and Avni who were waiting for their 10th results. Prasad was in the second year of Mechanical Engineering so was Sam. Aman was another future CA just like Radhika; he was doing his article-ship and had to appear for the exams. Among this group there was one person who had gone to his hometown. Harsh had built up tones of appreciation for his fellow so I was eager to meet him, his name was Anup. I wanted to meet this guy as Harsh said was the best guy of this group. So I wanted to know him. During this time Prasad was very keen and interested for a night out plan for Mahabaleshwar. But somewhere the plan was not working as many were not interested in coming until then.

"Where are you Dhruv?" Radhika called up. It was 8.00pm.

"I am in class, why? What happened?" I said.

"Nothing I am coming to the class."

"What are you serious? Where are you? Do you even know where my class is?" I said in a tensed voice.

"Mottu you have to guide me I am near the Karisma Society." She said some way I was happy that she was coming to meet me but at the same time was worried.

Every year we have the processions of Saint Eknath and Tukaram in Pune. This year there was huge rush and crowd in the city which made me worried. I informed everyone Radhika was coming to meet and went to pick her as she had gone in the wrong direction. Seeing her I was happy and smiled while I got her to class. Everyone was excited to meet her. Preeti had just left so it was Prasad, Aman Sam and Harsh. I introduced them one after another and within seconds she was friendly with them. I guess she had a magic in her of making people friendly within seconds. They were chit-chatting with each other just in the same way as she and Parth did when they were together. I brought up the plan for Mahabaleshwar and to my surprise everyone was ready to go to Mahabaleshwar. I was stunned to see that everyone was ready to come. I told her how everyone was giving reasons to not come.

"It's ok Mottu now that everyone is ready we'll have fun." She said.
"Mottu why do you call him that." Aman enquired.
"Well, that's his name. Only I call him that." Radhika said.
"Oh! That's great maybe true love and all. We like to call him Max." Harsh added.
"Oh! Thanks Harsh I am obliged." Oh I never said that instead I said, "Oye Harsh keep that funda of true love and all aside do I look fat by any chance and look at her she ends up calling me Mottu. It's really embarrassing at times."
"Oh! it's embarrassing for you Dhruv. I'll make sure I don't embarrass you anymore." She said in anger.
"Radhika I was joking, you can call me that I love it, have no problems with it. Ok, nobody will say anything." I said and hold her around her waist.
"When did we say anything? It's you who is continuously talking." Aman said making a straight face.
"Ok fine I'll stay quiet." I said and everyone started laughing.

After a while we all left and while I was driving Radhika started." You were not happy to see me here, right Dhruv? You felt embarrassed to introduce me to your friends. I am sorry I came without informing you." She said.
"Are you crazy Radhika? Why will I feel embarrassed to introduce you?" I said.
"Yes you were Dhruv and I told you thousands of times we won't go to Mahabaleshwar still you made this plan and made a fool out of me."
"It's not like that Radhika everyone wanted to meet you as I had already told them about you. I was worried as you were coming alone and there was no

other reason. And about Mahabaleshwar if you want I will cancel the plan don't worry." I tried to convince her.

"No Dhruv you will again make me the culprit for cancelling the plan." She said and I kept quiet in order to avoid any further fight with her. When we reached home I informed her that the plan won't be cancelled because of her.

I was searching for reasons I will give all the friends in order to let them know that the plan is cancelled. Next day morning Radhika called up, I disconnected her phone as was going in MAAC and thought of calling her back once I reach home but her cell was switched off so I wrote a mail which I never knew would land up me in trouble. I complained that the plan was cancelled because of her. Although I had no problem if it got cancelled, but I didn't want Radhika to cancel it. I also mentioned that every time the plan is cancelled because of her or Parth. I knew I had writing stuff I shouldn't be writing but still without giving a second thought to what I have written I clicked on the send button and within no time I had a reply from Radhika.

YA ITS ALWAYS ME... who cancels the plan. Thanks a lot for coming that day. We planned it for you as the plan you make gets cancelled every time. The plan for Mahabaleshwar is not cancelled it's postponed for a week. I thought we are going to Singhagad fort on Sunday. I am telling you from the last few weeks that Mottu am short of money, and don't want Parth to spend every time. Just calculate the total expenditure per head. Approximately it goes around 7 to 800 bucks. Right? I feel ashamed at times saying no to you!!! That day we cancelled the plan for movie due to the high rates but I spent around 500 bucks. Just for you... You don't know how I am cutting off my expenses for all this (you were telling me the why I don't drink milk when Devika is gone, or why don't I have breakfast while going to bus stop. This is the damn reason, I drink complain with warm water instead of milk.) I never said no to you when you wanted to buy Happy Meal at Mc D. What do you think I like wearing glasses? It's just that am not in a position to afford monthly lenses. I stopped buying my eye-drop because it's 170 bucks twice a month. My dad is not a millionaire who can afford so much luxury for me. He has to run the house, pay for my brother's medical class fees and hell lot of expenses. I told you dad is not well, so many tests are going on. He would never utter a word but I know the charges of each tests. I told dad not to come but as he wants to be with me on my birthday he is not cancelling the plan. Maybe this is last time am celebrating my b'day with them, coz I will be on job here from next year onwards. But I am fool; I booked the tickets for them on 4th all because of you. I could have been in Jabalpur and mom dad wouldn't have to come. I don't want to say this to you. It feels so cheap *and I feel ashamed of myself. I bought jeans/top coz you wanted me to dress good when we go out. You liked the top I was wearing so I bought it, knowing I am not going to wear it a single time at home. I feel like a fool thinking so much for others. Now on, I am not going to miss a single class. Think whatever you want. I told you not to make night out plan two days back because of money problems. Still you made the plan yesterday in front of your friends. I am really very sorry for cancelling your plan once again. I have done all this because I love you and don't like saying no to you. As you always say to me!!! But what I get in return...So much pain...It hurts Mottu.*

==

I read the mail twice and didn't know how exactly I should react. I was stunned! I went in the kitchen drank a glass of water and sat down back on my chair and read the mail again. Somewhere I knew she had written this because somewhere I might have been wrong. But the fact that Radhika gave me the complete explanation of every single penny spend on me made me feel bad. It was horrible I remembered how I used to spend money on every person who was with me and never calculated money in any relation. One thing I knew was money screws up everything in a relation and I hated when people showed me the calculations or the money they spent on me. Radhika knew this very well but still she wrote such a mail. That moment I felt as if she actually showed me my place where I stand in terms of money. Being jobless felt like a curse to me after reading that mail. Later, I replied to the mail in anger and wasn't expecting any reply. I thought things would be fine till the evening but when Radhika came home she showed eccentric behavior. She spoke little and tried to stay as far as possible from me. I tried to cheer her just in order to make her talk with me but she didn't utter a word.

Does she really love me? If she does why is she behaving like this? These thoughts continued in my mind as I decided to stay away from her for some time. Next day was Saturday Radhika went to Parth's place without informing me. I decided to give her some space and went to class. Her thoughts were still in my mind. She didn't talk so I stayed away from her in anger. Somehow I didn't want to initiate the talk. She came in my room while Krish was doing something on the computer. I pretended to be sleeping on which she left the room and went back to hostel. This time Radhika was adamant and I knew she would never initiate to talk first. I did feel bad for ignoring her but I thought everything would be fine. I cancelled the plan for Mahabaleshwar but they came up with a plan to Sinhagad fort. I didn't want to go as Radhika wasn't talking with me. The plan was almost cancelled as my cousin didn't turn up to give me his bike until Vishal called up. He asked me if I was free on Sunday and we could go out somewhere. I told him about the plan for Singhagad which got cancelled. He told me we could take his bike and my approval happened to be the biggest mistake of my life.

21ˢᵗ June 2009, Sunday I left for Singhagad fort. I thought of calling Radhika but it skipped my mind I thought I would let her know once we reach the fort but there was no network as we reached. Like always she came home for lunch in the afternoon and she asked mom about me. I didn't know how she would have reacted that moment when mom told her the truth as I was busy clicking pictures. Somewhere I felt I should say sorry to her and probably sort out everything but Radhika ended up crying the entire day. She always wanted to be at Singhagad along with me but I left her crying just for one stupid mail and maybe that ego within me which kept saying 'I am not wrong she doesn't love me. Had she ever loved me she would have never said those things.' I was cursing myself the moment Radhika came to know I was here. I knew things would be worst but I wanted to sort out everything that was messed up. Radhika was everything to me but I couldn't let go off my anger and left her crying. Later, I tried to convince her through mails. But I had to get an awesome reply to it, no matter how hard I wanted things to be normal.

===

I said those things because I never mind sacrificing my happiness on you, never ever counted the money I spent on you. Dhaval bhai was always reminded me to save, but I was happier seeing you enjoy with me than the interest earned in saving money. I don't like people spending on you as they discuss that thing one or the other way which you never understand (they make fun of you Mottu, or they pity on you). When I hear all this, it makes me sad, thinking of the days you use to spend on others. You know something, I was not ignoring you. I was not able to make eye contact with you due to the reply I sent. I was so guilty I thought you should have not read it. I tried to recall it through outlook but failed. I didn't want to write all that rubbish it's all because I found it necessary to give the explanation for cancelling the Mahabaleshwar plan.

I just wanted to ask you one question. How could you go without me? How Mottu??? Not even once you thought what will I Radhika if she knows this. I am begging from the last 2 years to go to that place. But you went there without me. How? Why? If you think you saved my money by not taking me, you are absolutely wrong. You know what I'm crying from the very next moment kaku told me and I'm still crying. I took bath 4 times because I was felt the hatred for each of my body parts you touched. I felt like a fool, who didn't go with her colleagues on Saturday to Singhagad. I thought if I go without you, you will feel bad. I cancelled my Essel world plan. I think of you hundred times before eating pani-puri alone because you it. I stopped going to McD alone, which I used to go before I started roaming with you. Even yesterday I went to get bhel but recalled last Sunday we ate together, so how can I have alone.

You tried so many things to cheer me up... By biting me, by not calling me. Not replying to my messages. I asked you whether you were going to CCD because I wanted to come with you. So that no one had to pay for you accept me. You asked me on Saturday lets go in the rain. I shut the computer and came immediately. But you went without me. I called you 100 times in the morning just to ask why you did this to me.

You always do this to me. Always leave me alone. We were supposed to go to see our, I mean your new home. What happened? Did you forget? At least there my money wouldn't have been spent.

Parth asked me lets go to Singhagad on Sunday you, me and Dhruv. I refused as we were going with your new friends, and Parth won't be comfortable with them. Parth stopped talking to me after our night-out because he thinks relation is being spoiled because of him. I accepted thinking maybe he is right. But, what happened? How can you do this to me? I am asking this question to myself every single second. How can he do this to me? You don't love me Mottu; you just don't... because I am not that kind of girl you wanted. You were not worried about me when I came to your class. You are ashamed of me. I know this. I don't know what the reason you choose me is. Maybe you wanted to have someone rather than staying alone...or something else.

But let me tell you one thing I love you so much that I can never eat anything in my life alone which you like, I can never go to a movie without you. McD will be the last place I would like to go, tandoori, Cad B, pani-puri. I just can't have them without you. I just can't think of going to Mahabaleshwar without you. The 1ˢᵗ thing which comes in my mind when I heard all these things is you Dumbo. I don't know when my tears are going to stop, but I want them to flow because it may be the punishment of loving someone so much. That was the last Saturday Sunday I had to spend with you guys. But it's ok Mottu. Thanks for such a lovely tearful Sunday...

Hope you get a beautiful wife
Love you

===

I wasn't sure how exactly I should reply to her mail. I kept thinking about it the entire afternoon and later started typing. I wanted her to know how I felt the moment she had mentioned about spending money upon me. When we love someone we never think about the things or the time or money wasted on them. Firstly, we never waste anything it's the moments that are cherished together, that's the way I look towards any relation. I never wanted this in any relation whether I was in relation with Mahi before or whether it was with Radhika. I had always given my fullest to each. Although I knew I hadn't been fair enough with Radhika but I had always loved the moments spent with her. She was important to me today but it was the anger that made me say everything to her and it was the anger that stopped me from taking her to Singhagad. Had I learnt to control my anger these things wouldn't have happened. Most important I was never able to tell her how important she is to me in my life and maybe that's why she always felt that she was just a replacement over Mahi, which wasn't true. I never proposed her until Mahi was gone forever. I never wanted Radhika to be a replacement as I had always liked her. But it was difficult for me to explain this to her. I tried hard to let her know it was my biggest mistake for leaving her alone on Sunday. I explained it to her in many ways so it was one mail after another but I failed to justify myself. Radhika's mail had hurt me a lot and I was angry on her. But after reading the very first mail I had realized my mistake and I badly wanted things to be normal.

Radhika brought up the past again in front of me, the things I did with her when I was with Mahi. I would read her mails and try to clear my point, but one thing which I always knew. No matter how hard you try to explain, the person will always listen to only those things which he/she wants to listen. Everything else is a sheer waste of time and words. So I did say sorry and said I would not repeat the things again but then, I gave up. I wanted to ask her that one thing but I didn't. She had completely lost faith in me. She wanted Parth to be with us every time I had to plan out something. I never said anything about it as Parth was my friend but sometimes I really hated when these two left me alone to just listen to their talk. But I never said anything, I stopped replying to the mails.

After sometime I got another mail from Radhika. I opened it.   'Just scroll down' it said and I began to scroll down to read the contents which said. 'A very special good morning to a very special person in a very special way'. I didn't know how to react as she had pasted one of her funny photo showing her tongue. Radhika was always unpredictable and this email showed it. I decided to give my complete efforts to make things normal. I knew it was difficult but not impossible. I would never say sorry to anyone even if it was my fault but yes I did bend on my knees and asked for her forgiveness when she came back home in the evening. I sat on my knees and hold her hand and asked her to forgive me. I didn't let her go until she forgave me and things were back to normal thanks to Parth who had advised her to give me that one last chance.

23rd June 2009, Parth, Abhi, Radhika and I had planned a surprise for Riya. Abhi brought his car and then later we all went to Hinjewadi to pick up Radhika from her office. On our way Riya Parth and Abhi were shouting on me one after another. Reason was simple I was not treating Radhika properly. "Dhruv you should understand she is your girlfriend now and not just any friend. You should give her some time." Riya began first.
"I really didn't like the way you left her alone and went to Singhagad." Parth added while he was seated beside Abhi driving the car.
"And what about the things she said to me, how was I supposed to react." I said never letting anybody know about her mails.
"What did she say, maybe you ignore her I do this, I do that and you never give time for me. Right?" Parth started again.
"No it was something more than that Parth."
"Hey what did she say Dhruv let us know soon?" Abhi said trying to be funny.
"She is a girl Dhruv, she will definitely do all kind of crazy things, and you know me how I was in office." Riya said.
"Yours is a different thing Riya."
"Nothing is different Dhruv. Promise me you will take good care of her and hence forth I don't want you guys to fight." She said holding my hand.
"I promise, I will never hurt her again."
"By the way show me your Abs Dhruv, I want to see those six packs. And now leave my hand we are here and smile don't keep that sad face when she comes." She said and tried to check my abs while Parth added his witty comment.
"You must be feeling very good, Riya touching your body."
"Shut-up Parth don't be jealous." I said while Riya immediately moved her hand away from my stomach.
"Its nice Dhruv let's see how many days you are able to keep them." She said and as we reached I called up Radhika. She came within the next 5-10 minutes and said, "what's the matter why is everyone so serious."
"I love you Radhika." I said and hugged her while Parth shouted "Woo hoo come on Duksey". Radhika was clueless of what happened between the three

of us but I had made up a promise I would never hurt and be angry on her for stupid reasons.

Later we had lunch together; well it did take a while for us to find a nice restaurant. We were happily chit-chatting and maybe the last memory to share with Riya as she was finally married and was about to leave for Kerala forever. After lunch, I blindfolded Riya with my hands and took her near the car.
"What are you doing? Dhruv, I will fall."
"Don't worry Riya, you won't and come here we have a surprise for you." I said while Abhi opened the back-door of his car and there was the surprise.
"What is it?" Riya asked as she was not able to understand anything. Finally I took the gift out and kept it in her hands. She was still not able to understand what we were up to.
"Ok Riya, this is a new guitar and we have bought it for you. A gift for someone I love I mean someone we love." Finally the surprised expressions were out.
"Oh my god are you serious?"
"No I am joking guys she doesn't want the guitar I will take it home." I said when everyone started laughing
"Thank you guys and Dhruv if it's for me I will take it and not you so give it here." She said and pulled the guitar from my hand. One of the best moment when Abhi clicked pictures of Riya holding the guitar and trying to play something out of it. She was thrilled excited and very happy for the gift.
"I had told you she will like this particular gift." I said when Riya added," I loved it guys this is one of the best gift, thank you very much."

Later she hugged everyone and we dropped Radhika back to office and came to Aundh. I took my bike and was about to leave when my bike got punctured and I was like. *"Can't things end properly with me?"* I said with a smile and then later pushed the bike in order to get it fixed. Next day, Radhika and I went to meet all my guitar class friends. Preeti was so excited that she hugged her as soon as I introduced her to Radhika. These people were unpredictable especially Preeti. Well girls are always unpredictable. They bought a surprise gift for Radhika, a fur toy which left me speechless at that moment.

"This one is for you Radhika from all of us." Preeti said while she gave the soft toy to Radhika.
"Hey was this necessary?" Radhika said.
"Yes it is you are leaving Pune and it's your birthday next month we came to know you won't be here on your birthday. So yes it is necessary." Preeti explained everything with a cute little smile on her face. Later Harsh introduced me to Anup the person whom I was waiting for a long time to meet. He was

6feet tall and was slim like I guess I never had a comparison for him. I kept wondering how was he the best in this particular group, but maybe first meeting won't give me all the answers. We moved to Mc Donald's where Radhika gave a treat. I was very happy that Radhika had many friends when she was about to leave Pune and I had already started to miss her. After all that fun we came home and mom again had a question for both of us. I wanted to use my favorite line here 'Ab meri personality hi aisi hai na… But then then line suited well for Radhika at that moment." We didn't say anything just smiled looking at each other. Mom didn't ask anything else.

*****

Chapter 15

Radhika's Birthday...

27th June 2009, we were finally leaving for Mahabaleshwar. Radhika informed mom that she is going to Lonavala with her relatives. We had to reach near guitar class around 4.00pm. That time Diya had called up Radhika. I wanted to meet her too but, maybe it was my ego that stopped me or was it something else. "Radhika when you meet her just ask her one question, is she happy there?" I said before she left to meet Diya. I reached Deccan to my cousin's garage and took his pulsar. Around 3.45pm I picked up Radhika near the Z-bridge and we headed towards the guitar class. As usual I was late.

"We were supposed to leave at 4.00pm." Sam said as we met everyone.
"I know but I was stuck with some work and had to get this bike." I said.
"And where is your guitar?" Aman asked.
"I forgot to get it also this bag was very heavy."
"So what even our bags are heavy." Sam said.
"He never gets his guitar and we end up getting our guitar like fools." Prasad added.
"Ok fine now let's not fight and better we leave or else we would be late." Anup said and our journey begun.

So, it was Sam, Anup, Prasad, Aman, Radhika and me for the one-night trip to Mahabaleshwar.
"Mottu finally we are going to Mahabaleshwar." Radhika said while she hold me tightly around my waist.
"Yes Radhika we are." I said and asked her about Diya. She informed me that she was very happy in her life which brought a smile on my face. No matter how easy it seemed to pretend I didn't care for my sister anymore but, I missed her a lot.

We reached the Khambatki Ghat where we took our first halt. The perfect time to view and enjoy the sunset. We continued to click some of our best shots. Whereas driving the pulsar on the Highway was the best feeling as Radhika was with me. We shared a lot of stuff on our way as we reached Panchgani the place we were to stay. We had to meet a person who would arrange a flat for us, but due to some problem that didn't work. So Anup and Prasad somehow managed to get two rooms for the six of us. I should say the bungalow which he searched had an amazing view but he made it a little complicated for me.

"Dhruv we have managed to get the rooms but there's a problem. We told the owner Radhika is your sister as they were not allowing any girls." Anup said as he came back to discuss with us. Everyone started laughing.

"Oh! Wow! How the hell did you say that? You couldn't think of anything better than that." I was annoyed the very moment, but it was of no use we all were tired after a long drive. I was working late night a day before the trip and didn't get much time to sleep as I woke up early. The bungalow was owned by the Oberoi couple. Aunty seemed to be extra caring but talkative. She showed us the entire bungalow and our rooms. The entire bungalow was made of marble and was simply wonderful.

Later Prasad and Sam went out to arrange dinner and a birthday cake for Anup. We had planned to cut it at midnight. Radhika went downstairs to talk with the Oberoi's when Aman was all set to tease me.

"I will sleep with you both today Dhruv." He said while he hugged me.

"No ways you are going to sleep in that room. Only Radhika and I will sleep in this room." I said trying to free myself.

"Dhruv we are good friends and you are like my elder brother I won't leave you." He said again trying to hug me. I knew he was fooling me still I told him not to be with me. It all stopped after sometime when Radhika came upstairs.

We finished our dinner around 9.30pm and I was totally exhausted and wanted to sleep. At that point of time Preeti called up on Aman's cell, he was talking with her for quite a long time. It sounded fishy but then we all spoke with her one after another. After the dinner we played cards. Later, when the clock stuck 12.00 we brought the cake and wished him for his birthday. Anup fed the cake to everyone one by one when finally I said.

"Chalo, I am going to sleep."

"We all know why you are in a hurry but wait for some time." Prasad said while everyone started to laugh.

"I am completely exhausted and its nothing like what you guys are thinking."

"Ok fine go sleep peacefully with your sister."

"Shut-up she is not my sister."

"Yes we all know, go and tell this to the Oberoi and we all will be on street in this freezing cold weather." Anup added.

I knew it was hard to beat these guys so I finally left and went to the other room. Radhika joined me within few minutes on the bed and this was something unexpected.

"Mottu don't sleep come with me." She said and took me on the terrace in the rains. She wanted to spend some time with me in the rains. I hate rains but that moment felt awesome with her. After spending about 10-15minutes in the rain I got her inside and later we both were sitting in each other arms besides the window watching the rain. On the other hand I could hear the giggling sound and the laughter from the other room as these guys were busy with their own gossips.

We kept watching the rain when I started dozing on her shoulder.
"Lets sleep Dhruv." She said and we moved on the bed. Well my body was freezing after spending the time in the window, whereas Radhika's body was pretty hot. Well should say she was looking hot in the one-piece she wore as soon as we closed the door. I took her close in my arms when we noticed the bed was making some crackling sound. We moved on to the other side and I kissed her on which she reacted quickly and kissed me back. Within moments we were lost in each other, kissing and hugging while I remembered Radhika's words we would make out in Mahabaleshwar and we were actually doing it.

Later she took a ring out of her finger and tried to roll it in mine. I found it difficult to keep it on my finger as it slipped the very next second as she put it in my ring finger.
While placing the ring she said,
"Dhruv, this ring I had bought it for you. Promise me that you would always keep it in your finger and would never lose it. Most important Dhruv this ring will remind you that I am the only person in your life and you would never let any girl come close to you." Those words meant a lot to me. I knew she loved me from the bottom of her heart and I never wanted to lose her but like always I continued.
"Radhika I will keep but if it continues to slip from my finger how would I be able to keep it forever." I said trying to get a smile on her face but instead she got angry and took the ring back.
I kissed her on her forehead and took the ring back and said,
"Radhika I won't lose this, it will be with me forever." I took her in my arms and finally went off to sleep as I was no more able to control my drooping eyes. Radhika kissed me and closed her eyes. She was lying close to me in my arms. Never wondered how time would fly. It was almost 4, by the time we both slept. It's one of the best moments when you wake up and find the person you love sleeping right next to you in your arms. I kissed her and wished her Good morning. She kissed me back and I pulled her closer towards me.

Later I checked my watch it was 6.00am, we had to get ready soon. I brushed my teeth and went in the other room.
"So how was your night Dhruv?" Aman asked me with a smile.

"Oh! It was awesome. I went off to sleep as soon as I left the room." I said.

"You are hopeless Dhruv. You did nothing yesterday."

"No I said I was tired and sleepy."

"You are hopeless Dhruv." Sam added while he was still sleeping.

"Actually hopeless that's the right word." Radhika joined in and they all started to laugh.

"Radhika…" I stared at her. "Even you joined these guys."

"Yes Dhruv now let it be…. Raat gayi baat gayi." She said and joined everyone to make fun of me. Anup had gone downstairs, whereas Prasad was brushing his teeth.

"What happened? Why are you people laughing so much?" He asked as soon as he entered the room.

"Nothing we were discussing about how hopeless Dhruv is." Aman said.

"Actually hopeless…" Prasad added brushing his teeth. I continued to look at everyone when I picked up a piece of cake and started to eat.

"Tu bas cake hi kha. Aur kuch nahi kar sakta tu." Aman said again.

"Arre shut-up you people and stop pulling my leg early morning." I said and left the room in order to get ready. Radhika joined me and locked the door and caught hold of me from back and we began kissing again.

"I love you Mottu. Last night was the best night of my life."

"I know it was the same for me and I love you too." I said and kissed her again. Soon we all got ready and were all set to leave the place. We reached Mahabaleshwar by 11. We decided to have lunch and then visit all the sights. So it was the birthday treat from the birthday boy we ordered every possible thing we could think of in chicken whereas Sam and Aman ordered veg. At that moment Prasad gave his favorite statement," There's nothing like chicken. Chicken is GOD, GOD is chicken." We couldn't understand anything why he would say so but that statement added a smile on our face.

While we were still waiting for the food Radhika and Sam went together for a walk. I checked if they had gone nearby.

"Sam won't kidnap your girlfriend, stay cool don't be so tensed." Prasad said.

"It's not like that, the food is here and I thought should call them." I said.

"So you can use your cell phone." Prasad replied and I called up Radhika. She came and sat when my phone started to ring. It was Mahi.

"Where are you?" She asked.

"I am in Mahabaleshwar."

"What are you doing there?"

"Nothing I am here with my friends I told you on Friday." I said when Radhika gave me a stare.

"Ok fine. Is your mom home?"

"Yes she will be, why? What happened Mahi?"

"Nothing I will talk to her bye." She said and kept the phone she sounded tensed.

That one phone call changed the expressions on Radhika's face whereas I cursed Mahi for calling me at the wrong moment. After the lunch we headed towards the Golf point. Later clicking some pictures on the streets we moved towards Arthur Point one of the famous point in Mahabaleshwar. The foggy whether had made the environment awesome as we were not able to guess the exact time. I was so attracted by the beauty that I completely forgot Radhika wanted to click photos with me. I was walking ahead of everyone and didn't notice Radhika getting slipped on the muddy ground. Later, we headed towards the next point. I couldn't recall the name of this particular point but the best part of this point was its famous fresh strawberry cream which we all ordered and enjoyed a lot. So viewing the deep valleys and dense forests we finally reached the famous Mapro gardens. We ordered something to eat and bought the famous jelly sweets and then headed towards home. We reached Pune around 9.30pm, Radhika still wanted to spend some time with me, she wanted to sit alone somewhere where we could talk. I couldn't think of any such place so we came back home.

Within a few days, Radhika left for Mumbai to meet her parents and other relatives. On the other hand I started gathering all her photos to make an album just as I did for Riya and Mahi. This one had to be different and beautiful. So I started to think for some creative ideas giving my brain a hell lot of work. Something that was different and she would like it as soon as she sees it was in my mind. I decided to buy some A4 pages of different colors and then decorate them in such a way that when I paste the photos on it should look wonderful and creative. Now that was going to cost me a lot and I was running out of money. That time the money saved in my books helped me a lot. I had my own unique way of saving money in every book in my cupboard whenever possible. Fortunately, I was lucky enough to gather a decent amount that would help me buy all the essential stuff required to create the photo album. I knew she had cried a lot because of me and this was the only opportunity for me to make her smile and happy. After I was done decorating the album I had to get a spiral binding done for all the pages but I was again short of money. So I searched my entire cupboard again and found a 20Rupee note which I took and went to get the spiral binding done. I knew after spending this, I would run out of money but I never cared. For me money was never important than any person and when it was Radhika I never gave another thought and handed over the 20Rupee note to the shop owner after he gave me the album. It was looking amazing but there was some more work left on it.

While Radhika was in Mumbai enjoying with her parents she was in contact with me through regular sms or a call at times. She came back on the 2nd of July her birthday. Parth and I went to pick her and her parents from the station around 8.00pm. Radhika and her parents sat behind whereas I was seated next to Parth. Her father looked like those typical Bollywood movie any rich actress father who doesn't want his girl to be around any poor guy like our Indian Hero. Her mom was beautiful and was very quiet. It gave me a feel of Jaya Bachhan from Kabhi Khushi Kabhi Gham. Somehow I would never stop comparing people with movies. But that was the way I always related my life and the others involved in it. It was a strange feeling; I had to kill the silence that was getting created as soon as Parth started the car. I took the bouquet which was kept near my legs and gave it to Radhika and wished her Happy Birthday whereas Parth started the formal small talk with her father.

We reached to a hotel and the family got settled. Now while Radhika's mom was getting ready Radhika came downstairs in order to call us up in their room. We both wished her while Parth hugged her. Later in the lift I hugged Radhika and kissed her on her cheek wishing her Happy Birthday. It was really strange how things changed. The talk with Radhika become more formal. I had informed that I was going out with Parth at home. After sometime Radhika and her mom got ready while her dad stayed in the room. We went to a restaurant and ordered dinner. Radhika sat next to me when Parth's friend Shiva and Vrunda joined us. Well they had to as they had become close friends with Radhika. Her mom was very impressed but it wasn't me it was for Parth. I wondered how I should talk and kept wondering whereas Parth was successful in making a mark on her mom. I really had no clue how to initiate a normal talk.

Next day, Radhika came home along with her parents. I was busy working on her album giving it the final touch and checking every page carefully to ensure I haven't missed anything. I locked my door from inside when I heard Radhika's voice while. Radhika started banging the door but, I kept her waiting outside while she was eager to know what I was doing. Few minutes later I came out and handed over the album to her. As soon as I gave her the album her face was enlightened with a sweet smile and she was very happy.

"Kya baat hai Mottu, photo album for me? This one is amazing. How did you manage to make such a beautiful album without my help." She said.

"I had to do it coz it was for you, had to be the best." I said while she smiled and said, "Its awesome Mottu." She was happily turning every page showing it to her parents whereas; her mom was annoyed as she kept calling me Mottu.

"She always calls him Mottu." My mom said while Radhika's mom scolded her. My mom was ready with compliments for Radhika. I took the album back and said I had to write something on the last page and came inside. After I was done writing I called up Radhika and gave her the album. While she was about to leave I pulled towards her hand hugged her and gave her a kiss.

"Kya kar raha hai Mottu… Our mom and dad are sitting outside. We'll be dead if anyone comes inside." She said while I continued to give her another kiss when she immediately ran away saying I love you Mottu. I finally managed to get a smile back on her face and make her feel happy. I came out and found that her hostel friends had joined us. They started to view the album and there were praises for my creativity. Later Radhika took her mom to see her hostel while her father was still seated talking with my father.

Next day Parth made plans to visit the nearest Balaji temple along with Radhika's parents. On the way we stopped at the construction site of our new house where dad gave them a view of how the building was getting constructed. On the other hand Radhika and I continued making plans about which room should is ours (once we get married) standing away from everyone as nobody could hear us. Later we moved towards the temple and reached around 1.30pm and due to the huge rush we three men decided not to go and where seated in a hotel, whereas Radhika and her mom visited the temple. Like always I sat quiet when Parth was continuously talking with her father trying to make an impression. I tried to talk in between but it was very less compared to Parth. We came back around 5.00pm and Parth dropped us in camp as her parents wanted to do some shopping. During this time Riya and Abhi came along to meet Radhika. Riya gave a box of liquor chocolates to Radhika.

"Riya Radhika doesn't like chocolates. She doesn't eat chocolates." I said.

"Oye Mottu I like chocolate don't you dare think I will give them to you. "Radhika added immediately and we all started laughing. Meanwhile her parents were walking down the streets and we four were walking behind them. Later we crossed the streets and then proceeded towards Abhi's car and we hugged each other and that was a final good-bye from Riya and Abhi to Radhika as well as me.

After that we joined Radhika's parents who were very angry. Radhika father started yelling on her in their native language Bengali, I failed to understand but I knew something was wrong. He was shouting on her as it was already 6.30pm and they were not able to shop anything as we went to drop Riya and that was the perfect reason for her father to get angry. I tried to convince him but it was of no use. He informed me that the train is at 8.00pm and he would not get any time to shop which they wanted to. I couldn't say anything, they took a rickshaw and went back to the hotel. I messaged Radhika to inform me when they leave so that me and Parth can meet her for the last time while I was walking back home.

I got fresh and started surfing on the internet, tried to check the social networking website Facebook which I was never able to understand. Within few minutes I logged out and came out of the room when mom informed me that Mahi had come along with her parents in the afternoon. I missed the opportunity to meet her parents so I called her. She didn't respond properly on the phone. Something was still in my mind for her even though it wasn't love anymore I wanted to finish it off but then Radhika was leaving and I had no time for such thoughts.

Parth came to pick me soon and we both went to meet Radhika for the last time. As we reached there I saw Radhika was sitting alone on a bag reading a novel. Her face was dull and sad whereas her parents were sitting way away from her. I could still sense the anger on her father's face. As soon as we both went near, Radhika's face glowed with a smile.
"I didn't call them now." She said immediately as her father gave a weird look. I knew something was messed up really bad.
"Yes uncle we just came to meet her for the last time she is our best friend and we'll definitely miss her so just walked in for the final good-bye." I finally said it to her father I couldn't understand how I managed to speak, but must say it bought a smile on his angry face. The train arrived and we helped them get their luggage in the train, while this guy came running towards Radhika, he was Sahil. Radhika gave me a strange look as even she didn't expect him. I was surprised to see his strange behavior, as he started touching her parents feet as soon as Radhika introduced him as her class-mate. Parth and I were just not able to understand anything what he was up to.
The train was about to leave, we finally said our final good-bye to Radhika and were about to get down when I turned back and asked Parth to wait and headed towards Radhika again. She was trying to get settled on her seat and was surprised to see me back.

"Uncle I am sorry because of me you people were not able to do any shopping in camp. But trust me I didn't mean to do purposely." I said to her father and Radhika was stunned at the moment.

"Its ok now we just thought we could get but something for our relatives."

"I know uncle but you can but some stuff from the train." Oh that was something horrible that came out from me.

"Arre Mottu are you crazy." Radhika said while her father had a smile on his face so did her mom.

"Uncle, please don't keep any hard feeling and it was really great to spend time with you people. Please do come back to see our new home. Aunty you have to come back." I said addressing both her parents.

"We'll try, now get down quickly off the train or else you will have to come to Jabalpur." Her father said shaking my hand. Oh that was amazing, Radhika's father finally cooled down. Well he was not that bad.

"I don't have any problem uncle will get to know your city." I said and made them smile again and later got off the train. We left the station when Parth wanted to know what I was talking with them.

"Nothing." I said and we got out of the platform as the train left. Sahil came along with us and as soon as he left Parth started.

"Are you crazy Dhruv? You can't even talk with her father just were laughing like a fool." Firstly I was shocked why he said that but I soon realized he was addressing the time spent at Balaji temple.

"What should I do? I don't know how to talk with people whom I meet for the first time." I said.

"If he would have been Meera's father I would have kept him above my head."

"I know Parth you would have done that, but I am not you." I said when Parth had no words to say.

"Ok fine now she's gone get back to work we'll meet later." He said and dropped me home.

So that was it. After spending a real good time with Radhika and her family here I was alone once again. I looked up and prayed to God when Radhika come back let her be the same girl who just left now and whom I knew loved me more than her. One thing I came to know after being with her family she needs someone who will love her like crazy the way her father loves her. I wanted to be that person, it wasn't difficult I just had to start working back on my showreel get a job and knew everything would be fine.

*****

Chapter 16

Finally we met...

Next day I went to the guitar class in the evening. Radhika had messaged me as she had reached Jabalpur. I had decided to work on my showreel work and also complete the guitar course so one day maybe I could compose some songs and play them on the guitar for Radhika. It was never difficult with these new friends everyday was enjoyable and fun to learn guitar. I was able to get more help on the leads and chords I failed to play in the class. But the best part was everybody in the class would be eager to meet each other and never minded spending a lot of time in class.

6th July 2009, we celebrated Preeti's birthday which was quiet memorable for all of us. Thanks to Aman and the new member who was introduced to us by Preeti on her birthday. Her name was Akshada who had one of the best thing in the world her laughter, which could make even the saddest person laugh. She was wearing a Punjabi suit and within a fraction of seconds we totally forgot that we never wanted to get introduced to her and soon she was a part of our group.

My time was spent sometimes at the construction site with Krish and later in the evening at guitar class. We were daily headed towards McDonald's or the famous Durga Cafe shop in Kothrud where we always found Aman and Preeti holding each other's hand. Once I did click a picture through my mobile giving everyone a chance to burst out into a big laughter where on the other hand Preeti started to blush in embarrassment. Akshada met us whenever we came to meet Preeti on Monday or Tuesday during her dance class. Sometimes she would join us during weekends.

Few days later, Parth called up and we visited a place near Tamhni Ghat. Some plots were for sale at really good price. So it was Krish, Parth and his friend Shiva and me who went to see the place. The entire day we enjoyed a lot and Radhika was all set to get angry as we enjoyed without her. I missed her a lot but her messages and calls never made me feel as if she was away from Pune.

This year on my birthday I got stuck with cold and cough which later turned out into high fever. I wasn't happy about it but Radhika kept me going as she sent me a black t-shirt all the way from Jabalpur. I slept the entire day before my birthday as Radhika's strict instructions kept me awake till 12.00am. 'Mottu don't sleep and if you sleep I'll never talk with you.' I sneezed every other minute as I tried to concentrate on the showreel work. It was the third time I was ill on my birthday. I had planned to enjoy with the new friends as I was missing Radhika but she had something already planned for me.

"What are you doing Mottu?" She asked as I picked up her call.

"Nothing special… I am working and it's not fair, its just 11.50pm and you called up, don't want anybody else to wish me first?" I replied in a funny way.

"Mottu, your watch always runs slow, anyways go out and check someone's there for you". She said.

That moment I visualized her, outside my house waiting for me. Immediately, I ran out to check if that was true and came back in my room. I picked up the phone and said,

"There's no-one, don't fool me Radhika!"

"I am not fooling you, did you really check outside the window?" she asked again.

I continued talking with her as I checked once again if there was someone waiting for me.

"Ok then, go check your fridge." She said.

"What's in it?"

"You first go and see I have kept something for you."

"Wow! Radhika how's that possible, I mean, you are not here in Pune and you keep something inside the fridge when I'm at home. Don't you fool me."

I said so but still checked the fridge and pulled out a box kept inside which had a black forest pastry in it with a quote 'HAPPY B'DAY MOTTU'. I came back to my room with a smile on my face and picked up the phone.

"When did you plan this? It's awesome!!!"

"So did you cut the cake?" She said.

"No…Everyone's sleeping, will cut it tomorrow".

"Ok, and is it 12.00 in your watch, or is it still running slow?" She asked.

"It's 12.00 and my watch always shows the right time.

"Ok Whatever, HAPPY B'DAY MOTTU".

"Thank you Radhika and. . . I miss you." Well, I never said anything about missing her but it meant a lot to me, I did miss her.

"I planned this one month back before I left for Jabalpur. Didi helped me. Hope you liked the surprise."

"You are just too good; anyways it seems Riya is calling me I need to talk with her it's been a while I haven't spoken a word with her. Can I please?"

She agreed, as I promised to callback but Riya's call got disconnected. I thought of calling her but waited thinking she might call again but such things never happen. After a while, my phone was silent, I was blank in front of my computer, trying to think about the next move on the showreel work when my eyes started to get wet and the very next minute tears began to flow in full swing. Maybe the feel of being alone, not well or maybe somewhere I was still expecting a phone call from Mahi. I tried a lot but was not able to stop them when Radhika called back.

"Mottu I was waiting for your call", she said.

"I forgot, stuck with this work and also am not well." I replied wiping off my tears.

"What happened Dhruv?" she asked as she realized within a minute.

"Nothing Radhika, I am fine just stuck on this thing don't know what to do next".

"Are you sure Dhruv?"

"Yes. Everything's cool."

"Ok, then I am sleeping as am very tired and my cell is about to die so will switch it off, will talk to you tomorrow."

"Ok, no problem."

"Once again Happy B'day Mottu".

"Good Night Radhika and Bye". I said and hung-up the phone.

Later, I washed my face, drank a glass of water and started typing this message to Radhika.

"Hey Radhika I know your cell would be switched off but I would have been happier had you been here with the cake. It was an awesome surprise & the best thing for my B'day to begin with. I don't know but being left alone made me cry a lot. I am dying to talk to Riya from a couple of weeks but she never called back. My phone is silent as always even today as I thought it won't because my friend circle has increased, well I've just received few messages that's it. Anyways I am missing you a lot today. Bye, good night." I was about to send the message when Prasad called up. His reason to call up late was he didn't want to disturb me and Radhika. That did help me forget everything and I was in a cheerful mood after talking with him. Then came Natasha's message and it was unexpected as she was the one who always called up first. A bit of anger raised for her but it vanished soon. Somehow, I managed to get out of my loneliness and finally sent the message to Radhika followed by another one which said 'I

am cool now' and went off to sleep. I struggled a lot to sleep but the headache got on my nerves. I took a tablet and went off to sleep around 4.30am.

I still felt some weakness after I woke up but I got ready and went to gym. When I came back and was replying to the birthday messages happily. I decided to go to Dagdushet temple with Devika after her college so I had enough time to rest till evening but I avoided. I went to the ATM center to withdraw money when my bike was caught from the no parking zone. I called up Radhika and told her everything.

"Stop laughing. You know what, I am not well and I am roaming on the streets without my bike and it's my birthday today!" I told Radhika.

"Dhruv I don't understand why such things always happen to you." She said giggling and munching something.

"By the way, what are you eating?"

"The chocolates that Riya gave when I was leaving."

"Sahi hai, I am walking here on the streets and you are enjoying those liquor chocolates, by the way you still have those chocolates left?"

"I wanted to keep some for today's awesome incident when you are running for your bike. Ha ha ha."

"Very funny, anyways I have reached here, we'll talk later bye." I hung up.

Things were pretty strange today; somehow, I managed to get rid of them. Fever increased so I went off to sleep. I had invited all my friends at home in the evening. Before they came I went to Dagdushet with Krish instead of Devika. Oh well! I couldn't take a risk of going with her as Radhika had warned me. While returning home Mahi called up, the call I was eagerly waiting for but I didn't pick up thinking I would receive the next time she calls but she did not which raised my temper for that moment. But Radhika was more important for me now. Even though she was not in Pune she never let me feel her absence. Her frequent messages and calls kept me happy throughout the day. Later all my guitar class friends arrived with a big black forest cake. I felt good as this year I had the opportunity to cut two cakes in a day and everyone's presence did make me forget my illness. The enjoyment continued till 7.30 and everybody left home except for Enosh. I was waiting for all the late comers Suresh, Ajit, Abhishek and rest of my college group. Mom asked Enosh to take me to the clinic as I was not well. So I injected the doctor as the fever had increased to 102!

Ah sorry...! The doc injected me. I was also advised not to eat pastries or cake or any cold stuff for the next 2-3days.

"Wow!" I said, "It's my b'day today and I can't eat any of those stuff".

"Chill Dhruv maybe next time you can have that cake".
"Shut up. I am not listening to that doctor". I said to myself while I was cutting the cake into pieces to serve everyone.
"HAPPY BIRTHDAY." Pooja shouted and wished me with a cheerful smile on her face which made me turn back to her with a piece of cake. But, she took the piece of cake and fed me. That was amazing, the perfect moment to be captured in a camera and to be treasured. Being Mahi room-mate I hardly knew her but still was a reason to put up a smile on my face. The enjoyment continued with everyone so did Radhika's text messages. She enjoyed with her family, as he bought chocolates and Chicken Tikka for her, added to a conclusion she was missing me and so was I, she helped me to keep a smile throughout the day. The best part was everything happened in a way I had never expected, the way everyone treated me gave me a reason to say, "I am the best". This certainly had to be the best day for me although it was full of rush and excitement and Radhika's last message explained everything.

This is my last message on your b'day... So many times you've gone out of your way to make it nice for others, to bring some extra happiness to someone's special day. Now it's your day to let others DO NICE THINGS FOR U...
So today though I'm not there, I wish for everything happy everything good everything beautiful to be a part of YOUR WORLD and with this I promise you that your next b'day will be the best as we'll be together...PROMISE...!
This message set a lot of expectation from her. Even though many things didn't happen the way I wanted, I enjoyed my day as she made it the best remembered even in her absence.

Next day Mahi came home and I was confident that she never came to meet me. But, still I went in the living room to meet her. I came inside immediately and started working as I thought she didn't react properly.
Later she came inside and said, "How are you Dhruv?"
"I am fine, what would happen to me?", I replied rudely.
"I am leaving Pune next week". I was surprised and a bit shocked so keeping my work aside I started talking with her and immediately my cousins went out of the room leaving us alone.
"Are you serious Mahi?" I asked.
"Yes, I won't be coming back to Pune again."
Now that was really strange. Mahi was out of my mind but still when she was leaving why the hell I found myself worried for her? I asked her to meet me

before she left. My questions were still left unanswered, so she agreed to meet and said will call later and left.

I couldn't wait any longer to meet Mahi to get the answers to all my questions but she wasn't picking up the phone. I tried calling 2-3times but every time she disconnected the phone. Finally I gave up when her message came. *'Duffer I am in class will call you later.'* After reading it I was continuously waiting for the call. She called up around 6.30pm and decided to meet on Monday. So I eagerly started waiting for Monday. In the meanwhile, Anup made up a plan for the movie 'Love Aaj Kal' along with me it was Aman and Preeti who were coming for the movie. The entire night I was not able to sleep as I kept wondering what I would talk with her how our meet would end up, where we would meet and most important will I get the answers to all my questions which I had in my mind for her. At that moment a thought came in my mind and I messaged Preeti that I need her help, I never bothered to look at the time it was 4.00am.

Next day when I met Preeti I asked her if she would help me in my new venture. Why I made of taking her help I didn't know, whether it was the right decision or not. But I had something in my mind writing a book, something really unexpected from me.

Monday- 3rd August 2009, I was waiting till evening and as soon as the clock struck 4.00pm I began to get ready and within few minutes I left the house. I had to reach Kothrud where Mahi was staying these days.
"Where are you?" I said as I called up Mahi after reaching Kothrud.
"I am in the hostel; you come near one of these hotel Rugved or Vedant." She said. The names I had never heard but somehow was able to find the second hotel Vedant and stood there for some time waiting for her. Within the next 5 minutes she showed up on a grey colored bike. She was wearing a 3-4th jeans and a lousy top. I wondered why she was dressed up like this.
"Hey you finally bought the pulsar." She said.
"No it's my cousin's."
"How is Aarosh?" She said.
"Who? His son, he's fine."
"His eyes are really amazing, see I still have his picture in my cell. And how is kaku and kaka?" She said.

"They all are fine Mahi and probably we are here for some reason what's the point discussing these things." I said trying to change the topic.

"Ok then let's go inside we can't keep talking here. And listen I just have 5-10 minutes so whatever you want to talk make it quick." She said as we moved in.

"What the fuck? Am I here for just a 5 minutes talk? I feel like killing her right now." I said to myself and followed her with a smile on my face. We took the corner table. I was continuously looking at her while she continued to play with her cell. I felt as if I should grab that cell phone of her and throw it on that lizard that began to stare at me next to the side wall. I guess she was here to listen what would happen today.

"So tell me what you wanted to ask?" She said keeping her phone aside and opening the menu card.

"You very well know what I want to ask Mahi." I said.

"No. What do you want to ask and I really don't want to eat anything, we'll just order tea. Bhaiya do chai." She said after asking me if I wanted anything else, she was really pissing me at that moment same as the lizard who continued to stare.

"Mahi I just have one question. Why you did this with me? Why did you leave me when you always loved me?" I asked her while she didn't bother to answer anything. I asked her again but she kept changing the topic. She tried to explain various things but never made an attempt to answer my question. The tea was here and I again asked," Mahi there was a time when you never liked any girl around me but it doesn't matter to you at all if I go with any girl."

"It's your life Dhruv what am I supposed to do with it."

"How did you change so much? I never expected this from you."

"Yes, you are right even I never expected people calling me a thief in the hostel. I have no regrets now whatever happened I know happened for a good reason. You know the best thing we are allowed to keep pets at this new hostel and I am very happy here. I have made new friends here they are very nice and caring."

"And, what about Mohit?" I asked.

"I have stopped talking with him. "She said later sipping the tea. Mahi had called up in Mahabaleshwar to talk about it. She was being blamed for the things being lost or stolen from hostel which continued even after she left. Mahi wanted to talk with me but that day I ignored her even though I knew something was wrong. That day Radhika felt I was ignoring her later at Mahabaleshwar because I spoke with Mahi. That incident had changed Mahi completed and she hated Radhika as much as Radhika hated her.

It was 5.30pm we had spent around 30minutes, I was still waiting for my answers when finally Mahi spoke.

"Chalo, I'll tell you the reason, why I left you, maybe I need to get out of it as well."

"Yes I am waiting. What was it that made you behave in such a manner?"

"Dhruv I was going crazy in love with you and it was getting very difficult for me to stay away from you. That started creating problems between me and Gaurav. So I had to do it."

"Mahi, I had told you whenever you feel I am coming in between you two guys let me know. I will get out of your way." I said.

"I know Dhruv, but I didn't have that guts in me, it was impossible for me to face you at times. I wanted you to be out of my mind. So I got involved in Mohit so that you would hate me."

"I don't hate you Mahi."

"But now you don't love me Dhruv."

"I have no answer to this Mahi. I guess, after this we won't be meeting anymore. Things will change and it won't be like before." I said and finished my tea and looked at the lizard. She was trying to move away from us. Maybe her mission was complete or the reporter's story was complete.

"It's not like that Dhruv the hostel incident has screwed up my mind. Give me some time we'll definitely be good friends. I don't want to lose you as a friend. We have so many beautiful memories to share. I never want to lose them" She said and I began again.

"So what if in future we meet will you ever say hi to me or even bother to look at me Mahi."

"Dhruv I'll definitely meet you, will greet you nicely and we will be good friends. But not now and anyways did you see the movie 'Love Aaj Kal'." She said

"Yes I did it was amazing." I said as I had watched the movie half in the cam-print I downloaded last night.

"So consider this tea as our break-up party." She said and started laughing.

"No ways I want a bigger party Mahi."

"Forget it you will never get it." She said and I paid the bill and left the hotel. I wondered we had actually spent an hour as she had warned won't spend more than 5minutes. I was happy that she finally told me the reason; I had decided never to forgive her. But that meet helped me forgive her.

The next few minutes she left and there was no more hugging or a hand-shake we just said bye to each other and I moved on my bike towards Dev's where Preeti was waiting for me. On my way I kept smiling as I knew now

Mahi was completely out of my league and it would be just me and Radhika.
I reached class and met Preeti.

"I need a hug Preeti." I said as she hugged me.

"Bhai finally you did it. Now tell me whatever happened." She said with a smile on her face.

"Oh well, now that you read it in my book." I said and we both began to laugh.

"Bhai this is not fair." She said and hugged me again as she was really happy for me so was I when I messaged Radhika.

'The best thing has happened today for which I was waiting for a long time I am very happy Radhika.' Within few minutes a reply came *'What did you do? Did you fight with Mahi or did you hit Mohit'.*

I began to laugh and said bye to Preeti and went home.

*****

Part - 2

You're my Dream
Come true... What would
I be without you....?

Chapter 17

Back To Work...

'Mottu bata na what happened? Did you fight Mahi or Mohit?' Radhika's message had flashed on my mobile screen as I reached home. I got fresh using the new face-wash Krish had bought for himself. It smelled great! Later, I picked up my cell phone which was completely charged and turned on the computer. I began to read the messages from Radhika and began to laugh.
'Mottu you can view your Mona darling's painting later, reply to my message.'

Well Mona was this new girl in her hostel and was a Fine Arts student. I had been talking about her with Radhika recently. Anyways let's keep her aside for some time and where was I, yes, I read the first message and then the other.
'Ok fine don't tell me Mottu, but if you are happy I am happy for you.'

That message put me in a dicey situation as I didn't know how I should reply. I started typing a reply when Radhika had lost her patience and called directly. We spoke for some time as I cleared her doubts after which I got back on my showreel work.

Later, Pooja knocked in my room and so did Mona after sometime. Seeing me work she sat watching me.
"Dhruv! What are you doing?" She asked
"Nothing..." I replied immediately. "Just working on my showreel?"
"Showreel?" She sounded confused. I knew she wouldn't know anything about it as even I was unaware about it until I selected animation as a career.
"Well showreel is like a small project. We create a demo video file which focuses on a particular field of specialization."
"Now, what is a specialization." She seemed very keen to know every aspect of it.
"Well specialization is nothing but, ok let me explain." I said and turned my chair facing her and said.
"The process of creating an animated movie begins with a story and a story-board, which are the drawings or rough sketches of the characters and scenes. These story-boards and character references are passed on to artist(modelers) who create these scenes and characters on the 3D software and the next are

the texturing and lighting artist who take care of the colors and background lights."

She was listening very carefully as I tried to explain everything as much as possible in order to make it simple for her. She was taking much interest in it and wanted to know everything.
"So what is character animation?" She asked.
"Yes I was coming to that, the characters which are created are lifeless and the act of making them walk, talk, act, sing and dance is done by a character animator. Just like this one which I am working on." I said and showed her the moves which I had prepared. Both watched the scene and complemented on my work which made me feel happy. Well not to forget the guitar playing session which added more compliments. As soon as they left I did shout for myself 'I AM THE BEST 'which I always did whenever the feel of happiness revolved around me. Later I had dinner and began to work and day ended with a good night sms from Radhika.

Radhika had changed my life and things were not the same. Well, the change was good for me as long as she was with me. I was getting serious about my work even though I was not able to give my complete time to it. Everyday Krish would take me to the construction site to accompany him even though I hated it most of the times. Few days later I started attending the TATA AIG Life Insurance training near Koregoan Park. A new venture to earn some income, while I was preparing my showreel for the animation job. Life had so much to offer at every point of time. Every weekend including Thursday and Friday would be enjoyed along with the new guitar class friends. Aman and I used to spend most of the times together in Landmark where we would never miss the Live Concerts except reading books. I must say I had developed a kind of addiction towards books thanks to Radhika and Devika who were always found reading novels.

One evening I was sleeping restless on my bed and was thinking about the past events when I checked the calendar on my cell phone, the day was 13th August 2009. A year back Diya had left home and Mahi came in calling for her. Recalling the past event same time I was depressed. I tried hard to avoid the thoughts in my mind but was not possible. Later, I typed a message. *'It's been a year that Mahi came home running calling your name when I was sleeping. I can never forget how horrible that day was for all of us. I miss you but I can never forget the way you left, will never forgive you for this ever in my life.'*

This was the first message after a year to Diya. I sent another message to Radhika. She always knew how to keep me motivated.

'Dhruv your past was beautiful with Diya as the best sister and Mahi as the best girlfriend. Remember the sweet memories and be happy, rather being depressed. Be strong and live in the present, past will never do any good. But it's up to you to welcome the future with a smile or cry about the past and screw up your life. The decision is yours.'

I read the message again and again. I knew I had to live in the present as it was Radhika who was with me always. She knew that I would still be depressed so she called back immediately.

"Kya hua Mottu?" She asked.

"Nothing, I am missing you." I said.

"Don't lie Dhruv…" She said as there was a moment of silence between us. "You are missing Mahi and Diya. I am pretty sure about this."

"Radhika it not only about Diya, it's about everyone. Every day was awesome, Mahi along with those stupid Devika and Mentos just walked into my life. They treated me as their friend and brother. But now, it feels like I was never a part of their life. It was just a dream." I spoke about them instead of Diya.

"Dhruv you gave your best. Now it's time to work hard and show it to that girl Mahi. You have to do something that she would one day realize she made a mistake leaving you. And forget Devika and Mentos you very well know how they behaved with me."

"Yes I know, but I am also thinking why does it have to rain in the evening. Why can't it rain at night?"

"Dhruv, you are impossible. Can you ever be serious?"

"Yes Radhika I was a few moments back, you know I can't handle the seriousness for a long time." I said while she laughed.

"You are seriously impossible Mottu. Anyways work hard and keep these things aside as your hard work would decide our future. If you get a nice job I would be able to talk with my father or else nothing will be possible." She said.

"I know but you have to talk with my mother and father as well."

"Why will I talk with your parents?"

"Because they like you and I won't be able to say anything and your father, he is a Hitler. He is always angry." I said while I was trying to make her laugh along with me.

"Dhruv you know it was our fault."

"I know. I don't think he will ever accept me as his son-in-law."

"That's why I am telling you work hard. If I say he will get convinced. I can convince him, only if you get a nice job, so study Mottu. Work hard." She said while our talk continued and it was quiet dark in my room I turned on the lights. I asked her to continue with her studies as I wanted her to study hard as well. I knew if she was expecting me to become an Animator I wanted her to become a CA. One thing was sure, I couldn't gather that courage to let her know it was all because of her I could stay focused. Had she not been with me I would have lost myself in some place I could never come out. So, finally keeping all the negative thoughts away I said, "I love you Radhika and I miss you a lot." She smiled back and replied the same before she hung up. Later, I cooked noodles and along with a cup of coffee and sat down in front of the computer watching the next episode of LOST. My new companion, in order to relax myself from work. The series did give me many nightmares, but still I enjoyed watching it.

Aman and I spent a lot of time together and shared most of the things. The best part was whenever we made plans for a movie; Aman would end up buying last row corner seats for the two of us. Something happened during these days when Preeti and Avni stopped coming to class. My daily schedule was still the same. Sometimes, the day would begin with me visiting the construction site with Krish and later evening in class. Sometimes, I would work in the evening avoiding guitar class or if attended, I would work till late night. I knew this won't take me anywhere. I had to concentrate more on my work so I avoided them and stayed at home and continued with my work. By the time I made this decision, the Ganesh Festivals were approaching.

I invited everyone from the guitar class and only Aman turned up to show. Krish brought his friend Neha home. I always ignored her as I never had any intentions to talk with her. But when you are destined for something you can never ignore. She was presently working in some Marathi films and I happened to ask her. I was eager to know what she was into and how she achieved it. "Dhruv spoke with me today." This was the only response she gave me after sharing all the information.
"It's not like that, whenever you came home I was busy that's it." I replied.

Neha later asked me to give my pics and also asked to edit some of her pics to which I agreed. She informed me about an audition and had asked if I would like to apply. I ignored it for some time as I was busy enjoying the Ganesh festival and hopefully the audition was two days after the festival. On the last day we have huge processions lined up on the Laxmi road and a day when we would have many foreign tourist in India especially in Pune. I and Aman were enjoying it till late night when we called up Radhika. She was studying and on the other end was unhappy to miss the fun. I assured her once she becomes a CA I would take her everywhere to enjoy her life to the fullest. That day I told Aman I had the best girl in my life…Radhika. We continued to have fun the entire night and went home by dawn. Two days later, I went for the audition Neha had asked to attend. I just happened to inform Radhika about being selected as I wanted to know her reaction and her message said it all.

'I am very happy Mottu but tell me something how many things you would be doing. Animator plus actor who writes songs plays guitar. I am really happy that I have a multi-talented boyfriend. But Mottu concentrate on one thing first, it shouldn't happen that you go behind everything and get nothing. Please take care about that I love you and miss you.'

I knew that animation was the only aim in my life but if I was getting something more I never had any problem with it.

I decided to stop going to guitar class and concentrated more on the showreel even though I used to visit the construction site everyday along with Krish. Few days later, I completed few walk cycles of a character as well as animated few motions for a character. I took the work to MAAC to get some feedback from Sir, he gave me some tips to improve my work and also asked me to read the 'ANIMATOR'S SURVIVAL KIT'. A book which every animator needs to know in and out before he begins animating characters. I wondered why we were never told about it during the lectures. A bit frustrated I came home and called Radhika. Our regular message chats and calls continued as we never left each other. But it decreased as her exams were approaching. Later, that evening I went to guitar class as I wanted to meet everyone, well even if it was a day not been with these guys it always felt like we haven't met for years that was the real strong bonding with each other.

As I opened the door of the classroom, my eyes began searching my friends. I found Prasad playing his guitar seated right next to another slim girl. I doubted if Avni was in the group just because of him. So not going into any more details, here was the new member of our group... Aaliya. The squared shaped specs well suited her tiny round face. Her smile always make her two bugs bunny teeth visible. Not to forget, her laughter that could squeeze her tiny little eyes. So the overall package of Aaliya... She was cute and cute people were always invited in our group. She was an engineering student and like us she was here to learn guitar. I Think!!!

Few days later, my college friends came up with a plan to visit this place named Shivtharghal suggested by Rahul. Like always Rahul organized things in such a manner that he always got picked up for birthday bumps. Nevertheless, due to his planning we college friends were always found together exploring new places and enjoying the drizzling rains. The place was amazing and as I was seated behind Enosh, it had to be the maximum count in terms of photographs. Once back from the trip I started going regularly to the guitar class once again. Aman would always pick me up from home whenever I didn't have a bike all the way from his office. I started composing few lyrics as at times it was Anup whose guitar inspired me to write something. Whereas once when Preeti was seated along with us I wrote a song for which Sam was playing the chords. Everything seemed to be fine except for the fact that I used to miss Radhika but never let anybody know about it.

2nd October 2009, I and Aman went for the movie 'Wake-Up SID!'. I was always passionate about movies as I always thought every movie had something to learn from it. During the movie I recalled Riya calling me a kid and how I would try my level best to let her know I was not a kid. These same things were being projected in the movie, so immediately after the movie I called up Riya but her phone was not reachable. While coming back Aman did say it to me 'Wake-up Max'. I knew I should start working or else I would be left back. So, as I reached home I turned on my computer and downloaded the 'ANIMATOR'S SURVIVAL KIT' written by Richard Williams and began to read. Every day I used to read few pages and try to work on the character animation. Slow and steadily I found improvement in my work with the help of the book. Had I known about this before I could have been better was always a thought I had. A month passed by and during Diwali festival I was missing Radhika where I enjoyed the movie 'All the Best' along with my entire family.

Aman, Anup and I were at Landmark store watching the Jazz Concert. I had never been to a Jazz Concert before, so this was my first time. Within few minutes, I was the only one who was trying to convince that it would be good some time later. Aman was busy playing games whereas Anup was checking out the latest cell phones. I couldn't abide Jazz anymore so I called up Radhika. "Hi Radhika, what are you doing?" I said as she picked up the phone.

"Watching a movie." She said.

"Your exams are in few days, why are you wasting your time."

"I was getting bored and anyways you are enjoying the Jazz right!"

"Ya! It's simply amazing I got my handy-cam to shoot it. But there's only one problem. It is so boring that I haven't even turned on the camera. I am going crazy"

"Ha ha ha! I already knew you would be bored. Jazz is mostly enjoyed by elderly people. Anyways, what's my janemann doing."

"He is busy playing games, why are you always calling him janemann?"

"Just like that I love to see you get angry when I call him so." She said while she continued laughing.

"Radhika, listen Prasad is calling, he might have reached. I'll call you later." I said and picked up the other call. He came along with his room-mate.

"Abe ye kitna bore hai re." Prasad said in a moment as he heard the band.

"Yes it is dude, that's why I was away playing games." Aman added as he approached us.

"Tu toh bachha hi hai saale game khel raha tha." Prasad commented back.

"Abe kya bore kar rahe hai ye log. Harsh would play better than them."

"Yes, which is that song he always plays?"

"Sayyoni, that's the one. Please guys don't compare these people with Harsh they are always better than him." I was amused at the two of them.

"By the way where is Anup baba?" Prasad questioned.

"He was roaming somewhere... Ah! There he is coming, right behind you." I said pointing towards Anup.

"Prasad is this the time to come." Anup said while he smacked his back.

"Anup Baba...here you are."

"Baba ki jai ho!!!" With that coming from Aman, Anup was bestowed 'Baba' permanently. We tried to enjoy the show for the next few minutes, then finally we left. My planning was somehow screwed, thinking the show would be for an hour. As I reached home I was tired and went off to sleep. Radhika was angry on me for this reason as I had promised her will be back soon and begin to study. I woke up late the next day when Radhika called up. Also, I made it clear for myself that I would never attend a Jazz concert again. Though it was good not many people enjoy, but I had liked a few songs.

8th November 2009, another movie 'Ajab Prem Ki Gajab Kahani' in the corner seats with Aman. I always wondered how he actually managed to get corner seats every time when asked to buy tickets. The movie was hilarious as we both enjoyed it. I did miss Radhika; her company definitely doubled the fun.

But she was busy with her exams and I didn't wanted to distract her. I had to wait till the 15th of this month. But the question here was, what was progress in terms of my work? Would I be able to answer her if she questioned me about my showreel? These thoughts flowed in my mind, while coming back home, but the smile couldn't fade away from my face thinking about Radhika coming back.

*****

Chapter 18

Radhika is back...

History Repeats Itself In Various Forms...! I made this statement when my judgment about things became precise. I knew everything that happens, serves for a reason and if you aren't able to understand that instant, things will repeat in the same manner but in different forms. Radhika was back in Pune after her exams along with her father. Oh my God! She was actually back in Pune. I was so excited to meet her but we couldn't meet, till her father left back to Jabalpur after confirming his daughter was settled properly. 15th November 2009, I remember, in the evening as soon as her father left she had called me.

The burning desire to meet her after a long time had a smile throughout the way. Many things kept flashing in my mind on my way to Station. I was dressed up properly to look good to make an impact on my already impressed girlfriend. As I reached the Station gate I saw Radhika in her sweet simple attire. The only thing which hadn't changed about her was her smile. Every time we met Radhika would smile and wave her palm lifted a few inched in the air followed with a Hi. The same happened again and I was left with a smile and a thought that said Radhika will never change I just love her.

"Radhika, motti ho gayi tu." I said as she sat on my bike.
"Ab ghar ka khana you know. All I would do is eat a lot. What about you Mottu? Where is your six-pack? Have you stopped going to the gym?" She said while her hands were wrapped around my waist.
"Actually, gym membership is over. I'll start again once I get a job."
"So what's the status of your showreel?"
"Radhika... let's talk about something else, anyways one most important thing I forgot to ask you. How are you Radhika?"
"I am fine Dhruv. You know something Dhruv I was dying to meet you. Pooja, my room-mate kept asking me, why I was so eager to meet you."
"Then, what did you say?"
"Dhruv, its four months we haven't met each other. So I was jumping out of joy that we would be meeting today."

"I know... Anyways how were your exams?" I said as we reached SGS mall, I was interrupted by the security guard. I drove towards the parking lot after the security check. Well, after the Mumbai 26/11 blasts the security checks happened in every mall and hotels. But the worst part was to watch the security guards checking every single person sometimes drained out of their daily routine.

I remember saying out loud to every guard," yes check quickly or less the bomb would blast." That silly joke would sometimes light up a smile on those poor guys. But these thoughts about thinking something good for others had to vanish within a few moments as I walked upstairs where Radhika was waiting for me.

"Ok, now tell me. How were your exams?" I said as she pulled me towards a vacant table.

"Let's sit here Dhruv and would you like coffee." She said ignoring the topic.

"Wait I'll get it." I said and ordered two coffees.

"Dhruv, my exams were horrible and I don't want to talk about it. But, one thing I know I will somehow pass." I was shocked for a moment, but soon she changed the topic.

"Hey when did Landmark store move here in this mall."

"It's been a long while. I had told you about this but you know the worst part now JM Road and FC Road follow one-way traffic."

"So many changes happened here. I want to see everything now."

"You will Radhika, very soon, it's just the first day today. I'll take care of it." I said while we continued talking with each other till it was 8.

Later, we headed towards home and everyone was surprised to see her back. I went in my room turned on the computer while I changed my clothes. I could hear Radhika giggling with everyone which made me happy. After four months I felt my house was complete. I drank a glass of water while Radhika was talking with mom about our new house which was still under construction. I remembered that I needed to show her the house. But keeping all my thoughts away I got back to my computer and began to check the stuff I was working on.

"Kya kar raha hai Mottu?" Radhika said as she entered my room after sometime.

"Mottu, after a long time I heard this." I said while she rested her hands on my shoulders.

"You still apply this chameli ka tel."

"Its not chameli Radhika, its jasmine and anyways, will please stop ruining my hairstyle." I said taking off her hands away from my hair. Well, I personally liked it but my rule was never let the person know what you like and what you don't due to which they could never understand me completely. My rules had its own good and bad effects.

"Now give me those stickers you bought for me." She said trying to open my cupboard.

"Did I? When? I never bought anything."

"You liar you told me that you've bought some Disney stickers for me. I want them."

"Arre those I think I should not give them, I have decided to keep them." I said while I removed the stickers. I gave them and the smile on her face made me happy. She stayed with me till 10pm had dinner together with the entire family and later went back to her hostel. Well, our talk never ended as it continued on the phone when I was down with my pets. Well, I should say that my life was back as Radhika came back.

Some things never change, mostly our fights could never stop even on silliest topic on earth. Our fight was sometimes through emails or messenger chats. Today's topic was simple: Radhika met Sahil before meeting me. It made me feel a bit insecure at that moment, which led into a small fight which was sorted away from my mind and we both were back to normal.

"Dhruv... What are you doing in the evening?" Radhika called me one evening.

"Nothing special...Why? What happened?" I asked.

"I wanted to finish off everything with Sahil and I want you to be with me for moral support."

"What will I do there, Radhika?" I said as I wanted to avoid the scene between the two.

Sahil...Remember that guy touching her parents feet while they were about to leave Pune, well he had proposed Radhika. She refused immediately as for Radhika, Sahil was her best friend. Radhika had always been crystal clear about her relations and yet another reason why I loved her. She was never confused about any relation like I was. But it was not something about the proposal, Radhika was angry on him for some other reason which she had in her mind for the last four months. She was waiting for her exams to get over so that she can vent out her anger on him. I had to go as I couldn't directly say no and she was successful to convince me.

In the evening we both were wandering in the Archie's Gallery, Sahil called up and she took me outside.

"Hi!" Sahil said while he waved his hand with a smile as he looked at us.

"Hi!" Radhika replied being normal, so did I. I thought this would be the normal start of the conversion but something surprised me.

"Kya re chapree, Motti ho gayi hai tu."

"Aur tu bhi to Motta ho gaya hai chapree." I wondered why they were calling each other by that particular name. It was their own unique way of greeting each other. I stood quiet listening to them as soon their conversation became serious when Radhika said the most unexpected thing.

"Sahil I am not going to meet you again ever in my life. You were trying to hit on me when I said no, you started bitching about me to my childhood friend."

"Radhika I never said anything to her." He replied.

"Don't lie Sahil. I can call her right now if you want to hear the truth."

"Why are you over-reacting Radhika?"

"I am not, you hurt my feelings Sahil. I always treated you as my best friend, but not anymore. I don't want to see your face again..., please leave Sahil."

"Radhika! Can't you give me one last chance? You've given Dhruv so many chances even if he has hurt you thousands of times." He said realizing his mistake. But I wondered how he knew everything about me. Oh! Yes Sahil was Radhika's best friend. I again stood quiet as Radhika raised her voice.

"Sahil, don't compare yourself with him. I love him and he is my boyfriend, you have no rights to say anything about him." Well, I was left speechless and it felt good after that comment for me. Radhika took me aside and asked me to say something so that we could leave the place soon. Their loud conversation was magnetizing many people around.

At times, I felt I would have forgiven him or any person who would have asked me for forgiveness. But that wasn't the case for Radhika, once a person was out of her mind she would never forgive him/her ever in her life. I was looking at Radhika as well as Sahil both were quiet. Radhika looked at me and smiled and looked back at Sahil with the same expressions she had carried few minutes ago for him.

"Sahil, I always treated you as my friend and you have lost all the respect I had for you. Nothing can be normal as it was, please leave. We have to go, Dhruv say something."

"Sorry Radhika. It won't happen again." He pleaded.

"Again?? It's over Sahil...Our friendship is over. We are never going to meet." She said and picked up her ringing cell phone.

"Sahil, if she doesn't want to meet you again. Just leave her alone. I don't want any trouble for her. Radhika doesn't like someone cheating on her which you did I guess! Even if I would do such a thing she will not spare me. So leave it man you will get many more friends in life." I said and was confused if whatever I said was right. Finally, he decided to leave but waited till Radhika was done with the call.

"Ok then Radhika I'll leave... you're just not ready to listen to me." He said bringing his hand forward for the final shake hand.

"Sahil if you wouldn't have done what you did with me, we would have been friends. But it's all over. Bye." She said with her hands folded.

"Let's leave Mottu." She said looking back at me. We both started walking while Radhika seemed very happy after she let off her anger.

"Thanks Mottu for being with me and supporting me." She said holding my hand.

"I don't think I really helped you Radhika."

"You stayed with me that was all I needed or else, I wouldn't have been able to say anything to him."

"Oh! So me being there caused that fight between you and your friend. Is that so? Good." I said while I looked at her with a smile.

"Mottu it's a compliment for you and not a complaint, and everything is GOOD for you. Right!"

"Right. And if it's a compliment then I'm the Best." I said and continued to walk with her. I wondered whatever happened today wasn't right but I came to know Radhika's behavior. She would never spare the person who hurts her feelings and is completely terminated by her mind.

I looked up at the sky and said, "Please never let this happen to me, I should never hurt her. Please take care of that." Well, I always prayed to God whenever I found myself in trouble but never thought would end up hurting her feelings in a few days to come.

Few days later, after the Sahil incident Radhika accompanied me to the guitar class. Aaliya was very happy to meet her as she found Radhika to be cute and I to be the luckiest person on earth. Yes, I had that kind of a feeling when Radhika was with me. Radhika would come home regularly and one day we finally decided to visit the construction site. Radhika wanted to see the new home so I left home along with her informing mom about it. Now the way we convinced her was simply amazing that she never had any kind of objection of Radhika coming along with me. I told her that we had some work and also need to visit the construction site. Well, it was a week after Radhika was back and one of the best times when we kissed each other for quite a long time.

Parth bought a new bike on his birthday for which he had waited for a long time. Somewhere he was still fighting over to forget his lost love. But, Radhika was at her best helping him to get out of it. Well, the best part was he never smoked in front of her as she would hit him hard and that would be the best thing to watch when we three were together. Parth met us at Deccan few days later. I was excited to see his bike and drive it when we met, whereas the strange thing was Radhika had already seen his bike as well as drove the bike along with him. It did irk my mind but I ignored it. He gave his bike keys and as pushed the starter I was expecting Radhika to sit behind me.

"I am not sitting behind you...Mottu!" She said.

"I can drive the bike properly, don't think I can't." I replied immediately.

"Parya, I'm telling you he will hit somewhere." Radhika said again and I turned off the bike.

"Why are you saying like that Radhika? He can drive properly, go sit behind him." Parth replied and I was annoyed at that moment thinking whether I should actually drive his bike. I started the bike and continued to drive while Radhika sat behind Parth as he was driving mine. We exchanged the bikes as I didn't feel like riding it within few minutes as I wondered why Radhika didn't sit behind me. She always said she doesn't trust me and had proved it to me that instant, but I ignored everything and continued to carry a smile on my face and remained silent.

Few days later, it was Suresh's marriage. 29th November 2009, we college friends were meeting each other after a long time, so it had to be full of fun and enjoyment. Well, nobody misses a chance to tease each other on such great occasions. I left home along with Abhishek accompanied by Rahul and Rohit. Rahul has always been the target but for that day it was Suresh who was about to lose his freedom of being a bachelor as he was getting married. Well, whenever I was with my college friends I never thought of anybody else. But this time don't know why...I was dying to meet Radhika. I tried to plan to meet her in the afternoon but couldn't meet her the entire day. In the evening when finally we were up on the stage with the bride and groom I was still thinking of her. All the thoughts were lined up in my mind which were all about marrying Radhika and spending life with her. She was special for me even though she didn't believe in me. I wanted to call her and tell her everything at that very moment but kept my thought to myself. The sweet thoughts about Radhika kept me glowing with a smile and I continued to watch everything that was lit up around especially the smile that was on Suresh's face. Well, marriages are good in their own ways.

Another incident took place 2-3 days later, which had an adverse effect this time I was at fault. Radhika and I had decided to go for a book launch at Landmark. I had made up a plan with her, but we ended up fighting and my mood was screwed. It always took quiet a long time for me to get normal and by that time everything was totally screwed. The fight with Radhika would turn up to be a mission of not talking to her till she feels guilty for her acts. Well, but later I would realize that the anger was for no reason. I tried to control my anger and it would never happen. The only thing which was out of my control. I would always tell Radhika, we get angry on people whom we love and being angry on her showed how much I loved her.

The next day when Radhika came back home from office, she informed me she had to meet Parth. I had just woke up and was tired to go anywhere also had to work on my showreel, so I avoided. They had filled the forms to participate in the Pune International Marathon 2009. I asked Radhika to fill in my form as well, but she didn't, saying you won't wakeup early Dhruv. I knew I was sleeping late till 9, but if it was something to be with Radhika I would have kept myself awake the whole night. I wanted to participate in Marathon and this was a chance to participate along with her. I thought she will fill the form for me and as she left I started searching my cupboard for the money and I was happy that I could gather around 6-700bucks for the form fees.

Later, at night Radhika didn't come home for dinner and informed she had filled in a form for her and would not come in the morning being Sunday. I enquired about my form, but she hadn't filled any. Next day early morning, I woke up at 7am with the loud voice of the television showing the Marathon live. How strange was it to be left alone when your girlfriend is out with your friend and his friends? Was it only because I was jobless I was left alone? These thoughts kept bugging me the entire day, so did my anger which had reached to its extremes. The worst part was I was alone after 3pm at home so I had to vent out my anger and it did on Radhika when she came home to meet me.

"Hey Mottu! What are you doing?" She said.

"Can't you see am watching TV." I replied in a rude manner.

"Why are you talking like this? See I came to meet you as soon as you messaged me."

"Wow! Thanks a lot Radhika. I am glad you realized I was missing you. I got a really bad feeling for myself today. It's like just because I don't have money

I am nobody." Now that was something I should have never said. Radhika got angry and left the house within a minute.

"That's so cheap Mottu. I never expected you would say that. I didn't want Parya to spend so I said no to your form." She said in anger and ran all the way back to her hostel.

I tried to stop her but couldn't stop her, so I banged the door and sat watching the TV. The next two minutes I started pulling my hair and turned off the TV, threw the remote on the floor and began my self-conversation.

"Cheap...Wow! If I say so that's what she calls. I collected money I was never going to let her pay, as if I am a beggar." I drank a glass of water from the kitchen and sat back in the living room staring at the remote.

"I wanted to go. She says I can never wake up on time. But see I was awake at 7."

"Like it's only me, who is at fault. What about her? She once said those things about spending money on me. Wasn't that supposed to be cheap?" I said in anger and punched m fist on the wall. Well, it did hurt.

"AaooooccH!" I shouted.

"Well, now Dhruv pick up that remote and think about what you have done?" A voice came from within.

"I haven't done anything."

"Do you remember you had promised Riya...You will never hurt Radhika? What the hell have you done now? Dude you love her. So what if she didn't take you with her. She came to meet you and see how well you greeted her."

"I am sorry."

"Don't...Sorry me. Go, call her."

"Yes...I am an asshole. Radhika I love you and I'm sorry."

I said to myself and picked up the remote and ran inside my room. I picked up my cell phone which was still charging and called up Radhika.

10th December 2009, we were searching a gift for Aman and Aaliya. Well, the lucky ones shared their birthday on this day. After a long while we found some nice gifts and then we headed towards the guitar class to meet everyone. Well, Aaliya was very happy to receive a gift and meet both of us or simply Radhika. We were waiting for the cake to arrive, whereas Radhika wanted to go home. I somehow convinced her to wait for some time for which she agreed. We had a tradition; to get a surprise birthday cake for everyone on their birthdays.

"So, Aaliya you can wait for some time your surprise cake is on the way so is for Aman. We are getting two cakes today." I said as Aaliya winked her eyes with a smile. Well, there was another smiling face and that was Aman. It had to be, Preeti was here for his birthday with a red rose for him.

After spending some time with everyone teasing each other, clicking pictures together we were all about to move for the party. Radhika, I didn't know why she was not comfortable with everyone. Aaliya tried to stop her, but she kept saying her hostel in-time is 9.30pm and wanted to reach early. I was surprised as why she wanted to leave early.

"Mottu! Why was it so necessary for you to eat the cake?" She said while we were on bike.

"Why? What happened Radhika? I love cakes. You know." I said trying to be normal. I knew she was upset by something, maybe she didn't want to stay. Why so? I had no answers to it. Maybe, she did.

"Dhruv everyone was making fun of you especially Sam. How can you tolerate that."?

"Come-on Radhika that is normal. We all make fun of each other."

"Well, that would be normal for you. But it's not for me. I don't like anybody making fun of you."

"Okay, I will take care of that. And Should I drop you till the hostel or will it be fine if I drop you nearby."

"Now, how can you go when I am not with you? Is it so important?" She shouted again.

"Well, Radhika everyone wanted you to stay. But you want to go back home. They want to celebrate it with us. What wrong in it?"

"Nothing is wrong. Go enjoy with your friends. After all they are more important than me. Right!" She was sounding possessive and I couldn't get the reason behind it.

"Radhika it's not like that. Okay fine I won't go. I'll drop you till hostel and go back home. I will tell them something."

"So, again you will fight with me that I spoiled everything. Right Dhruv?"

"What's happening to you? Why are you behaving like this? I will give some reason."

"It's okay Dhruv, drop me here and go back. You have already told your mom you won't be coming home for dinner."

"What about you? I told we both would be eating out."

"I'll eat something." She said as I stopped my bike.

"Come-on Radhika, we'll have fun." I said trying to convince her again.

"Mottu every day I go late in hostel. Today I have no reason for coming late and I have lots of pending work. You go have fun."

"Are you sure?" I asked her.

"Yes, I'll go from here."

"Okay, then I'll leave. Give me a call when you reach hostel. Bye!" I said and started my bike and left as she started walking back towards her hostel.

After driving for a few seconds I immediately turned my bike and went to see Radhika. She was walking across the street talking on her cellphone. I smiled at her and waited for a moment till she was out of my eye-sight. Later, I came back to the hotel where everyone had ordered something to eat. As I was about to sit my phone rang. It was Radhika.

"You reached hostel?" I questioned her.

"Yes and did you?" She asked back.

"Yes and whom were you talking with Radhika?"

"When did you see me?"

"I saw you." I said with a smile when everyone was staring at me.

"You should have been here Radhika. We miss you." Shouted Aaliya. Well that was unexpected.

"Did you hear that? Everyone is missing you here. By the way what are you eating?" I said.

"Nothing. I'm planning to cook some noodles."

"Radhika… You should have come."

"I know. Maybe next time. I'll talk later when you come back give me a call."

"Okay!" I said and disconnected the call. Now, I had no clue why everyone was so excited to know what I was talking with her. So for the next 10-15minutes our talk was all about Radhika. I was very happy that I had someone so special that I always loved to talk about her with my friends.

We finished our dinner and I came back home late. As I changed my clothes I called up Radhika. She sounded sleepy so we spoke for some time and then I began to work on my computer. During that time some thoughts kept rolling in my mind about Radhika with a smile on my face. No matter whatever stupid reason it was for the fight with her I knew it would never forget the wonderful moments spent with her.

*****

Chapter 19

Getting a Job...

The next day I woke up when Radhika came home early morning banging the staircase. She shook me and said, "Wake up Mottu." Well, that was one of the daily routine which I liked the most. I opened my eyes and saw her when she entered the kitchen and went off to sleep again. Usually, when she came out she would again wake me. But, today as she came out she kissed me on my cheek and asked me to wake-up. That brought a smile on my face and before I could say anything she ran near the staircase and went to office. I closed my eyes again and was still in a sleepy state when my phone started ringing.

"Mottu wake up. You have to go to MAAC and you were looking cute while sleeping."

"Oh that..! I am, right from childhood." I replied.

"That's your favorite line as always."

"I know. Anyways I have to go at 11. It's only 7.30am. I slept late yesterday, was working on that showreel. Can you call me later?" I said and she got angry.

"Ok fine! Bye." She said and hung up the phone. It didn't take a moment for Radhika to get angry upon me. But, couldn't give a much of thought over how to convince her back as mom came out from the kitchen to fire upon me some of her regular questions.

"Who was it?" She said. Now I just couldn't blindly say it was Radhika as her next question would be "Can't she live without you? She just left the house. Didn't she?" But to avoid it I replied," Just a friend from MAAC."

Well, I had totally forgotten I had to go in my institute to know about the CDT (Career Development Training) which was on the 15th. Radhika reminded me about it, so did my mom.

"You have to go for an interview. Right!" She said.

"Yes. It's on Tuesday." I replied.

A CDT is a compulsory program for the entire student studying in MAAC. It's held in the head office located in Mumbai. Mom and let's say my entire family had been cribbing over and over again on me to apply for a job or get back to the call center industry. I had no intentions to go back from where I had started but, it was very difficult to explain this to them. So, I had to say I was going for an interview in Mumbai. My mom's questions continued as finally I gave up my sleep when I wake up at 8.30am and messaged Radhika about the same. I got ready by 10 and went to class. Now, it was sometimes really weird when in MAAC I was never able to find any of my friends. Yes, I was able to make two friends. Once I reach MAAC, I would first search or sometimes make a call before leaving from home which I did today. As I reached the institute I spent my time starring at the notice boards later reading the animation magazines. Later, I called up Radhika and spent my time talking with her till the lectures were over. I went inside the classroom and met my faculty in order to show my work.

The task was difficult though my work was appreciated I wasn't happy as it was incomplete. Afterwards, I met my friends and one of them help me understand the way to the head office and also drew the map towards the same. Also he mentioned some useful instructions to follow which completely screwed my mind and I called up Radhika again.

"He showed me the way but it all went over my head." I said while she was unaware what I was talking about.

"What happened Mottu?" She said.

"Radhika you have to come with me to Mumbai. Do something. I'll be lost if I go by the instructions my friend gave." I said.

"It's not possible Dhruv. Its year-end, you know how much work I have in office. And what will I do in Mumbai." She asked.

"Radhika you can meet your brother and spend the day with him. You will have fun after a long time. Even I will get to see your brother."

"Ok fine! Let me see. I'll call him and let you know in the evening."

"Ok no problem." I said and hung up the phone.

Later, I went home and laid on my bed for a nap. I was waiting for Radhika in the evening. She came home but informed that she wasn't able to call her brother. Later she came inside with her dinner plate and sat next to me.

"Mottu put on that movie we were watching yesterday." She said.

"No Radhika watch this one it a real good movie." I said turning on another movie.

"Dhruv you have shown me three movies till now which I haven't watched completely. Starting with Love Aaj Kal then again so of those stupid movie and yesterday's What's your Rashi? I want to complete that, only then we'll go for a new movie. Don't you dare watch the movie without me."

"This is not fair Radhika. You leave the movie incomplete and I can't wait till the next day."

"Come on Mottu every-time you put on a new movie and I don't get anything what's going on." She replied and our discussion continued when finally we saw the movie of her choice. I was still not sure whether she would come along with me to Mumbai. Well, I had never been to that city and she knew it very well. On the other hand, I also had to convince mom which I was successful. Radhika informed me a day before which made me happy and had finally decided to leave.

15th December 2009, Radhika called up early morning around 4.30, to wake me up. I wondered if she actually slept that night. We had been talking on the phone till 12.30 midnight, later I was collecting my resume and the showreel work.
"Wake up Dhruv." She said.
"Radhika it's just 4.30. Let me sleep till 5. I have put the alarm." I replied with my eyes closed and still trying to sleep.
"Mottu wake up! You will take time to get ready and we have to buy tickets."
"Radhika I will be ready soon, just few minutes." I replied and tried to sleep again.
"Dhruv wake up. You have to go for the interview. It's 5.30 already." My mom tried to pull the blanket off my head while I still had to phone on my ears. I always wondered which time zone my mom followed when it was just 4.30 her clock already showed 5.30.

"Stop laughing Radhika. You people don't even let me sleep." I said on the phone to Radhika.
"Who is it?" My mom enquired when I already felt being tortured early morning by these two.
"It's Radhika." I replied to mom and answered the phone.
"Radhika am all awake now. Thanks for calling me and good night. I mean I will call you when I am ready. Come home and then we would leave." I tried to sleep again as my mom went inside when Radhika called back again.
"Mottu wake up! Don't sleep." She said.
"I am not sleeping." I replied closing my eyes wearily.
"Dhruv I know you are still sleeping."
"Radhika bye I will call you on time." I said and hung up the phone and pulled over my blanket. Within the next few minutes mom was out again calling my name.

"Dhruv… Are you awake? Get up or you will be late." She said and pulled the blanket again. I was pretty sure Radhika wouldn't have stopped laughing if she was still on phone. I cursed myself as to why I have to go to Mumbai. Somehow

I had to give up and folded my blanket and went straight into the bathroom. I got ready by the time it was 5.30. I called up Radhika and it was quite obvious that she was sleeping.

"Radhika, don't tell me you are sleeping now." I said.

"Who said that? I am awake." She replied.

"Is that so?"

"Yes…!"

"Then, why are you sounding sleepy. Wait… let me guess! You aren't ready yet."

"Mottu I was ready within 10mins and I knew you would take at least an hour so I thought of taking a nap."

"Wow! Anyways I am ready and come home soon. And I don't take time to get ready." I said and connected my cell phone back to charge the battery. While I was still combing my hair Radhika arrived and well still loud enough as usual her voice helped my father to wake up from his sleep.

"Mottu…Stop applying that makeup. We are not going out in search of your bride." She said.

"What if…? I get one." I replied

"Come-on you two finish the breakfast and go fast you would be late." Mom shouted and we quickly finished the breakfast and proceeded towards the station. But, an unexpected surprise was waiting for me. Radhika had called up Parth and had asked him to get the tickets. He had been to station and bought the tickets and later came to pick me and Radhika. I was never able to understand why Radhika could never trust me.

"Why did you call Parth?" I said while walking towards the rickshaw stand.

"Dhruv…I knew you would not wakeup early and we might not get the tickets so I had told Parth."

"What the …?" Could have been my next statement but like always I gave her my innocent look and said, "Radhika? I did wake up early and its good you called him. Now we won't have to go all the way walking till Station."

"See… I am smarter than you. That's why I called him here." She replied.

"Okay…" I said but that moment I didn't like her calling Parth. At least she could have informed me. I was angry at that moment as well as hurt but as always I kept quiet and said nothing about it.

I behaved normal and greeted Parth with a smile. We waited there for a moment and later Parth began, "Come-on Duksey we both will go and Radhika will join us as she will come walking."

"Parya, I called you here and you are going to ditch me." Radhika replied with a frown.

"I can't leave my friend alone. You can come alone walking."

"Okay fine I am going home." She replied.

"Radhika I can't go without you." I said holding her hands.

"Chill dude…! We are all going together. But we won't be able to go to our restaurant." Parth added.

"Why so?" Radhika asked as I interrupted in between.

"What about the tickets?"

"The train is at 6.15am and it's already 5.45." Parth replied.

"I knew this and that is why I had told Parth to get the tickets."

"Okay fine…lets go." I said and we three sat on his bike and left. I kept quiet and kept thinking over and over again why exactly I had called Radhika to accompany me when she doesn't trust me. I was about to be lost in my thoughts again when my brain replied. *"Its simple Dhruv you love her and stop thinking too much or else everything will be spoilt. You trust her that's more than enough. She should trust you, is what you are expecting from her. Don't run behind expectations it could ruin everything. And now smile…"* Yes, I smiled after that and shook my head when Radhika asked, "What happened, Mottu?"

"Nothing…" I replied.

We reached Pune Station and after drinking a cup of tea. Now, this was the very first time I and Radhika were together early morning seated close to each other headed towards Mumbai. Well, the city I had never been to but was eager and excited to be along with Radhika.

"Radhika am very happy, firstly you came with me and second is that we are going together with my mom's permission, too good just too good…" I said holding her hands.

"Mottu…Control, we are in public." She said with a smile. The feel was different being with her at that moment kept me excited. I knew it would have been difficult for me to attend the CDT alone as I would have failed big time in searching the Head Office. Radhika was seated along the window corner whereas, I was seated close to her holding her hand.

"Radhika…You know something, today nobody can say anything even if I hold your hand throughout the train journey and I won't leave it." I said holding her hands whereas we couldn't ignore the people staring at the two of us. But the moment I said I won't leave her hand my mobile starting ringing. I left her hand the very next moment as it was my mom.

"Hello!!" I said.

"Yes, Dhruv did you get the train?" She said.

"Yes I did." I replied as I couldn't stop Radhika gazing at me with that weird laugh.

"Okay, I called up to know whether you guys got the train."

"We are in the train." I replied and later kept the phone.

"So…Where were we?" I asked Radhika.
"You were never going to leave my hand." She replied with a smile.
"It was mom's phone. So just for that time now I won't leave it." I said holding her hand back again.
"Like your mom was going to know you were holding my hand." She said.
"I know." I replied and we were busy talking with each other during the journey. Not to forget her brother calling her to interrupt our conversation. Her brother hated me and today I was going to meet him. Why did he hate me? I really had no clue. Yes, maybe for my stupid behavior with Radhika when I was with Mahi. But that was past I guess and things would be normal I hoped and was excited to meet him as well.

Sometimes when you are with the person you love, even the shortest time spend together are treasured as memories. Well, for me this journey was memorable as I couldn't stop being mischievous whenever I got a chance. Sometimes, I would put my head on her laps and sleep for a while and sometimes it would be Radhika's head on my shoulder. We would tease our fellow passengers who were more concern to watch the two of us. Radhika was the only girl in that particular compartment, so the journey till Mumbai was fun. We reached Dadar station around 10am and later were waiting for her brother at the ticket counter on the platform.

The station was heavily crowded and I had never been in such a crowd before except during the Ganapati festivals. We were being carried along with the people who were almost running to reach their respective offices. I wondered how could people actually survive in such a crowded platforms. Our wait was finally over so were my thoughts when her brother arrived. We greeted each other with a formal Hi-Hello and he ended up giving me that creepy smile(As if he would kill me the very next moment…But he seemed quite decent). He informed us about the tickets we need to buy when he and Radhika were in the queue. I watched them like the kid who is told not to move from his place. Later we had to rush as the train was about to move in 5minutes. Again a long run in the crowd frightened me, so I was holding Radhika's hand while her brother was walking ahead. Every time he turned back I would leave her hand and the moment he was looking ahead I would hold her hand again. Finally I was pushed into the train and few minutes later got place to sit. This time it was a 20minute journey till Andheri where I was sitting quiet as I failed to understand their talk. But seeing me quiet Radhika would initiate a talk with me and I would smile if at all had an eye contact with her brother. He was very helpful as he accompanied me along with Radhika till we reached MAAC's head office. I was happy to see Radhika's cheerful face to meet her brother, at the same time I got to know she was really lucky to have people around her who really cared a lot for her. I waved off my hand as the two left and I entered the MAAC premises.

I registered my name in the registry book and enquired about the training. I wanted to know the schedule for what I was here for. I was informed that there would be a mock interview session followed by the seminar at 2. I was asked to be seated in the lobby where I began to prepare myself for the interview. Till the time my name was called I kept gazing at every person who came in and out of the campus. Well, not to forget Natasha's favorite statement about me 'Dhruv has a crush on every girl who walks into his life'. I happened to recall this statement when I saw one nice beautiful girl walking inside the corridor. Immediately, I called up Radhika and wanted to know what she was into, I knew this might irritate her brother but, still I called.
"What are you doing Radhika?" I asked as soon as she picked up the phone.
"Nothing we are going to Juhu beach then later we might go to Marine drive. Why? What happened?" She replied.
"I am bored, waiting for my name to be called."
"Mottu is your training is cancelled?" She was concerned.
"No, it is at 2. Before that we have a mock interview where we would have to show our showreel."
"No problems Mottu, give a call if you get free early."
"Yes…I will. Okay bye." I said and kept the phone and began thinking what I would do next, when the person next to me tried to converse with me. We spoke for a while and within few minutes we became good friends. My name was called and I had to go in for the interview. I was asked some basic questions and was told how I should face a real interview. Later, I was waiting for Ranjeet. Oh! I forgot to tell his name before, yes he was the same guy I was talking few minutes ago. We went to eat something before the seminar began, during which I again spoke with Radhika and she was on Marine drive.

The seminar began at 2.15; we were seated in the auditorium. The interiors of the auditorium were impressive. The seminar was conducted by one of the faculty members who once conducted a seminar on animation in the JM road branch. I was sure that I will get to learn a lot today. Well! I was right, we were informed about various things that were important in order to present our showreel to the production studios as well as some of the work were appreciated. My doubt about working on the animation clip of a song was cleared and appreciated. I was told that I need to present it with a copy of my demo-reel(showreel). It gave me a ray of hope that once I go back everything will be fine as I would be working on it in full swing and will get a job soon in the field of animation. So, after the seminar was over I called up Radhika and she asked me to meet at the Andheri Station. I took the bus and proceeded towards the station along with this new friend Ranjeet. We exchanged our numbers and yes I always knew I would contact him someday if at all I come back to Mumbai.

As, we reached Andheri Station my eyes began to search Radhika and there she was coming along with her brother.
"Mottu you should have come early. We just ate ice-candy." She said as she met me while her brother was busy talking on the phone.
"The seminar was from 2 to 4 and I left soon after that. We were asked to wait to get our work checked but I was exhausted."
"Mottu, you should have shown your work, we won't be coming again." She scolded on me.
"Chill Radhika. I have received many tips upon how to finish it and present it. So I am not worried about it. By the way look at your lips all red. Can I kiss you?" I asked her softly in her ears.
"Are you crazy Dhaval bhaiya is here."
"Okay then we'll do it in the train."
"You have gone mad Dhruv."
"Don't be serious I am joking. Let's eat something, I am very hungry." I said pointing her towards McDonalds
"No way Mottu I have had a lot of stuff. Am not hungry at all." She replied give me a huge list of stuff we had along with her brother.
"Radhika. I didn't eat anything the whole day and you've enjoyed your day."
"Anyways I think I should buy something from here. Would you like to have something?"
"No Mottu you buy from yourself, I'll go and find where my brother is?" She said looking for him here and there.
"Okay, no problem when you find him come inside the restaurant." I said and went inside.

"Wow! Why is everything so crowded in this city?" I said to myself as I entered inside the restaurant and saw the huge crowd. Within a moment I dropped the plan of eating here as I knew it would difficult to get a table round in any corner of the restaurant. I took a value-meal parcel and came out sipping the coke.

"What happened Mottu?" Radhika said as she stood right outside waiting to enter.

"The place is very crowded, I felt suffocated so I took a parcel.."

"How was your training?" Her brother asked.

"It was good." I replied.

"Okay now come with us. We need to do some shopping." She said and I followed the two. Radhika had planned to go shopping in the most crowded area where I was following her but the best part was the see the siblings helping each other without any hesitance. Maybe that was the reason her brother was the most important person in her life. I found him very kind and helpful with her and he never showed any signs of hatred for me the entire time I was with him rather was with Radhika. So maybe he liked me. No ways, a girl's father and brother are the most difficult people to impress. Well, her mom was impressed the time they were in Pune but with Parth. I remembered the moment when they were in Pune for Radhika's birthday and I had been a shy guy, also I recalled how Parth burst on me the moment they left. So, this time I was trying my best that whenever I talk with her brother I talk sensible. But, I was quiet watching them as I had always been whenever I met any new people.

This was my only time when I could impress him, talk with him and get to know him more but none of these things happened due to my shy nature. Finally, after roaming around the crowd Radhika decided to leave for the Station. We had to run all the way to get ourselves inside the train. So here I was…In a train crowded with people with no space to sit after waving the final good-bye to her brother I thought I have really made up a bad impression on him once again. I knew that one day everything will be fine, maybe someday I will be treated equally or just like Radhika I would also be a part of Radhika's family one day. It was difficult but not impossible.

Radhika looked at me and smiled whereas those thoughts were still running in my head and my eyes were gazing around the people who were standing beside me. I smiled back at Radhika and she asked, "What happened Mottu?" Now, why the hell should she call me Mottu in front of so many people? I was sure that many would have laughed and might be many would have just ignored it. I nodded my head to say no with a smile.

"This train is so crowded?" I said

"I know Mottu, but what happened to you?"

"Nothing." I replied and said, "I am hungry I need to eat something."

"Mottu we will get some place to sit then you can eat." She said and we waited for some time as I continued to say, "I can't wait any longer. I am going to eat this burger." I said as I removed the burger from the pack. I took the first bite and offered Radhika, she took a bite and there were many mouth-watering faces staring at us. Later, we got some place to sit next to the lady who never wanted us to be near her. She gave Radhika some place to sit and later I sat next to her. "Radhika I'm still hungry. I didn't eat anything the whole day." I said as I could see some people still struggling with each other balancing their weights as they had to stand the whole journey.

"Mottu…Why are you always hungry? Wait for some time, we'll be home soon." She replied holding my hands.

"I know but at least I can eat one biscuit." I said again.

"You're impossible Mottu."

"I know still I'm the BEST" I replied and took the pack out of my bag. Well my back was fully loaded with eatables that day while returning back home. And once again I had people staring at me and the poor little boy sitting right in front of me.

"Mottu why are you teasing that poor kid." Radhika whispered as the kid was continuously staring at us..

"I am not teasing him Radhika….I'm just! You know…Look at him." I replied with a smile.

"Okay fine." I said and put back the packet in my bag. The train journey was getting more exciting as the kid started begging his father to give him something to eat and I wasn't able to control my laughter. Some new people joined us whereas the standing committee finally decided to sit in the walking space of the train. Some were cursing the rail-ministry for not providing sufficient space to sit.

The fun ended when we both took a nap in each other's arms and by 10.30pm we reached home. Mom was waiting with her questions piled up one after another.

"Did you get the job? How was the interview?" She asked.

"It was good. Don't know if I would get it?" I replied while eating dinner. Radhika stayed quiet as I could see she was tired. I loved her for accompanying me today but never did I say it to her. A thank you note would have been a lot to let her know but I saved it as a message and didn't send her. She went back to her hostel and I was back on my computer searching for some job requirement.

Next day, I was busy checking my mails when I found Ashwin online. I called him as I confirmed his number.

"Chinki…! How are you?" I said.

"I am fine. How are you bro?" He replied.

"I am fine. What's with you where are you these days? How's the Bailgaddi working?" I said and he was quiet for a moment and then began laughing.

"These days I am working with Ventura." He replied.

"Okay I should inform Nishant about it."

"So are you still working for Microsoft?" He asked.

"Actually I am working on my demoreel. It would take time so I'm hunting for a part time job somewhere." I said.

"Demoreel ? What is that?"

"It's that short animation video which we have to present for the interview. It's like a project you can say. Anyways do you have any vacancies in your new office."

"Yes we do." He said and gave me the entire information of his work environment. He also gave me the contact number of the consultancy office through which I could apply for this particular job.

I needed a job in order to take care of the home loan as the monthly installments were rising and so were the expenses. I had a long way to go along with my demoreel as I knew I was still in the basic phase of animation. I had made up my mind to join a BPO for a tech support once again. So Ventura was the option I opted to go for. I called up the consultancy and they asked me to visit the office. I got myself dressed up in the formal attire so that I could make that first impression perfect. I always believed in first impression has to be the best. I was right I was selected by the recruiters in the office. They informed me about the interview the next day in the Ventura office.

19th December 2009, here I was driving all the way towards the office with Radhika's wishes along with me and a hope in my mom's eyes-the financial problems would seize if I get the job. I was confident about myself as I knew I had always cracked the interview on the very first go. The interview went well and I was nostalgic for some time with memories of Microsoft interview. At Ventura I was been asked more about selling skills rather than any technical stuff. But I cleared all the hurdles of the interview and came out blushing with a smile and a nice package to make everyone happy. I tried to call Ashwin to thank him for making it easy for me, later I called up Radhika.

"Radhika…Guess! What?" I said.

"You got the job?" She creamed from the other end.

"Yes I did and do you know what package I got."

"It would be above 25K I guess." She replied.

"Arre are you crazy not so high but it's 18K/month. So 15thousand would be for the housing loan installments then one thousand saving and two thousand will be enough for us. Right?" I asked her in excitement.

"It would be more than enough Mottu and I am very happy for you. Congrats Mottu."

"Now you won't have to spend money. I'll do it for us and I am sure everything will be awesome after this." I said and continued to say, "Radhika we have to go to guitar class to give everyone this particular news and it's been a long time I haven't met them. And I am going to call Parth after this don't worry."

"Why should I worry about it? Anyways did you tell your mom first."

"I'll go home and tell her. You know it's always good to see the reactions." I said.

"Okay Dhruv and come to pick me at office." She said.

"Yes I'll be there within the next few minutes." I said and went to pick her from office.

Later, we went home and told mom and everyone about the job. Well, she was happy about it. But at the same a bit disappointed as I was taking Radhika along with me to meet my friends. But that was normal I was able to manage everything at that moment. Like I said before, getting a job changes everything. We reached the guitar class and told everyone about the new job. So it was Harsh, Aman, Aaliya, Akshada, Prasad, Sam and Preeti who all screamed in chorus, "Party!!!" and I said, "Let me first get the salary."

I remember after that it was the very first time I kissed Radhika in front of everyone in excitement. Well, in front of my friends and it was on her cheeks to be precise. We all enjoyed the moment and later went to drink cold coffee and came back home. I had to finish my showreel work as soon as possible before the joining date as I knew I would never get time to work on it later. So Radhika was after me to finish my work. She would wake me up early morning before going to office. Sometimes it would be just shaking me, sometimes her loud voice and sometime that cute peck on cheek. I would begin my day with sometime getting on my computer with a motto to finish the work. I also accompanied Krish on the construction site. Our house was on the final phase of construction and we had to select the proper bath fittings and color for the walls. Few days later, 25th December, finally after a long debate we ended up watching Avatar over 3Idiots and then spending the day with her.

*****

Chapter 20

The New Year's New Job and Radhika...

When the year is about to end how exactly will you like to end it. Well the year 2008 ended pretty well for me and the entire year was amazing. My so called best friend Radhika turned out to be my girlfriend who never like being credited on this. I knew I was getting so attached to her that I wasn't able to think of anything without her. Let it be hanging the Christmas tree picture on my wall or giving a bath to my pets she would be with in every act of mine. I loved her every moment but the only thing that missed was I never said it to her always thought she will understand how much I love her. Was she just my need in finishing certain tasks of was I just getting used to the fact that someone was always there with me.

So just like that last year's new year celebration I was waiting for Radhika. But she was busy with her work in office till then I was roaming with Aman and Abhi(Riya's best friend). He had started working in Bangalore and was here for few days. We three were roaming on the streets of MG Road and later went to JM Road as Abhi's friend joined him. It was 11pm when I called her and confirmed her arrival at JM Road even when mom had warned me. So we were waiting for her as Abhi's friend somehow convinced him for a treat(now it had to be for the new job and the biggest reason was we were tempted by the smell waiting outside Pizza Hut). Abhi ordered a parcel and had to wait for the next half hour till then Radhika was there.

"Radhika how much do you work dear?" I said as soon as I ran towards her.

"I know I am very tired now just want to sleep." She replied and we came towards these guys.

"Hello Abhi..!" Radhika said as she saw him.

"Radhika would you like to order something we already have ordered a lot. But you can still tell us." I said as Aman and Abhi's friend continued to smile and Abhi face turned into a frown.

"Okay Dhruv, you guys have already cut down a huge bill. Anyways Radhika what would you like to eat?" He asked her.

"I just had my dinner in office. You guys can carry on. And Dhruv, when will we go home?" She said.

"Who we??? Radhika I came with Aman I don't know how you will go." I said being sarcastic.

"So you should have told me before I would have gone to hostel." Radhika said in anger.

"Chill I will leave you I was just kidding." I said keeping my hand on her shoulder.

We waited for some more time for the parcel when the clock struck 12. I thought how strange life could be, a year back I was bugged off with the loud music in the pub and today here I was with friends on JM road waiting for the pizza.

"What happened Dhruv?" Aman asked me as he found me nodding my head and smiling as I was lost in my thoughts.

"Nothing, Happy New Year…!" I said and wished everyone. We all wished each other and that moment thought of calling some friends when I first name strike in my mind and I dialed the number.

"Happy New Year Riya…!" I said as Riya picked up the call.

"Same to you Dhruv. How are you? You know what, I was just going through that photo album you gave me and was missing you." She replied.

"Am fine and Riya you should come here, see I called you on the right time. I miss you too. Come back to meet us." I said and I could hear Riya being silent on the phone. A few seconds later heard her cry.

"Riya…! Why are you crying?" I said.

"Nothing I was missing you. You always make me cry Dhruv."

"What did I do? I called you to wish you. I was also missing you I always do. Anyways you know what we are going to eat pizza in few minutes."

"Who we?"

"Me, Radhika, Abhi, his friend and my friend Aman."

"Abhi's treat and we have ordered a lot of stuff. Here, talk with him he's dying to talk with you." I said and handed over the phone and signaled him that she was crying. Later, I turned back to Radhika with a smile and said, "Kya yaar you girls always have to cry for some stupid reason."

"Mottu you won't understand. Let it be." She replied.

"Okay, no problem." I said and checked if Abhi was done talking with her.

"Oye don't finish my balance, I want to talk with her." I said and few minutes later he handed over me the phone. Well, Abhi was trying to convince Riya all this time to stop crying as she was alone at her place and her husband was out of town. We talked for a while and a smile was back on Riya's face as even Radhika wished her. Later, Radhika was busy talking with her parents when our wait for pizza was over. We enjoyed the pizza and finally after dropping

Radhika to her hostel I could say that this New Year's start was not so weird as I thought it could be.

1st January 2010, the very first day of this year, I had made huge plans that would work towards my success in life. Those plans included me getting a job as an ANIMATOR, shifting to the new house and enjoy its ambience and most important being with Radhika. But, yes did I forget I had to go to the Dagdushet temple today. It was possible this year thanks to Radhika; she accompanied me to the temple. As we reached there we found that there wasn't much crowd in the temple. But I could see many people properly dressed up devotedly lined up for the queue to go inside early morning. As we went inside I joined my hands and began to pray,
"Bappa thanks a lot.
Finally Radhika is with me.
Now, please help me complete my showreel, so that I can get a job in animation.
And please...
Please...! Please...!!! Please...!!!
Let Radhika be with me forever. And also don't forget my showreel thing you need to help me in that.
Okay! Now I'm going bye." I said and opened my eyes. I saw Radhika was still praying. Immediately, I closed my eyes again and said, *"Bappa the most important thing.*
I forgot. Radhika, do help her she should become a CA.
It's her dream...Please fulfill it."

Radhika looked at me and said, "Kya hua Mottu?".
"Nothing … Let's go and tell me where I should drop you?" I said.
"Same place where you always drop me?" She replied.
"Okay! No problem let's go." I said and we both sat on my bike. I dropped her near her office and then came back home. I had my breakfast and later sat down to work and after some time I went off to sleep. It was 11am when Radhika called and I woke up.
"Hello!!!" I said trying making my dull voice strong not letting her know I was sleeping.
"Mottu can you ever be serious in life?" She said.
"Why? What happened Radhika? I replied.
"You're sleeping Dhruv when you are supposed to be working." She said raising her voice in anger.

"No I was not sleeping just that I was sleeping sleepy. But I was working, see I finished animating that character up to 10frames."

"Wow! Dhruv, 10frames in last 2hours. It's simply amazing." She said.

"I know, but it is a bit difficult to animate that's why it's taking time."

"You very well know Dhruv once you start working it will be very difficult for you to give time. So instead of sleeping, please concentrate on work."

"I know, anyways it was because I woke up early so I felt sleepy. I'm..." I paused.

"Even I woke up early Dhruv, that's not a valid reason for your laziness." She said still being frustrated on me.

"I'm going to work. Don't worry, I was just sleeping for 10-15 minutes." I continued as I was again interrupted by her.

"I know you very well Dhruv. Anyways I had just called to tell you I won't be coming home in the evening today."

"Why? Where are you going?" I said being confused.

"You know my friend Adeena. She is in Pune and I am going to stay at her place."

"Okay! But, when are you coming?" I said as I got up from my bed and turned on the monitor.

"I will be coming on Sunday evening." She replied.

"Are you crazy Radhika? Why are you staying there for two days? One day is enough come back tomorrow. Why didn't you tell me in the morning?"

"I forgot to tell you. Anyways do tell kaku, I won't be coming home for dinner." She said.

"I won't tell anything. You call her and we were going out this weekend." I said in anger.

"When? You never said anything." She replied in a calm voice.

"Is it that every time I should tell you. Can't you understand. Okay fine! Do whatever you want I don't care. Go to hell and I won't tell anything to anyone." I replied in a rude tone.

"Okay fine! I'll call kaku you enjoy your sleep. And you didn't tell me about any plan so I made up this plan. I am sorry I forgot to inform you in the morning. Anyways, bye!!!" She said as I knew I was successful to make her angry once again.

"Yes, okay fine but I'm not sleeping..." Before I could say this she had disconnected the phone.

I was angry with her behavior, I went outside and found that mom had left for work. Krish and dad might have gone to the construction site, I guessed. I drank a glass of water and came inside my room. My pet Sweety had been sleeping near my legs as I was angry I hit her hard and kicked her out of the bed. She looked at me making innocent face then later went out growling at me. I had decided to take her for the Dev's music concert but her decision made me angry and I kept cursing myself as my thoughts began to curse me.

"Dhruv! How is she supposed to know what's in your mind. She might have thought of spending time with her friends as she is meeting her after a long time. What's wrong in it? Even you spend time with your friends. So why the big mess if she wanted to spend her time with her friend. You go...Meet your guitar class friends today everything will be fine. Most important your mood will change. Maybe, then you would feel whatever you did wasn't right."

That thought from my mind helped me forget many things but I knew my stupid behavior had screwed up the very first day of the year with a fight with Radhika. I kept walking in and out of my room, sometimes in the living room and later I sat next to Sweety. I couldn't sense her eyes to be wet and maybe the anger in her eyes. I called her near and even though I had kicked her she forgot everything in a moment placed her head on my laps. Strange how dogs could be I thought. As I rolled my hand over her fur, the other one (Pluto) came running and sat on the other side beside me wagging his tail.

Sometime later I was in front of the computer and continued with my work. I knew I had messed up by being angry on a stupid reason but at that moment I thought it was Radhika who was wrong. Later in the evening I went to guitar class and wished everyone Happy New Year. I tried to convince my stupid mind that I can enjoy and be happy without Radhika. After spending some time everyone got busy with the practice. Aman, Anup and Prasad were busy playing the guitar chords and lyrics along with a new guy named Adesh. Sam was busy setting up the pitch of his guitar along with some unknown girl whereas there was another girl named Sawari who was standing next to Anup and both seemed to be talking a lot with each other. So maybe my guess was right these two were the new members of our group.

The practice was in full swing were I and Aaliya continued to watch them play. Later Preeti joined us and hugged me and Aaliya and said, "Happy New Year Bhai." I felt great about everything that my friends were into a live performance, at the same time I wished I would have been with them in the practice. Later, Preeti left for her dance practice and few minutes later Aaliya got busy making the guest list and the speech ready as she was anchoring the show. I tried my luck if I could be a part of the show it her. Somehow it didn't work for me.

"So, Aaliya how' s the practice going on." I asked as I found her free.

"It's cool Dhruv. I wish you would have been with us. We could have great fun. It's only you and Harsh not participating in any event." She said.

"I know!" I made a sad face with a fake smile and said, "Maybe, next time we would." The fight with Radhika had been no good for me so did coming here to class. I was missing Radhika and regretted for fighting with her the very first day of the year. That moment, I understood the fact of being lonely even if you are surrounded by your friends. Before Aaliya could get back to work I wished her Happy New Year and said, "Hey I need to go home. The practice won't get over. We'll meet later."

"Okay! But you are coming to the concert right?" She said.

"Don't know. Maybe, I'll try." I replied.

"Dhruv do get Radhika along with you. We'll have fun."

"I know but we just had a fight today. I am not sure if she will come."

"Why do you always fight with her?"

"I don't. But today it was a very stupid reason, I wanted to spend time with her and she wanted to be with her friend."

It's okay Dhruv. Let her do what she wants to do. Anyways, how's this guy?" She said pointing towards a boy.

"He's good. Wait. Let me guess! Is it like you guys dating each other and stuff going on?" I asked curiously.

"No. But I'm thinking about it." She was smiling. I could sense that from her tone even though she showed a blank expression.

"Good. Keep it up!" Well the word 'good' was my favorite word on every occasion and Radhika would be annoyed with it a lot but still I would never fail to use it as I was fully addicted to such things. I nodded my head to make sure there was a smile on Aaliya's face.

"Okay Aaliya it's getting late. I'll have to leave, but you do inform the others about it."

"Okay I'll inform everyone and you talk with Radhika. You guys are that perfect couple. Don't fight unnecessarily."

"I will." I said with a smile and left from the room waving my hand to everyone. Immediately Anup followed me outside the classroom and said, "Dude! Why are you leaving? Wait for some time."

"No it's already 9. I told mom I will be at home by 8. Also I have work to do." I said and he didn't insist much to stay and finally I left for home. That day their practice continued till 11 and on my way back home I kept thinking about Radhika and to interrupt my thoughts it was Aaliya for whom I wondered. Within no time she had become a part of the group and had been sharing a lot of secrets with us(with me to be precise). Maybe, I am the best but I miss you

Radhika I said and wanted to pacify her but somewhere my ego and attitude was stopping me to do so.

Next day I was watching my cell phone every single second waiting for that one message or at-least a miss call from Radhika. But she never called and I continued to pick up the phone every second. A message finally came from Airtel to download new hello-tunes and to show me that my cell phone was alive. I couldn't wait any longer and I decided to call her.

"Hello!!" The voice of Radhika from the other end finally raised my heartbeat and so I continued with my normal tone.

"Radhika you can't even give a miss call. I was waiting from morning."

"I just woke up and I didn't have balance in my cell." She replied in a normal tone as well.

"You know something Radhika. You always keep fighting with me and always call me so I was waiting."

"Yes!! You are right. I fight with you and I have to call you back. Why should it always be me Mottu?"

"Because I don't know you have to call and how will I know if you have a balance in your mobile or not. Wait I'll recharge your phone from here."

"No need I'll do it later."

"Okay but you know me. I don't know how but aisa hi hoon mein." I said.

"I know and that's why I hate you." She replied quickly.

"No... Radhika. You love me"

"Yes. Maybe, that's why you always take me for granted. Anyways why did you call?" She was back in that same old mood and I always loved her to trouble her at such point of time but more often I loved her with that anger on me. Anger is always shown on the people we love. Isn't that right ? I never told her this but yes where was I?

"I was missing you Radhika so I called you." I replied.

"Is there nobody at home?" She said.

"No, I mean yes... No I mean do I always say this when nobody is at home."

"Yes. That's right!"

"No you are wrong. I was missing you and anyways nobody is at home." I replied

"See I told you." She replied with a smile

"But I am missing you and Radhika when are you coming back?"

"I told you Mottu. Sunday evening."

"Come in the morning, we'll go to the Concert."

"Not possible Mottu. I and Adi are going out for shopping in the morning tomorrow. She needs to buy some stuff. Anyways I'll get bored, I hardly know anyone there"

"Radhika you know everybody. Aman, Anup, Sam, Preeti and Aaliya, she wants you to be there for the show. Come it will be great fun." I said trying to convince her again.

"I know Dhruv but we have already made a plan and as it is I am meeting her after a long time."

"Ya right." Well I said this to myself. We spoke for some more time where I still tried to convince her to come but nothing worked so I gave up the plan of going to the Concert. That evening I was at my relative's place but every moment was thinking of Radhika. I never knew why I was becoming so mad about her.

3rd January 2010 the day of the Concert. Being Sunday I had to give bath to my pets. I wasn't thinking about it the Concert anymore. But as there was no other work for me the thoughts about missing the Concert kept lingering in my mind. After finishing my breakfast, I took Sweety inside the bathroom. Everything was normal the only thing missing was Radhika who would be here watching me give them bath and say it in her cutest tone, "Kya kar raha hai Mottu?" keeping her hands on my shoulder and watching my pets.

People always go crazy when in love and I was supposed to be the craziest person on earth thinking of her while my pets would keep rotating their head as if there were reading my mind. Crazy…Isn't it? But someone had to get me out of it Harsh did for me when I picked up my ringing cell phone.

"Hey Max! Was sup?" He said in his unusual tone.

"Nothing you say." I replied.

"Nothing man! I just called up to ask if you were going for the Concert."(Now that's why I always need such friends to make me recall the thing I want to wipe off my brain- I going to the Concert).

"No. I don't have the tickets for the show." I said being calm.

"Arre we don't need tickets. We just have to flash our I-cards and we get direct entry to the show. Also we can get anybody along with us."

"Great Harsh!! You are telling me this today at this last moment." I said.

"I know man. But I just got to know about this last night." He replied.

"Cool then we both will go together, but do you know the location." I said being excited about watching the show once again.

"I'll check with him again and will call you within 5minutes."

"Okay! Give me a call soon. I'll be waiting. Bye!" I said and was back with excitement. I was all set to go for the show. Maybe, I'll get to see my friends perform and I won't feel bad, things will be awesome. But, yes to do so I had to finish bathing my pets first and then get ready, which I did and was waiting for his call. But a message popped on my screen, it was Harsh: *"Hey Dhruv I can't come. You go."* My mind was screwed and I decided to call him immediately.

"Dude what happened? We both were supposed to go. I was waiting for your call and was about to get ready." I said as soon as he picked up the phone.
"I know that's why I messaged you I can't come." He said.
"And that's why I called you. What happened all of sudden? You were excited about going there some time before."
"I know. But I gave a thought and felt if we go, we might feel bad that all our friends are performing and we are just sitting in the audience to cheer them."
"Well...That's the point Harsh. Someone should be there to cheer them. So what if we are not performing. We will enjoy." I said that to change his mind.
"No I won't like it as it is you know something..."
"What?"
"Nobody bothered to call us or tell us that we could watch the show without buying any tickets."
"Chill Dude...! They must be busy with their practice." I said but he wasn't wrong.

Nobody can be so busy that they can't inform their friends. But I didn't want these things to circle in my mind so I gave up the thought of going to the concert and ended the conversation with Harsh with an approach maybe next time. After that I took a bath and it was already 12. The other girls came home as usual for the lunch and mom asked me to have my lunch with everyone which I did. The lunch was heavy and I felt asleep after that for the next 3-4hours. As I woke up in the evening it was already 6, I washed my face and that afternoon sleep helped me a lot as I continued to work late till 3 at night when finally I got back to bed.

I woke up with the sound of footsteps. It was Radhika, same time as every morning she would come running to take her tiffin.
"Aa gayi tu...!" I was just about to say this to her but mom said it before me as she entered directly into the kitchen.
"Haan..!" She replied and it brought up a smile on my face.
"Where were you two days?" My mom asked.

"I was at my friend's place. My school friend is here for her training."
She said and yes I should say, both my mom and Radhika had that unique
inbuilt increasing sound system in their vocal tone which would never need
a microphone if they had to speak in a crowd. Their voices could be clearly
heard even in huge crowd. But that's not the only point, the thing was even if
I forget to turn on the alarm on my cell phone their talks would wake me up.
Anyways as I saw Radhika coming outside I closed my eyes and pretended to
sleep when she took the newspaper and sat next to me on my bed.

"Wake up Mottu..!" She said. I opened my eyes smiled at her and closed my
eyes. Radhika waited for a moment and kissed me on my cheeks and again
tried to wake me up.

"Kya be…!" I said as soon as she kissed me with a smile and continued, "Read
my horoscope loudly."

"You can read it later." She said.

"I won't get time. Both our sun signs are same so read it." I insisted.

As she began to read, I began to roll my fingers slowly on her back inside
her top. She was looking amazing but within a fraction of seconds she stood
up as mom called her inside and began laughing at me. I loved her a lot and
sometime even the shortest moment spent with her was a sweet memory. She
took her tiffin and went to office and I got out of bed after sometime with a feel
that everything was back to normal. That entire week I would try to wake up
early when Radhika came home but would always fail and was never able to
get out of bed before 10. The schedule was fixed for the week. Work the entire
day, sleep for some time in the afternoon and spent time with Radhika in the
evening watching some movies. Later work late-nights. This was the last week
at home before the joining at Ventura so I never wanted to do anything else.
Except that I also had to visit the construction site once. But Radhika had some
plans for the weekend made up with Aman and I was totally unaware of it. She
informed me on Friday evening that we had to go for a movie. We couldn't talk
much as mom called her for dinner and she left home soon after dinner as she
had some work to do.

Later around 10.30pm I got a call from Radhika. It was a conference call
but I never knew until Aman spoke.

"So Dhruv, What have you decided?" She asked.

"About what?" I replied.

"About the movie. Are you coming or not?"

"I don't know. I won't be able to wake up so early." I said as I knew at that
moment I was short or money. But Radhika was never going to listen.

"You have to come Dhruv. I don't know anything. We have to reach there by 8.30 only then we will be able to get the tickets. Also I won't be there on Sunday." She said and yes she had another reason for me to convince- she won't be on Sunday.

"Wow! If you have made such plans why to go on Saturday You can leave right now." I said.

"Okay! fine then, I'll go with Aman."

"Now where the hell did he come from?" I said and was interrupted soon.

"I was here listening to both of you." Aman said laughing.

"Saale Kutte …You were listening to everything" I shouted.

"Yes and anyways you don't come I and my janemann will enjoy the movie." He continued to laugh.

"Chup kar saale." I replied.

"Okay! But anyways what I was saying Radhika we would take the corner seats. Those special balcony corner seats right in the very first line. It's amazing."

"Yes and also we'll have caramel popcorn together." She joined him to tease me.

"Caramel I don't like them much so we'll buy cheese once." He said.

"No ways cheese… I am allergic to them, but never mind we'll share it. Or maybe we'll buy both." She added.

"Oye chup karo Saalo! Stop fooling me." I said after listening to all their crazy talks.

"We are not. We are just planning what we would do if we go together." Radhika replied whereas Aman continued to laugh.

"Okay! I am not laughing we are serious." Aman said.

"Fine…! I said. "You people enjoy, I don't have any problem. But I wanted to see that movie. Anyways you people carry on with your plan."

"As it is Mottu you have already seen it after downloading it right."

"Wrong Radhika I just saw a part of it. I didn't see the entire movie."

"Then you can watch the remaining part at home tonight." Aman teased me again.

"No I want to come with you people and okay fine I won't come you people enjoy. I'm keeping the phone." I said.

"Mottu we were just teasing you." Radhika said.

"He kept the phone I think." Aman said as they were not able to hear my voice and I disconnected the phone.

Immediately Radhika called back. I picked up the phone.

"Arre Mottu why are you getting angry we were just teasing you." She said.

"Who said I am angry? I was just about to go upstairs. This Sweety Pluto were behind some dogs so I disconnected the call. Anyways you people enjoy." I said again.

"Okay fine you are not angry but you are coming with us tomorrow." She said.

"Aur haa jyada nautanki mat kar. Otherwise I'll go with her." Aman said it again.

"Chal be saale I am coming. But how are we going together." I asked Radhika.

"I'll come directly to the theatre."

"Okay done. Now disconnect the call I have to do some private discussion with Radhika."

"Okay bye..!" He said and pretended to disconnect the call.

"Radhika you people always make a fool out of me."

"That's because you are easily caught into such things…!" Radhika replied with a smile and Aman began to laugh.

"Aman I told you to disconnect the call. Radhika I think I should call you later he won't hang up." I said.

"Ha ha drama king… Anyways don't ditch or else I and Radhika will enjoy the movie together."

"No ways, this won't happen I am coming. Bye!"

"Okay bye…Bye Janemann…!" He said to finish off with his final round to tease me.

"Bye..!" Radhika said while I cut her in between.

"What bye? Did he really disconnect the call this time?"

"Yes. Now say what did you wanted to say?"

"I love you Radhika…!" I said it with a big smile on my face.

"Is nobody next to you?"

"No…! I am on the streets with Sweety and Pluto."

"That's why you are saying it so loud. I thought so." She said.

"But you know Radhika you should say I love you too and not ask question like who is next to me and stuff like that. You know."

"I know…Very funny Mottu."

"Anyways why so early. You know very well I can't wake up so early. Can't we go a bit late." I asked her again.

"The prices will be too high and I won't be able to afford it. So we are going early. And I don't want anyone else to spend on you so I told Aman we three would go."

"Ok no problem. I'll try."

"No try Mottu, you have to get up anyhow."

"Okay fine and I love you." I said and after 2 seconds of silence.

"I love you too." Replied Radhika.

"I love you two three four." I said which I did every time she replied I love you too.

"So it seems nobody is next to you Radhika. Right?"

"I came outside my room to see you in your shorts." She said laughing.

"Okay bye…I am keeping the phone or else you will start again. Bye… Bye… Bye!" I said and she instructed me once more to be ready tomorrow.

"Don't ditch Mottu… And bye…Good night." She said.

"Bye Radhika..!" I replied and kept the phone.

I came back home along with my pets and later sat down to work on my computer. Around 12.30am I decided to sleep as it could be difficult for me to wake up early in the morning. I setup the alarm for 6.45am and pulled over my blanket. That night I continued to get nightmares that I missed the show and kept sleeping. I used to woke up every 1-2 hours check my watch and then again close my eyes praying to God to wake me up on time. Finally 6.45am alarm began to ring. Unfortunately I pressed the stop button instead of the snooze. I was back into my dreams again where Radhika was trying to wake me up as I was sleeping and was late for the movie. Minutes later I woke up and yes to my surprise it was 7.15am, so I had to immediately jump out of bed and get ready. I took a bath and after wearing clothes I called up Radhika.

"Wake Up Radhika…!" I said as I heard her sleepy voice.

"It's just 8am Dhruv, the movie is at 9.30. Let me sleep for some time." She replied.

"What???" I yelled back to her, "You people fooled me again. You know what I haven't slept the entire night fearing that I might not wake up on time. If you would have told me the exact time atleast I would have slept for some time."

"I know Mottu…But we thought you would be late so we didn't tell you the exact time." She said trying to avoid her laughter and bring some seriousness in her tone. "Anyways I'll be ready soon and will meet you by 8.45. Now let me sleep for some time. Bye!"

"Arre Radhika…! What will I do till then? Wake up…! Get ready and come soon by 8.30 or else pakka I won't come this time." I replied.

"Okay fine…No problem." She said and kept the phone in her own unique way. Well that was her kind of a signal to let me know that she will be there on time and yes that did happen. She called up at 8.30 to confirm if I was ready.

"Five minutes…! I'll be there." I said as I was combing my hair.

"Mottu you are still not ready." She said.

"I am ready…Okay now don't waste my time or else I'll be late." I said and was about to leave when mom's last minute questions were on their way.

"Whom are you going with Dhruv and which movie are you going?" She said.

"3 Idiots" I said searching for my bike keys and avoiding any eye contact with her. "I told you yesterday itself I am going with Aman."

"Radhika is also coming with you?" Now that was the question I was waiting for. "She is at her friend's place." I replied and tried to escape her questions but, you know my mom was always piled up with many questions whenever I was about to leave my house with friends.

"Why are you taking your bike? Can't he come here "This was her next question I mean one after another. I gave her the reason he would be coming directly to the theatre and finally left the house and met Radhika near the Apollo theatre. After narrating her the entire scene at home she had that same old question for me.

"How does your mom know I would be with you...?"

"I don't know." I replied and then we went directly to the movie hall. Aman came directly. Well the movie was a real treat, simply amazing as Amir Khan always rocked so did Radhika for making this movie experience a lifetime memory for me.

11th January 2010, the joining in the new office. I was excited to go so was Radhika for me. I had to reach office by 10am. I woke up with the sound of Radhika's footsteps at 7. Her loud voice always added a smile on my face and I loved this everyday wake up alarm. I spelt for a while but Radhika had to wake me up again through her call. I got out of bed and began to get ready and reached the office by 10.

I approached the help desk and I was asked to reach the 7th floor. I gave a surprised look when I reconfirmed the number. Later, I followed the HR who was walking along with two other guys and we reached the floor where we entered a huge hall. Some new recruiters were seated along the two group of chairs on either side of a projector. We grabbed chairs at the back row while the HR walked along in the front. Within a few minutes she checked up the cable connections and the slides to be displayed and opened one of the introductory slide of the company. Everything was new and yet another experience for me to begin. I was excited but it didn't give me much positive vibes as I had while I was joining Convergys. Well, every company has it's unique code of conduct. But the best part to distract me from my thoughts were girls. Yes, as I had heard early about this company I could see many beautiful faces around. I was waiting for next slide to begin when the slides were interrupted as we all were asked to introduce ourselves. I was listening to every single person the way they introduced themselves till my turn. I began,

"Hi! My name is Dhruv."

"We cannot hear him." A sound came all the way from the front row. I wanted to see who that girl was but at the same time I had to concentrate on my introductory speech so that I shouldn't be a reason for anybody's laughter.

"Yes buddy, your dear friends cannot hear you. Can you speak a bit louder please!" The HR insisted and I wondered when exactly did I make any friend. I tried to speak a bit louder, "My name is Dhruv.. And I was working previously…" I began and the fear within me vanished as I was done introducing myself. I felt a part of these newcomers and felt more relaxed. The session continued where we were guided through the company history and work policies. But being alone I couldn't resist my boredom and wanted to call up Radhika when I heard.

"Ok guys let's take a 20mins break and we will meet up here again where our facilities manager will talk to you."

"Ok whatever just leave us now we are bored." A guy sitting next to me whispered when I looked at him and smiled. Soon I was out and could see many of them rushing towards the washroom. I removed my cellphone and dialed Radhika's number.

"Hello!" She spoke in her usual tone and said, "So Mottu how's the first day going?"

"Radhika this place is horrible. I am bored." I replied.

"Why? What happened?"

"Nothing. I didn't like this place at all. When, will I get a job in animation?"

"Aah! That…" She paused and said, "You will get it once you complete your showreel."

"I know that, what should I do till then."

"Dhruv I was after you to work on your showreel before you join the office. You never felt the need to work on it." She said and immediately she skipped the topic and said, "Why don't you make some new friends Dhruv. You will feel better, maybe then you will like this place."

"I know let's see! But Parth was right this place has awesome girls." I said, "That girl I tell you…"

"What?" She interrupted me and I could sense her tone change which provoked me to continue further.

"I just recalled that song 'Mere Khayalon Ki Malika…' She was that beautiful. Just too good…!" I continued.

"Good…Enjoy then." She said in a jealous way.

"Arre listen there's more…" I tried to annoy her more.

"Ok tell me." She said.

"As this song was still running in my mind there entered this other girl and you can't believe the song that ran in my mind. She is a trainer and she was so hot! No other song suited than this one…Aye Sanam Tere Pyar mein tere ab toh jeena marna hai."

"Good… Enjoy then."

"You are sure that you are not angry Radhika." I tried to confirm her level of anger.

"No. Why will I get angry?" She replied in a calm voice.

"I just thought. Anyways you know it very well I am innocent." I said and began to laugh.

"Yes I know Mottu you are innocent." She was still busy with her work. I sensed the way she would be working in front of her computer with her formal tone. "Ok you continue I have work will talk later."

"Radhika… I knew you would be angry."

"No Mottu I'm not. I seriously have a lot of work."

"I miss you Radhika." I said, "You know the worst part of this company."

"What?"

"The shift-timings from tomorrow. It's 6.30pm to 3.30am. You would come home and I will go."

"No problem Mottu. We'll enjoy the weekends."

"Yes we will, anyways you continue with your work. How much will you talk?"

"What?"

"Nothing, bye."

"Bye Mottu we'll meet in the evening." She said and kept the phone.

I still had some time so was scrolling through my contact list and called up some college friends to inform them about the new job. Later, I went back to my place and was checking the pictures of Radhika and me.

"Girlfriend…?" Well that voice wasn't familiar. It was the guy sitting next to me.

"Ah..! Not… Exactly…! I mean yes she is." I replied and wondered why I was hesitating so much. Well he was a stranger. And I can't just tell every unknown person about my relation. But yes I did tell him.

"I guessed it…! The way you were smiling on every pic you scanned. Anyways I am Ajay." He said.

"Hi…!" I said, "I'm Dhruv. Actually was just going through some old pics. As it is these people are irritating."

"Yes but, just for today. Anyways you are here for I-Yogi right?" He said.

"Yes…" I replied and finally made a new friend at the first day and it ended well.

Next day, I woke up as Radhika gave me an early morning wakeup kiss. Well, I was sleeping in the living room and as there was nobody in the room Radhika didn't want to miss the opportunity to kiss me. Somehow I always loved this early morning wake up kiss. I got up and we talked with each other for a while as mom was filling her tiffin. Later she went to office and I spent the entire day at home.

I was about to leave for office around 6. I wanted to meet Radhika before leaving. She came by 6.05 and we began to talk, as mom was behind me to leave for office. As it was just 15-20mins drive, I thought I would make it in time but I was late. So as everyone always loved to say Dhruv can never be on time, I always lived up their expectations. I rushed to office and met Ajay who was walking along the corridor. We entered into a training room where everyone was seated. The arrangement of this room was different I felt I shouldn't compare it with the training rooms of my previous company but I couldn't help myself. Although I liked the arrangement. The computers were arranged in such a manner close to the walls leaving an empty space in between where the trainers could walk up to each desk. We couldn't grab chairs as the room was over-crowed. We waited till our names were called up by the trainer. I had to stay in the same room, whereas Ajay walked into the other training room along with the other guys whose names had been called. A feel that I wouldn't enjoy the training vanished when our trainer spoke. His name was Arvind and he made the entire batch more lively. So ours was the batch of 20guys which had three girls in it. Arvind gave us the brief idea about the training material and within the next few minutes he gave us our first break. It was hardly an hour we came and had our first break. I felt excited about it as I took my phone to call up Radhika. She was in her hostel reading novel and not a my place, well the reason was simple- I was not at home. Later I made two new friends with whom I played snooker.

Within a flash the first day was about to get over. It was Friday night when I was dialed Natasha's number. Radhika had gone to bed and before I could forget I had to call Natasha. As soon as she picked up the phone I wished her- Happy Birthday. She got happy and to my surprise I was the first one to call her. We spoke for a couple of minutes and later I kept the phone. I was about to get into the training room when one of the three girls from our batch came close to me and stopped looking at me. I was confused!!!

"Hi! My name is Vrushika." She said and let her hand out.

"Hi! I am Dhruv." I said and we shook hands. That felt great…Strange actually.

"I know…" She said, "we three are always talking about you whenever we see you."

"We three?" I questioned when the other two girls came forward and introduce themselves to me. Madhvi and Trupti, they said. They also introduced Zahir who was standing next to them. After the introduction was over I stood quiet staring at each other's faces, I wondered what should be done next.

"Ok…fine! We are here… You know it." Vrushika broke the silence.

"No…I don't know." I replied.

"Come-on now. Aah…!!" Vrushika said being irritated. "We want to be friends with you." The moment she said this she started blushing which made everyone laugh. Friendship with girls in this office would begin in such a way I never thought, but yes, I did feel good. I wanted to call up Radhika but it was late so I tried to control my emotions and when I was about to leave for home Vrushika waved her hand for good-bye and I smiled at her craziness.

Next day morning, as soon as Radhika came home I wanted to jump out of my bed to narrate the entire scene that happened in office, but she was in a hurry. Every Friday she had to reach Hinjewadi and was getting late and my half-sleepy eyes didn't brother to open till she ran downstairs. Later as I woke up I called her and narrated the entire scene. Once I was back in office our trainer gave some good news about the shift timings. 9am to 6pm sounded great! But, getting up early morning was a problem. Not till I had Radhika's early morning ever banging footsteps and my mom's loud voice to wake me up.

I was used to listening Radhika's early morning wakeup sound, it was Saturday and we had no plans except that Radhika informed me about her result which would be declared the next day. I was happy that she would become a CA. On the other hand Radhika was tensed and worried about her result. Her result was very important for both of us. Most important I would proudly say my girlfriend is a CA. Secondly, she will not be leaving Pune for the next one year as she wanted to continue working with Kimberley Clark. That very feel of Radhika becoming a CA gave me a happy feeling and I was lost in my thoughts after I hung up. I prayed to God the next moment closing my eyes for a minute. *"What if Radhika really becomes a CA? Will she still be my girlfriend? Obviously she would. Also, she will be earning much higher than me. But that would never create any differences between us. Right? Never… as she loves me more than anyone."* I said to myself. Radhika was staying at her friend's place for the weekend. I continued with my regular work that day.

17ᵗʰ January 2010, the day finally came. I was excited about her result and had expected a lot from Radhika. But sometimes our expectations take us a long way on an uncertain path that cannot be predicted. Well, the same way one cannot predict Radhika's nature. I called up Radhika but the results were yet to be announced, so I informed her to callback once the results were declared. She called up later.

"So CA …What is the percentage you scored?" I said as soon as I picked up her call. She didn't respond for a while and then replied, "I didn't clear the exams. I failed in both the groups Mottu."

"Radhika don't lie. I know you won't fail." I said.

"I'm not lying Dhruv. I really couldn't clear my groups. I didn't become a CA." She said and started crying.

"Radhika…It's ok. Don't cry." I said trying to stop her from crying. I wanted to meet her so I said, "Let's meet Radhika. Where are you exactly?"

"No Dhruv I don't want to meet you and it's not ok. I have failed the CA finals. It was important for me."

"It's ok…Will you pass if you continue to cry? There's always a next chance. You will get good marks."

"People like Sahil have cleared CA and Shreya also cleared one group. It's me who has failed."

"It doesn't matter Radhika. He passed because you helped him, he wouldn't have done it on his own so be relaxed don't cry." I said and tried to console her through frequent messages throughout the day. Later when Parth called up I made up a plan to meet her. I wanted to be with her during this time as I was equally responsible for her failure.

Later when me and Parth were about to leave she called up Parth and informed him not to come. This was an unexpected change I saw in her for the first time. Though she kept saying, "Mottu I have let you down, that's why I don't want to meet you." I wanted to let her know that was not true by being with her but she completely avoided me that day. As a result I and Parth cancelled the plan to meet her and came back home. Radhika's friend took her to a pub to enjoy that day and to make her feel relax.

Next day, Radhika came home early morning and I was waiting for her to come close to me. Instead she took her tiffin and went straight to her office. Later, I called her to ask the reason for not talking to me.

"You were sleeping Mottu and I was getting late for office."

"It never happened before Radhika. Even if you were late you always try to wake me before you leave." I replied.

"It's not like that." She said, "Anyways I'm waiting for my tickets to be confirmed, I forgot to tell you."

"Which tickets?" I asked.

"I am going back to Jabalpur on the 1st." She said.

I was shocked and surprised that she took a decision to go back home without even discussing it with me. Who was I really in her life? I question stood in front of me. Some questions which never had any answers kept rolling in my mind. I wanted to ask her that very moment, but I kept it for myself. I had to be supportive in her decision so I accepted the fact that she would leave Pune and me once again soon.

*****

Chapter 21

The Last Few Days...

I came to office and Radhika had called up to confirm if I reached on time I had reached before time and was alone in the room. Vrushika entered the room and greeted me good morning, but I didn't respond on which she said. "Where are you lost Dhruv? Everything's fine?"

"Yes. Actually it's Radhika I was thinking about." I said. "Nothing, forget it." I continued.

"Radhika...Is she your girlfriend?" She asked. I smiled and that gave a reason for her to tease me. "What? You actually have a girlfriend?"

"What do you mean? I have a girlfriend. Shouldn't I?" I replied.

"Hey Madhvi listen Dhruv has a girlfriend." She screamed as soon as Madhvi turned the room.

"Are you crazy Vrushika?" I said.

"Wow Dhruv!" Madhvi started. "Who is she? What does she do?" I was trapped and there was no way to escape, so I began telling them the truth.

"Her name is Radhika and yes she is my girlfriend." I said.

"Where did you guys meet?" Madhvi asked.

"Home"

"Home?" Vrushika shouted on top of her voice.

"Come-on now, stop blinking eyes at each other and I'm not telling you anything." I said.

"Why you can't blink your eyes." Madhvi asked

"I cannot." I said and they started laughing.

"What's so funny in this to laugh?"

"Nothing, just that you can't blink an eye is funny." She said and both of them started laughing.

"But seriously I really can't do that." I tried to defend myself.

"Ok Dhruv we are not teasing you and we really want to know about your girlfriend." Madhvi provoked me to continue.

"Come-on Dhruv, we are your friends. You can tell us." Trupti replied as she entered the class. "By the way what are you guys discussing?"

"Dhruv is telling about his girlfriend." Vrushika said and we were again interrupted by the guys entering the class.

"Good morning Guys!" It was Anurag who greeted us.

"Good morning." We replied in chorus.

"Hey Anu could you please go outside for some time, we are discussing some serious stuff here." Vrushika said and asked him to leave.

"Ok fine. Let me know when you guys are free till then I have a drag and come." He said and left.

"Come-on Dhruv you continue before everyone else comes." Vrushika said holding my hands and the other two forced me to continue.

"Ok, but leave my hands. Why are you holding my hand like a girl?"

"What do you mean? I am a girl." She said and punched me on my arm. I got up from my place and began to tell them everything

"Mom runs a household mess and we have girls coming home from the nearby hostel and that's how I met Radhika." I said.

"Your mom runs a mess, that's great. She must be a good cook." Madhvi interrupted.

"Yes, she is cooks great and should I continue." I waited for a reply.

"Yes you continue…" Vrushika replied and looked at Madhvi, "stop interrupting Madhvi everyone will come soon and we won't be able to know everything." I continued to tell them more about Radhika but had to stop as everyone else started coming.

"Dhruv we want to meet her. Can you call her to office?" They said in unison. I looked at the three and thought what I should reply.

"Please don't say no." Vrushika said.

"Ok fine I'll talk with her and let you know." I said and they all went to their respective places I was thinking of how I would tell this to Radhika but yes thinking about Radhika and people who want to meet her made me feel proud for myself and Radhika.

"Where are you Radhika?" I called her as she was on her way to my office the very next day.

"I'm about to reach Adlabs. You come there I won't be able to find your office." She said.

"No problem. As soon as you reach there give me a call." I said and was excited that Radhika was here to meet my friends the very next day. I informed the girls and they were excited too. I went to get Radhika and informed everyone to be present at the gate. She was standing near the Archie's Gallery; I wanted to hug her at that moment but then I just walked towards her with a smile as she waved her hand.

"What did you tell your friends about me?" She asked.

"Nothing…! Actually… everything. They know you are my girlfriend and maybe that's why they wanted to meet you." I replied as we started walking towards my office gate.

"Is it really necessary I should meet them?" She again had a question.

"Come-on Radhika you will like them."

"You and your friends…"

"See here they are." I said and left her hand as we reached. We were greeted by Vrushika with her smile.

"This is Vrushika, Madhvi, and Trupti and then this is…Arre… What's his name? Titan…Oh! I'm sorry he is Raymond and this is Zahir. And everyone this is Radhika." I said.

"Hi…!" Radhika said it with a smile. I was very excited but I tried to resist my feeling within me by just smiling but, I couldn't stop myself from saying anything.

"You will like this guy…He is typical your kind of a guy." I said when everyone was staring at me. "He is an NDA cadet you know."

"Shut-up Mottu." She replied immediately.

"No he is, just that he ran from the training." I said and finally she believed when he spoke and they both started a new conversation.

"My father works in the military as well." She said.

"Where?" Raymond asked.

"Jabalpur."

"Cool!" He said and Vrushika interrupted them.

"Why do you call him Mottu?" She said.

"Because he is one." Replied Radhika with a smile.

"Come-on Radhika… Do I really look that fat?" I said and everyone started laughing. Madhvi remained quiet and kept listening to everyone. We spoke about the movies we watch during the training sessions and the main thing was what Vrushika said changed the entire view point of Radhika which I couldn't do anything,

"You know what your Mottu and me are always roaming in the office holding each other hands. We always call each other girlfriend and boyfriend." She said.

"Although she has a boyfriend." That was the only thing that came all of sudden at that moment from me to handle the situation.

"Good…I didn't know that." Radhika said with a change in tone.

"Arre don't' worry they are just good friends and she is trying to pull your legs." Madhvi finally spoke and did say the right thing to save me.

"When are you cabs leaving?" I asked in order to change the topic after that.

"Actually we are late. Come-on you guys we should go." Vrushika shouted immediately. "Hey Radhika it was really nice meeting you and you have a nice boyfriend.

"You should say I have a nice girlfriend." I said holding back Radhika.

"Yes you are right... You are lucky in that case. Poor Radhika.!" Trupti said and everyone again laughed, I just smiled knowing the joke was on me.

"Okay then we'll leave. We'll see you in the office tomorrow." Vrushika said.

"And Radhika we really enjoyed meeting you, at least I did."

"Bye!!!" Everyone said and so did Radhika with a smile. They all left for their respective cabs and we both started walking towards my bike which was outside the office.

"You know something Mottu last time when I was leaving for Jabalpur there was one girl. Now I am more worried that I am leaving you along with three girls." Radhika said.

"Radhika learn to trust me, I only love you." I said.

"I doubt you don't." She replied.

"Come-on Radhika I brought you here to meet my new friends. Why are you saying like this?"

"Just kidding Mottu. Where's our bike?" She said holding my arm with a smile. I wondered if that was just a joke or did she really mean it.

It was Saturday, after finishing her half-day shift Radhika and I were roaming on my bike. She had her arms wrapped around my waist and I was driving in slow-motion. Well, it is rightly said when in love...life starts rolling in slow-motion. But yes I should confess I always drove my bike in a slow speed. We were about to reach the construction site where the work was in its final phase. The painter had given the first coat of color to the walls. Most of the colors were selected by me for the inner bedroom, kitchen and the living room. We still had to finalize the exterior paint. The color Krish chose for the outer bedroom was looking awesome. We couldn't stop ourselves from clicking pics in that room. I took Radhika's individual pics so that she could upload it on Facebook website and I could on Orkut as I was still having hard time to understand Facebook.

Once the photo session was over Radhika began clicking my pics in the other room where the painter was still working on the final coat. We were waiting for him to finish the work so that can lock the room and go elsewhere or rather we could spend some time together. Radhika was wearing a green t-shirt and blue jeans and I was in black shirt and blue jeans as usual. She was looking hot and I couldn't stop myself from kissing her after the painter left. Later we spent some time on the terrace watching the sunset.

"So where are we going?" I asked Radhika as she sat behind me after we locked all the rooms and were about to leave.

"Anywhere...You say." She replied holding me tight.

"Should we go to guitar class. I haven't met anybody for a long time." I said.

"Not there."

"Why?"

"I don't like it there. I get bored." She said pulling her hands behind.

"Why will you get bored? Everyone likes you and you know them very well."

"We'll go somewhere else. Mottu...I want to spend time with you and not your friends."

"Ok then, you tell me where to go."

"I don't know. Let's go anywhere else."

"We'll leave in 5minutes Radhika. Till then you decide where we can go. I don't recall any place where we haven't been yet." I said and turned my bike to reach the guitar class. I was waiting for some suggestions from Radhika when she replied. "Fine.." The only word when said by a girl a boy should understand it a warning on a board which reads 'Enter at your Own Risk'. I took the risk and tried to check again if she really meant what she said.

"Are you sure, you are not angry...We will leave in 5 minutes. I promise." I said and as she didn't reply in any negative tone I considered everything was normal and grabbed her hand and continued to drive with one hand.

We reached Dev's and were greeted by Harsh. He took us on the 3rd floor and informed us that it was Ajinkya's b'day treat today, so everyone was to meet today. We met Sam and later wished Ajinkya as he joined us. He told us that Aaliya and the others are coming within the next 5minutes. I looked at Radhika and went close to her.

"Can we wait for more 5minutes? Please..." I asked her.

"Ok no problem." She replied which added a smile on my face. We waited for 5minutes when Aman arrived and that helped me as Radhika didn't feel bored or irritated after that. Within the next 10-15 minutes we gather downstairs in the building parking. In between, I continuously kept asking Radhika whether we could stay or leave without meeting the others. She agreed to stay and meet everyone else and as we reached downstairs. Anup, Aaliya, Prasad and Sawaari joined us. Meeting everyone I felt happy as we were pulling each other's legs.

Later, I got a hint from Radhika's face that we should leave so I told everyone that we are leaving.

"Where are you going?" asked Anup.

"We have to go out as we had made some plans earlier. We had come to meet you guys on our way."

"So you are not coming for the party?" Aaliya interrupted.

I wanted to stay but what happed on Aaliya's birthday I never wanted to repeat things again.

"No…!" I replied.

"I tried to convince him but let it be. Let's give the couple some privacy." Harsh added and everyone laughed. Maybe Radhika didn't like it. Aman and Prasad tried to convince Radhika but I stopped them by saying we had an important work. I began to shake hands with everyone as we had formed up a circle. It felt great to meet everyone after a long time but yes the best part was when Aaliya hugged me instead of the shaking hands which actually made me feel confused.

"I am still confused… Why she hugged me?" I said as we came near my bike.

"How would I know? She is your friend." She replied in a rude tone.

"What's wrong? Why are you talking like this?" I said while I started my bike.

"I asked you twice if we should leave or we should stay. You could have told me. We would have left long back."

"I wanted you to meet your friends. Later you shouldn't say I didn't let you meet your friends." She said as she sat behind me.

"Aren't they your friends?"

"No Dhruv they are your friends."

"But can't you see how happy they are to meet you. Anyways did you decide where we are going."

"No. I don't want to go anywhere." She said and I turned off my bike.

"What happen now, Radhika?'

"Nothing, I just don't want to go anywhere. Let's go home. Drop me to my hostel."

"Radhika I asked you to decide a place. You never come up with an option. Also if I say we'll go to CCD, you won't, because you feel I will only keep talking about my past (Mahi) and the time spent with her."

"Am I wrong about that?" She said, "Answer to me Dhruv."

"Fine…! You are right. I'll talk about her, but I'll do it once…twice. Maybe third time I won't talk about her as we would gather our own moments there. We hardly ever talk with each other in such restaurants. All you come up with is we'll go to that garden near Central." I wanted to say everything at that moment in anger but all I said was. "You suggest some place then Radhika."

"I told you we'll go to that garden near Central. But you never like it there."

"Radhika whenever we want to talk we are always in that garden. Can't there be some other place, except that garden?"

"I don't know any such place in Pune, Mottu you have been living here not me."

"I've never been out of my house for the past 20 years. How will I know?" I said, when the fact was I could never come up with a place at any particular moment where I could take Radhika where money won't be a problem. Why was I never able to recall any such place? I always cursed myself at such moments.

"Let it be Mottu. Let's go home. As it is my mood is totally screwed. Thanks to you." She said trying to calm her down.

"Ok fine." I said and started my bike. On our way home we didn't speak a work to each other and I kept thinking. Why do we always end up fighting? I really wasn't able to recall any place where we can go. Maybe I should have agreed to the park. But anyways she won't agree to come now. Maybe, I should wait till her anger is gone. Or should I try to calm her down. Let it be she will fight more. Why should I? I am elder to her and she never listens to me. I don't want to recall Mahi, but she always reminds me of her. What am I doing wrong? Why does she behave like a kid at time? My thoughts couldn't end till we finally reached her hostel.

"Are you coming home for dinner?" I asked as I stopped my bike.

"I don't know." She replied.

"Good. Bye then." I said and drove back home. Maybe, it always that male ego sometime or can say my stupidity that I would never say sorry when it is actually required to make a girl happy. Or maybe I never know I should say sorry for spoiling things at that moment.

Radhika didn't come home that night. She asked her room-mate to get her tiffin and she ate dinner at hostel. Don't know why but I slept without eating anything.

"Saale K K…" Radhika said as I picked up her call early morning. KK which actually meant Kutte Kamine, the only abusive words in her dictionary which she loved to express her anger in joy. "Why didn't you call me?"

"Just like that…" I replied. "Even you didn't call me. I was waiting for your call and for you at home."

"I was busy with office work. I had told you." She replied.

"You never said anything about work."

"I did tell you yesterday that's why I wanted to come home."

"Oh I forgot! You had told me when we were at our new home. But you were angry yesterday."

"I was not angry Dhruv. I just didn't want to meet your friends. I wanted to be with you and spend some time together. And why do you always keep forgetting things?"

"That's the way I am."

"Like always your favorite line. Anyways you know I didn't even eat anything yesterday. Don't tell kaku."

"Good. Anyways she is here; you want to talk with her." I said as mom entered my room.

"Who is it?" Mom asked.

"It's Radhika." I said.

"Doesn't she have any work? Come home quickly. I have to go out in the afternoon." She shouted.

"I don't have work. Today it's Sunday." She said and I repeated her words back to mom. Mom gave me a weird look and went out. I never had to repeat what mom said. Her loud voice can be easily heard by the person on the other side of the line.

"She left." I said, "I forgot to tell her. Anyways you tell me the reason and I'll let her know."

"No please Mottu don't tell kaku. She will kill me."

"Good. Anyways can you tell me the reason?"

"I was working so I wasn't aware of the time. I called up Hema didi she was at your place so I told her to get the tiffin. But later didn't feel like eating it alone."

"Good."

"Everything is good for you. Even if worst things happen the only word you know is good."

"Aisa hi hoo mein…But did I tell you not to eat anything. Mom Radhika didn't eat her dinner yesterday." I shouted.

"Mottu are you mad. I won't talk with you…Bye."

"Relax Radhika there's nobody in the room. Anyways what is your plan today?" I asked.

"Nothing as such. Maybe will go to camp with Adeena in the evening around 4. Parth had also called up so will be meeting him as well." She replied.

"Good. Enjoy then." I said and stayed quiet for a while my computer restarted.

"Look who is fighting and getting angry now." Radhika said immediately.

"I'm not fighting. You have made your plans so enjoy."

"Ok then, I'll meet you in the afternoon when I come home will leave for camp."

"Good." I replied.

"See again 'good'. How many times you use this word?" She said.

"Ok bye I have work to do, will meet you in the afternoon." I said and immediately kept the phone. I wondered why I did this then figured out was missing on something so immediately picked up the phone and dialed her number again.

"Are you seriously going?" I asked Radhika.

"Yes Mottu. I have promised them."

"Good then enjoy." I said again and kept the phone. I moved the mouse cursor on the screen. I right-clicked and selected refresh. I did this this for about 10-15times and pushed the drawer back and dialed her number again.

"Radhika I know you are doing this purposely. Can't you avoid that friend of yours for few days. As it is she is coming to Jabalpur the next week. You can meet her there. I won't disturb you guys." I said.

"I know but I've promised her."

"Good" I said and she started laughing.

"Again good Mottu…" She said and continued. "I'll meet her late. Now you decide where we should go."

"This is not fair Radhika. Every time I have to decide. Ok fine let's go for a movie."

"No Mottu, I don't have money for a movie."

"Ok fine then let's go to Pantaloons. I have to buy a kurta for myself."

"That will be fine. Even I have to buy something for bhaiyu." She said. That lightened a smile on my face and finally things were again sorted out properly. I put on some music and then began to give my pets a bath. I was rubbing soap on Sweety's body when Radhika stood behind me and kept her hands on my shoulder and said, "Kya kar raha hai Mottu?"

"You came so early."

"Yes." She replied.

"Where are you roaming Radhika?" Mom asked her.

"Nowhere Kaku. We are just going to eat breakfast." She replied.

"When will you people come for lunch?"

"We'll come soon." She said and left. Later, we both left for Pantaloons after lunch and continued to peek into the variety of clothes which were on display there. I got a black top and asked Radhika to try.

"Mottu it's too short." She replied immediately.

"You would look amazing in it."

"But where will I wear it and go?" She said still hesitating to wear the top.

"That's why I'm trying to tell you. Wait till 14th, we'll go out for a candle-light dinner." I replied looking at some unique collections.

"No Mottu I have to clear my CA finals this time."

"I know and I won't be in contact this time like before. You have to study really hard this time. Anyways go and try it once." I said and dragged her into the trail-room. Few minutes later she called me while I was checking something, right next to the trail room. I looked at her and my mouth dropped out. I went close to her and before I could say anything Radhika spoke, "I'm not looking good in this."

"Should I tell you the truth?" I asked and waited for her reactions.

"Yes." She said and screamed like a child. "Quickly I'll change."

"I feel like kissing you this very moment Radhika. You look amazing." I said and I went more close to her.

"Kuch bhi yaar." She replied.

"No. Seriously, let's buy this one."

"I don't have money Dhruv."

"So that's the reason I am telling you. Wait till 14th, I gift you this with my first salary." I said.

"It's too costly Mottu. Let it be."

"It doesn't matter. Anyways if not this Valentine, then next Valentine or maybe on your b'day I'll gift you this one."

"But you are going to gift me that teddy right?"

"Which teddy?" I said when she walked out of the trail room.

"The one you clicked my picture with."

"So what are you crazy? You would only get a photo frame of that teddy." I said and we left Pantaloons still arguing about the teddy. Later we went to the construction site where Krish had called up a plumber to get the final tap fittings done. Till he came Radhika and I enjoyed kissing each other and later were waiting for him on the terrace. I was happy that Radhika didn't meet her friend and spent the entire day with me.

25th January 2010, there was nothing special about this day but some incidents make a day special in its own way. Maybe sometimes the worst day to forget, this was one of it. It was just a normal morning day shift in office. The training was going normal when our trainer felt the need to talk.

"How many of you actually like this shift?" He said. Everyone was quiet and didn't utter a word.

"It means nobody likes this shift." He said again. "Come-on speak up guys as I really hate this shift it makes me feel sleepy."

"It's not like that Arvind we like this shift but only problem is getting into the cabs early morning." One of us finally said something. I was quiet and continued to listen.

"So you people want to get back to the night shift? Or do you want to continue this shift?" He asked everyone.

"Actually night shifts are better Arvind. We can atleast enjoy the movies." Vrushika said and everyone laughed. I felt a need to participate and put forth my opinion before he changes the shift timings. I had no problems as I could get time to spend with Radhika in the evening. But before I could stand up to say anything Arvind spoke so that we do not get diverted from the topic of discussion.

"It's not about watching movies. There's hardly anything in the training course. If we work in night shifts I can take you guys to WI jack the calls and you can know how stuff actually works on the floor. After all it how you crack a sale even if you are not technically sound."

"We have no problems Arvind. We actually love to sleep in the morning." Someone spoke again and I wondered why these people were generalizing their statements. They could simply use 'I' instead of 'we'. But after sometime Arvind went outside to discuss with the other trainer and the shift timings were decided-8.30pm to 5.30am. I didn't like the decision but now I had no choice. Also 26th January would be celebrated as traditional day was announced by Arvind.

I came back home in the evening and took Radhika and Krish along with me to buy a traditional kurta. We were roaming in Pantaloons and after a long search we finally found kurta. I pointed out to the black top while Radhika was standing beside me. Krish was clueless what we were up to. We soon came back home and mom was waiting for dinner. Dad had gone out for some work. We were quietly eating watching the television when suddenly Radhika recalled something.

"Kaku I am going to adopt your son." She said and I continued to stare at her with my eyes popping out to check if she actually meant it. But then she continued to give her reasons for the same.

"Yes take him and keep him n your hostel." My mom said which confused me on what these two were up to.

"I wish I would have but boys are not allowed in our hostel, or else I would have taken him." She said and it reminded me about the famous TV serial Sarabhai vs. Sarabhai and the guy who always would end up saying momma in his own unique tone. I could have said the same but I ended up saying, "Are you crazy Radhika? I won't come with you. Come on finish your food."

"Nahi kaku I'll take him once I get my own flat." Radhika was in her own mood today as she said this.

"But God only knows kya hoga Dhruv ka." Mom said.

"Why?" Radhika asked and I wanted to know why my mom said so.

"You always underestimate him kaku." She said and I was happy she was talking for me. Like I always said History repeats itself in various forms. Few months back it was the same discussion between mom and Mahi and now it was Radhika who was talking about me. Maybe that's why I always loved these girls they couldn't tolerate anybody underestimating me, even if it was my mom.

So the discussion between mom and Radhika continued and I never thought the funny talks would turn up into something serious and would change the entire mood of the environment.

"She only has problem with my friends coming home." I said to some point of the talk.

"Yes, even I have seen this myself. Parth came home and you didn't even ask him for tea or coffee." Radhika tried to support me but that turned on Krish and he got angry.

"How dare you talk like that? Do you know anything what she does and what she doesn't?" He shouted on Radhika.

"He ends up getting every friend at home. I'm not a free person to run behind every friend of his. But still I do for everyone." Mom's tone changed and everything seemed to be getting tensed.

"Come-on she was just kidding." I said and tried to calm down everyone.

"No but who gave her the rights to say anything like this to mom." Krish said and I felt like smashing his face at that moment for continuously cribbing on stupid things.

It's rightly said angry spoils everything and that's what happened, these two got angry on some stupid remark passed by Radhika and it changed everything. I wasn't able to talk on behalf of Radhika even though I wasn't in favor of mom and Krish. I knew Radhika wasn't wrong but the thing was she spoke at the wrong time. She left immediately after she finished her dinner and didn't talk much just said sorry to Krish and mom.

"You know it's been like this right from childhood. Vishal doesn't come upstairs for the same reason. But forget it Radhika it wasn't your fault." I said while I was trying to stop her from crying.

"Where are you?" She said.

"I'm downstairs with Sweety and Pluto." I said.

"Good. Then it's ok or else she would have problems with you talking to me."

"Forget it Radhika."

"You know Dhruv if this continues we better stay away from them I can't handle such things."

"As you wish Radhika." I said, "But at least smile now."

"I am not crying Dhruv. I felt bad and didn't expect such things to happen."

"Neither did I Radhika." I said and wondered if I would really stay away from my family or will things be back to normal. A small fight can't change a person's way of thinking for others like the way it changed in this case. Radhika started ignoring mom and mom didn't find her a nice girl. Why? Because, she said something that was right or maybe it was totally a wrong timing. Something were meant to happen but I wasn't ready for this and never wanted such things to happen.

Next day being the republic day I woke up with the loud noise of patriotic songs being played in the next lane. Also I was able to see the schools kids going to their respective schools. Sometimes these things lead us into the nostalgic moments of childhood. But soon we are brought back into reality when I recalled things that happen last night. Soon my mind was diverted to last night's incident which made me think more about Radhika. I knew that somewhere in the corner of my mom's heart she liked Radhika and always expected something from her. Well we also keep expectations from people whom we like and who are important to us. I still thought things will be fine soon and everyone would forget what happened last night. I was trying to deviate my mind while I was in the window watching everyone. But as I failed to bypass my mind I came back to bed and started folding my blanket. Krish came near and showed me a message on his cell phone. "I'm sorry Krish. I didn't mean to hurt you. You're just like my younger brother with whom I share a lot of stuff. This won't happen again. I'm really very sorry."

I gave back his cell phone without saying anything. Stupid crazy Radhika I can never understand this girl, why does she have to say sorry when it wasn't her fault? I said to myself as I went inside and kept my pillows and blanket properly on the rack.

"See she didn't even come today to take her tiffin." Mom said as I was searching for tooth-paste. She was busy preparing food and maybe she was expecting Radhika to come as she always did every morning.

"It's 26th January. She has a holiday." I said as I began to brush my teeth.

"Ok! So is she coming in the afternoon?" She asked.

"I don't know. Maybe she will come." I replied.

"I am not going to cook rice. Tell her to eat whatever I have prepared." She said and I recalled Radhika never had a problem with whatever mom cooked she had always praised the food she cooked even if mom had cooked something I didn't like, Radhika would always like it and would always say kaku this was very good. But today why was mom had to say these things?

"What time is she coming?" She asked again.

"I don't know." I said and was trying to concentrate on brushing my teeth.

"She was going to come early today, she didn't even call me. Just look how much ego she has…" She said and spit the water out sensing did I hear something stupid.

From the day Diya had left mom's nature had always been unpredictable. She always needed her daughter who could help her and from the day Diya left mom was doing the entire household work alone. Mahi used to help but later it was always Radhika. But as the girls kept leaving one after another it was getting difficult for mom to manage all the expenses and would soon make her angry. Maybe yesterday's fight was the outcome of the same. I wanted things to settle down things as soon as possible but till the time I don't get a proper job it was difficult to manage. Radhika came in the afternoon for lunch and later we spent some time together. Mom was out for her work and came back in the evening. Radhika didn't come in the evening as I wasn't there and she asked her friends to get her tiffin in hostel. As I reached office I was able to see that Madhvi and Trupti ditched Vrushika and came in their regular attire. Vrushika was wearing a nice saree and she looked different. She complimented me for looking nice in the new kurta, whereas many asked me from where I bought it. Later Vrushika and I went together to drink coffee as our trainer gave us a break. While we were drinking coffee I thought of clicking some pictures together along with Vrushika, Madhvi did the honor for us. There I saw the most amazing girl walk into the pantry in a beautiful while silk saree. She was from the other batch. Vrushika spoke with her and I came to know her name. Mridula- it sounded strange but I had never heard such a name. Well every girl I knew had strange names. She left within a few minutes so did the thought of staring her wiped of my mind. Never did I bother to go and peep out the pantry for the last time to get a glimpse of her. Later we went to the training room and the traditional day ended with watching a movie and getting some more knowledge about the process from Arvind.

Next day, it was 7.20am when Radhika came home. It was quiet early than what Radhika would usually come. Her normal time was 7.50am. This time it wasn't her sound but my mom which made me wake up.

"Why do you get so angry?" I heard my mom say to her.

"No Kaku I wasn't angry."

"So why didn't you come home yesterday?" She asked her.

"I was at my friend's place." Radhika said and she came out. "Wake up Mottu."

"Let me sleep." I said while I hold her hand and mom came out. I left her hand and Radhika stood up.

"If Kaku gets angry and scolds you is that the way you get angry?" She said and I loved the way they were arguing with her. Maybe the same like the mother and daughter relation. Daughter –in-law to be precise.

"Kaku I am not angry and I said sorry." Radhika said and went close to mom and hold her hand.

"Sorry won't work. You have to get ice-cream."

"Tomorrow on you birthday. Pakka!" Radhika said immediately.

"Radhika!!! Chocolate ice-cream!!!" I shouted.

"Dhruv not you, it's not your b'day." She said and continued, "We don't like chocolate ice-cream. Which flavor you want kaku?"

"Butterscotch!!" Mom replied.

"Ok I'll get it and don't give to this Mottu. He's getting fat day by day."

"I'll eat it anyway. Aren't you getting late for office?" I said and got up from bed. Radhika took her tiffin and went to office. I drank a glass of water and went back to sleep after messaging Radhika to call me after some time to wake me. The smile on my face concluded that I was happy for whatever happened at this moment and maybe things couldn't be more perfect like these small fight. Just forgive and forget!!!

"So where are we going Radhika?" I asked Radhika.

"We have to get my sweater from my cousin in Pimpri." She said.

"It's too far." I said while we were still discussing where to go. Radhika would hold me tight and try to convince me as I continued to trouble her by saying we'll go somewhere else. Finally after a few minutes I got her to the road which led us directly towards Pimpri. That had brought up a smile on her face and she hold me more tightly with her arms around my waist. I was driving my bike with normal speed so as there wasn't much traffic on road I hold her hand close to my heart and kissed it.

"Radhika...I'm hungry. Let's eat something first." I said after a while.

"Why are you always hungry Mottu?"

"I haven't eaten anything. Ok fine go and ask that guy if he knows about the building we are searching for." I said as I we had reached Pimpri. I saw the way the guy was guiding her making various hand movements and I made me realized we had come far from the destination.

"Mottu we had to take a right turn from that signal." She said when she came back and maybe we hadn't come too far.

"Ok fine." I said. "But now we'll have to go straight and then take a U-turn." On our way I saw Mc Donald's restaurant which tempted me and asked Radhika if she could get a parcel. I stood on my bike as there wasn't a place to park. She quickly went inside a brought a parcel for which I felt like kissing her in order to thank her. But again I kept my emotions away by passing some sarcastic comments.

We immediately headed towards her cousin's place; Radhika went upstairs to meet her cousin and gave me the parcel. It smelled great and I couldn't wait much longer. Every time I avoided the smell my hands would still try to open it. But I would still control them. But after a few minutes I wasn't able to control myself and was about to pull out a finger chip when Radhika came out with a guy.

"Who's this?" I said to myself dropping that chip in the box.

"Mottu meet my cousin." She said, "Yes this is Dhruv." I liked the way she stressed herself with a smile on my name. Few minutes of talk and we were back on our way still deciding where to go and when I began to sing.

'Hathon ki lakeeron me aa chupa le mujhe,
kar na paye fir koi juda bhi hamein,
Ho... Ho... Ho...
Hathon ki lakeeron me aa chupa le mujhe,
*kar na paye fir koi juda bhi hamein...*One of my favorite song by Falguni Pathak.

"Mottu why are you singing this song from morning? That too the same line again and again." Radhika interrupted me.

"That's because I like this song...*Hathon ki lakeeron mein...*" I began singing again. It was getting cold and Radhika had her hands inside the front pockets of my jacket. She gripped me tightly and said, "Arre Mottu why are you singing that same line again and again. It's so irritating."

"Ok fine. I won't sing again." I said and was still humming the words softly.

"Nahi na Mottu. Please!!!" She said and I finally stopped singing. I never knew why I was singing this particular song but yes the lyrics had a strong impact on me. I didn't want her to leave me and only wanted her to hold me more tightly just the way she was at that moment. We reached the park near Pune Central on the University road and we finally ate the burger and chips. I was holding her hand after feeding her a bite from my share. People who were in the park form their regular evening walk continued to stare at us. I knew we hadn't done anything great but, being with her made her feel special which I could see it in her eyes that day.

"Come-on let's leave." I said and we left. She bought the ice-cream and we reached home where mom was waiting for us.

31st January 2010, the final day to spend with Radhika. I didn't made any special plans even though I wanted to. So it was just the normal Sunday where I was giving bath to my pets when Radhika came home. Every time she came home I always had that dying smile which would light up as soon as I heard her voice when she walked in through the staircase.

"So are you done with your packing?" Mom asked her.

"Yes." She replied.

"When are you coming back?" I don't think mom really wanted to know the answer for this question, but as soon as Radhika said four months, I came out and pushed her from back.

"Go right now. Don't come back." I said in order to tease her.

"I won't be coming back for you. I'll come to meet you kaku." She replied back.

"Ok fine." I replied but wondered if she really meant it.

"You will have to come to our new house now." Mom said.

"When are you shifting there?" She asked immediately.

"Next months." Mom replied.

"Why do you want to know? We'll go whenever we feel. You go home." I said again trying to interfere. "What is your problem Mottu?" She said, "Kaku just look at him how he is teasing me."

"You are leaving Pune so that's why he is teasing you." She replied.

Later I continued with my work and we all had lunch together along with Radhika. Maybe that was the last lunch along with her in this house. She went back to her hostel and we made up plan to meet up at the bridge spot. I made an excuse of going for guitar class, although mom enquired why I was leaving at 4. Radhika and I went to the new house, I had got the bedrooms cleaned we could sit there talking with each other. I rolled out a mattress on the floor and got Radhika to sit beside me. Few minutes later we both laid down into each other's arms. I kissed her on her forehead and grabbed her more close to me.

"Don't go Radhika…I will miss you a lot." I said.

"I know Mottu. But it's just a matter of few days." She said and we continued to talk with each other and soon I was able to hear every single breath she took. Her heart-beat would increase rapidly as I began to move my hand around her bare skin. Goosebumps piled up on her body and as I moved my hand around her face to move the single bunch of hair Radhika gave me a naughty smile. I kissed her and she responded back quickly with yet another kiss. We were once again lost into each other and I forgot that Aman wanted to meet Radhika and I had told him to come here. Radhika got her hair tied up properly and we folded the mattress back and went upstairs on the terrace. Aman came within the next 5minutes and later I clicked a picture of the two without giving them prior intimation about the same. Radhika shouted back not to click any picture but I wanted to capture her into my mobile camera just to remember this moment we spend together.

I knew Radhika would go back to her hostel after some time as her train was in the morning the next day. I wanted her to be with me for more time and then go late to her hostel which she always did. But she wasn't ready for it. I was thinking of something to convince her while she was talking with Parth on the phone. Aman continued to smile and I couldn't make from her funny smile why he wanted to meet Radhika the so called janemann as the always said to each other. Parth always had some crazy plans even though I wasn't in full favor of them I had to agree to it.
"Parth is coming to pick you at Somwar Peth." Radhika said as soon as she kept the phone.
"Why? Where are we going?" I asked.
"Mahabaleshwar.!" She said.
"What??" I shouted back. "Are you guys crazy? You have a train to catch tomorrow. Right?"
"Yes, but he said we'll go to Mapro garden for dinner and then come back. So I said its fine with me."
"Wow!! Fine with you." I said and paused for a moment. "Is he crazy? Anyways why didn't he call me?"
"Your phone was out of coverage."
"Oh!! Ok I had turned the offline mode on for some time..." I said and stopped myself as I noticed we weren't alone. Aman was standing right next to us. Even though the plan sounded weird I agreed to go as maybe this could be the last night out with Radhika.
"You coming?" I asked Aman.
"No. You guys enjoy I'll go to class."
"Ok and tell everyone that I am not coming today."

"Yes I will tell them you are going to Mahabaleshwar along with Radhika."
"Oye don't or they will start it again."
"Come-on Radhika. Let's leave or else we would get late." I said in excitement.
We left the place soon and Aman left for guitar class. As soon as I reached home
I turned on my computer and started selecting songs to make a mp3 disc. As
Parth came home I took my blanket along with some bed sheets. I also took the
keys of the new house. Mom was out so I informed dad that I was leaving for
Mahabaleshwar along with Convergys friends. I got into his car and later we
picked up Radhika who was waiting for us away from her hostel.
"Here this one is for you. I have added all the songs that you like. Also I have
added some of my favorites. You would like them" I said as I gave the mp3 disc
to Radhika and gave another disc to Parth which he inserted into his music
system.

Finally we left for Mahabaleshwar and I was happy that I would be able to
spend the entire night along with Radhika, thanks to Parth. We shared a lot of
things together while I was still trying to find out that one song which I had
selected for Radhika.
"Ye kya songs hai. Can't even understand a single word. Radhika don't listen
to that disc. Horrible choice Duksey." Parth said
"Come-on people these songs are from that new folder I got from a friend in
Ventura. I am still trying to figure out the good ones. My choice is not that bad
Radhika knows it." I tried to defend myself.
"Ok fine. Atleast change the song and put on something which we can
understand." He said.
I continued to skip the tracks which were new until I found the track I was
searching for.
"Hey Radhika this song is dedicated for you." I said and I relaxed back
increasing the volume a bit. Radhika was seated next to Parth and was watching
through the window. They continued to talk with each other while I wondered
if she would listen to the lyrics at least once. '*Why you wanna go...*'

At that moment, I just wanted to hug her tightly and tell her not to leave me
as I would miss her a lot. I wanted to shout it loud enough to let her know my
inner feelings. How much I care for her…And how badly I need her. But then
boys never disclose their emotions so easily and hence I controlled my emotions
and changed the song.
"What happened? Why did you change the song?" Radhika said.
"Just like that. It's boring. Anyways we'll listen to some Bollywood tracks."
I said with a smile. After a while I was quietly listening to the songs while I

kept my eyes constantly on the highway and the car's speedometer as Parth was driving with quiet a good speed.

"What happened Duksey?" He said to which I replied nothing with a smile. I was lost in my thoughts and while we were just a few kilometers away, Parth raised the volume of his music system as the song began to play. *'Tu hi haqeeqat ...'*

It was one of my favorite track and while Parth was driving on the curvy roads I was eagerly watching as I was tired sitting in the car for a long time. It was dark everywhere and I checked the time it was 8.45pm as we finally reached Mahabaleshwar as the song ended. We reached in time as the Mapro garden was just about to get closed. We gave our order and were waiting for it. Most people were on their way back home and the place turned to be quiet.

We finished eating and later I sat inside the car on the driving seat. During this time I recalled the previous night-out when I and Radhika were on the back seat kissing each other. I wanted to leave the place soon but Parth sat behind and within seconds he was off to sleep. Radhika sat beside me and I held her in my arms and watched the within covering our car slowly. After a while Parth woke up and we left for Pune. Radhika went off to sleep on the back seat.

Parth began to drive the steep slope with constant speed as I watched the deep valley lightened up with few lights. I turned back to Radhika and noticed her sleep like a baby. I moved the hair back from her face and was again lost in my thoughts. Radhika was my dream come true. I said to myself and I had become totally dependent on her. I would never let her go away from me. And if she did I would lose myself and maybe everything I want to achieve in life. While I was lost in my thoughts I totally forgot Parth was sitting beside me and was watching me smile and talk to myself.

"What happened Duksey?" He asked.

"Nothing. Just look at her how she is sleeping like a baby." I replied.

"Let her sleep. She has to leave early tomorrow."

"Yes I know." I said and lowered the volume.

"What's going between you two?" Radhika said opening her eyes.

"Nothing Radhika. You sleep we weren't talking about you?" Were we?" I said patting her back.

After some time, I dozed off while Parth continued to drive without disturbing the two of us. Later he woke me up as we came close to Pune and I was surprised he got us back within 2hours. I showed him the way to our new home and finally we were back in town. I got down to open the gate while Parth helped Radhika to get her bag off the car.

"You guys sleep. I'll come back by 5.30am." Parth said after I opened the gate and kept Radhika's bag inside.

"Are you crazy? Where are you going?" I shouted immediately.

"I have some work to do."

"At this time. Don't lie Parth."

"I'm telling the truth Dhruv. My friend just called up. Don't worry I'll be back on time." He said while Radhika was listening to us.

"Parth if I miss my train. You have to come all the way to Mumbai to drop me." Radhika said as she stood close to me.

"Parth come late. We'll go to Mumbai. But why the hell are you leaving?" I said as I didn't want him to leave. I had planned the entire night out in such a way that once we reach home we would be playing cards and would spend the entire night talking with each other.

"I seriously have work to do. You guys enjoy." He said and I like a dumb wasn't able to understand what we two would do. Obviously I would go to sleep. But somehow I liked his decision as it strike me later that now I could spend this final night with Radhika and there would be no one to disturb us.

Parth left us with a promise that he would come soon and I still had few more hours to go. We went upstairs and kept her bag in the living room and went upstairs in the bedroom. Radhika changed her clothes and came inside wearing a loose white t-shirt and 3-4th track pants while I was setting up the mattress for us to sleep. She looked amazing. Immediately I hold her hands and hugged her. Later we both got into a single blanket as it was very cold outside. Within the dark I could still feel her natural beauty. I gently moved my hand over her face and kissed her and she hugged me tightly.

"Radhika this time when you come back I promise that everything will be fine. I'll work hard to get a job into animation. You study hard and become a CA." I said.

"Yes Mottu I will." She said and I kissed her again. She moved more close in my arms and within some time we both were into deep sleep. After some time I woke up and could sense the most amazing feeling of Radhika being in my arms. I could feel every particle of air inhaled and exhaled through us as if the time had frozen for us. I wiped of the tear drop that rolled down my eye and moved back the hair off the face.

"Kya hua Mottu?" Radhika said as she opened her eyes.

"Nothing. Don't ever leave me Radhika."

"I won't." She said and kissed me again. This time we kissed over and over again and every time the kiss were getting better than the previous ones. We were lost into each other as I later checked the time. It was running fast. It was already 4.30 and Parth would call up soon. I closed my eyes and later my phone began to ring. It was Parth. I wasn't able to understand how an hour vanished within a flash of second.

"Hey Duksey I'm reaching there in 10-15minutes. Be ready." He said as I picked up his call.

"Ok!" I said and cut the call. I kissed Radhika again realizing maybe she won't be here or maybe I didn't want to waste a single moment of my desperation. My phone rang again and as I picked up the call Parth informed me to come down.

I got up and saw that Radhika was already dressed up so I got ready and we came downstairs. We got her bag back into the car and reached Station. Parth parked his car and we got her into the train. Now it was the time to wave off the final good bye. But before I could say anything Parth began giving instructions. "Radhika… Take care and study hard. Give a call when you reach home and start studying seriously. Don't eat anything from the train. Take care." He said and I knew Parth was always this caring right. I never knew what exactly I should say when someone close to our heart is leaving us. Just don't leave me would come from my side. But these thoughts again were in my mind at the wrong time. I realized there were many things that I needed to tell Radhika. About every moment I hurt her and made her cry. I wanted to tell her that she meant a world to me. And now that she would be gone I would be left alone. So as Parth shook hands with her I wiped off those thoughts again. Radhika knew I would hug her at that time.

"Mottu not here. People are watching." She said.

"Forget it I don't care." I said and hugged her without listening to her. She hugged me in return. Radhika would never show her affection in public and I always loved her for that. But this time she did and I liked it.

"Bye Radhika…Take care and call me when you reach home.

"Don't keep calling her Duksey. Let her study this time." Parth said as he punched my arm.

"I have promised her. I won't. Come-on let's go." I said and we got off the train. The train left for Mumbai and as we came out of the station I recalled the last time I came to drop her when she was leaving with her parents. This time she was alone so I was a bit worried but, something else was still in my mind. I look up at the sky.

"No… I don't want such things to happen. Whatever thoughts you are putting in my mind, get them out. I love her and want her back. She should come back for me." The fear that she would change once she comes back was there somewhere in the corner of my heart. I never wanted to lose her so I didn't talk much about it even with Parth. He dropped me home and I went off to sleep when again Radhika woke me up. This time it was her sms… 'Mottu I reached Mumbai.'

*****

Max

Chapter 22

Missing Radhika...

1st February 2010...Radhika had reached Mumbai and was still travelling towards Jabalpur. I wasn't able to focus my mind as continued to think about Radhika the entire day. As I reached office I sensed something different today. I gave the strawberries to Madhvi I got from Mahabaleshwar. It made her smile and I informed her to keep it with her so that we can share it with Trupti and Vrushika as they come. Later when I was trying to concentrate on the topic taught by our trainer I saw the three enjoying the strawberries. I felt a bit weird as I found out that the three had begun to ignore me. I wasn't able to understand the reason behind it so I decided not to pay attention to them. I called up Radhika in the break but her cell was out of reach. Maybe, she might have switched it off or maybe network issue. I felt alone so went upstairs and joined the guys playing pool. Somehow I forgot what happened downstairs and was happily enjoying or rather was forcing myself to enjoy. Somewhere that question kept hammering in my mind, 'what did I do wrong for such a strange reaction from these girls?'

The break ended and I went downstairs but found that the break was extended so the guys left for a smoke. I went into the pantry to grab a cup of coffee. There I found these enjoying their talks and stopped as soon as I entered. I tried to push the button for coffee when Vrushika said that the machine wasn't working. I cursed it in my mind and came outside without uttering a word. Vrushika could bare this kind of ignorance and came behind me. She called my name and I turned back with a fake smile on my face.

"What happened Vrushika?" I said.

"What's wrong with you Dhruv? Why are you ignoring us?" She said.

I smiled at her and said, "Wow! I am ignoring you....?"

"Yes you are Dhruv." She said.

"I'm wondering about it the entire day. What exactly did I do wrong? You girls are ignoring and not me."

"We are not ignoring you Dhruv. We just wanted you to be with other guys as I thought you are only roaming with us and not your friends. That's why we wanted to stay away from you for a while, but you took it the other way round. I never thought you would completely ignore us in such a way." She said and

I was carefully listening to her thinking maybe she was right to some extent. Maybe I was giving too much of important to these girls. But then she was completely right.

"You actually thought that way Vrushika? Then you really don't deserve to be my friend in that case. Let me decide whom I should be with and I hate when people ignore me for such stupid reason. You should have told me I would have stayed away from you people." I said.

"I am sorry Dhruv. I didn't mean to hurt you." She said and I was left back with a thought that just ignoring these girls made Vrushika fight with me and now she was begging for forgiveness. I forgave her and later things were back to normal as Madhvi and Trupti joined us and we were into the training room. Later I decided maintain the distance. I wanted to talk with Radhika so as soon as her messaged popup on my screen I dialed her number and came out of the training room.

"What are you doing Radhika?" I said.

"Nothing. Was reading a book, will sleep after sometime." She said.

"Which book?" I asked immediately.

"2 States."

"Hey I want that book after you come back." I said and hearing her voice made me feel relaxed and happy and I told her about the incident that took place and later told her how happy I felt from inside when Vrushika was begging to forgive her.

"You are so rude at times Dhruv." She said.

"I know...Aisa hi hoo mein. But you know I didn't like the way they behaved so I ignored them and my trick worked." I said.

"Good." She replied.

"Anyways why aren't you sleeping?"

"People are snoring so loudly that I couldn't sleep. Also I didn't feel like sleeping. Anyways you continue with your work."

"What work? We are watching a movie right now." I said.

"Do you people ever work?"

"We do Radhika but anyways you sleep and call me later."

"Yes, but I'll call you once I reach home." She said.

"When will you reach Jabalpur?" I asked.

"Tomorrow morning."

"Fine then this is the last call and start studying once you reach home. Bye good night."

"Bye Mottu." She said and I disconnected the call. I was about to enter the room and Vrushika opened the door and came out.

"What are you doing out? Come let's go for a walk." She said in her unusual tone.

"What?" I shouted.

"Let's go for coffee." She said. I walked along with her and somewhere in my mind was still thinking about Radhika and waiting for her call.

Next day morning, I woke up at 7.30am, same time when Radhika would come home banging the steps. I was going to miss that early morning moment when she would come home for her tiffin and sometime would kiss to wake me up. I couldn't say this to anyone so I kept it for myself and slept back. But some things never change I woke up again as my cell beeped. It was a message from Radhika. 'Mottu I reached home. Will call you later as am very tired. Will start studying soon as Dhaval Bhai is coming next week. I am so excited. Love you bye.'

Anything that came from Radhika early morning always lit up a smile and a message that carried *'Love You'* along with it doubled the ratio of my smile. But somewhere down the line there was yet another thing for me to worry. Her brother would be along with her soon. I wasn't getting a good feeling about it. Still, I tried to wipe off the negative thoughts away and got up from bed. I continued with my regular routine as I had already promised Radhika I wouldn't call her often. I began spending a lot of time with my new office friends. I used to wait after office to workout in office gym. Later a cup of tea at the shop near office would make me recall the moments spend along with Riya, Parth and Abhi. The mates in my batch used to discuss a lot about their current relationship status; they hardly had any other topic of discussion left among them. Especially these three girls who would often be talking more about the girly stuff like getting up a new make-over. The new shades of lipsticks, lip-gloss, eye-liners, powders, creams and many more which would keep me away from them most of the times. I would thank god that Radhika would never be into such a girly stuff or else it would have been very difficult to handle her. But sooner or later I used to think that once she comes back I'll ask Vrushika to take her along with her and give her one of the best beauty tips which would make her look even more beautiful than what she actually is. So maybe mom would find her to be the best girl for me and won't think of searching any other girl for me to get married. But will Radhika ever go along with her would be the questions next my mind would keep in front of me and be lost in my own thoughts.

So life in office was being difficult as I would feel left alone most of the times. But changes happen, some are good and some are bad. We only need to adjust ourselves to those unexpected change that's what life is all about. So along with the boring routine in office the only good thing to happen at that time was, we moving to the new house. Mom and dad planned out the house warming ceremony inviting a few relatives. I was missing Diya at that moment along with Radhika. My house was incomplete without my sister Diya and Radhika had become a part of family so I wanted her to be with me. But things never work the way we want them to and when we are busy these emotions are always over looked. The same happened with me when I was piled up with work one after another. Krish was still working with the plumbers to check the final fittings of the taps in every bathroom and the kitchen sink. Along with showing the house to the guests I was also clicking some pictures along with my cousin Sana who was recording the entire function on the handy-cam.

After a long wait of one complete year we would finally be shifting into the new house made me feel excited and I was overwhelmed with joy for the same. So the house was constructed in a way that we had the car parking on the ground floor. The living room and kitchen on the first floor, two bedrooms on the second floor and finally a nice terrace on the third floor. Once I reached my bedroom I started building up my own dreams. I reading a novel along with a cup of coffee seated on a bean bag whereas Radhika pulling the novel from my hand and asking me to get ready in order to go out. And I would say- "Radhika…I am just about to finish the novel." Soon Radhika would reveal the ending climax of it and I would run behind for spoiling the fun of reading. Then mom would shout you guys go out and get the vegetables from the market or else no dinner for you two. I smiled with this strange thought in my mind. Everything can be so perfect when you are given a freedom to build up your own dreams with your imaginations. But during this time my phone rang with that perfect timing of Radhika when I was only thinking about her.
"So how is it going Dhruv?" She asked.
"Good." I said.
"What happened Mottu?" She asked immediately sensing that something was wrong.
"I'm missing you Radhika." I said and checked if I was still alone in the room upstairs. "Why did you go so early."
"I had to study Mottu or else how would I come back in Pune again forever."
"I know. Anyways you study hard and I was busy with work so I couldn't reply to your message." I said as dad came upstairs along with my uncle as he was free from the puja. I had to wrap up the call soon but before I could say

anything Radhika heard his voice and said, "Mottu you enjoy. I'm going out with dad to eat pani-puri. And guess what Dhaval bhai is coming tomorrow. I am so excited."
"Cool..!" I said. "Now you would study along with him and I'm sure you won't call me after that."
"I'll call you when I'm not studying. And I'm leaving will call you later." She said and kept the phone. I went downstairs to meet others enjoy the sweets with a smile.

Time passed and it was 10, everyone left leaving behind me Krish and my parents. We thought of staying back when mom asked to come back to somwar peth as we had to pack all the things properly to get them shifted to the new house. So we both left along with them. Also our pets were waiting back at Somwar Peth which now would be called up as our old house. It was the time to wave of the final good-bye to everyone who stayed nearby which included Natasha, Vishal and Abhishek. Soon they won't be the ones staying nearby but yes would always be friends. Abhishek helped us moving everything into the new house. We also took our pets along with us after waving off the final goodbye to the old house. Mom and dad brought some nice pav-bhaji parceled which we ate after placing the things into the desired places. My pets were still trying to adjust themselves to the new surroundings. After the diner I had to get ready for my office for the night shift. As I reached office I noticed that it was very far from this new place.

Some good will happen someday, was the feeling I used to get even though I didn't like much in this office. Nobody that I could trust as a friend were the thoughts running in my mind as I was walking upstairs after parking by bike when someone hit me from the back. I turned back and wasn't able to recognize the person and soon I shouted back, "Chinki" I said and ran towards him and hugged him. It was Ashwin and I was finally meeting him after a long time.
"So finally joined Ventura? He asked.
"Yes, I did. All thanks to you." I replied.
"So enjoying the training."
"Yes watching all kinds of movies. What about you?"
"I'm taking calls." He said and I wondered how formal the talk becomes between two friends when we meet after a long time. Why can't we just stop these boring talks and directly tell them how much we have missed the fun we used to have before. But then all our feelings and emotions are shown in the form of smiles and laughter which we began to share after sometime. We spoke

with each other for the next 2-3minutes as Ashwin was late for work; I joined a friend in the smoking zone.

Later when we reached the training room our trainer decided to combine both the batches together. It was a good way to know everyone better in the other batch. This was the last week of training and we were also sent to wi-jack the calls on the floor. Morning I came back home and the new home gave me a peaceful sleep. I woke up late in the afternoon and then the new house felt like a haunted castle. Nobody on the streets as I peeped out of the window. There was silence everywhere and I didn't know how to spend the rest of the time as there was nothing to do. I felt like running back to Somwar Peth. Mom came back home from her office and then I felt a bit fine. Two days passed and I was still trying to adjust myself to this new surroundings when I called up Radhika. "What are you doing Radhika?" I said as soon as she picked up the call.

"Nothing… I was getting ready to go out. What happened Dhruv?" She asked.

"This place sucks Radhika. I don't' like this place at all. It feels like a haunted castle."

"Why? What happened?"

"This place is so quiet and there's nobody on the streets. I don't understand what I should do. It feels so lonely out here."

"Why do you feel like that Mottu? Start working on your showreel. This time you have to get a job before I come."

"I know. But you know something, every time I feel like working all I see is you and me making out in this house and I the moments we spent together while we visited this house." I said.

"So it's good Mottu. We have some good memories you can recall and you would like it there."

"But this is a problem Radhika I am not able to concentrate on my work because of this. Whenever I think of the moments, I miss you more."

"Mottu don't do this to me. Even I miss you but I have to study only then we can be together, you know that. Right?"

"Yes Radhika, But… Ok fine I'll try not to miss you but I'm sorry that I'm calling you always but please talk to me whenever it is possible as I really miss you a lot.

"Ok Dhruv I will and listen I'll call you later. Mom is waiting for me."

"Ok fine bye…I love you." I said.

"Hmm… Bye!" She said and kept the phone.

At least she could say I love you too. I thought maybe she doesn't love me or maybe I'm behind the wrong girl. A thought came in my mind as soon as she kept the phone. Soon a message popup on my mobile screen. *'I love you Mottu. Just two months and I'll be back. Plan out something where we can go once I'm back and we'll have fun.'* It brought up a smile on my face and I cursed myself for thinking rubbish about her.

The talk with her helped me a bit but I was still inside this haunted place. I wanted to get out of this place, so I took my bike and went to Aman's office to meet him. Soon we both went to guitar class and I spend the rest of the evening along with guitar class friends and was back home.

You can call it faith or just luck but I would say I was lucky to join the company which has a party just after we finished the training just like Convergys. This time it was Ventura's anniversary party on 13th February 2010. The place was far away from the city and I was on my way. I wasn't interested at first but Vrushika had forced to come so I had no other option. I had left home at 6 in the evening and
was driving along the same road and soon found out there was a huge traffic jam on the entire road. I thought that maybe some politicians might be visiting the city today. Somehow I reached the place and was very late. I called up Vrushika who was busy on the dance floor. So I called up Radhika.
"Parth was right. Ventura girls are hot and all I could see is sexy leg piece Radhika." I said to her.
"Good Mottu. So you reached the place finally."
"Yes it took a real long time to reach here."
"So enjoy the leg piece Mottu."
"What enjoy Radhika. I'm bored."
"Why?"
"I can't find any of my friends. Maybe no one turned up for the party. You know I'm thinking of drinking a beer." I tried to tease her again.
"No Mottu. You have to drive back home."
"I know. OK fine no beer only sprite." I said as I picked up the sprite bottle. My eyes were still searching Vrushika.
"Good. Where is Vrushika and your other friends?"
"I don't know. Maybe they didn't come…Ok wait I can see Vrushika. Oh! Man she is looking so hot I tell you Radhika." I said and Vrushika was walking towards me. She was wearing a black skirt and top and was looking beautiful. As soon as she noticed me talking with Radhika she wanted to talk with her, so I gave the phone to her.

"Radhika your boyfriend is never on time. I was waiting for him for the past 2 hours." She said and I continued to stare at her with expressions that made her smile and lie more about me.

"I wasn't able to find the place. And I'm always on time." I said to defend myself.

"Shut-up even your girlfriend is laughing when you say you are on time. Anyways Radhika your boyfriend is looking very handsome today. You're lucky to have him." She said and it made me smile and she gave the phone back to me.

"Mottu send me the pics and by the way what are you wearing?" Radhika said. "Nothing …I mean I am wearing something. Oh! What am I wearing…Arre that black shirt I wore on the 31st last year." I finally was able to say it properly. You know sometimes when people praise me I get flattened and that make me go crazy at times.

"Good Mottu you enjoy. We'll talk later." She said.

"Ok bye." I said and hung up the phone and turned back towards Vrushika who was eagerly waiting for me to finish my phone call.

"Why the hell you have to tell her am not punctual? She already knows that." I said to Vrushika.

"Poor girl…How the hell is she still with you? I would have kicked you for being late. Anyways you're looking really nice today." She replied.

"Oh! Thank You and even you are not looking bad today. So finally you managed to take a bath right?"

"Shut-up Dhruv! I'm not like you. Come-on lets go to the dance floor." She said pulling my hand.

"No…I can't dance and let's eat something first am very hungry."

"Oh GOD!!! I really pity Radhika for having a boyfriend like you, who is never on time and always hungry."

"Oh Come-on I didn't eat anything since afternoon and first of all I wasn't able to find this place so I was late or else I would have reached before you."

"Ok Let us see what's there for the dinner?" She said and we proceeded towards the food counter. After dinner we took some pictures along with each other. She took me with her to dance and I had to match up with her. I am a really bad dancer. Madhvi and Trupti didn't come and so were many people missing from our batch. All I was able to see was some real nice faces from the other batch and many hot girls around me made me miss her a lot. I took my cell phone out and found a message from Radhika. *'Hope you are fine. There has been a blast at German Bakery Pune.'* I was shocked the moment I read it. Immediately I called her.

"How did you know?" I asked.

"I saw it on the news." She said, "You must be there so I thought of messaging you as I was worried."

"Don't worry I'm far away from office and no wonder there was a traffic jam while coming here."

"You are safe right." She asked again.

"Yes Radhika. I am."

"Anyways Mottu message me when you reach home safely. I'll call you back." She said.

Later, I asked everyone about the blast if they had any clue about it. Many said it was a gas leak. Some said it was a religious attack whereas the truth was something else which was revealed by the newspapers and TV channels. People here in the party were least bothered to know what would have happened they were just happy to enjoy the party. I messaged Radhika as I reached home but it was too late so couldn't talk with Radhika.

Next morning Valentine's Day, I wished Radhika was with me for this day, but she was studying for her exams and I had to let her study I just wished her and was trying to enjoy the boring Sunday at the new house helping parents to get the required things for the puja next day. This was the same puja where once I was competing Radhika for eating maximum gulab-jamun for the first time. I and Krish called up our friends and the only difference here was my friends came empty handed whereas Krish's friends bought a gift along with them.

That time I felt bad as everyone was continuously praising Krish as this house was possible because of him.

"Didn't I give my time every day in order to see this house build?" I said to Radhika when she called up.

"I know Mottu but let it be now. Why are you getting so upset?" She asked.

"Everyone is praising Krish for the house. It's like I never did anything for this house."

"I know Dhruv what you have done and how you have sacrificed your time for it so it doesn't matter if nobody cares about it. Work hard and become an Animator then everyone will be proud of you. Most important I'll be happy and I know you can do it."

"I know and that will surely happen." I said with a smile.

"That's it keep up the spirit and you will be successful." She said and later everything was fine with me. I didn't have to bother for being discouraged or if nobody cared about what I did, as long as Radhika was with me I had nothing to fear. She was always there to motivate and encourage me even when I felt lost and very few people are lucky like me.

As I reached office everyone congratulated me for the new house. We were done with the training and this was our second day on the floor. I was on leave the other day so for me I still had to begin with the calls. Even though I had worked before I was a bit nervous about taking that first call. We had to take calls for four hours and the rest of the time was for training. The first four hours would be enjoyable as both are batches would be clubbed into one training room and we had to share our experiences on the calls. Later we would be guided and instructed accordingly to boost up the customer satisfaction level and achieve sales. The latter half would be challenging as would be on the floor taking calls. For me it was difficult to crack a sale as most of the times I would end up troubleshooting the customer's computer instead of convincing him to buy the support plan. So for me it was getting difficult as I wasn't with my team-mates anymore. My shy nature would always keep me alone from the people who were ready to get friendly with me.

Two days later I was in the smoking zone along with a friend from my team who was talking with the girl whom I wasn't introduced yet. She was the same girl who wore the white colored saree on 26th January. But their talks helped me to know her name. Mridula- it was a nice name. While I was still trying to get to know her through her name slowly. Something else was planned for me at a much faster rate. Mridula wanted to go home and yes I was along with Sudhir and her. He directly told her that I would drop her home. Now why would I do that if I didn't even know her? But soon she was sitting behind my bike as she stayed near my house. Strange how girls could easy sit behind anybody. I always thought she was some kind of a very rich girl whom would never talk with a guy like me. But I was wrong as next day she asked for my number and soon she became my new friend at work. She began to send me some cool messages which I would soon forward them to Radhika.

"Abe kya bache ki jaan lega?" I shouted as Aman was driving his bike on top speed. We were late for the movie and he didn't want to miss the movie. Most important Preeti had been waiting for us at the theatre for a long time and we had to reach there before it was too late. I was continuously asking him to drive slow as I hate speed and was terrified by the way he was driving. Suddenly he applied brakes and asked me if she was still there.

"She had been waiting there for a long time. She is showing her own attitude that she has been waiting there for a long time." I replied while he took a sharp turn and slowed down his speed a bit. I felt relaxed for a moment.

"Balls to her fucking attitude... Nobody told her to reach the theatre at 11, when the show was at 12." He replied and increased the speed in anger. Please slow down Aman I was saying it to myself as I wasn't able to speak much.

Aman had made up a movie plan considering that I was free on Sunday and so was Preeti. He wanted to spend some time with her as he was leaving for home the next day. But thanks to me we were late to reach the movie hall Aman had lost his temper as Preeti left. I was never a fan of SRK but Aman was and had selected this movie-'My Name Is Khan'. The movie was nice and did put me into a thinking mode as, is it really that important for a person to prove his love to such extremes even after losing the person he loves. Well, Radhika knows I love her a lot and I knew will never have to prove it to her, so I gave up those thoughts as the movie changed Aman's mood completely. Although he was still angry about Preeti he never showed it.

"What happened to you?" He asked as we were walking towards the parking zone.

"Nothing the movie is too good. I told you Shahrukh Khan's movies are always good."

"C'mon I don't believe this. Anyways when are you coming back."

"I'll come one week before my exams start but I won't meet you guys before my exams are over.."

"You all CA people are crazy for those exams. I wonder when you guys would be free from it."

"Once we become CA." He replied and smiled.

"Anyways I am driving the bike and not you." I snatched the keys from him and came home.

Yet another friend left home. I wasn't sure if I would ever stop missing them. Radhika and Aman were closest to me and knew most of my secrets. Well many of my friends knew a lot about me but these two were different. I used to call them Cartoon Artists who were busy in their own world of studies to become a Chartered Accountant someday. But I was lucky that I didn't have to be alone atleast at work as most of the time would be spent along with Mridula and many other people. I was trying to make my own mark at office. A month passed and it was time for Holi and this year it had to be the best- new house and some cool friends. I still wished Radhika and Aman would have been when I was enjoying it along with the guitar class friends. We took many pictures and soon I uploaded it on Orkut. The internet world was moving fast and everyone had made their accounts on Facebook but I still preferred Orkut. I messaged Radhika to check the pics and soon there were a lot of comments from her.

*****

Chapter 23

Back To Work Phase-2…

It was high time for me to get back to work as promised to Radhika. I had to clear my graduation exams, which I had been dealing for the past two years. I got my leaves sanctioned for the next twenty days before the exams. But when you start working it's very difficult to get back to studies. Same happened with me although, I had no other option. I had get over it as this was my only chance to prove myself.

It was weekend when I came back home and had already planned for the pizza party at home as promised to my class friends for getting this job. "Aman and Radhika are going to kill me when they know I have given you guys a party without them." I said to everyone as Aaliya took the initiative to gather everyone and reach my place.

I called up everyone at 4 in the evening but my friends had learned from me never to be on time. They came around 5 and had many reason blaming one another. I didn't mind and asked everyone to be in my room. Later I asked Aaliya to accompany me in order to prepare the pizza. She stood up and immediately Anup spoke, "Yes Aaliya go and help him… The pizza should be delicious." We both came downstairs into the kitchen and I showed her the box which I had already ordered from Dominos.
"You ordered a pizza Dhruv…" She said in a surprised tone. "I thought you have got the pizza base and other stuff to prepare it."
"Yes… I did think about it but then a readymade pizza was much better option. I thought so ordered it. Don't let anybody know upstairs." I said with a smile.
"Ok! No Problem. But can I get some water to drink."
"Here" I said and gave her a glass of water and we went upstairs with the bottle. She gave the bottle to Anup and I kept staring at her. As how wonderfully she was instructing everyone.
"Hey guys listen! This is the last bottle of water left at Dhruv's place so we have to use it wisely." She said. I smiled at her and said, "Don't worry friends we just have to use it properly till 6."
"That's ok but where is the pizza?" Anup asked as he finished drinking half the bottle.

"It's in the microwave and let the others drink some water Anup." I said and Harsh immediately grabbed the bottle from Anup.

"I'll come to help you?" Preeti asked in an innocent tone to grab my attention. She was reading the synopsis of a book I gave to her so I asked her to continue with the same. I turned back to go downstairs when Harsh shouted back. "Hey Max! I'm taking this book home."

"No you are not. And don't make those funny expressions. It won't work on me."

"Why do you always have to behave like a kid Harsh? Are you a girl?" Prasad began to pull his legs and we all broke into laughter. "Anyways, you go Dhruv get the pizza we are hungry." He said and I came downstairs along with Aaliya. I serve the pizza into two large plates and Aaliya helped me to carry them upstairs along with the coke. As I reached my room everyone was surprised to see it in my hands. Anup immediately grabbed it from me and we took some pics together before we began to eat. Everyone praised me for the delicious pizza and finally I told them I had ordered it from Dominos.

"So what's the next plan?" Sam asked me.

"Nothing. Let's play cricket."

"Sure" Everyone shouted together except for Preeti and Aaliya, but they had no problem being the audience to watch us play.

My cousins Shivam and Sana had just arrived so Shivam joined us to play cricket. Later I went upstairs while Shivam continued to play with my friends. Time felt as if it was running fast so I was planning for my next surprise for everyone. I was preparing cold coffee with ice-cream on it when Preeti and Aaliya came upstairs.

"Hey listen Dhruv we have to leave soon as it would get late by the time we reach home." Aaliya said on behalf of everyone as she saw me in the kitchen. "Anyways what are you doing Dhruv?"

"Nothing." I said as I turned back towards her. "Just a bit of cold coffee for you guys after game."

"You should have called us. We would have helped you." She said immediately.

"Ok help me. Inform everyone to go upstairs and I'll be there soon." I said as I began pouring the coffee in each glass. She went and informed everyone and came back again to the kitchen and began to lift the glasses.

"Arre wait…" I said. "I still need to add ice-cream in it."

"Dhruv how can you do so many things. You're just amazing." She said and smiled. We took the glasses upstairs and I informed everyone to be careful with the glass and handle with care. We all sat on the terrace were the cool breeze kept blowing making the atmosphere lovely and enjoyable. I was happy to see all the surprised faces waiting for me to come. Their faces were lit up with smile while they enjoyed the coffee. Later we kept the glasses close to each other in order to keep them safe. We kept talking with each other and I didn't want anybody to leave at that moment. Maybe I could do something more so that everyone would stay for some time longer. I thought as I would soon get bored in this house after they would leave. But everyone was getting late so all got up together and a glass broke with a slight push from Aaliya dress. This was unexpected everyone burst into laughter when I had warned them about it.

"Mom will kill me if she comes to know about this broken glass." I said.

"I am sorry Dhruv I didn't do it purposely." Aaliya said with a frown.

"It's ok now just see how you can dispose the glass away from here." I said as even I couldn't control my laughter after seeing Aaliya's expression. I knew I would be able to handle this properly as for me a thing isn't that important than a friend. Well that doesn't mean my friends can come home and break everything in my house. (Just being sarcastic...) We all continued to tease her for quite a long time.

I left the house along with everyone and told mom will be back soon. As we reached the guitar class everyone left except for Anup, Aaliya, Harsh and me. We four continued to talk with each other for till 9 and later I came home. I knew that these moments would never come back and if I need to keep them alive I have to work hard and achieve something in life. It wasn't difficult as on my way back home I started preparing a schedule I would follow in order to study and clear my exams.

When you have a particular aim in life and are dedicated towards it nobody can stop you from achieving it. I did believe in this a lot and it had to be true as I was becoming very serious about my graduation exams this time. I began to study hard as there were 5 backlogs which I wasn't able to clear even after attempting the papers again and again for the last 2 years.

I planned my studies properly and began to work hard towards it. During this time I hardly interacted with Radhika. No phone calls or messages. It was just the subjects of Computer Science that were in my mind day and night. I used to wake up early and sit down reading the old class notes and stay awake late at night. For the first time it felt that I could have cleared them a long time back had I given it a little push. But this time it was different and was getting much easier for me. I wasn't thinking of anything else but clearing the papers.

At times there were guests at home, I used to collect my stuff and go to Somwar Peth my old home to study.

The fear had gone away from my mind as I started attempting the papers one after another. With the last paper I came out of the college with a confident smile that I will be a BCS graduate this year and Radhika will be very happy about it. The entire month had passed and I didn't even respond to the messages sent by Radhika so her messages had kept decreasing day by day. I thought she might have got herself busy with studies.

That day after I left college I called up Mridula and asked her about the shift timings. We were still into the same shift timings. So I got ready soon in the evening and went back to work. Everything seemed to be changed within a month at office. I was able to see some new faces on the floor and it seemed much crowded than before. It felt great being to office after a long time. The best part was I wasn't taking calls as I had forgotten everything about the process. My team manager asked me to wi-jack the calls for a day so that I would be familiar to process soon. As there was a very less class flow I moved up from my place and sat next to Mridula and kept talking with her when soon my eyes were rolling in all the corners of the floor and I saw Ashwin.

"Chinki…" I shouted and went towards him. "How are you? Seeing you after a long time."

"I was on leave. Just came to office today." He replied.

"Why? What happened?"

"Well…I just got married." He said with a smile.

"Bloody hell!!! You got married!! Are you serious?"

"Yes."

"Whose that lucky girl?"

"Neha. My girlfriend." He said as I saw her name engraved on the gold ring he was wearing.

"You never told about her. Since when?" I asked.

"How will I? You were always busy with Riya."

"Riya was just a friend. I mean she still is…" I said as Ashwin got a call and went towards my desk.

"Dhruv let's take a break." Mridula said.

"So early?"

"Yes I am hungry and will get a call."

"Ok let's go." I said and as we were walking together I looked at Ashwin and shouted,

"Chinki we need to talk about this later."

Later, when we came up my manager asked me to login into a system and take calls. Soon I logged into a system and as there were no calls coming I began surfing the internet. I came across an opening in Animation. I checked the information about the company and soon decided to visit it the next day to see if the last date for the openings.

Next day, I went to the Animation Studio to make inquiries about the job. I was informed that there would be openings for the post of 3D Animator in the month of June and was told to come on the 15th of June for the same. I was happy to hear this as I still had time to prepare my showreel and apply for this particular job. The thoughts about getting this new job was not letting me concentrate on the current job I had. I needed to focus myself properly and at the same time had to begin working on my showreel. My team manager had already informed me that I won't be allowed to take leaves for the next 2 months. Apart from this I was able to see that some of my batch-mates had already started filling the form for appraisals. They had performed well for the past two months so they had a chance to see themselves promoted to a higher level. I couldn't apply for it as I was on leaves for my exams. So there were two options running in my mind at that moment. Either work hard for the next 2-3months and get myself promoted soon or maybe just concentrate on the showreel and start working seriously upon it. I often used to discuss this with Mridula seeking help from her. She used to come up with idea for me like work part time and then give rest of the time for the showreel. But in Ventura there was no such policy and even it was I still would have to work for 6 hours which wouldn't take me anywhere.

She was right about one thing that if I quit the job it would be difficult to survive without any money. Where on one end I was becoming serious about my life there were people on the other end who would still think that there was something going between me and Mridula. I would really pity on the people with such great imaginations. A girl and boy can be good friends. It never has to be always the other way round. So I decided to stay away from her when in office in order to avoid the gossip behind my back. I didn't want any trouble for myself. So when I wasn't on call I used to be surfing the web. I used go through DreamWorks official website to see their work and used to dream of working there some day. Yes I had seen this dream quiet a long time before I joined Ventura. I used to visit this website frequently when I was in Convergys. Always thinking how I would get into DreamWorks. But there always is a huge difference between dreams and reality. Reality was that I was confused with what exactly should I be doing. So one weekend I went to meet my guitar class friends. A new face had joined up our group and soon I came to know that Sam was in love with her. I spend some time along with them and that moment I missed Radhika a lot.

I wanted to talk with her so I picked up my cell phone and dialed her number but soon disconnected it as I knew she would be studying. I knew she would definitely give me an appropriate solution for my confusion and so I just messaged her that I was missing her. I wanted to start a proper conversation so that I could talk with her whether I should continue the job or quiet. I never asked her directly. I would always create some excitement first among the person then would say that's in my mind. The same I did at that moment but I got a strange reply from Radhika. I couldn't stop myself and sent another message to her.

'Radhika I miss you a lot. I want to marry you and I love you a lot. Don't want to lose you in my life.'

She replied back and I was shocked with her reply.

'Dhruv this thing marriage cannot happen between us. Stop thinking about me! I am sorry I got you into this situation maybe you need to find another girl and get settled with her. It won't be possible for me to marry you with strange things happening in my place.'

I wondered what possibly could be the reason behind such a reply. Is it because her brother is around her. I replied back that she would be the only girl of my life and maybe we would talk about this once she is back to Pune. Few minutes later a message popped up on my screen. It was from Radhika but it wasn't her.

'Please don't send such messages to Radhika. I know how much trouble she is going through. She is here to study so please don't call her or message her till her exams are over.'

This message was sent by her brother. I got angry after reading the message. I read it again and again and it only made me angrier. So is it like Radhika typed every message in front of him. Was she telling him the entire conversation over the messages to him? And if not, who gave him the rights to read her messages. Or maybe once again was I behind the wrong girl. Were they both enjoying making fun of my feelings? I couldn't understand what was happening with me whether it was right or wrong. How I should react to this? Somewhere I was worried about the interview. How would I make it for the interview if I am not able to complete my showreel? I wanted a solution from

Radhika but this is what comes from her. Maybe, she doesn't love me at all, she never did. Why does this happen with me? I love her and this is what she thinks about me. Just make a fool out of me. I read the message again for the last time putting an end to my thoughts and replied back to it.

'*Ok! I am sorry.*' I replied.

After that I decided not to message or reply to Radhika's messages and focus more on the showreel. I made up my own mind to quit the job and maybe later find a part-time job while I work on the showreel. Few days later, I received a message from Radhika. For a while, I was happy that I got a message from her. I read it twice. Soon I recalled the message from her brother. I knew I should have cleared it with her. Did she know that the message was sent from her number? But I didn't bother about it and I replied. '*Please don't message me. You are there to study.*' These were the same words that were sent by her brother and were hurting me a lot. I knew that it was a very rude reply but I couldn't stop myself. Later I regretted a lot about it. What if her brother succeeds to wipe me off her brain completely? I won't be able to live without her. I want her to be a part of my life. Rather she was my life. But still soon I got over the thoughts and began planning my showreel work.

The last working day of the month arrived. It was Friday and I had already received my salary. With all the installments done I had informed Krish and mom that I would be leaving the job soon. I was talking with everyone on that day and was sure none of them would miss me except Mridula I thought. We both stayed back after office and were enjoying the chocolate pastry early morning. Later we both left home and while returning home we were listening to the songs played on my cell phone with one ear-plug in my ear and the other in Mridula's ear. Life had once again brought me into a situation where I had to leave job to focus on animation. This time it was for a job and not for the completion of my course. Well, the course wasn't complete yet as I still had to attend the last batch of the post-production software Fusion.

As we reached Mridula's home she was holding my hands like she always did in office. She was still trying to convince me not to leave the job but I was only seeing a bright future ahead instead of her. She smiled at me I thought maybe it's the smile which says Dhruv I'll miss you. But she did say anything except, "Best of Luck Dhruv and don't forget me once you get a job."

"You know it very well Mridula. I am doing this for Radhika. I have to get a job before she come back. As it is I have made her angry by sending some stupid messages."

"Ok no problem and in case you change your mind and wish to come back to office. Give me a call and come to pick me. Don't go alone." She said and we both laughed at each other.

After coming home, I took a bath, then had my breakfast and then went off the sleep. This had been my routine every morning after I dropped Mridula and came home. But today was the last day of this routine. I woke up at 4 in the afternoon and later went to the guitar class. As usual everyone was practicing on the guitar scales and chords. I sat next to Sam and he was playing some chords of a known song so was Anup along with him. The music inspired me and I began to write a song that could fit properly into the chords these two were playing. Within few minutes our song was ready and we played it again and again matching every word of the lyrics I wrote to the chords. That moment was wonderful and al I said to myself was this song is for you Radhika. Later, after the class was over I informed everyone that I won't be seeing them for the entire month as I had to work on the showreel. Coming home I started downloading some reference showreel in order to work and create some concept. Later, I sorted out and finalized some scenes to work upon in order to make my showreel.

Next day even after avoiding everyone I was at some place called Level-9 where once Radhika had brought me and Parth together. I didn't like the place much but today it was Aaliya's plan and we all were here up on this roof-top restaurant. I took pictures of everyone as usual to add up into my memories. When I came back home my relative were already at home and it was very difficult to get all my cousins off the computer in order to get back to work. Somehow I did and began with my schedule which I prepared for myself. I had planned things properly in such a way that I will be able to finish the showreel by 30th May and before Radhika was back in town. I started up with waking up early in the morning by 7, take a bath and finish off with my breakfast throwing away my laziness and by 8 I would be seated in front of the computer. I used to work till 1 and after lunch would usual take a nap which would wake me up late. Later in the evening I would continue again and work late till 3 at night sometime maybe 4. I wondered if at all I would have worked this way before I would have definitely got a job as an Animator somewhere. But considering the fact that I was doing this for Radhika I was very serious about it this time. But this seriousness would cease down during the weekends as my relatives would be at home and usually I would be with my guitar class friends.

The occasion was Akshada's birthday and to give a surprise Aman was back in town. I quietly whispered into Aaliya's ears when we both came out. Something which was completely unexpected for me. She went all the way running towards Aman and hugged him for quite a long time. I didn't get a hint at that moment but yes Aaliya was in love with Aman. Yet another love-story to begin in our group. We came in and somewhere I knew that the enjoyment with everyone was at one end and my work was at other and things were getting mixed up. I didn't want to lose my focus still we all were out for a movie during the weekend-'Badmaash Company' after which we all were at Aaliya's place. Aaliya stays with her family in an apartment which was well furnished. I liked it very much and also I did acknowledge it to her. It was 9th May 2010, that day and I had realized that time was running very fast. I hadn't made any progress in my showreel, still I never wanted to crib about it in front of anybody. I was enjoying the moment even though somewhere in my mind the only thing running was the shots I had to work.

Even though I was trying hard to get myself out of everything I had many obstacles on my way. I tried to continue with my work with the same routine when on 15th I received a call from an unknown number. I picked up the call and wasn't able to guess who it was at first when later I shouted back.
"Duffer!!! When did you come back to Pune?" It was Mahi.
"I came a long time back. What are you doing?"
"Nothing was working on my showreel." I said.
"Can you come to meet me near Inox?"
  "Now?"
"Yes, I don't have time later." Mahi always had that strong influence. I wanted to stay back and ask her to meet me in the evening as I knew meeting her would kill my time but still I went to meet her. As I reached Inox I found her shopping in Pantaloons. I waited for her to finish her shopping as I stood away from her. I was going through the new arrivals and noticed that Mahi was looking different today. Being a Fashion Designer student I wondered why she wasn't in her best outfit like always. I was observing her for the past 10minutes and later felt I should talk to her so I approached towards her when she was at the billing counter.
"How much time will you need?" I said when she turned back and looked at me.
"Chee! What have you done to your hair?" She shouted loud enough to grab everyone's attention and make me feel embarrassed.
"What's wrong with my hair?" I said.
"Go get a haircut, long hair doesn't suit you." The lady at the counter kept staring at me and I felt maybe I should have waited till she paid the bills.

"Anyways do you have 10Rs change?"

"Yes." I said and gave her the money and waited away from her so that she doesn't say anything else.

Later, we went into McD and while eating I had to make sure I didn't make any sound as Mahi hated a lot.

"Why do you always shout on me Mahi? We are meeting after such a long time and all you do is shout on me for no reason."

"Aisi hi hoo mein." She said with a smile.

"Don't copy my dialogues."

"Your dialogue… Really? Since when?"

"Right from childhood!" I replied and we both smiled at each other. We continued talking with each other and later she cancelled all her plans and came along with me to see my new home. I wanted to show her before but due to her friend Mohit and many other problems it was never possible. That was something I never wanted to recall as it would remind me how rude I had been with Radhika. So I ignored the thoughts as we reached home. Mom was happy to meet her and so were Krish and dad. Well meeting old people always lit up a smile of happiness as it evokes the happy moments spent with them. I was happy even though I wasn't into any relationship with Mahi, seeing her smile lit up a kind of positive energy within me. She was insisting everyone to come to Ajmer for the wedding. I wanted to attend her wedding but then Radhika would be back in Pune and I didn't want to leave her. Now my priorities had changed as first it was Mahi but now it was only Radhika. I wish I could tell her this.

In the evening Aman called up to ask if I was coming to class to which I agreed and asked Mahi to accompany me. She agreed and we both were on our way towards class. I introduced her to everyone and she was very happy to meet them. We didn't spend much time and I was again with Mahi to drop her home.

"I am very happy to meet you after such a long time Dhruv." She said. I smiled and didn't say anything. "I never wanted to spend the entire day with you but then I didn't feel like going back."

"I know ab meri personality hi aisi hai. You know people don't want to leave me." I said.

"Very funny."

"Even I am very happy to meet you Mahi. That time when you shouted on me in the morning I thought you have changed but then you are still the same."

"I am sorry Dhruv I wasn't there with you but truly I wanted to be away from you as later it would have been very difficult for me."

"I know. But Mahi, you left me at that time when I needed you. If it wasn't Radhika at that time I would have lost myself. She loves me a lot and I had always been rude with her when you were around." I said and stopped my bike at the signal. I waited for it to turn green and looked at Mahi in the mirror. She seemed sad as I found her eyes wet.

"Radhika had always been there and I never want to lose her now. When you were not with me she used to take care of me. Later I found these friends and now when Radhika is back to Jabalpur I enjoy with them." I said as I started my bike when the signal turned green.

"It's really nice Dhruv that you had someone with you when you were not alone." She replied wiping off her tears.

"You are right but the thing is I don't want to lose Radhika. We are thinking of getting married soon."

"Hey that's great and even your mom likes her right!"

"Yes but you know there has been a problem between these two." I said and told her everything about the fight or rather the conflicts that happened between mom and Radhika before she left for Jabalpur.

"She should have known that she should not talk in your family matters."

"It wasn't like that we all were discussing about my friends coming home and it all broke up into fight due to some misunderstandings."

"If you love her I wish that everything will be alright anyways you can stop here." She said and got down from my bike as I stopped near her hostel.

"So when are we meeting again?" I asked.

"Make some plans for tomorrow. I do want to spend some time with you."

"Let's see. I'll ask all my friends?"

"Yes. I would love to spend time with them as well."

16th May 2010, the plan was finally made. I had asked everyone to gather near Dev's and later we would be going to Level-9. I was pretty sure Radhika would have killed me had she known this. But everyone has promised me they will seal their lips, provided I treat them. Now that wasn't a big deal. We spent quiet a good time together and later I left along with Mahi. I had to drop her and comeback to drop Akshada. On our way Mahi said that she really enjoyed being with me. I asked her if she would do me a four on which she replied immediately.

"No Dhruv. That will never happen."

"But... Why Mahi?" I asked.

"Because, what you are requesting will never happen. I never want to see her or talk with her. I am happy that she is always with you. But I can never forgive her."

"Come-on Mahi… It's been a year now. Why can't you forget that thing and you two be friends?"

"Because…We can't Dhruv. As it is I won't be coming back once I get married. So meeting Radhika will never happen." She said.

"What if I marry her and I invite you to the wedding? Will you still not talk?" I asked immediately while I was still driving back to her place.

"It depends on the situation Dhruv. I won't comment on it now."

"Ok fine. But you know one thing if Radhika leaves me like the way you did. I'm thinking of marrying Natasha. What you say?"

"Are you crazy Dhruv? How can you even think like that after what she did with you? She doesn't trust you. How can you forgive people so easily?"

"I can you know just like the way I forgive you for what you did to me."

"Very funny!!!"

"No but seriously tell me what if Radhika leaves me. Should I go for her?"

"NO!! NEVER!!! Radhika is much better than her." She replied in a loud voice.

"Ok. But see you like Radhika. Still you want to fight with her.

"Yes, she is nice but still. Ok Now change the topic."

"But tell you something honestly."

"Yes Dhruv."

"I have always loved being with you but, now on I just want to be with Radhika. I don't want to loose her as I love her. I'll go mad if she leaves me."

"She won't leave you Dhruv. Come-on now drop me here." She said as we had reached her hostel. She got down from my bike and I think I should have wished that her last statement she made should have come true. Radhika wouldn't have left me. But everything is planned and you can't do anything about it.

Mahi gave me a smile and asked me to be present at her wedding. I got back where everyone was waiting for me. I drove fast and this time it was dust and nothing else.

"Don't cry Dhruv. I know she is a nice girl. But it's ok, she's gone." Aaliya began to tease me as Aman and Akshada joined her.

"Come on you guys. I am not crying."

"Anyways she is a nice girl. But you shouldn't be crying for her." Aman said in a very sarcastic tone.

"Shut-up Aman. And Akshada, aren't you getting late now or should I go home directly."

"No, Let's go. Ignore them and Radhika will come back soon Dhruv. You shouldn't be crying for any other reason."
"Ok fine am leaving you go home on your own." I said.
"I am joking Dhruv. Ok now don't make fun of him. Come-on Dhruv let's go." Akshada said and everyone burst into laughter. Her unique way of expressing that statement made everyone laugh including me. Soon I dropped her home and I was back in front of my computer.

The scene I was working on was half done and I still had few more scenes to go. I had planned my work accordingly and I knew it would be complete in more 10-15days calculating the possibility of the electricity failure at my place. Ever since I had moved here I had always been a victim to power cut which made me hate this place even more. But, I was sure that I would get the job before Radhika would be back in town. She had told me while leaving; she would be back by the first week of June. So as most of the afternoons were spent doing nothing because of the power failure I decided to look forward on Aaliya's suggestion. After a long week struggling with the power cut and finishing the entire scene, I went to her office early morning. So as soon as she saw me she came running and hugged me. I was clueless at that moment; maybe it was her excitement to see me in her office.

Her boss took my interview and was pretty impressed with my resume and work experience. I still remember his words though.
"I would be glad to have you work in our company but with the talent like that I think you deserve much better options. Work hard on your showreel and definitely you would become an animator someday. Make your dream come true." I smiled at his statement and left without feeling bad about not getting a job. Well his words did say a lot even though he was nobody to me. I had to make my dream come true but with the savings decreasing every day I was recalling Mridula's words. It will be tough without a job. I never talked about it to anyone. I was mentally prepared for it as long as I wasn't deviated from my work.

After reaching home I began working on the showreel along with the music I was addicted to. It was Taylor Swift at that time I would be listening while working simultaneously. In between I used to be on Facebook to play games and one day I read a message:
"Oye mere lal...How are you? I miss you so much. I tried calling you but your phone was switched off. I was waiting for a Sunday to talk with you, but everything was a big flop. Anyways how are you?"

Well that was Riya-my only unique friend who always meant a lot to me. That message added an instant smile on my face and I quickly replied back. Later, I saw Radhika online which increased the ratio of my happiness. I began to chat with her. She informed that she will reach Pune the next day. I couldn't ask her the time as she logged out soon. I thought of calling her back but stopped myself thinking her brother might pick up and can make me angry. Also I thought she must be kidding as she was supposed to come in June. I needed some time before I meet her as I wanted to show my work as soon as she was back. But she was coming the next day.

*****

Chapter 24

Break-up-The other side of Radhika...

26th May 2010, we were celebrating Sana's birthday at our home. We all were busy chit-chatting in my room while Shivam was checking his Facebook account. I found Radhika online in his friend's list. I asked Shivam to begin a chat with her and then I continued the chat. She informed that she was back to Pune in morning. I couldn't make out why she didn't bother to inform me. It kept me bugging the entire day. I wanted to call her but was not sure which number she was using at that time. Finally the day was over with the party, clicking pictures with the family and I was back to work at night.

Next day I could not stop myself the moment I saw Radhika online, I began the chat with a normal 'Hi'. She replied back the same and I just couldn't stop myself from asking her.

"Why didn't you inform me that you were back in town?"

"Why should I? You should have checked the train arrival time and should have called me." She replied back which sounded weird.

"How am I supposed to know Radhika? I wasn't sure if you came along with your dad, like you did the last time."

"You could have called me."

"On which number Radhika? Every time you come back you contact me. What happened all of sudden?"

"Yes. You are right. I contact you. That's what needs to be changed. Why can't you contact me? Anyways I've got work. Need to go. We'll talk later" I could sense she was avoiding me. Somehow I convinced her to meet me after office. She was staying at her friend's place. Adeena the girl I never liked at all. I confirmed the timing with her and later in the evening was all set to meet her.

That day being Sam's birthday I went to meet him near Dev's. I informed everyone that I was going to meet Radhika and had to leave early. Sam forced me to be at his place for some time and then leave. I wasn't sure if I made the right decision at that moment saying yes to him. Well, letting everyone know that I wanted to leave so that I can meet Radhika gave them a reason to continuously tease me while I was about to leave.

"Wait for some time Dhruv. Why are you so crazy about your girlfriend? She won't go anywhere." Aman said to again stop me.

"No. She will be angry if I don't show up on time Aman." I replied and was interrupted by Akshada.

"Let him go… Do you want to make him a Devdas like you, who keeps wondering from here and there?"

Aman felt bad and he spilled the glass of water on her. Yes this was his instant reaction as he could never control his anger. I thought for a moment and decided to wait for the next 5-10 mins for Aman and to make sure they don't end up in a fight.

Sometimes you never think of the consequences while making such quick decisions. I never thought this one decision could change my entire world. Later, Anup and Sam forced me to sing the song I has written for Radhika before I leave. I began to sing as I wanted to leave quickly. So by the time I left it was almost 10.15pm. I called up Radhika and informed her that I was on my way as I picked up a red rose for her from a florist. I reached her friend's place by 10.30pm. I was late…Very Late!!!

"Sorry Radhika. These people were not letting me come. Please don't be angry. Just meet me for 5-10mins, I can explain." I said as soon as I called her. She didn't want to meet me as she was angry on me being late. Somehow I convinced her to come downstairs for some time. I parked my bike and sat on the stairs of the building. I saw all the shops getting closed except for the medical store as there were still few people in there. My eyes were searching for Radhika everywhere. She came from a gate on my left and as usual gave me a smile and waived her hand saying hi, like she always did. I smiled back and was very excited to see her after a long time. I wanted to hug her at that moment with any hesitation but her words stopped me.

"Why did you come Dhruv? I was about to sleep."

"How could I go without meeting you Radhika?"

"I know Dhruv. But have you seen the time? You were supposed to come at 8.30."

"Sorry Radhika. But these people were not letting me come. They all wanted to listen to the song I had written for you. But I knew you would be awake so I came to meet you."

"No Dhruv. This is not done. I was about to sleep. I can't take this anymore. You always do this." She said raising her voice. I could see the few people staring at us as her voice increased. So to cool her down I gave her the rose. But the rose didn't make any difference as she had already planned something else.

"Why didn't you tell me Radhika that you are back in town?" I asked her.

"I did tell you Dhruv. You should have come to pick me. I knew you would not come. That's the reason I didn't call."

"How will I know if you don't tell me Radhika?"

"Why should I tell you? You should have checked the timings online and come to pick me." She replied back. Well that sounded weird as I was not able to find from where this was all coming from? Was it her brother or her friend? I was not sure, but whatever was coming I wasn't prepared for this. Something kept telling me inside this is not the Radhika I know. Something has changed her attitude and the way she was talking with me was simply not accepted. I pretended to be normal to fool myself. Radhika was angry only because I was late. She asked me how my job was going on. I didn't say much about it as I didn't want her to be more angry if I told I wasn't working anymore.

"Dhruv you were supposed to gift me that black top. Remember?"

"Yes, but you went home, I wanted you to stay."

"So what? You could have got it and kept it with you and given it when I came back to Pune." Well she had a point I could have done that but considering not receiving my complete salary from the day I joined Ventura it was hard for me to do any saving so I couldn't get her that top. But the thing was not about the money, I had completely forgotten about it the very next day we had been to the mall. Somehow she reminded me about it but I never gave any explanations. I told her about the interview on 15th.

"Dhruv, I am not going to meet you from now." She said and I thought was it because I didn't get her that top?

"Are you crazy Radhika? Why would you do that?" I asked immediately.

"It's because I don't think you really care about me Dhruv. I am not at all important to you."

"It's not like that Radhika. I told you these people were not letting me come."

"Why was it so important for you to go and meet them? You were supposed to meet me."

"Radhika I told you, I was about to leave in 5-10mins and meet you directly..."

"But you didn't." She interrupted me. "You always do this Dhruv. I am never in your priority. Your friends come first. Then me, if you get time."

"How can you say that Radhika? I have been with you even before I met them."

"Yes and that's the reason you didn't take me along with you to Sinhagad."

Now, if I can forget the thing about buying her that black top the very next day. How was I supposed to recall what was the actual reason to not take her along with me. I was seriously not able to understand why I failed to recall things and why I always kept forgetting things. Maybe I needed more almonds in my everyday meal. But this was not the time to think about the stuff to make my memory strong. I wanted her to realize that she meant the world to me. I was not here to prove whether I was right or wrong. I knew somewhere down the line I didn't turn up on time and had not talked with her properly while she was in Jabalpur, when her brother texted me. I did try to ask her about it. I thought maybe I should give her some time. I didn't mind she met Parth the moment she reached Pune. I always wanted her to be happy. I had to accept my mistake that I was late and had never been punctual when Radhika had planned to meet me. I tried to get back our discussion on a normal track when I told her that I would be busy with the preparation of my showreel. She was disappointed as it was still not complete and I knew this was meant to happen. I was cursing myself from within while I put up a smiley face talking to her.

"Dhruv you should go on. It's already very late." She said as I checked my watch. 11.30pm it showed.

"Ok no problem. Let's do one thing Radhika. I won't meet you till the time I finish my showreel. Till then you can cool yourself. I will meet you with my demoreel. Then everything will be fine."

"I won't meet you Dhruv, even after you finish your showreel. I am never going to meet you."

"Why are you doing this Radhika? Ok fine, take your time I know you are angry I will meet you soon." I said and stopped her from saying anything. I was trying to fool myself that nothing was serious, whatever had just happened. I waved my hand as I started my bike.

"Message me when you reach home." Radhika said as I finally looked at her again and left. I continued to curse myself for being late and continuously thinking about her on my way back home. I messaged her as I reached home and was back to work when there was again a power cut.

Next day, Aman called me as he was eager to know about Radhika. The most important thing was 'Prince of Persia' the movie we had planned was released. I informed Aman I won't be able to come for the movie on which I had an instant reaction. He knew how to convince me and I could never say 'no'. Watching the movie did strengthen my decision to stick to the animation field and work even more hard. I was working late at night even though my relatives were at home. I wanted to stay back home and cancel my plans to the trip which my family had planned. A short trip to visit all the 8 Ganapati temples also known as Astha-Vinayak Yatra. This had happened for the first time that I was saying no to visit a Ganapati temple as I wanted to finish my work soon and get back to Radhika. We all left home early morning on Saturday the 29th May 2010, where I was still lost in the thoughts of Radhika watching the scenic beauty on the road early morning. We had reached the first temple before 8 in the morning, so I was sure we would be home before sunset and was trying to be happy although was worried at the same time. My mind kept thinking about Radhika and the work I had to complete. I kept forcing everyone to be quick at every place. On our way to the fourth temple the topic of discussion at one point of time came to my marriage. I was least interested in it as I was not ready to accept any other girl in my life than Radhika. Some point of time the topic was moved to Radhika.

"So what's wrong in Radhika?" My uncle asked my mom as they had always seen us together. Everyone liked her.

"She is a nice girl and gets along with everyone so easily with everyone. What is the reason to say no?" I was so happy to hear that from my aunt, that I could hide my blushing, which was screwed the moment I heard mom's reply.

"I don't like her."

"Now she would always say that. It's only because Radhika doesn't help her in any of her work. She is not nice; if she does she is definitely to be nice for her." I tried to defend Radhika. Everyone was convinced and I was sure mom would be convinced as well soon. But my thoughts were soon moved to one thing. What about Radhika? She doesn't want to meet me or talk with me, who will convince her?

Somehow there was nobody to answer this. I could not ask anyone from my family the same. So I tried to keep my thoughts away and would continue to enjoy with everyone and often check my phone if there was no miss call or maybe a sms from Radhika. But my phone remained silent.

May ended and I felt time was running fast for me. I began to stretch for long hours on my computer, till the time there was no power cut. The power cut would make me go crazy at time as I used to sit for 3-4 hours doing nothing or spending that time in sleeping which I wanted to avoid for few days. The work was almost 80% complete when Radhika came home. It was 13th June 2010, Sunday Krish and I were busy cleaning the underground water tank in the parking space. We were almost done when Radhika came along with her room-mate Hema to visit our new home. She spoke with me and it was a formal talk when she went upstairs in the living room. I finished the work and went upstairs to meet them; Radhika didn't seem to be interested in talking to me, so I went in my room. I started working on the scene with music turned on. I wanted her to come up to talk with me but she was completely avoiding me. Later she and Hema came upstairs along with mom to see the house. My eyes were set on Radhika and she continued to avoid any eye contact with me. After some time they went down and I was back to work. Mom asked Radhika to call me for lunch when she finally came up.

"Mottu!!!" She shouted from behind which gave me Goosebumps as I turned back to see her standing near the door and not stepping in. It was a very long time when I heard it from her. "Come down your mom has asked me to call you." The way she said sounded rude, so I kept my work aside and asked her, "Why are you ignoring me Radhika?"

"I am not ignoring you Dhruv."

"Yes Radhika. You are ignoring me. You are not calling me, neither are you replying to my messages."

"I guess you were the one, who told that you won't contact me, till you work is over. I can see you are still working."

"Yes I am working but it almost done; now working with the final corrections. But if I said don't contact me, does that really mean you should not contact me at all?"

"Yes Dhruv, have I ever said no to anything you demanded?"

"Ok fine, in that case I want you to be with me."

"Sorry Dhruv that's not possible, I know it's difficult for me as well, but I have decided to stay away from you. I can't but, I will."

"Come-on Radhika. Don't do this to me."

"I have not forgotten what your mom once said. She will not let anyone come upstairs. That's why I didn't come."

"Are you crazy Radhika? She didn't actually mean those things."

"But I felt bad Dhruv that day, so I won't come again. And please, leave my hand everyone is waiting for lunch."

"I am not coming." I said leaving her hand.

"Good. As you wish." She said and left.

"Radhika" I shouted and she came back.

"Come down if you every loved me Dhruv."

"I am seriously not hungry Radhika."

"Ok I don't care bye." She said and vanished downstairs. I kept thinking about the fight between Radhika, Krish and mom before she left Pune. Many days had passed away but Radhika didn't forget anything. I didn't want any of this to happen. I just couldn't ignore her and decided to go downstairs. Everyone was sitting in the living room. I sat behind Radhika on the bed that was kept in the living room to trouble her for a while. Moments later I picked up her cell phone and began to read her messages. I had already read one of the most important messages which I was not supposed to read. She turned back to see what I was doing.

"Don't read my messages Dhruv."

"I am not. See." I said and showed her the pictures I was scrolling on her cellphone. Mom raised her eyes that said I should not touch Radhika's belongings. Also her behavior forced me to keep back the cellphone back on the bed and went back upstairs. I prepared a file for the final render while everyone else was done with lunch. Mom had asked me to have lunch with everyone but something was stopping me to be with everyone. After I kept the file on final render I kept thinking about the message I read: *"You mean a lot to me Radhika. Take Care of yourself."*

The message sent from Parth kept me bothering while the words kept circling my mind in bold. *"YOU MEAN A LOT TO ME..."* I used to say this to Riya always so I tried to be positive about his message to Radhika and tried to forget. Finally they were leaving back I peeped out of my window and saw Hema who waved me a hand as Radhika was still wearing her shoes. I came inside and later peeped out again when they had walked ahead a distance along with mom who went along till the bus stand.

15th July2010, supposed to be a big day for me. I was gathering all my work as I had to reach the animation studios by 11. The studio was located near Radhika's office. Unfortunately, she was working in Hinjewadi office, so there was no way I would get a chance to meet her. But some things are always unpredictable, one of which it always been Radhika. She called up to wish me luck that morning which encouraged me and gave another reason to give my best. After having my breakfast, I reached the studios and submitted my showreel at the reception. I was asked to wait for some time. While I was waiting I was mentally preparing myself for the test. I wasn't sure what would be asked. Whether I would clear the test? Whether it would be simple? Will I get the job? These thoughts were running randomly in my mind while I was going through some of my notes I had prepared for the last minute study. An hour passed by and I completely forgot I had been sitting here without anyone giving me the further instructions. I got up from my place and asked the person at the reception. He said I would be called soon and asked me to wait again for some time. After a long wait I was asked to leaves as the HR would call me for the test next week. I was annoyed with that statement. I had been preparing myself for the set for the past few hours doing nothing else. I began to ask the reason and almost had a verbal fight with them. Finally, I left the studio apologizing for my behavior.

Later, I went to MAAC to meet my faculty and check if there were any other openings. I had to wait till the lecture finished, so I called up Radhika. "Hello!!!" I said as she picked up.

"Hi!" She replied normally.

"What are you doing Radhika?"

"Work"

"Oh! Ok."

"What happened in the interview?" She asked.

"It got postponed."

"Good."

"What good?" I have to wait till they call for the test, which was supposed to happen today."

"Good. Enjoy then."

"What enjoy? Aren't you worried for me?"

"Why would I ?"

"I thought…. Maybe that's why you called me today. Right?"

"I called you for the sake of humanity. Anyways I have lots of work." She said and kept the phone.

'SAKE OF HUMANITY…!' What the hell was that? I said to myself as I wasn't able to understand why she was behaving like that. I was upset that the test was cancelled, but the talk with Radhika made it worst.

Completely disappointed I was only waiting to get a feedback for my demoreel. The lecture got over and I went inside to meet Sarang Sir. He saw the demoreel twice and then looked at me. I wasn't sure what he would say, when he said, "Good Job." He smiled at me and said, "Keep working hard. See how well you have improved your work with continuous practice."

"Thank you Sir. I will." I said as it was made possible only because of Radhika. I came downstairs and got myself busy with few friends in the practice lab. I showed my demoreel to one of a friend while the others were super excited to view the reel. So there faces were turned at the computer screen when he played it on the computer. But soon they got back to their work making a sulk face. I wasn't sure why this happened. Only two of them continued to watch my work carefully, here I was introduced to this guy who was working as an Animator in Anibrian Studios. I couldn't remember his name but he was the one who helped me find out few corrections (actually there were many). He gave me some tips in order to improve my work. He also showed me how to implement the principles of animation in the workflow. Soon I figured out that I was a complete disaster in terms of my demoreel work. He informed me that I need to start working on the demoreel right from the start at least for the next one year if I intended to get a job in any of the animation studios. That moment I was completely shaken, thinking why didn't Sir tell me the truth? I could see my future in darkness as my confidence was broken completely. I couldn't take this as a positive comment but rather got de-motivated and could see myself nowhere. I tried to keep that smile alive till the time I spoke with him and later returned back home.

21st June 2010, somehow I was able to convince Radhika to meet me in the evening. Radhika had been avoiding me completely since the interview day. I continued my job search in animation ignoring the fact that my demoreel was a total disaster. There were no openings and I kept losing hope. I felt lonely even though my friends were with me. They had planned a short trip. Aman's behavior changed when I said no for the trip. So later I joined him but it couldn't make me happy for a long time. He knew I was missing Radhika and wanted her to be with me. But still he wanted me to forget everything and enjoy. Ever since she had gone to Jabalpur I kept thinking that maybe we could go out somewhere to spend some time and have fun. But she was least interested to go anywhere. That day, I kept thinking what I could say to her when she would meet me. I did call up Parth to come along. We had decided to meet up at Landmark by 7. While I was about to leave I got a message from her to come by 7.30pm. So I reached accordingly on time and saw her peeking through some books, while she had gathered few in her hand. That moment I felt nice as she always said she wanted to buy books for her someday.

I stared at her for a while then went close. She kept the book aside and gave a smile. Don't know why but my heart beat raised that very moment.
"Hi!" She said.
"Hi! So, finally buying a book?" I replied with a smile.
"Yes, it has been a long time I haven't read any."
"Good, let me see." I said and she gave me the book.
"So, where are we going?" She asked while she was still searching some books.
"You say…" I said and looked at her in a hope that she would look at me.
"No Dhruv. You tell me. You are the one who wants to talk and where is Parth? He said he will be here soon. I called him and he said will be here in few minutes. Ok let's wait near Naturals."
"No problem." I said and gave her the book. She then headed towards the billing counter and I kept looking at her. Once in a moment she would look at me I would smile but there was no change in her expressions. The distance between

us had begun to increase. I felt the talk was becoming too formal. I need to do something I said to myself and waited till she purchased the book.

"So... What's going on?" She asked while we were walking towards Naturals.

"What would I do without you?" I said.

"Come-on Dhruv don't talk rubbish."

"I am not Radhika. I seriously don't understand why you are avoiding me? No messages, no phone calls, not even a miss call Radhika... What is in your mind?"

She didn't say anything; she saw my bike and sat on it while I kept staring at her. She then looked at me.

"I can't take this anymore Dhruv. Every time I have to wait for your time when someday you would come and we would spend time together. I am never your priority Dhruv."

"It's not like that Radhika. You are important to me and I know you are angry about that day I came late to meet you. I am sorry."

"It's not about that day Dhruv. Every time I want to be with you, you never have time for me. It's like I mean nothing to you."

"When did I ever say that Radhika? You mean a lot to me."

"No Dhruv that's not true." She cut me in between and continued to talk about how every time I failed to live up to her expectations. So whether it was spending time with her or not, I had always ignored her according to Radhika.

"Dhruv you asked me to come along with you to get the gift for Riya. But as soon as you saw Mahi you forgot me. You took her along with you instead of me. You didn't even bother to think how I would feel when you asked her right in front of me."

"That's not true Radhika. I didn't do it purposely. I didn't realize it at that moment. I completely forgot that I had asked you when I saw Mahi."

"So that's what it is. I mean nothing to you. You've always taken me for granted. Whenever you want you can take me with you, whenever you feel you would ditch me. Like a fool I keep telling myself that someday this will stop but no, you never changed. That day you asked me to come along with you to the new house. I packed all my work and came to your place. What you did was, you went along with your friends instead of me." While she said this I was still trying to recall if I had actually treated her in this way. I was not able to recall any of the incidents while she kept bombarding one incident after another.

"I've always wanted to go to Singhagad along with you, but you went with your friends. What would have happened if you would have taken me along with you? That was the worst Sunday ever for me. I kept crying the entire day but you didn't even bother to tell me that you are going along with your friends. Friends, yes your friends are more important for you always and not me. I was about to leave for Jabalpur, all I asked was spend some time with me as we won't be able to be together once I leave. But for you spending time with your new friends was more important." I was still trying to recall. What was the reason I didn't take Radhika along with me? I failed to recall and was left with no explanation.

"Mottu." Oh! She actually called me Mottu I was surprised for a moment I heard it.

"In Mahabaleshwar we spent an amazing time at night, but then you have to screw it up the next day. I was with you still you called up Mahi. I decided to roam around with Sam as you were busy talking with her."

"Radhika that's not fair, you asked Sam to come along with you. I would have been very happy to be with you but you never asked me."

"That's the problem Dhruv; I have to ask you every time to be with me. Why can't you always be with me without me begging you for it? I am happy with you but it's like only for some time, because you screw it up the very next moment. The moment I feel I should forgive you as am happy being with you that very moment you would do something that will screw up things between us."

"It's not the way you think Radhika. I never want to hurt you."

"But you do Dhruv, every time. Do you even remember I fell down in Mahabaleshwar?" She said. When the hell did this happen? I thought and never gave a thought that I shouldn't ask this question but I did

"You fell down? Where and when did this happen?"

"You were busy clicking photos. You were not even there for me. Aman was there by my side, he helped me to get up and not let me fall." I wasn't sure how I should react. I began to feel guilty for my behavior and thought how I could be so dumb. She continued to talk not giving me a single opportunity to explain myself. On the other hand I was not able to recall any of the incidents she put in front of me. I tried to convince her to forget what happened in the past. But she was least interested in my pleadings. I tried to let her know that she is leaving me at the time when I am trying to straighten everything between the two of us.

Somehow I felt that someone should come up and help me so I called up Parth. He was on his way to meet us. Within few minutes he met us and Radhika began to talk with him instead of me. They continued to talk as if they were the best buddies and I was a third person who was completely ignored by Radhika. I kept thinking and hating myself for my behavior with Radhika. I looked at her to grab her attention but she would ignore me and continue to talk with Parth. Finally I decided to break my silence.

"You are you so quite Duksey?" Parth asked.

"What would I say Parth when she is not talking to me?" I replied back.

"Come-on Radhika talk with him."

"I am talking to him."

"Wow Radhika the way you are talking if that's called talking I seriously like it. Parth please tell her, I can't live without her. Why can't she understand?"

"I don't want to talk about it anymore Dhruv. I guess we finished talking about it."

"No Radhika we have not I need to tell you one thing here. You are punishing me for things that happened long time back even before we were into a relation."

"What difference does it make? You will never change." She shouted back.

"Come-on Radhika I told you that I am trying to change. Why can't you believe me?" I tried to plead.

"I don't trust you Dhruv. Not anymore. I have given you many chances but you can never change."

"I am Radhika and if you have given me so many chances why not one last chance. I promise you would not regret this time."

"Why should I listen and act according to you?"

"Because…" Well I never had an answer to that question of her at that point of time. Parth spoke in between while he was continuously listening to the argument. He asked her to give me another chance which denied.

"Parth are you leaving me home?" She asked him.

"Yes Parth leave her. She doesn't trust me." I said even thought I wanted to drop her home instead.

"Are you crazy Radhika? Why would I leave you when Dhruv is standing right here? Also I have some important work so I will leave you guys carry on. Dhruv will drop you home safely." He said and asked me to drop her home. Later I took him away from Radhika and asked him if he was actually leaving as I wanted to talk with him. He asked to drop Radhika and come back he wasn't going anywhere.

She finally sat behind on my bike and we left. The silence between the two of us was hurting me. So I took a long route rather she told me to. *Come-on, talk something Radhika, your silence is killing me* I said to myself. I wanted to say it instead just kept mumbling. We reached near her hostel, she got down and waiting in front of me.

"Can things never be the same between you and me Radhika?" I asked her.

"Mottu you were always like a kid to me whom I took care more than myself."

"Then why are you leaving me? You should learn to forgive kids. Right?"

"I did Dhruv; many times I have forgiven you. But not anymore, I can't handle it."

"Radhika so things can never be the same between us again. At least we could be friends."

"Yes Dhruv we will be friends, but for that give me some time."

"So can we talk just like friends at least?"

"We will Dhruv, just give me some time." She said and was about to leave. It was getting difficult for me to leave her and go but it had to be done. I assured her that we would only behave like friends and nothing else. I turned back and then went to camp where Parth was still waiting. He spoke with me for a while and then left. Next day I thought of meeting Radhika, she agreed and we met after her office in a park. She was seated beside me but the distance between us was unbearable for me. I took out the holi thread I had brought for her and then tied it on her wrist. There were still some negative vibes at that moment or you could say the distance between the two of us let me think that way. Any other person could have easily sat between us I thought at that moment. The distance was killing me from inside. So I decided to leave within the next 10-15minutes as soon as I was finding difficult to continue any conversation with her. I dropped her near her hostel and came back home and soon messaged for Aman. The moment he came home I went along with him. We both were seated at a place where Radhika always wanted to come along with me. I told Aman that I wanted to cry that very moment and let everything out. But it never happened. Aman shared some of his childhood memories and cried recalling them. I convinced him and I felt I was normal and came back home.

Some things actually make us think to such extremes that we could actually lose ourselves. The same happened with me that night. I was still searching for any new openings in Animation but there were none. Radhika had informed me that I can message her anytime I want, so I sent her a text. She replied back formally. I replied with a smiley on which she asked me what happened.

"Please Radhika, don't do this with me. I really miss you a lot." I messaged her.

"Dhruv I am in the hostel meeting right now, please stop this nonsense." She replied after a while. I kept thinking inside my room with the mobile in my hand. The television sound in my living room was loud enough to destroy the silence in my room. I had locked the door from inside still I could hear the sound and all the minute details inside my room. Within the next 10-20seconds I sent another message to Radhika. There was no reply.

"Radhika please reply. Your silence is killing me. Please... Please... Please. I miss you a lot. I am sorry."

I typed again and the tear drop was on the verge of falling down. Please reply Radhika Please...I am sorry Please reply back." I kept saying to myself after which I received a reply.

"Dhruv I am in the hostel meeting. Stop this nonsense right now or I won't talk to you ever." The message broke me into tears and I dropped the mobile on the bed. Tears began to flow as I cried, cried till my heart beats increased so did the pain. Please Radhika I am sorry, I need you. I need you, don't leave me. Please come back... Please come back. I couldn't stop myself after that. I tried to wipe off the tears and stopped myself from crying but every time I did I failed to stop the watery eyes. There was a deep silence and darkness in my room. I could feel every beat of my heart. Radhika has left me. She has taken her decision now I have to face it. I have to assume she was never there. It was just a bad dream. I should forget her. I persuaded myself and tried to sleep.

Next day, I woke up at 7am with a fresh state of mind. My motto for the day was simple, get ready quickly and then start hunting a job in animation. I believed I had a showreel that will help me to get a job provided I could find an opening. I took a shower and then went downstairs. Mom was in the kitchen making breakfast when she asked me what I would like to eat.

"Mom, please talk to Radhika. She is leaving me forever. She would listen to you and things will be back to normal between the two of us. Please convince her, I can't live without her." I wanted to say the moment mom looked at me. But then I couldn't control my tears.

"I don't like this house. I don't want to stay here. I want to go back home." I said. Immediately mom took me in her arms and asked me what happened why I am crying. I kept repeating again and again. I don't like here. I want to go back to Somwar Peth.

"Why are you saying this Dhruv? You were so happy when we moved to this house. You would gather your friends and stay here before we moved in. Then why do you say like this?" Mom replied wiping my tears.

"And we are here. Me your dad, Krish, we all are here with you then why do you feel this way." She continued while dad came out of the bathroom. Mom pointed out to him and he asked me the same question to which I never had an answer.

"I don't like to be here." I replied. Mom wiped my tears again and hugged me tightly.

"Do you want to talk with Diya?" She whispered into my ears. I nodded back to her yes. Why I did so I could never understand, but yes I knew I could express myself completely only to Diya. Mom told me that I am in the house for the past 2months and maybe that's why I feel this way. She also asked me whether I wanted to go along with Pal to freshen up my mind. I was completely clueless as what was happening to me. Was it real or just another dream? But

yes this was all real and somehow that helped me get myself back to normal.
I had breakfast and by that time Krish and rest of my relatives came to know
I cried early morning reason being I don't like my new house. I was still in a
state where I didn't know what would be my next plan of action.

I picked up my phone and began typing a message, *"All this while I have
always been wrong now I can understand what was in your mind. Please meet
me today I am very sorry for whatever I did to you."* That message was for
Diya. After mom asked me if I wanted to meet her, my mind started to think
about her a lot and that was the thing that came out of it. She replied yes and
asked me the time and place to meet. Mom took me to aunt place where I met
Pal and she asked me to come along with her to Mumbai. Mom then left along
with aunt and later I told everything that happened between me and Radhika.
Pal knew Radhika very well and also liked her. Well, nobody in the family ever
had any problem about me meeting Radhika. But then I kept thinking was I
doing the right thing by telling everything about Radhika and me to Pal. She
did promise me that she would not disclose it to anybody but then I wasn't sure
for how long would that be. After spending some time, I asked Pal to get ready
and then left her home to see Diya. We had decided to meet her at McDonald's
restaurant on JM Road. Diya was standing at the entrance of the restaurant
when she waved us. I smiled and Pal went towards her while I went to park my
bike. My heart beat increased as I was confused what I would talk with her
meeting her after such a long time. She hugged me and was very happy to meet
me. Meeting her made me a bit nervous as what's next. We ordered some food
whereas I was in no mood to eat. Diya forced me to have a burger and then
later we found some place to sit. She kept staring at me and I wasn't sure how
to begin and tell her that I need her help very badly. Then Pal broke the silence.
"Dee it's Radhika." She said and then continued. "Bhai is in love with Radhika
and now she is leaving him forever. So Bhai was crying in the morning." I kept
looking at the way Pal began to explain everything. But there could be some
other way to say it. Obviously Diya had to laugh.
"Seriously? When did this happen?" She asked trying to control her laughter.
"Two years." Pal replied.
"Ok now there's nothing funny in it to laugh." I spoke in between.
"Ok fine. Tell me everything. I want to hear it from you Dhruv. What is the
exact matter?" She said and began to tell her everything that had happened.
Now I was telling the same story again which I had told Pal some time ago. Only
this time I was being more precise in telling it. Diya was listening carefully
and her verbal nodes assured me that she will help me in every possible way to
get her back. I was feeling very relaxed after telling her everything. Somehow

she was still confused as why would Radhika leave me if Mahi was getting married. She knew unless she talks with Radhika nothing will be sorted out, so she assured me that she will talk with her as soon as possible.

Pal then forced Diya to come along with us to Mumbai. I wasn't sure if I was going along but then I had no other plans. We had decided to leave in the afternoon so I packed my bags and came back to Pal's place. Just before we left I saw Radhika online on Facebook. I told her that I am going away from her forever. Within few minutes Parth called me up.
"What's wrong with you Dhruv? Where are you going?" He asked.
"Just like that I won't tell you."
"What happening Dhruv? Why are you behaving like this? Firstly you created a big scene in the morning and now you are updating those freaky status messages. Why are you behaving like a kid?" He asked and I wasn't happy with his approach towards me I wanted to just cut the phone but then he said that Radhika was worried for me stopped me from doing it. I told him that I was leaving for Mumbai and will be back in two days. I asked him to talk with Radhika on behalf of me. He kept saying that he will try his best. It was Pal and her friend along with Diya and me who went to Mumbai. We stayed at our relatives place and enjoyed the stay in Mumbai. It was a wonderful experience but it kept reminding me of the very first time I had come along with Radhika for the CDT training.

June was almost over and it was a bright sunny first day of July. I called up Aman to check if he was free. He had work in office which was going to keep him busy for the entire day. So I called up others and checked if anybody else was free. Sam came along and we both went to buy a gift for Radhika. I had planned to give her the photo frame of her photo along with the teddy bear which I had clicked in the month of December. Sam helped me select the frame and also suggested some quote to write along with the card. Sam and all the others of the guitar group always liked to see me happy. Rather everyone was ready to do anything for each other's happiness. Thanks to these friends I would get enough courage to fight back again in order to convince her. I planned to meet her on her birthday in the morning and gift her before she left for office. So I somehow had to catch up with her at around 7 so that I could get at least an hour to spend along with her. I tried to convince her but she was adamant. She never wanted to meet me so I got her convinced through Parth. Strange irony of my life my best friends would convince her in order to meet me. She was so close to Parth as if he requested she would be ready to do anything and yes he convinced her and she was ready to meet me.

I had to make sure I was on time and was not even a second late in order to meet her. I woke up at 6 in the morning and got ready as fast as possible. I called her and wished her. She hesitated to meet at first but later asked me to come near her hostel. I then left home and reached near her hostel around 7.15. She made me wait for another 15minutes before she showed up.
"Why do you want to meet me Dhruv?" She said as she came walking towards me.
"Come-on Radhika it's your birthday today. Let me make it special for you."
"It's no need Dhruv; you might just spoil it for me cribbing again for me to come back in your life. You very well know that it will never happen."
"I know Radhika I won't do anything like that. Come-on sit on my bike we need to go somewhere."
"Dhruv my cab will come in sometime."
"Relax Radhika I won't take you any stupid place. Trust me once I promise you would like it."
"Okay but you only have 10mins. You have to drop me back where my car comes to pick me."
"Okay." I said and took her along with me to the Dagduseth temple. There was no rush in the morning so we could go straight into the temple. For a change it has started drizzling. Somehow it changed Radhika'a mood.
"Thanks Mottu. Because of you I was able to come to the temple early morning or else I would have missed it." She said.
"I know that's why I got you here. I knew you would want to go to the temple. So... How you feeling now? Still, angry on me? Here this is for you."
    "I can't take any gifts Mottu, please you don't have to." She said and I tried to force on which she accepted the gift. This time I didn't gift her a flower as I didn't want it to be thrown in the dustbin, like she did the other day when I went to meet her all the towards Aundh. She called her cab near the temple. Somehow I could feel the change in her behavior, except that she instantly freed her hand when I tried to hold while crossing the road. I told her to open the gift later. I asked her if I should drop her to office. She hesitated although she loved roaming on the bike in the rains. Her car arrived and she left within a minute. I was happy when she turned back and looked at me with a sweet smile. I wished her again and left behind the car for some time, I tried to follow her. I stopped when she called.
"Mottu I liked the gift, but you were supposed to gift me that teddy instead of this frame."

"I told you I will gift you this frame on your birthday. Anyways there's one more picture of ours behind that picture. Whenever you feel you love me you could keep the picture or else you could just tear it away. But please keep this photo of yours along with the teddy. You look beautiful in it." Okay I never said the last line neither did she utter anything after seeing that picture. She hung-up and I could sense that she was happy to see it. I just wanted her to be happy.

Later I went to meet the guitar class friends who were eager to know Radhika's reaction on receiving the gift. I told them about it and also that Radhika has asked me to meet in the evening. I decided that once I reach Aundh at her friend's place I will ask Aman or the others to get a birthday cake for her. But something else is always planned, I called Radhika when I was about to leave for Aundh. She informed me not to come as something changed her mind. I didn't know what happened to her all of sudden when everything was fine in the morning. She said she doesn't want to meet her but I just wanted to see her. I reached Aundh and called her she came to meet and again the reason was Parth. He asked her to talk with me for a while and then maybe they would go for a party.
"Why did you come here Dhruv?" She asked.
"I wanted to meet you Radhika."
"I already met you in the morning then why do you want to meet me again."
"What is the problem Radhika? You were so nice in the morning. Why do you have to so rude now?"
"I don't want you here. I met you in the morning as Parth asked me to do so. I have plans with my friends I would have taken you along but I don't want to. You were supposed to give a party on my birthday, do you remember Dhruv?" She asked to which I had no answer as I never recalled saying anything to her. "Dhruv I would have taken you along today but you started the same thing. I am not coming back. I want to stay away from you. Please get lost from here Dhruv." She actually shouted on the last statement. I felt bad but I didn't show anything on my face.
"Okay Radhika if you really don't want me to be around you I will leave. Have fun, enjoy your day. Sorry I spoilt your mood." I said and left. Her words kept echoing in my ears. GET LOST she said. I laughed at it and wondered had I really been so bad to her that she had to say this to me.

"GET LOST it is. Dhruv get lost who have screwed her life and now it's her turn to screw yours"

Next day, I logged on to Facebook and saw Radhika had uploaded few pictures of her birthday party along with her friends and Parth. Her friend Adeena his boyfriend and my friend Parth, where was I? Sitting at home and liking all her pictures. So now that her birthday was over I was still in a dilemma whether I should meet her, talk with her and maybe again make an attempt to get her back. So again a meeting happened with Radhika a friendly meeting assuming she is just a friend. I was waiting for her at Kothrud, while she was sipping a cup of coffee along with a colleague from her office. I wanted to break his face to doing so but I didn't do it. I waited while she came back. I spoke to her in a normal tone. She enquired about the animation job on which I informed that there are few jobs I have applied for. I knew there were no jobs and this was something I wanted to tell her. We spoke for some time and then I asked if I could drop her.

"Strange it is Radhika after being in a relation together I have to ask this question to you."

"It's okay Dhruv I will come along with you, drop me to hostel."

"Radhika just imagine we are friends, good friends. We meet each other once in a while after you free yourself from the coffee dates."

"Okay now no need to mention the coffee date." She interrupted me.

"Okay no coffee date, only we meet once in a while a month or so. What after this Radhika? I am planning to write a story on us. What would be the end Radhika? Please tell me." I asked. She remained silent and didn't say anything. I knew she wanted to be back but she was not making any attempt to make thing they were before. She was fighting for a change in her life, a new life in which there is no Dhruv. A single independent life where she could do anything she wants. I dropped her back in the hostel and came back home. She promised that I could chat or talk with her once in a while like normal friends do. I was struggling on my end to be normal.

The next day we all met near the guitar class to celebrate Preeti's birthday. I wished her and after a while called up Radhika.

"Radhika you should have been here. We are really enjoying a lot." I said.

"I wish Dhruv I know last year you guys had fun and I do remember my birthday celebration as well."

"I know and I am very tired clicking picture and we are having so much fun. The cake is awesome, everyone is missing you Radhika."

"I am sure, but you guys carry on I have work, we will talk later." She said and hung up.

"Why did you lie to her Dhruv?" Akshada shouted on me. "You are not at all enjoying we all are here and you are only thinking about her who isn't bothered to talk with you."

"It's not like that she is busy in office."

"Come-on Dhruv stop fooling yourself." She said and I tried to join them and try to forget the thoughts in my mind. I wanted someone to help me maybe mom but I was not able to tell her anything. So I decided to Google something and I found a book, 'How to win your Ex?' I began reading and found it very helpful. But was difficult to follow everything mentioned in the book but I decided I will. I avoided dialing her number and even messaging her until she calls back. At the same time I found something that got tears to roll down as I read, "Opening in Animation." That very same day, Krish's friend Neha had come home. She was currently working as a Counselor for NIIT and wanted to know if I would like to work along with her. I had no clue what I would do so I didn't say anything to her. I applied for the interview which was in Mumbai on Saturday, 10ᵗʰ July. The interview was for Prime Focus Studios in Mumbai. I tried to check if I could ask Radhika to come along with me for the interview. But then I was avoiding her until she called me the next day.

"Where are you Dhruv? You are so busy, that you are not replying to any of my messages."

"Yes Radhika, I am searching jobs."

"I wanted to meet you Dhruv I was here in Somwar Peth and thought maybe we could meet."

"I just left Radhika." I said although I was in Somwar Peth. I wanted to go right away and meet her but I didn't.

Next day I was preparing for the interview when my aunt called and asked me to come at her place. I left my work and went as she informed it was urgent. Later as I reached her place she asked me everything that was going with me and Radhika. I tried not to say anything but Pal had already told her everything.

"Dhruv speak up. Do you really want to marry her, because that will never happen."

"Why?" I asked.

"Your mom came the other day when you cried and she told me everything about you and Radhika. She told me that she would kill herself if kept going along with Radhika." I was shocked. My mom said this to her. I wanted mom to help me. Now whom should I trust, I kept quiet and kept listening to whatever aunt had to say. I didn't utter a word, just told her that I had broken up with Radhika and there is nothing between her and me. I had nobody left whom I could trust and share my feelings with. So I called up Diya.

Diya asked me to meet at her office. I was visiting the office after like almost 5 to 6 years. I used to go when the office was located at a different location. Now it was in a shopping complex at JM road. I was scared at the first as well as nervous a bit to go there. Somehow it was one of my hidden talents you could say but I was able to hide some of my feelings at times. (Yes, I did say it at times or else anybody could read my facial emotions within a moment). She asked to me to come inside I guess nobody was in the office.

"Where is everyone?" I asked.

"They have gone to the exhibition hall." She said and it confused me so she explained it.

"We have arranged an exhibition of Vastushastra (home science) culture and some of the paintings." We waited for a while as she had come to take the files. We then moved towards the exhibition hall. There I saw her husband's first wife. To my surprise as soon as she saw Diya she pulled her and took her along to get some work done. I waited while she was back along with her. Both of them looked really happy together. I was surprised to see how happy they looked together as if they never had any issues. I wasn't wrong. They were living together and were really happy. I felt that Diya had made the right decision. She took me along with her and showed me the exhibition. It was nice and they were getting a very nice response from the people who was at the exhibition. Later she asked me if I wanted to meet her husband on which I hesitated first then said yes. We then moved back to the office where I finally met her husband. Immediately he cancelled the next appointment as we entered the cabin. It was a very nicely maintain cabin not like the first office. This one had a pretty rich look and feel, everything was organized properly. My eyes kept rolling in all directions as I entered the cabin.

"I am very happy that you came to see me." He said.

"Yes it had to happen one day." I replied.

"I know it is hard for you to come and meet me after what we have gone through in the last few years. But I am sure everything will be fine." "I have no clue about it maybe it will take some time. At least, you should have told my parents about it."

"What would I tell them Dhruv? It took such a long time for you to understand her situation so how will your parents understand at that time." He said and had a point I agreed.

"Dhruv it was a very bad phase for me and my family that time. I was given electric shocks as I was not able to understand anything. I wanted to be with you sister, although I knew I am married but I couldn't stop myself from her. I lost everything that time. I didn't have money even to stop my car which was taken away by the bank as I was not able to pay the EMI. I lost respect in the society my family. I wasn't even able to earn properly. So I just made up my mind that I am never giving up on her. No matter what happens I will marry Diya and look towards I have my own Benz and a bungalow. What I am today it's only and only because of her. I love her and was able to get to this place only because of her." I listened to every word he spoke and felt proud that my sister gave him a reason to fight back and win her. I wondered if I will be able to fight in that manner. Later we discussed many things and I felt from the office. Diya asked me if I had money with me as I had to go to Mumbai for an interview. She handed over me some money and said that she will talk with Radhika once I am back.

After I left from her office I went to MAAC. I checked with one of the faculties if I was eligible for the interview. The interview was held in Prime Focus Studios at Mumbai. The faculty told me that they were hiring some Rotoscopy artist and not animator so I was again depressed so I came back home. The day was spent doing nothing. I wanted to talk with Radhika so I tried to call her but her phone was out of reach. So I tried the next day. She didn't pick up instead she messaged me that she was in Mumbai and will meet me once she was back. I wanted to avoid her, never wanted to call her as I was strictly following the book on How to win her back. But I messed it up by calling her. So the entire Saturday I kept thinking only about her. I had absolutely nothing to do. I wasn't able to figure out how and from where I should begin to search job. Next day as promised by Diya she was ready to meet Radhika. So for that I had to call up Parth who would be there to support me. I met him in camp; he told me that he was with Radhika in Mumbai as she wanted to meet her. I told him that I need to meet Radhika as Diya wanted to talk with her. Diya came to camp and later he called up Radhika. She asked him to meet near Law college road. He did not tell her about me and Diya. We waited till she came and later she was shocked to see me and Diya.

"Parya why did you lie to me, you should have told me that Dhruv is with you." She said. I knew she would do this, but then, she calmed down when she saw Diya.

"Hi Dee, how are you? Long time it's been I have seen you." She began her normal conversation. She behaved as if nothing had happened to her. This was my last attempt to let Diya talk with her and maybe she would realize that I really love her and will do it forever. She was normally talking with her until Diya began to ask her about me and our relation.

"Dee I can't be with this guy, I am never important for him, he has his own priority." She said, I heard and could stop myself from replying back immediately.

"It's not that way Radhika, you are important for me."

"Dhruv don't talk in between let me talk with her. I know him Radhika very well. But at the same time I could sense it that he is telling the truth." Diya tried to say it for me and I felt good for a moment. But it wasn't for long.

"I don't believe him Dee he has done this with me many times I can trust him this time. I have given him many chances." Diya understood her frustration level with me when Radhika tried to explain all the incidents again to her. That moment I understood one thing that if I cannot convince her, nobody else would be able to convince Radhika. Diya was listening to her and later kept giving me strange looks as how much of the truth I had actually told her. That moment I decided that nobody should talk on behalf of me even though I wanted them to. Parth was quiet and didn't utter a word. That time he asked if we would like to eat anything. That very moment Radhika and I said SPDP (Shev-Puri Dahi-Puri it's an Indian Snack), our very favorite chat which we never missed to order if we were at this location.

"See even our taste is the same and still, you want to break up with me." I said.

"Parth please order something else for me I don't want to eat what Dhruv is ordering."

"Ok fine I won't eat anything." I said.

"Shut-up you two, Dhruv you go along with him till I talk with her and Radhika eat what you want to eat don't change your mind because Dhruv is ordering the same." Diya shouted and we didn't utter a word. I went along with Parth and they continued to talk. We were back in few minutes and then the conversation again turned out to be a normal talk. I needed to speak, so I took Radhika along with me and said I want to talk with you. We walked away from them and began to talk.

"Dhruv why are you doing this? How many people are you going to get to convince me?"

"I don't know Radhika, I just want you to be back with me."

"You very well know that this will never happen."

"I know and maybe that's why I have decided something. I want to tell you…"

"What is it Dhruv? She said while it stuffed her mouth with SPDP. Diya and Parth were watching us as I continued to talk.

"Radhika ever since you made this decision of staying away from me I am not able to concentrate on anything. I am not able to focus. I need to focus and work on my demo-reel get a job into animation, but it's not happening."

"So what should I do Dhruv?"

"I want you to give me some time like maybe 6months. I will prove myself, will work hard get a job, I will do something that will make you feel proud for me. But I am not able to do so as you are stuck up in my mind. Give me a feel that you are with me at least for one day and maybe don't meet me for the next six months I will prove myself worthy for you. Then you decide whether I should be in your life or not."

"Six months will change nothing Dhruv. I am not coming back."

"I know but still for me do this please. I just can't be your friend. I need you to stay away but I want to spend a day with you first. Please let me feel that you were there with me and I was the one who messed up and need to work for it." She kept listening and maybe was convinced. She agreed and that time we decided to go together. She had to get dinner for herself and then go to her hostel. I told Diya and Parth and we both will leave together and will drop Radhika at her hostel. Diya seemed worried for me as I didn't let her speak with Radhika but was assured as Radhika herself told that she needs to spend time with me.

We took a rickshaw and left while Diya and Parth went home. Our conversation continued in the rickshaw were I told her many things.

"You know Radhika, there was a time when I was happy when every morning you would come home and wakeup me in the morning. I would be very happy to see you early morning. But these days you are there only in my dreams I wake up and realize that you are nowhere. I try to search for you. Then later I get ready and just sit on my bed sometimes on the chair thinking what's next. What should I do? Where should I begin? I am not able to understand what has happened to me I am not able to take any decisions for myself." She looked at me came close and hold my hand.

"Dhruv I am here. I am with you so what we are not in a relation, I am still here you can call me anytime."

"No Radhika you are not here, I don't feel anything. You know something I felt bad on your birthday the way you behaved, you tried to get rid of my hand when I was holding it while crossing the roads."

"Oh! So you noticed that."

"Yes Radhika and it was very bad I wanted your birthday to be the best day for you but sorry I spoiled it." I said and she came closer to me. I grabbed her hand tightly and looked at her, she had her eyes wet and later began to cry.

"Why are you crying Radhika? You have not lost anything. It's me who has lost you."

"I am sorry Dhruv but you are really making me feel guilty of what I have done to you."

"I am not saying this to make you feel guilty Radhika. I seriously need you in my life. It's incomplete without you."

"I know Dhruv but I can't."

"What is stopping you?" I said she didn't utter a word, I wiped her tears and kissed her and grabbed her in my arms. She stayed there for a while.

"I am happy Radhika at least today you gave me a chance to be with you. Wipe off your tears we are here." I said and we got out of the rickshaw. We then went in the Bengali restaurant where Radhika and I used to come. She ordered a parcel and then we had some Bengali sweets together. Her presence made it special for me. I knew I would never come here again if it's not with her. We then decided to walk for a while together.

"Do you know Radhika I had written a song for you. I never got a chance to sing you for in Mahabaleshwar."

"You did have a chance but you never sang for me."

"It's not that way; I was tired and very sleepy. Anyways do you want to hear the song?"

"Yes." She said and I began to sing for as we were walking holding hands on the footpath.

"Kabse main baitha tha, teri yaado mein...
Tanha main kahi tha, teri yaado mein...
Na jaane ab, tum miloge kab?
Dhoondta phiru tumhe, mein toh ab hare k gali....
Kabse main baitha tha, teri yaado mein...
Tanha main kahi tha, teri yaado mein.
Ab toh janemann dil kahi lagta nahi
Yaad teri aati hai jab ye waqt katata nahi..
Aisa jaado chalake, chal diye ab tum kaha?
Mujhko apna banake kho gaye jane tum kaha....."

"So…How is it?" I said.

"Hmm, it's good but I didn't like it maybe the mood it not right for the song."

"Okay" I said and shouted to myself *"she didn't like that song!!!"*

We then almost reach Central when she pointed out the way the walk and talk. She tried to show me my flaws and the reasons why I cannot change. I tried to walk straight and maybe the way she wanted me to. Was I really acting as a kid? I questioned myself and didn't utter a word to her.

"Come-on Dhruv I only straight don't jump while walking and never told you to stop talking." She took my hand in hers and asked if we could sit near the park. This was her favorite place where she would always get me. By the time we had reached there it was already closed. So we decided to sit outside.

Everything was going nice when I had Radhika besides me. I felt good. We were seated close to each other holding hands. I kissed her twice on which she smiled. I told her that I am losing my confidence as she is not with me. She told me that make her my strength and not weakness. She had become my weakness and I was not able to get out of it. It was hard to make her believe. But then a strange thing was lined up for me. She was willing to start everything on fresh note maybe forgive me for what I had done. That moment I saw two cops on bike passing by. One of them saw me and stopped the bike. They came close and asked what we were doing. I started shivering and didn't know how to talk. I lost my calm.

"We were just leaving in a minute." I said. I guess he realized through my voice that I was scared so he tried to scare me more.

"Don't you know you are not supposed to be seated here? This is not the place for you guys. Anyways the police van will be here in a minute. We need to take you along with us." He said and I went into a complete panic mode. I should have not come here; maybe I should have gone to see the Lavasa city along with my family. This would have not happened. What will I do? What will I tell mom? Strange thoughts started flowing in my mind at a rapid speed. There was another guy and a girl who tried to say sorry as they were not aware of the fact. I tried to convince them but was not able to do so. Finally, they said it again, I said Radhika let's run away from here. We cannot stay on which she stood still.

"We have not done anything wrong Dhruv?" She said. The cops asked her what she was studying.

"I am a CA, I work with Kimberly Clark and I am completing my article-ship with them. It's Sunday so we went to get dinner parcel. We came walking as we didn't get any rickshaw, I was tired so we both sat here for a while and were about to leave when you saw us." She spoke softly and calmly whereas I was completely out of sync, I just wanted to leave from there I wasn't in my senses. Was this really me? The Police guy checked her ID and fortunately she was carrying it along with her. He then asked me what I did. I told him that I am an animator but it was hard to explain because he didn't know what animation was. I said I am sorry and let us go. He was adamant.

"You guys have to wait now and come along with us." He said.

"Radhika let's run, we can't go to jail." I shouted.

"Yes just try it once and I will see that I treat you as a criminal.

"Shut up Dhruv, Sir we are from a good family and he is just a friend. We were not doing anything wrong." She said. The other couple tried to say the same but I had already created a scene. Somehow he was convinced with Radhika and he gave us a last warning and asked us to leave.

"RUN??? Seriously Dhruv?" She shouted upon me as we walked away from them.

"And you wanted me to come back to you, you can't even talk Dhruv. Look what you have done today. Just imagine had there been 4-5 guys instead of the cops and tried to rape me? Tell me Dhruv what you will do?"

"I will die but won't let them touch you, promise Radhika." I said as I was already cursing myself for screwing up everything.

"Wow that's the best you could come up with. It's over Dhruv." She said and I began to cry. The tears were not for the reason what she said; it was for the guy who was lost completely. I screwed myself.

"What I did can never be undone, but please Radhika don't leave me." I said as we took a rickshaw.

"Don't you dare, touch me Dhruv. I don't want to see your face ever. Once we reach my hostel I don't know you. You do not dare to call me or text me. You can't talk for yourself."

"I am sorry Radhika."

"You're sorry will not work for me Dhruv. I am happy that this happened. At least now I know how I should react to a situation like this." She kept talking and I was not able to utter a word the tears kept flowing and I had nothing to say. We reached her hostel, I paid the meter bill and she left without turning back. She picked up her phone and dialed a number; I guess it was her brother. She went to the general stores took a packet of milk and didn't bother to look at me while she was walking towards her hostel. I tried to call her but she didn't look at me. Her face was lit up with anger. Immediately I called up Parth.

"I screwed up Parth."

"What happened Dhruv?" He said. I told him everything that happened and how helpless I was at the moment.

"Dhruv you should have told him let her go and take me along with you."

"I couldn't say a word Parth, everything was going normal. She had decided to come back but I messed up everything."

"It's okay Dhruv nothing will happen let me talk with Radhika and I will call you back." He said and kept the phone.

While he was talking with Radhika I called up Diya and told her everything that happened.

"I had told you Dhruv, let me talk with her. But you never listen. Now do one thing, go home and meet me tomorrow morning in the office we will decide what to do next." She assured me that we will find a way out. Parth called up and told me that Radhika was very upset and didn't talk much with him. He told with talk later. I decided to leave home as I had nothing left to say. I was broken, the break happened because of me. Thus I got to see the other side of Radhika. I screwed up our relation.

*****

Chapter 25

What's your dream Dhruv?

Everything was over. Radhika broke-up with me. I made this happen. The thoughts didn't let me sleep the entire night. I waited for the night to end and the day to begin. I got ready and told mom that I had an interview and left home. I went straight to Diya's office. A strange pain had started in my heart, I wanted to forget what had happened the last night but the images kept flashing in front of my eyes. As I reached her office she asked me to come inside the cabin and she locked the door.

"So tell me what happened last night after you left?" She asked. I started narrating everything when tears began to roll down my eye.

"Are you crying Dhruv?"

"No it's just dust in my eyes."

"Oh! Really?"

"Yes." I said and tried to smile. She asked me what's next.

"Talk with Radhika."

"And say what to her."

"I can't live without her."

"Yes I know that but that's why I had come along with you yesterday to tell her."

"Yes I know but please talk with her. Should I call Parth? Maybe he should have called her and talked with her." I said and dialed his number. He began talking normal and later was angry upon me.

"What have you done Dhruv? I cannot utter a single word in front of her."

"What did she say?"

"You tell me Dhruv. What should I tell her?"

"Parth you know that I love her."

"Duksey forget that thing she has removed you from Facebook. She only had one question for me for which I had no answer."

"Hmm…" I said quietly. "What was that?

"She asked me how I can trust him Parth he didn't had courage to talk properly with the cops. Had the scene been worst, instead of the cops there have been guys and tried to do rape me? What would have happened?"

"Nothing Parth, nothing of such happened?"

"Yes Duksey nothing of such happened but sorry dude I can't help you any further upon this. How can you act like a dumb?"

"I am sorry Parth, I would never do such a thing again."

"There is no chance for a next time. She doesn't want to see you face. This time I support her."

"Parth please, don't do this with me."

"I have not done anything; it's you who has screwed up things for yourself." He said and there was a long silence, by this time my tears had found the way out and I had nothing left to say. Radhika removed me from her Facebook account it was like she had thrown me out of her life. Parth said that he will talk with her again but not at this time. He hung up and said will callback later.

I had nothing left and the tears kept flowing. Diya tried to console me but it was of no use. I had never cried like this before. Although I had at home but this was with the never ending pain in my heart. Diya got up from her place and came close to me and tried to hug me and that made me cry more. I wanted her back. I was sorry for what I had done. Even God cannot get her back for me. I have screwed badly. Somehow after almost 10-15 minutes I stopped myself and said that she has given me six months, I will become something.

"Dhruv if that's the case work hard I am with you." Diya said and asked if I had eaten anything. She sensed it looking at me. She then asked the co-workers to order a sandwich for me. She asked me to eat when her husband came. He asked me everything that happened. Now telling the same story again got my eyes wet. I controlled myself and didn't cry although I sounded worst while explaining it to him.

"Don't worry Dhruv; this is the best thing that has happened. Now at least you know that you cannot react on such situations." He said and I was not sure if he was trying to make a joke out of my situation. He then told me to work hard and fulfill my dreams Radhika will come back. He assured that there are ways to figure out but first we need to set up a goal and work for it. He asked me to make myself busy and first to finish the sandwich. I tried to push into my mouth and later Diya and I went outside. She asked me to write down my dream on a notepad. I wrote 5 points of what I wanted to do.

I wanted to earn money, a hell lot of money.
I wanted to build a new house.
I wanted to become rich.
I wanted to marry Radhika.
I wanted to live forever with her.

I wrote the points one after another and gave it to Diya. She read them and said, "This is not your dream Dhruv. Please write down what your dream is."

"This is my dream, this is what I want in life."

"You are trying to write something which is completely irrelevant of your dream." She said and I was not able to understand what she meant. I tried to focus and write again. My hands were shaking while I tried to make and attempt to write. I again scribbled something and gave it to her.

"Dhruv let's do this, take time. Maybe an hour, think and then write it down because this is not your dream. This is only Radhika in your mind that you are trying to put on to the paper. If you want you can think over it and maybe tell me tomorrow. She confused me more and I was not sure if I would be able to tell her. This was my dream I wanted to be rich.

I then took my bag and went to Anibrain Studios located at Viman-nagar. It was difficult to find it. I went inside and found that it was an amazing studio; I felt if I would be able to get a job here it will be fun to work. I gave my demoreel work to the HR person. He took it along and asked me to leave for the day and will inform the day for the technical test after checking the work. I left and then I realized that I was not able to find my bike keys. It made me go crazy I started searching every pocket of my bag and my trousers. I was not able to find it. It made me worried and later someone came and handed me the keys. I had left it on the bike without locking it. This had never happened before. I decided to visit Abhishek and talk with him. I told him whatever had happened with me. He laughed at first and later told me not to utter a word to anybody from the college group.

"So what's your plan Dhruv?"

"Nothing I am planning to work upon my dream?"

"And what is your dream."

"I want to become rich."

"I still don't think you are serious about your life. Get out of the Radhika mode and think about your career. Think about your dream and then work for it." He said and again I was not sure what he meant to say. Was I really not able to recall my dream or were these two trying to play with me?

17th July 2010, early morning I received Mahi's wedding invitation from the postman. All I had to do was be at this wedding. She really wanted me to come there. If I had prepared myself I would have enjoyed the wedding. But I was busy convincing Radhika to be with me. I had lost her as well. I read the invitation her name was changed, she did tell me about it. I was happy that Mahi was getting married. But then my mind was full with many thoughts what If I receive a similar invitation with the name Radhika engraved in it. I would be broken completely. I had to stop this from happening. I continued with my day's plan where I visited Somwar Peth and later, I would drop a friend for his class and wait till it was over. During that time I began to scribble some pages. I had decided that I will be writing this story of Dhruv and Radhika. But where should I began was the question. I started writing from the day when she made my birthday the most happening day for me although she was not with me. Later, in the evening I went along with Aman at his flat for a night along with few other friends. We had fun rather I was trying to mold my mind into every conversation they came up with. Some realized that I was still in the breakup mode. While some offered me beer, I had made up my mind I would not drink at this stage or else I will never be able to stop myself from drinking. And thank God for the decision I made I am still away from drinking.

Next day, I woke up before everyone else did. I was lost in my thoughts I wanted to call up Radhika and let her know I was missing her. But I knew she would never pick up the phone. Aman saw me in the balcony and asked me to sleep as I had been awake for the whole night. I did respond to him instead kept thinking over and over again. I took the dairy which I had scribbled with my thoughts hoping that someday I might turn that into a book. I read everything I had written and tried to erase the unwanted part. That moment I made up my mind I will message Radhika so I started typing.

"This is the last message from me. I would not disturb you after this I am starting up with something. I am sure I will be successful in it someday. I know it won't matter to you but someday you will think over it."

Within a minute I received a reply from her. *"Stop messages me useless things. I am sure I will change my number after this if you don't"* Immediately I typed another message asking why she was doing this to me. I am sorry and many other things were lined up in the message. I was a complete melodrama with tears rolling again. She was least interested in what was happening with me or my life. She was enjoying with Parth and his friends. They had gone to Tamni Ghat to enjoy the rains. I on the other hand guess had turned myself into a girl who is demanding for some or the other support after her breakup. I had to break this image of mine that was being formed. This was not me. I cried for a while and then stopped myself, washed my face and turned myself into something that I always was. A happy person no matter what the situation is. I decided I will always carry a smile on my face. I had read this somewhere on Facebook. It always better to smile rather, to show people why you are sad. I asked everyone to wake up and later went out for breakfast and later came home. Mom asked me what I did the entire night and I answered we all enjoyed

a lot. I guess somewhere she might be happy to see me happy. In the afternoon
we all gathered for Anup's pending birthday treat. As always I was late and
everyone was waiting for me. Seeing me everyone had this one question.
"Dhruv, can you ever be on time?"
"If I come on time and break the trend, who will be late?"
"That's true." Anup said and everyone laughed. We ordered the food and
enjoyed. Anup thanked me for coming as he wasn't sure if I will turn up for
the party. This was maybe the last time we all were together.

Next day I started my plans I had to continue searching jobs as well as work
upon the showreel in order to make it better. Also I had to do some household
works, like getting the gas cylinder from the store. So I went along with Krish
and once I was back I got a call. It was Radhika. She had called to inform that
she failed in her exams again. I asked her to meet me once, as well asked her
why she failed if I never called her when she was busy studying. She had no
answers to my questions, neither was she crying. Maybe she knew that she will
fail again. The call didn't last more than a minute but it screwed up everything
for me. I was not able to work the entire day. Later in the evening I called up
Parth and he informed that he was in a movie along with Radhika. I told him
will callback later but yes, she was with Parth. Parth who make her feel safe and
happy. Parth who is very caring and a real good friend, but where did she get
this friend from it was me. I introduced her to Parth. I knew I will not always
be around her and maybe always fail to express myself but I never wanted her
to be left alone after all her friends from the hostel left her. But still who am
I nobody. I am left alone and was always compared with Parth. Be like Parth,
act like Parth. He is more caring and understanding than you. Seriously, but I
am not Parth I am Dhruv. I have a different way and approach towards life and
that was why she was in love with me. Where is this love? I guess watching
movie with Parth. I hated her that moment not because she was with Parth, but
I was not able to concentrate. My mind was diverted again with her thoughts.

Later, mom called me downstairs and told me that her trip has been
finalized and she will be leaving tomorrow. She was leaving for the Amarnath
yatra. The very fact that mom will not be at home for the next 10 days made
me sad. I said I will come with you I don't want to stay in this place. But then
she assured me that Krish and my dad are here and I can call up my cousins
over the weekend. She had to leave next day. So we all went to drop her to the
station, while returning back I again had many thoughts running in my mind.
I was sad that mom was not here, but then I still had Diya and I decided I will

go and meet her whenever I am not able to concentrate. I also met Radhika roommate once to check upon her but I was not sure if I did the right thing.

24th July 2010, I was working upon the showreel and was trying to get some information. Later, I was trying to figure out which would be the characters I could use to begin with the showreel. I was almost done with half the format, when Radhika called up. My heart started beating faster; I was not show what I should talk with her. I waited for a moment closed my eyes decided that I will stay calm and picked up the phone.
"Hello Radhika." She said the way she always said.
"Yes Radhika." I tried to be formal.
"I want to meet you." She said and I was not sure if I heard it right.
"I want to meet you." She said it again and without asking the reason I directly asked where.
"Can you come in an hour near Landmark?" She said.
"No problem." I said as I checked the time.
"Okay see you in an hour." She said and hung-up. Immediately I called up Aman.
"Aman Radhika called up today."
"Cool, but what did she say?"
"She said that she wants to meet me."
"I said okay but I am not sure if I should go.
"Go and meet her. Maybe she wants to talk with you something. Just make sure you stay calm and don't do anything stupid."
"Okay, let's see." I said and later reached near Landmark on time. I called up Radhika to check where she was, she was still in the hostel. I told her to talk her time and come and started looking at the new books in the store. She took almost 20-25minutes to reach here and later asked me where should we go. I asked her if she would like to eat something and we moved towards McDonald's restaurant. We ordered something well I don't remember what we ordered. Well actually it doesn't matter what we ordered the thing here was that I was waiting for her to say something. She sat in front just looking at me without saying anything. I recalled meeting Mahi the same way but then it was me who wanted to meet Mahi to clear my thought and now it was Radhika.

I waited for another 5 minutes when it became impossible for me and I finally decided to ask her.

"Are you going to say something or are we just going to keep staring at each other. Come-on Radhika say something." I began to ask her but she didn't utter a word. I know Aman had asked me to stay calm but I couldn't do that.

"Radhika what's wrong with you? Why have you called me here? You know something I am trying my best to forget you which is next to impossible task for me. These thought are killing me inside as why have you called me when you were never going to meet me again."

"Yes Dhruv you are right I was never going to meet you. But I have been thinking about this that how many people have you told about the incident that happened on that Sunday."

"Does it really matter Radhika? What will happen if people know it?"

"Nothing bad will happen to me, but something is bothering me that you might end up telling everyone and that will spoil your image."

"My image… Seriously? Are you sure what you are talking about. Why are you so worried about it?"

"I don't know but I don't want you to tell anybody about our relation and whatever happened that day."

"If you want I will not tell anybody but why should I?"

"Okay go tell everybody as it is it's your life."

"My life it is with you. It's nothing without you."

"Stop it Dhruv. Don't start it again."

"Radhika you still get angry on this thing and you are worried for me that shows you still love me."

"I don't love you Dhruv." She said.

"Oh! Is that so and maybe that's why you are not looking into my eyes while saying this."

"I don't love you Dhruv, not anymore." She said it right on my face looking right in my eyes. I was not sure whether I should say anything after this. There was a long silence in our conversation after this.

"I think I should leave I have to do some shopping until Parth comes to pick me or should I call him."

"Are you asking me or talking to yourself?"

"Both."

"Where are you guys going?"

"It's none of your business."

"Okay so call him and check." I said and she called up Parth. He already knew I was with her. I messaged him to come a little late. Later, I asked her if I could be with her till Parth comes. First she hesitated but then agreed. We went walking towards MG road and I followed her everywhere she went. She found a nice pair of sandals for herself. After a long walk she finally got it. During that time we talked about many things and I could sense the change in her. She had actually moved on with her life. I was stuck up with her but she had started living an independent life for herself. We had a small debate when she found that price high at one shop and other less. Well it was the business tactics of the shopkeepers. Radhika said that someone should talk and tell them what they are doing is wrong. She also told me that our thinking doesn't match. We don't make a good pair. We fight a lot. But then have we ever seen a perfect couple who never fought. Well we only fight with the person whom we love. But then that day I fought with Parth as well. After a while she called up Parth and got to know that he was already here an hour ago but was waiting for me as I had messaged him. She then told him to wait and we went towards him. I began to fight with him that maybe he should not be with Radhika when she broke up with me. Something is going between you two and maybe that's why you are behaving like this I said to him.

"Dude if there's anything going between me and Radhika we have balls to tell you that and you could do nothing to us." He said and so did Radhika.

"How cheap is your behavior Dhruv, you seriously think that way? Please leave this very moment." I had messed it up again. Aman had warned me not to do anything stupid but I did. Somewhere I felt that they are getting close to each other so I just said it without even thinking about it once. Radhika sat next to him in his car and asked him to leave. Parth assured me that there is nothing between him and Radhika but at the same time he was disappointed with me.

I didn't wait even for a minute after this as I felt bad for myself the way I was treated by Radhika and then Parth. Parth being my friend was supporting Radhika more than me. I needed him to be with me rather than her. I left home and wanted to erase the thoughts as I knew the more I think over it the more I will go crazy. I had to focus on my work but when I reached home I typed a message to Parth saying I am sorry I should have not said those things.

Next day, I called up Diya and told her everything that happened. She was sure this would happen someday. She told me to concentrate on the work and avoid them for some days. I got a new haircut and I should say that the barber messed up my long hair. I wanted to get rid of them as Radhika was no longer with me. I went to MAAC to check if I could finish my final software to finish the course. The Center head at MAAC told me that there was a batch starting Monday 28th July 2010 in the morning from 9-11am. I immediately agreed as I didn't want to keep the course pending anymore. I began attending the class and found that the three girls Palak, Neha and Anushka were too in this batch. I wondered if this was destiny or was it already planned for me.

31st July 2010, I had no plans this year Aman had told me that he would come to meet me and he did exactly at 12. We talked for a while and later I came upstairs and my phone rang I was expecting it to be Radhika but it was Natasha. She didn't forget the day, we spoke for the next 30 minutes where she wished me and then it was he talks about Radhika. Everything seemed to be messed up for me. I went off to sleep after that. Early morning I received a call from mom and I told her to come back soon. She informed me that she was in the train and will reach the next day. So it was decided that my birthday will be celebrated the next day. I wanted to celebrate my birthday my way so I decided that I will buy some chocolates and will distribute in the class just like we used to in school. I got my favorite 5star chocolates for everyone. Every other person was curious to know why I was giving them the chocolate. When I told the reason they wished me and I felt happy. Well few of them did fed me and tried to make me more comfortable. So maybe I got a chance to make new friends.

Later, after the class was over I was going home when Parth called up. I told him about the dream I saw the he and Radhika came along with a cake to celebrate my birthday. I asked him if he could make it come true. He said he will talk with Radhika and callback soon. Next was Diya and while I was talking with her it started raining. She wished me and asked me to come to her office as she had planned something for me. I reached home and got ready and was waiting for the rains to stop. So while I was still waiting I received a call it was from an unknown number. I picked up the call and to surprise me Riya called up. "Oye mera bacha!!! How are you? Wish you a very happy birthday. May all your dreams come true and you live an awesome life too. Oh I just rhymed it."
"Yes I know. Thank you, Riya."
"See I am amazing."
"That you are, always. I missed you a lot Riya thank you so much for calling me." I said and began to tell her everything. She already knew as she had called up Parth few days ago. I told her how I behaved with Parth. She told me to relax and also assured that Parth is doing it for me. He knows that I want Radhika to be happy and that is the only reason he is being with her. We then spoke with each other for almost an hour. The talk with her made me forget everything and I was very happy and a kind of positive energy ran through my body. Later I went to see Diya and she asked to come in a hotel for lunch. It was a nice 5star rated hotel which I had never been before. The ambience felt nice. After lunch Diya and her husband took me for shopping in the Mercedes Benz.

I had never seen a Benz before and sitting in it was like a dream come true for me. Diya got two shirts and a pair of jeans for me. I did try to say no but her husband was trying to make an effort to get the best for me. While returning back I received a message from Radhika stating Happy Birthday on which I replied thanks, her husband check it and tried to motivate me. I reached home in the evening and later left to meet the guitar class friends who had already planned the surprise birthday cake. So the birthday ended pretty well, nothing was planned except for the fact that I had decided I will keep myself happy and indeed was able to do so.

Next day being friendship day Parth called up and asked me to meet as Abhi was in town. We did spend some time together and later came home where my relatives and other family members had planned my birthday surprise. When I reached home I saw mom and was very excited and sat next to her. She was telling her experience she had in the yatra and how wonderful the feel was to experience it. After everyone left mom asked me whether I was able to get any job into animation. She then asked me if I could work somewhere else till I get a job. Krish asked if I would like to work as a faculty to teach the programming languages. The day ended with a movie along with Krish and later I received a message from Riya. I had sent those few pages to her and asked I this could be the beginning of the book. She liked it a lot she had tears in her eyes while reading it.

Next day I woke up and later went for the interview, Krish's friend Neha was working into NIIT as a counselor and said that there was a vacancy for a faculty. This job would give me new chance to explore life so I decided to try, I was not sure if I would be able to make it. I was stuck up with cold still I decided to go. Reaching there I met Neha and later the counselor took me in one of the classrooms for the interview. With few rounds of questions she decided to appoint me as a faculty to teach Core Java, C and C++. I felt dam excited and happy. The very moment I wanted to go and tell Radhika that I have got a job. In the excitement I completely forget she is no longer talking with me. I went directly to her office and called her. Luckily she picked answered the call and didn't agree to meet and hung-up. I tried to message her and convince to meet me but she was not ready. Later I asked if I should just go and kill myself on which she replied okay. What could I say after this? I was dead for her; it didn't matter if I was dead or alive for her. So I decided to leave and go home disappointed. Later Parth called up and asked me if I was still at her office. She had asked him to call me. I told him I was no longer near her office. He then asked me to meet in the evening so that Abhi Parth and I could talk upon this. I went home took medicine for cold and went off to sleep

-----

I was almost 4pm by the time I slept. I had set an alarm for 6.30 and decided to sleep peacefully for some time. After a while I could sense that I woke up and my room was completely filled up with fog. I tried to turn on the lights but there was still darkness in the room. I got up from the bed and went towards the bathroom. As it was already dark I turned on the lights of the bathroom and found that the bathroom was also filled up with fog I tried to wash my face when I heard a voice.

"Hello Dhruv."

"Who's this?" I said as the voice sounded creepy.

"Can't you see me?"

"No. The room is completely filled with fog."

"Okay no problem. I have a question for you Dhruv." The voice said again. I was still trying to search where it came from.

"What is the question?"

"It's the same one which Diya asked you. What is your dream Dhruv?" Okay I had completely forgotten about this. Diya never asked me again and never bothered to think over it. I checked the bathroom and the fog was disappearing and I could see am image getting formed in the mirror as if there was a guy in the mirror. But then how did he know this. I tried to keep cool and tried to answer his question.

"I don't know." I said.

"Why Dhruv? If you do not know then who else will know?" He tried to ask, I had figured out that it was a male voice so I wasn't worried about it. He tried to ask me many things like once Radhika is gone what will be the next plan of action. I had no clue of what he was relating to. I just wanted to get out of there but I realized that I was stuck up like someone was trying to pull me towards itself.

He spoke with me for some time told me that Radhika might never come back. I hated that voice when it said Radhika would never come back. After a while it told me about my dream. Yes, I was not able to recall what my dream was and why was it so important to everyone. He told me that there was a guy who was out of college with an ambition to earn for him and workout something that will make everyone feel proud for him. He had seen a dream to become an animator and yes that was my dream. How did I forget it? I was not able to recall it for so many days. Finally I got a chance to know my dream. I thanked him for letting me know. He told me many things like life is going to change. There will be many things that will come across me and maybe those six months I had promised Radhika would disappear within a flash. I had to work hard to make my dream come true someday. With that the voice disappeared and I started hearing something else. It was my alarm ringing, 6.30pm it was.

*****

Part - 3

More Dreams to Come...

Max

Chapter 26

Lost Confidence

The ringing alarm woke me up and I checked the time. It was 6.30 in the evening. Everything seemed to be the same way I had seen in that dream. I wasn't sure if the bathroom would also be filled with fog. So to get myself in proper senses I turned on the lights in my room and made sure there wasn't even a single amount of darkness around. It wasn't raining anymore, but it felt cold. I lot had happened today. I never thought Radhika would say those things to me. I read her message again, 'Ok Fine.' I couldn't believe her reaction when I said should I die. Somewhere the pain inside my heart was still unbearable when I thought about it. Radhika had changed and I never in my dreams thought that she would change into something like this. The medicine helped me get pass the cold. I got up from my bed and looked outside the windows. Somewhere I still felt that Radhika must be thinking about me. But all I would see was the building of the games council in front of me. No one around, just the unbearable silence. I wanted to run away from it back to Somwar peth in order to straighten things, but it was too late.

I turned on the lights of the bathroom and went inside. There was no fog and everything was normal. Whatever had happened in the dream did make me realize about my dream when I looked into my eyes in the mirror. I kept staring at myself thinking how I should begin and from where to begin in order to make my dream come true. But at the same time my mind had thoughts about Radhika which weren't helping me stop the pain. Did I really have a heart attack? Many thoughts were flashing one after another. I had to focus my mind and concentrate on what's more important. I now knew what my dream was and what is has always been. Falling in love with Radhika was one of the most beautiful thing happened to me. I still love her but now I am nobody for her. I had to setup things right as I knew time would be reckless upon me. These six months where I have promised her to become someone in life will get over with a blink of an eye. Like the mirror guy said, I had to focus more on my career. I got fresh and then went downstairs. Mom had just come home and was watching TV with dad. I went inside the kitchen and made coffee for myself and came upstairs again with the cup. I called up Parth to check when we were meeting for dinner. I had already informed mom about the dinner with them.

Parth also asked me to call Abhi. He informed that he would be free by 8.30 and then would meet us. So I still had a lot of time to be alone with my thoughts. It had become very difficult for me to find a right start. I was no more interested in listening to any kind of music or watching movies. The best Bollywood could gift me on my breakup were list of heart breaking movies. 'Break ke Baad', 'Milenge Milenge', 'I Hate Love Story's'. Was that all Bollywood could come up with? I had always been dependent on movies, as I could always be inspired by them, but seems like there was nothing inspiring left. My confidence was lost. I had to fight back as these continuous thoughts were taking me nowhere.

Later, Parth called up and asked to reach Deccan. We decided to go to Khyber. I was missing Radhika, but now I could tell this to nobody except me. Parth and I went inside and ordered chicken starters. Abhi was on his way and we both had nothing much to do till he came.
"You know Parth." I said as the manager took the order and went back.
"What?" He asked.
"That day when you told me about Meera, the very first person that came in my mind was Radhika. I knew only she would help you and nobody else could."
"Yes, she did help me a lot. I will clear my accounts this time. We didn't get much time as we began late."
"I miss her and I know it's very late."
"Let her finish her exams. We'll go and meet her again. Right now it's important that she clears her CA examination."
"I know and I'm sorry Parth I fought with you that day. I really didn't mean to fight. I was not in my senses."
"It's Ok Dhruv. I was never angry on you. I knew as even I would have done the same if I would I been at your place."
"I screwed up big time."
"Don't think too much about it now. We are here to enjoy the evening so let's not talk about it. He said as he saw Abhi coming inside.
"You guys ordered chicken before I came?" He shouted.
"It just starters, sorry we couldn't wait for a long time." I said and somehow our serious conversation turned into a funny one with Abhi who kept cribbing of me always being hungry. Well I didn't say much we order the main course and continued talking with each other.
"So, faculty in NIIT...! How does it feel Dhruv?" Abhi asked me later.
"I am not sure about it. I have not touched the books of programing languages for quite a long time. But I am sure I will be able to teach. I will be getting trained before I get a batch." I said.

"Good. I like your confidence." He said whereas Parth was busy with the chicken leg piece. Looking at him I remembered the New Year's night when we three were together. I wasn't sure if I was really that confident about the new job, but somewhere I knew I can do it.

We contributed the money for the bill and I felt good when I gave my share of money even though I wasn't earning anything. My new job had many things to offer and a huge responsibility was put in front of me. Parth and Abhi were happy for me but somewhere even they knew I wanted Radhika to be here at the moment. We came out and later Parth and Abhi congratulated me again for the new job and wanted me to work hard. I waited for some time after they both left and finally took a decision that I won't eat chicken for the next 6months, till I fulfill my dreams and get back Radhika.

'EYEON FUSION' the final software, could end my 3D Animation course in MAAC, provided I attend lectures regularly. Well, terms and conditions always apply in my case, as everything around me had changed. No more mobile messages during the lectures, nobody to miss me, no more surprise kisses to wake me up, nobody to say you're the best, nobody left around to say you're not alone.

Life had become so strange... I had the entire world around me, but when left alone, why was it so difficult to win it back...? These thoughts bugged my mind during the lecture. I had to concentrate, as this software could help me in my demo-reel. I jotted down everything in my notes, the things shown on the projector screen but failed to understand the concepts. Things were never difficult for me, but I just couldn't make them simpler.

"Come-on Dhruv...! Don't be a bore and concentrate on what's being taught. Within the next few minutes everybody will know you had a terrible heart-break, with, wow! . . . Should I take her name?" My mind started again.
"Oh! No need to take her name and please let me concentrate." I replied.
"Oh! Yes sure, concentrate dude, after all I am the cruel mind. Right? And I guess he's waiting to ask you the next question."

Well that gesture was right. The talk within me vanished, as sir fired the next question upon me.
"Dhruv...!" He said as I looked towards him. "What is your specialization?"

"Character Animation… Sir!" I replied and prepared myself for the further questions.

"So Dhruv you must have animated a ball in the previous 3D software. Right?"

"Yes. I did… Sir."

"Help us animate this ball in FUSION." he said waiting for my reply.

I looked in my book, then at the screen as everybody seemed quiet. I made an attempt to answer which turned out to be perfect. Later, I stayed more alert and ignored my thoughts. The lecture got over by 11 o'clock. On my way downstairs I could hear every single wicked comment about him as nobody liked him.

"Will this happen to me too? Will I be able to teach properly?"

The thoughts bugged me as I reached NIIT. I met the counselor in NIIT who always carried a smile on her face and had also helped me get this job.

"So Dhruv how does it feel? Everybody would call you SIR." she said.

"It's nice, let's see how it turns out to be. My brother is all set to call me 'MASTER-JEE'… A for Apple B for Ball." I said while she smiled.

"Your brother is crazy, but you seemed confident maybe that's how you got this job, you'll do well." She said and tried to boost up my low confidence. It was strange, people who hardly knew me believed in me than the people who have actually known me for years.

The Center Head came within an hour and informed me to take my first batch; she assured that she would put me through the faculty training the next week. My first lecture was at 7.00pm. I had enough time to prepare myself. I had to get rid of my fear, be confident, to give my best.

"Dhruv! Best of Luck. Believe in yourself. Everything will be fine. And the most important thing, don't be afraid of anything or else you would mess up everything." I said to myself as I never wanted to lose.

The students arrived at sharp 7; the center head came to me and said, "Dhruv, you have to impress these students as you would be teaching them for the next two years."

"Ok and how should I do that?" I replied a bit nervous and confused.

"It's simple! Be friendly, get to know them more and if you do well, I'll give you another batch tomorrow. And, I don't think you need any training, you seem confident."

That sounded weird but I had to do this. People around believed in me and I couldn't let them down. *"You have to do this Dhruv,"* I said to myself and went inside the classroom.

A bit of nervousness still lingered around me which disappeared as I began. Somehow, I managed to overcome my fear and began asking few questions. Later, I taught the concepts precisely feeling as if I was a master in it and around 8.45pm called the day off.

Here I learnt the most important lesson which life had to offer me, *'Never let the person in front know that you are afraid as he might be more afraid than you are.'*

On my way back home, my eyes got wet. I wanted to share my happiness with her. I missed her and was doing this for her. She was the one who had changed my life and whom I respected the most. It was her with whom I had gathered those beautiful moments of my life. I dreamt of spending my whole life with her. I truly loved Radhika, but today it was me alone. I kept the thoughts away and wiped off the tears as I reached home.

I went to bring candles from the grocery shop as there was a power cut in our area. On my way towards shop I wanted to narrate my first day experience to Radhika. I thought of calling her, instead called up Akash, he didn't pick up so it was Parth on the list. It was totally unbelievable how he made fun of my emotions by his wicked laughter. Finally I called up Diya who cleared up everything for me.

"What was so funny, if I say Radhika would have been very happy today and would have felt proud for me?" I asked her.
She waited for a second and said, "Dhruv I know how you feel but, if you behave like this, it will turn back to you. People will laugh and make fun. But keep in mind this is just the beginning."

I reached home and light up the candles. I still could remember how in Somwar Peth Radhika and I used to enjoy dinner together in the low light of the candles, whenever there was a power cut. Here the power cut would happen almost every day. I didn't want to eat but I took my plate and came upstairs after the electricity was back. After dinner, I started searching my college books and some references to prepare notes for my first lecture in java. The GNIIT batch that I took some time ago was an alternate day batch. I was not concerned about it much as I was about the next batch of Java. I got the books and started preparing the notes till late night as next day we had an off for the Fusion class in MAAC.

I woke up early and got back to prepare notes for the class. I was informed that the java batch would begin at 5 in the evening so I still had ample amount of time. I had to prepare myself to the fullest, but then mom asked me to get the bank work done. When we reached bank I was given a token number and was asked to wait. I was continuously mumbling sad songs in my mind and continuously staring at the woman working at the cash counter. She was taking her own time to collect cash from every person that stood in front of her when their token number was displayed. Mom was getting irritated and so were the others who began abusing her one after another. I was watching and stayed calm when Radhika's words echoed in my mind. *"Someone has to stand Dhruv to change it."* The entire scene of her shopping in camp stood in front of me. I got up from my chair and walked towards to counter.

"Madam!" I spoke softly at first. I knew this won't help so I gathered my courage and spoke a bit louder.

"Madam. How much longer are you going to take for every person?" She looked at me and didn't say anything and got back to counting the notes.

"Hello!!! I am talking to you. We are not fools to stay in this line for an hour. I have to go to work. Can't you work a little bit faster?" Seeing me the others joined me and soon we got her to work faster. Mom also had joined them and I decided to stay quiet once again mumbling my songs. I smiled at myself and said yes someone has to stand to change it. My number was called on the other counter and everything started working smoothly. By the time I got out I really felt good as I really made a difference. Mom kept talking about how people continue to work their way in the bank and I was totally lost in my thoughts. All I wanted to do was call up Radhika.

I reached NIIT in the afternoon and continued with the notes. Around 4.30 a guy stood next to me and I was scared for a moment. He smiled at me and then introduced himself.

"Hello Sir I am Sandy. I am in your batch."

"Hello!" I replied back in a voice that could sound firm and confident.

"What are you doing Sir?" He asked again. Was I really supposed to answer that I thought for a moment but then I smiled back at him and replied.

"I am preparing some notes for your batch. Go take a seat in the classroom I will come as soon as everyone is in the class."

"No sir I will stay here I want to see what you are writing." He replied back immediately. Now that was really weird. I wanted to get rid of him so that I can complete the notes quickly, but he made me feel uncomfortable. Being a faculty I knew I could get rid of him soon. But it was not easy until another guy walked along the corridor into the room. I asked them to be seated in the classroom and finally they went inside. There were 4 guys already in the class. I told them we have some more people joining and will begin with the lecture soon. I started the lecture when the batch was full. It was my second batch and I was still nervous. Previous day I had 3 students and now there were 8, which made me more anxious. But I had to behave normal and be confident so I introduced myself and later asked each of them to introduce them starting with name, college name and education qualifications.

They introduced themselves one after another and my face reading skills predicted that I might end up with few problems with this batch. Well nothing happened that very moment as I began the lecture smoothly. I introduced the basic concepts of java and the history and not to forget dictating the notes to them I prepared some time before gave me a real feel that I can get through this. The next 2 hours passed by and I almost dictated the entire notes. I informed them that the next day we would begin with the first java program. Everyone agreed and were about to pack their bags when the Center Head knocked inside the class.
"So class how was the first lecture?" She asked everyone.
"It was good except for the fact that we had to write a lot." One of the students said. I thought for a moment if this would be held against me.
"Notes?" She shouted as she looked at one of the books. "Good you people will get a practice of writing from day one."
"But, Ma'am Sir teaches really nice." Sandy said. I looked at him and said to myself. *"That was quick."* I never excepted someone appreciating me on the very first day.
"Good that you like Sir. What about the other?"
"It's just the first day. We'll come to know soon." Replied the same guy and I was right, my face reading never goes wrong. It never did for Radhika as well. But that time was wasn't thinking of her. I was more concerned how the center head would react to that statement. She stood calm and asked everyone to come tomorrow on time. Later she seemed to be impressed on the notes I prepared she wanted me to work hard and give me more batches. That was making me nervous as I wasn't sure I would be able to handle it. Later, I asked if I could take a break and go down to eat someone. She agreed and I was down in search of something to eat. On my way I looked at myself in the mirror of my bike parked in the parking and cursed myself for losing Radhika. I walked out and took a left. After walking a few distant I saw a street hawker. I asked the price of veg patty and asked him to give one. 7rs per plate seemed like a huge amount for me. I finally realized the value of money when I was giving him a 10rupee note from my valet. It had been difficult to digest the patties remembering how

my life was and what it has become. Every bite I took reminded me that I am person lost in the crowd. This was not where I wanted to be. It took me some time but, I got up with my fighting spirit saying everything will be fine and left back to the class.

I was yet to be introduced to the other teaching faculties. As I walked inside the corridor the other male faculty gave me an angry look. I wondered what I had done wrong. I sat with Neha and spent the rest of the time chit-chatting as I had no other batch. The GNIIT batch was an alternate day batch. The center head was busy finishing her work. She asked me if I wanted to leave early as there were no batches. I agreed and then left along with Neha. She asked me to drop her near her hostel. She asked me to drop her. We both left together and I dropped her at her hostel. While riding back home I noticed the traffic light signal turned green and it was blinking for the left turn. There was a car ahead of me while I took the turn the signal stopped blinking and I was stopped by the traffic cop.

"Show me your license." He said. I removed the license and showed him and waited for him to speak.

"You will have to pay the fine, as you broke the signal."

"Sorry." I said. "I never broke any signal. It was blinking and by the time I took the turn it stopped. How would I know if I was not able to view the signal? There was a car ahead of me."

"Sir the signal was red. You broke the signal."

"This is not possible; I never do such a thing. I didn't rather." I remained strong and confident over my point. Soon he understood that I was right and he gave my license back and I left from there. I don't know why he did it but the traffic cop; he patted my back and said that he liked my confidence. Yes my confidence which was lost somewhere when I was asked what I was doing outside the park. I wanted to shout at that moment where this confidence was when I needed it the most. Radhika left me because she thought I could not protect her. After few minutes I decided to go to that place. I reached there when my mom called. I informed her that I will reach home soon when I saw something that I couldn't believe at that moment. I saw the cop who had caught me and Radhika. He was asking a couple what they were doing at the park. I had noticed the boy and the girl holding each other's hand. I thought maybe the boy was trying to say something to her. The cop was asking them questions and I could see tears in their eyes.

I didn't know how this happened with me, but I decided to go and talk with the cop.

"Hello Sir. Is there a problem here?" I asked.

"Do you know these two?" He asked me.

"Yes and I also know you Sir." I replied. He stared at me confused to understand what I really meant.

"Sir few days ago you caught me along with my friend when I was seated here outside the park. I tried a lot to tell you I wasn't doing anything. My friend said that she is a CA and I am sure you were convinced by her and very disappointed by me at that time."

"What do you mean to say? Just get lost from here or I will have to take you inside as well."

"Sure Sir, you could do that. Being a cop you have the all the rights to do that. But on what basis would you arrest me. Just for telling you, that you are doing something wrong here."

"Just shut up and get lost from here. Shinde did you dial the call?" He shouted on me as well as on his colleague.

"Wait Sir." I said holding his hand. He gave me another anger looks and I pulled my hand back the guy and the girl stood there and the tears were still following from their eyes. "I am not done yet. Just listen to me I want to tell you something very important." I said and he asked me to speak.

"Sir that day I was scared because there was a girl along with me I was worried about her safety but I was not able to talk as there were many things running in my mind. I could see the same situation with my friends here. I had asked them to wait for me. I work as a faculty for a reputed institute. And I would like to say this again. There is no board here which says a girl and a boy could not sit here." The moment I said this he got angry and tried to be rude the same way he was before. Somehow the guy wiped off his tears and tried to say sorry and informed the cop that he would not sit here again. The cop left by saying this is the last warning. I was angry on him as he did the same as he had done with me. The moment he left the girl shouted. "I don't want to see your face again." She started walking in anger. The boy ran behind her. Somehow I felt the guy needs help so I parked my bike and walked behind them.

"Excuse me." I said. "Guys I just saved you from that cop at least you could say is thank you."

"Thank you but we need some space." The girl said and tried to avoid me.

"Wait a second; you guys were crying a moment ago. Why the hell are you showing that attitude now?"

"Well thanks a lot for that. But you won't understand." The guy said.

"Well then make me understand."

"I was trying to convince her as she is leaving me forever. All I said to her was, give me one last chance. I won't repeat my mistakes again."

"History repeats itself in various forms…" I said to myself as the girl continued.

"You would never change Ravi. I have given you many changes."

"Wait a moment can I say something." I said.

"No." Both said in unison.

"Ok, thank you. But I can see you guys are meant to be together."

"Why don't you give him one chance and see. Maybe this time he really wants to change."

"I have given him many chances." She said again and interrupted me.

"Wait a second, whatever just happened right now, everything had happened the same way with me few months ago. I think you should give him a chance. Look at me my girlfriend never gave me that one chance I deserved. Now I am all alone still thinking of her. Do you want to same to happen with him? If at all you love him you should give him a chance"

"I do love him but he would never change. He always avoids me, his friends are more important than me."

Before I could say anything I boy started to beg and was almost on his knees asking for forgiveness. I didn't know what I should do at that time. I asked him to get up and there were tears in her eyes as well.

"He always does this, I love him a lot but he never treats me properly, I will learn to live without him. I will not forgive him."

"See no guy would ever cry unless he feels guilty for what he has done and is hurt from inside. Give him one chance. Maybe he really wants to change." I tried to convince her whereas the guy still kept crying on his knees.

"It's ok. Stand up now or else I will cry again." She said and he finally stood up. He said sorry and she finally forgave him. I smiled at them and said, "The world is too small for such things, be happy and take care of her. Very few people get a second chance." I started walking towards my bike and once turned back to look at them. They both were walking together holding hands. It felt good. I didn't know how I gathered that courage to talk at that moment with those strange people. But it was a nice feeling, only if Radhika could see this… I got back my lost confidence.

*****

Chapter 27

Gone Forever...

Sometimes when things begin to pile up on you all you need is some time to sort them properly. Yes, I wanted time to prepare notes for these two batches as soon as possible. I had to give my 100% and had to be totally prepared for all type of questions the students would put in front of me during the lectures. C++ and Core Java these languages were not difficult to teach, but it had been a long time I had read my books on programming languages. MAAC added its own unique contribution that time which helped me for few days.

I was informed that there won't be any lectures for the next 10 days till August 10 as new students were to join our batch. Sir wanted to cover the previous topic with them so that all of us would be on the same platform. That gave me some time to finish up with the programming notes. But it had its own drawbacks. The more I was free my mind would continue to think about Radhika. I wanted her thoughts to vanish off my mind and concentrate on the notes. At the end I would always have a battle within myself. One part of mine who was dying to see Radhika's face, while the other trying to concentrate. That day when Sir announced the 10day leave we all left from class. Anushka asked me if I would like to join for breakfast. I was hungry but had decided to save money and was actually avoiding new people as friends.

Later that afternoon I went to NIIT and then I was informed to take a batch of C++ for a girl. I was confused as why this was happening with me. Yet another batch, I didn't want girls around me. But then I couldn't say anything. So that got me into preparing Core Java and C++ notes and also make sure I taught them without any errors. My life was getting into a strange path, I didn't knew where it would lead me. I kept myself focused and prepared myself for the next batch. So this girl for C++ was a year down student. This was one of the subjects she had to clear. She was skinny and had some curly hair and I guess that was it I would say about her. The other faculties were busy with their batches and I had no other option left than to start teaching her, which I did without any fear of making mistakes.

Next day, early morning I was in Somwar Peth standing downstairs when a car passed by my side. I ignored it at first but then I could believe my eyes when the car stood on the other side of the road. It was Radhika on the driving seat; she was actually driving a car. Parth was seated next to her. She looked at me and later ignored me completely. She drove the car in full speed and vanished away within seconds. I blinked my eyes and somewhere felt happy for her. Later I opened my eyes and found myself standing in the balcony of the new house. Parth came in his car and called me downstairs. I went running immediately as Radhika was along with him. I always thought about this happening someday. I asked Parth to come upstairs rather forced him as Radhika didn't agree at first. She spoke nicely with everyone in the family and then we came in my room.

"How long are you going to be angry?" I asked her. She just stood quiet and looked away in the balcony without answering me.

"Parth please tell her, I miss her badly. I can't live without her." Parth looked at her, she gave me an angry look.

"This was the reason Parth I didn't want to come here. He will continue to crib on how much he misses me. I really don't give a dam about it. Tell him Parth." She replied in anger. I still tried to convince myself she loves me and this is just the anger that's talking. I wanted to hug her that moment and let her know I was not cribbing, I really cared for her. She then came inside I was still watching her through the balcony. She turned on the monitor as my computer was already on. She logged into her Facebook account and started deleting all my pics from her account.

"Why Radhika? Why?" I said while tears began to find their way out of my eyes. I tried to stop her but she had already finished deleting most of them.

"Why do you hate me Radhika?" I asked while I hold her hand.

"Leave my hand Mottu...Sorry Dhruv. Leave my hand." She corrected herself and got her hand freed. Hearing the word Mottu added some extra heartbeats for a second. She got up and asked Parth to come down quickly as she left the room. This time I didn't stop her.

"Give her some time dude." Parth patted my back and followed her. I went down and watched them leave, when Parth stopped the car. Radhika stepped out and came walking towards me. She hugged me tightly and spoke softly into my ears.

"Stop dreaming Dhruv. Work hard if you really want me back in your life and wake up or you would miss your class." She then wiped off her tears and returned towards the car. I was blown away as I woke up. Yet another dream that left me silent for quite a long time. I checked the time. It was 7.30am, the time when Radhika would come banging the stairs to take her tiffin and wake me up by kissing me. The only difference now was she just came in my dreams to wake me up. Somewhere my heart spoke that Radhika still loves me and will never utter a word about it to anybody.

After the dream I began to miss her more. The classes were going normal but then, I was handed over yet another batch of Adv. Java; the batch which was handled by one of the faculty members here. The more I wanted to stay away from girls I was forced to be somewhere near them. This batch was of 5 girls. I decided to keep myself focused as I had to continue Advanced Java from the point where madam had stopped teaching. Pragati the girl from the C++ batch was able to read my expressions clearly.

"What happened Sir?" She asked.

"Nothing." I replied.

"You look tensed. Any problem Sir?" She asked again.

"No problem. I am fine. Let's continue where was I?"

"Sir you can tell me. I won't tell anyone. I promise. I know there is a problem Sir. You have been dictating the same notes again and again. I have almost written the same problem twice."

"Oh! Really." I was shocked to hear that. I immediately looked into her book and was totally surprised. I was actually not in my senses that moment.

"Sorry Pragati I am a bit tensed about this new batch of Adv. Java have to take over."

"Advanced Java? You teach that as well. Wow Sir!!! You are a genius."

"No I am not. I don't know what I would teach them. I hardly got time to prepare myself."

"When is the batch?"

"It starts right after your batch."

"So leave me early Sir. You would get time to prepare yourself, as it is I was not in a mood to study."

"Very nice Pragati." I looked at her angrily.

"Sorry Sir but I was not feeling well. So I didn't want to come today."

"You should have told me before. Anyways I can't leave you. We have to finish this topic today."

"Please Sir not today. I will tell Ma'am that I have some work, that's why you left early."

"Why would you lie? Tell her the truth." I said as I checked the time. I thought for a while and looked at her, she was still waiting for my answer.

"Ok then. Will see you tomorrow." I said.

"Thank you Sir and Best of Luck." She said and left. Actually I needed some luck at that moment. I checked the notes of Advanced Java. The syllabus had changed a lot. I had never learnt the stuff that was in the notes. But very soon the girls arrived and I asked them to be seated in the class. Unfortunately, I could read much and had to close the book and get into the class. I closed my eyes before I entered and tried to visualize Bappa's image in my mind when a voice echoed, "Best of Luck Mottu."

With that the fear within me disappeared as I entered the class. I was confident to face the class with these five girls. I asked them to introduce themselves before I begin. Later I asked them the topics covered by Ma'am. I introduced the new topic which I would begin to teach and at the same time I informed them to be prepared for the test the next day. This test was to judge them so that I could understand their level of understanding and it could have been easy for me to teach them further. The girls agreed and were curious about the test as what I would ask them. I now had a task for myself of preparing questions on topic which I had never read before. Advance Java had a syllabus that I had never studied or had any knowledge about it. But I couldn't tell them about this. I asked them to prepare for the test and was out of the class confident and smiling as the lecture went well.

Later I called up Mridula, to wished her.
"Happy Birthday!!!" I said.
"Dhruv. Where the hell are you?" She shouted first and then said thanks.
"I am in Pune. Why? What happened?"
"You've disappeared. What are you doing?"
"Well. I am working as a faculty in NIIT."
"What the hell?" She shouted back. "What are you teaching there?"
"I am teaching programing languages here."
"How come all of sudden? How did you land up into such a thing?"
"Just like that…" I replied with a smile. "BCS background. Remember?"
"Oh! Yes. I remember."
"What about Animation?"
"Still searching for a job in that."
"Good. And how is Radhika?" Just the question I knew she would ask me. She had called me up on my b'day but we didn't talk much about this that day. So the next 10-15mins our talk continued. I told her everything that happened in the past few days. I also told her that I still have 6months to prove myself. Mridula assured me that Radhika will come back if she had given me time to do something. I didn't tell her the later part that I was dead for Radhika. Mridula tried to build up a ray of hope within me.

2-3days later I spoke with Parth and for the first time talking with him gave me a ray of hope that maybe Radhika might come back. She had messaged

Krish that she wanted to meet him before she left Pune. I continued to contact her through emails but every email reply from her made me think a lot did she ever love me? If she did why is she is ignoring me now.

Few days later, I went to Dev's and asked Aman to come along for a movie. I wanted to give up all the thoughts and wanted to refresh my mind. I knew a movie can help me out. Akshada said that if my emails can upset Radhika, it means that she loves me a lot and will definitely come back to me. I smiled at her statement as I knew my friends were only trying to say things that will make me feel good. Maybe I was expecting too much from everyone. I had asked only Aman but then he gathered everyone along for the movie. Everyone enjoyed the movie making fun of each other. I wanted to talk with Aman to let him know I need a friend to support me in this bad phase, but somehow his reactions always gave me a feel that he didn't want to be with me or talk anything about Radhika. Maybe that's why I ended up saying human emotions play no role when people around are thinking of being practical. After the movie, I kept thinking over and over again. Was I really becoming an emotional fool? Or was I always an emotional fool. I had never seen myself into such a constant thinking mode ever. Continuous thinking about a person who isn't bothered to look at me or call me to check how I was living without her. I couldn't accept the fact that she doesn't love me anymore. That love where she said I will never leave you Dhruv. I will always be with you. Everything is over and now it's only me and nobody else. To add up more thoughts Parth called up. It was Saturday evening, I was back home from NIIT trying to do something on the computer.
"Duksey." He said as I picked up the call.
"Parth. What's up?" I replied.
"Nothing much. You say. How's life at NIIT?"
"Going good." I replied. "It's actually difficult to teach man. But it's fun as if I am learning something new every day.
"Good. So you are enjoying you job?"
"Yes. Kind of…You say, what's new?"
"Nothing much. Except that Meera got married today." He said without any feel of being sad about it.
"Parth I'll call you in a moment." I said immediately and hung up. I was shocked. I didn't know how to react. Meera had always been in Parth's mind. He had sacrificed his entire career for her. And now she's married to someone else without even thinking about him. I kept thinking about it for a while then called up Parth.
"How can you be so cool Parth? You didn't say anything."

"What should I say? She never loved me. You can never force a person to love you. Can you?"

"Yes. But… I know what she meant to you."

"Does Radhika know about this?"

"Yes she does. In fact I just dropped her some time ago. We were together." He said and I tried to sound normal.

"What did she say?"

"She continued to say one thing. I know Parth you are not happy. You will never say anything."

"Good. At least she understands your state of mind. Parth I'll tell you one thing. I won't be so normal as you are, right now. I love Radhika a lot and will always do. The only problem is she doesn't understand."

"She will, Dhruv. Give her some time."

"I wish she does. But Parth I am not you. I will go crazy if such a thing happens to me." I said as we continued to talk for quite a long time. I wanted Parth to talk to Radhika for me. In fact I wanted every single person on this earth to tell her how much I really care about her. If she can understand Parth's state of mind, why can't she understand me?

Monday afternoon, after the lecture I was surfing the internet. Well, I was now officially seating in the staffroom. I was finally introduced to all the faculty members. There were four faculties including me. Two female staff who taught VB.NET and Java along with C, C# and C++ and usually worked till 4pm. The other was Sudhir Sir. One of the most talented and brilliant faculty this center could ever have. He was an engineer who had cleared the CA finals and had knowledge of almost every programing language. So all he taught in class was VB.Net, Oracle, Java, C, C#, C++ on both windows as well as Linux operating system. Somewhere I always wondered why he always gave me an anger look. What wrong had I done to him? He asked me to sit in the staff room along with all the other faculties and that was when I was surfing the net. Radhika had already removed me from her Facebook account so I was checking the Orkut account. Radhika removed me from her Orkut account as well. I felt bad about it, but then it had to happen someday. She had told me she would break all contacts with me. Also my friends in her friend list would be removed soon. I closed the browser and got back to work.

Next day, I joined everyone for the breakfast after class as Anushka asked me again. I was introduced to the group. Well, the chocolates on my birthday did most of the things for me. I was not treated as an outsider anymore. So it was Anushka, Palak, Neha, Saket, Ketan and his girlfriend. Soon I became the part of their conversation and the jokes they would crack at each other. That time Ketan made fun of me as well when I said I was taking leave to prepare notes for Java. I was going nowhere, felt like time was running in full swing and there was so much for me to do. After the breakfast I returned back home and began studying Java and preparing notes on it. I had informed the Center Head about having a severe headache and cold. She asked me to take rest and I was busy preparing notes.

After sometime I had my lunch and was again back to work. The day ended and I was able to make proper notes that would help me for the next few days. Next day I called up Parth as I wanted to ask him how Radhika was doing. He informed me that she wanted to stay back in Pune as Kimberly Clark was her life. That added up a smile and a hope to fight back again to get her. Later, Diya called up to enquire how the preparations were going for dad's 60th birthday. I didn't say anything as I was lost in Radhika's thoughts. She was angry upon me, as we were not planning anything for dad. She really wanted to make his birthday the best and I was not able to understand her at that moment. Why did she care so much for him? In the evening, I was teaching Java and was interrupted by a student. This was the same one whom I thought would create problems for me on the very first day. So he began and another student joined him.
"Sir our hands are paining. Right from the first day you are only dictating notes. We haven't even done any programing."
"Have patience, we are going to start it tomorrow." I tried to defend myself.
"Why tomorrow? Why not today?"
"Because, I know what I am teaching you and I have planned it accordingly."
"Why can't you start programs directly? We need you to teach us the real programing. What you are teaching us is already been taught in college."
"Ok I see. But does everyone agree with him?" I asked and among the eight guys only two hands were raised. The rest didn't have any problems with the way I taught. I tried to explain them that one could only work on programs if the basic concepts are clear. The conversation continued and I was completely disappointed. I thought if this would actually stand against me. I told everyone that we would begin with programs only if everyone wants and called it a day off. Sudhir Sir told me not to worry about those students as they knew how to deal with such students. But somewhere the thoughts began in my mind.
"This is not what I wanted from life. Every day I am fighting to prove myself. Radhika please come back I am just a failure without you." I said to myself

while coming home. I thought again I couldn't give up so easily. I have to fight back and I will.

Saturday 28th August 2010, dad's 60th birthday, I wished him and well I didn't do anything else. But that day Diya had planned a lot for him. I was surprised too. Sometimes we can do anything but it's really hard to understand a girl. Diya was one such girl. No matter how much her father hated her after she left home she still wanted his birthday to be the best. That day I woke up early and went to class. Sir was teaching the concept of rotoscopy-one of the widely used concepts in movies and commercials. I went to NIIT after class and came home early. All my relatives had gathered home, the plan was to decorate the entire house with candles. But dad wasn't going anywhere. So my aunt took mom and dad to Saras Baug Ganesh temple. Once the three left we cousins began our work and started placing the candles all over the stairs. I was busy decorating the cake with candles and rose petals around it. We somehow managed to decorate the entire house pretty decent that too in a short span of time. Mom dad arrived and we switched off all the lights and lit up the candles one after another. By the time they came up in the living room we all started singing in rhythm, *'Happy birthday to you...'* Dad was surprised to see the nicely decorated cake in the middle of the living room. He then cut the cake and he celebration continued. Everyone got busy chit-chatting with each other. I clicked some pictures but then in every picture I clicked, I wanted Diya to be present. She was the one who had planned everything. Even the dinner was made by her. The moment I tasted it I knew it was not made by anyone else in the family. Diya used to cook different stuff and I could guess the food was prepared by her. Well at the same time I remembered Radhika and the celebration last year.

I came upstairs in my room and called up Diya.
"The veg-biryani was awesome. When did you make it?" I asked.
"How did you know I made it?"
"I can guess, it was made by you."
"Anyways you liked it?"
"Yes." I said.
"What about others?" She asked.
"They liked it too. Isn't this funny, people are enjoying your food and praising aunt and Pal for cooking it. Whereas they can't guess it was made by you."
"Let it be Dhruv. As long as everyone is happy, I don't care."

"You should have been here. Actually why are we doing this. This man, who screwed my birthday twice and kicked you out, how can we even think of making his birthday the best."

"You know Dhruv; mom has always taught us one thing. Always be nice with everyone even if they are not. Maybe someday they would realize their mistake and will be nice with us."

"What if they never realize their mistake?" I asked her and I knew what her reply would be.

"Dhruv this is the one basic thing of life. Never expect anything from anyone." She said.

"You know something; Radhika would always say the same thing. Always give your best to everyone and never expect anything in return. But she forgot something that she was always expecting some or the other thing in return."

"Let it be Dhruv. You liked the food right?" She asked and changed the topic immediately.

"Yes." I replied back.

"That's it. I'm happy. It doesn't matter if I am not there with you guys."

"You should have been here. This is not done."

"It's ok Dhruv. Just forgive and forget." She said and hung up as I was called downstairs to serve the ice-cream to everyone. Everyone was in their own world and nobody cared if Radhika was with them or not I mean if Diya was with them or not. I was missing both of them but I had finally learnt to be along with everyone with a smiling face, rather than letting anyone know my true inner feelings.

Well, am I forgetting something? Oh, yes! How could I? Two days later was my cousin's wedding at Somwar Peth. And yes I did forget to tell you about it. One of my cousins was getting married and his wedding was fixed within a month. Everything happened all of sudden so most of the people were busy with the wedding preparations although, I didn't miss the chance to check Radhika's status on Facebook. She had completed two years of her article-ship training and yes it was her last day in the company. I wanted to meet her before she leaves. So when I went to Somwar Peth along with mom my eyes were continuously searching Radhika everywhere. She had told that she would meet me once before she leaves. I would stay outside just to ensure I could get a glimpse of Radhika at least once. But I was never able to see her. Next day on the wedding day I was still in search of Radhika. I went all the way to her office and waited there for some time till I mom called me as were about to leave. Nothing was going right that day. My heart was pumping a lot more than usual. The thoughts of Radhika were not finding their way out of my mind. I was fighting with my mind, on the other hand I behaved normal as nothing had happened with me. We all left for the wedding which was away from Pune in our native place. It was a two hours journey; I kept interacting with my cousins. Laughing, teasing, playing, singing and doing all crazy things had become a part of fun to keep my mind busy. Although my heart was crying from inside I wanted to meet Radhika as two months had already passed I had not seen her. I wanted to get out of the bus and run towards her and meet her for the last time. I was getting some negative vibes that if it's not now, it will be never. Maybe she will leave me and will be gone forever. I stayed calm and didn't let anyone knew what I was going through.

We all reached the wedding place and were greeted by the bride's family. As I got off the bus my childhood memories of the village began to clash along with Radhika's thoughts. I went on the terrace of one of the room. It gave a complete view of the entire village. Due to rains, the entire village was looking green. Thank God it wasn't raining on the wedding day. Krish and one of my cousins joined me and after clicking few pics' we came down as the wedding rituals begun. First it was the engagement ceremony, followed by the Haldi and then the wedding. The rings were exchanged and then the rituals continued one after another. We all stayed together during all the rituals. By afternoon the wedding began where the bride and groom exchanged the garlands and sat for the pooja. We all cousins finished our lunch and decided to visit the Bhuleshwar temple. The temple is famous for its own miracles. It is said that if we keep some sweets with pure heart for Lord Shiva below the Shiv Linga it disappears within few seconds. I had been to this temple when I was a kid and the excitement was doubled when I came here after a very long time. We kept 5 pieces of sweets under the Shiv Linga. The Brahmin told us to wait for few minutes and later he removed the Shiv-Linga and gave us the plate. We all were surprised as it had only one piece left in it. He showed us that there was no hidden place below the Shiv-Linga except for an empty space in which the Shiv-Linga would fit. He told us that it was one of the miracles that happen within the temple for many years. Well if miracles like this could happen within a blink of an eye all I wanted to say at that moment was make such a miracle happen in my life. I need Radhika…Please don't let her go away from me.

Later, we all spent time in viewing the old carvings on the temple wall. Some of which were destroyed before independence. I clicked many pictures and let's say for some time the temple environment helped me forget the pain in my heart. We came back to the wedding hall where everyone was waiting for us to come. We had forgotten to keep a track of time; it was almost evening when we came back. We left the place with the new bride and reached Pune around 8pm. While removing the bags from the bus all of sudden I fell down. I tried to get up and life the bag and was not able to pick it up. I never felled so weak. I applied my full strength and then somehow kept the bag inside the house. I came out and soon called up Parth and tried to talk with him for some time. After that I called up Aman and asked him to contact Radhika. He agreed and then I hung up. My mind began to think again. What went wrong within a moment? Something was not correct. Aman informed me that Radhika's number was not reachable which made me more worried. My eyes continued to search her again and again till the time we were in Somwar Peth. Later as we came back home I turned on the computer and was copying the pictures on the computer when Krish showed me a message.

'Sorry guys, I am leaving Pune.

I was not able to meet you.

I will see you soon.

I'm going home for exams.' It was Radhika. I was completely shaken after reading this message. I didn't show it though. I gave the phone back to Krish and asked him when he received this message. He told that he had just received the message. He went off to sleep and I messaged Radhika, why she did this to me and also messaged Aman.

'I had told you give that letter to her before she goes. Why didn't you? Now she is gone home forever.' Aman called me immediately as soon as the message was delivered to him.

"Are you crying?" He asked.

"No I am not. I have decided I will not cry." I replied back.

"Are you sure?" He asked again.

"Yes I am Aman. I had told you to contact her. Why didn't you contact her?"

"The moment you told me to contact her, I was calling her. Her phone was continuously out of coverage. Seems like she didn't want to be contacted."

"I always knew she would do such a thing. She tells me to face problems. Now look at her who is running away."

"Maybe she has her own plans."

"Yes I know. Screw up my life and then get started with your plans. I know she is not like this, but she could have called me at least once before leaving." I said letting out the entire frustration within me.

"Listen Dhruv, give her some time. You know I thought a lot about it. Failing CA finals is like the biggest disaster that happens to a CA student. Ask me how I have been through it."

"I know that and I know she failed because of me. But that was not my intension that she should fail in her career path. Anyways I still think you should have given that letter to her."

"I know that but, I thought over it. I thought about you and about her. If I would have given that letter to her, maybe she would have read it and things could have been better. But what if they had gone the other way round?" Aman said and tried to justify himself. I never has asked for any justification. All I wanted was someone to stop her from leaving me. Aman did his role and I always knew he would never give her that letter I gave him. I was not sure whether I had made the right decision of giving that letter to him. One thing was very clear it's only me who could convince her but I had lost the confidence within me. I wanted everyone besides me to tell her I was not wrong I only loved her but always failed to express it. But then she had left me and Pune city forever.

*****

Chapter 28

The Show Must Go On...

2nd September 2010, I woke up, took a shower, got ready and went to attend the lecture. I wasn't listening to music anymore. But the sad songs still played in my mind. My heart still pained, the pain was unbearable. Many thoughts that flowed in my mind cried out one thing, Radhika please come back. I reached class and came to know that sir gave us a day off due to electricity cut-out. That time I was standing alone when Anushka asked me if I would like to join them for breakfast, rather I was waiting for her to ask me so. I wanted to get rid of all the thoughts that were running in my mind. Somehow I was not ready to accept that Radhika was gone forever and everything was over, so I said yes and joined them. It was Anushka, Palak, Neha and me.

"Come on so tell us who your girlfriend is?" Palak asked and before I could say anything Neha interrupted.

"Why will he tell us Palak? We are not his friends." That statement got me triggered and I replied immediately.

"You are my friends since the day we met during the clay modeling sessions."

"Nice line Dhruv." Anushka said and they all started laughing.

"So tell us Dhruv about your girlfriend. I am sure you must have one." Palak insisted again and told them about Radhika.

"She is a CA, currently working with Kimberly and has gone home to study for her final exams."

"Wow Dhruv your girlfriend is a CA?" She asked with surprise so were Anushka and Neha.

"So where did you guys meet?" She asked and with that question they were eager to know everything about her. Somehow that recalled few good memories and time spent with Radhika. They insisted a lot so I showed them her photo. Later I informed them that she was gone forever. Palak asked me not to worry she would find some for me soon.

"I don't want anyone just want her to come back soon." I replied quickly. We reached the hotel and order something to eat while we continued to chat.

This was the third time I was out with these girls; well the rest of the group had started bunking the lectures on a regular basis. I had started liking to be with them early morning, it kept me cheerful throughout the day. We continued to talk on various topics that day. Let it be Bollywood celebrities or Indian politics. The outcome of each topic was that someone needs to stand up to change or to bring the change. That moment I felt I should quickly go wherever Radhika was and tell her that she was not the only one who thinks that way. With that cheerful and sometimes a serious conversation, I got back to work. The next 2-3 days were spent at Somwar Peth attending the various events after the wedding. So it kept me distracted from Radhika's thoughts till 5th Sept 2010. Well, this day also famous for Teacher's Day and Akash's birthday. I called him up early morning and wished him Happy Birthday. Well he had his own plans for the day. He informed me that he would be going to the gaming zone along with his new girlfriend then lunch along with her, followed by movie. It sounded like a real good plan. But what was my plan for the day. Nothing! So I called up Diya to check with her. She asked me to come along at Pal's house. I got ready and reached her place, we decided to go for movie 'We are Family.' We went for lunch before the movie and the movie completely screwed up my mind. Well, aunt liked the movie and she made up a comment on my reaction. "You young generation would never understand how difficult it is to handle two women at one time. I really appreciated the way he took care of both of them." I didn't say anything, just couldn't understand one thing. If these people can understand and accept the situation of the guy shown in the movie so easily, why was it so difficult to understand the situation of Diya? And yes at that moment I did have an answer to Path's question. I did fell in love with two girls at one time. One of the dumbest things I could have ever done in my life. But I was sure that I loved Radhika more than anyone.

7th September'2010, I received my first salary cheque from NIIT. I looked at the amount and there were many questions in my mind for the salary paid to me. I went to the center head along with the cheque in my hand. Before I could say anything she began explaining it to me that there were complaints from the Adv. Java batch. The girls said that I was not sure of what I was teaching them. They were not wrong, I seriously was not aware of what I was teaching those girls. The Center head Sonal assured me that my salary would be increased soon if there was any improvement in my performance. I didn't know how I should react just thought for a while and then came back home. I gave the salary cheque to mom and I couldn't blame the reaction that I received from her, Krish and dad. The guy who once earned 30-40k per month was bringing home a salary cheque of 7000. Krish continued to crib that I should join his company till the time I get a job into animation. I didn't want to get into the profile which I had left behind. I wanted to move ahead. I knew life will be challenging, even though I was not prepared for it I wanted to face it without letting fear conquer upon me.

During that time I began to interact with Sudhir Sir and slowly got to know many loop holes in the NIIT administrative system which was handled by Sonal. The way she handled the front end of NIIT none of the faculties were happy with it. There always were huge clashes between her and the faculties. Sudhir Sir told me that all the faculties were informed that a Java Specialist would be joining NIIT, one who is an expert in Java. That was me. On the other hand I was told by her that I would be given proper faculty training before I begun to take any batch. With all the false and misleading information given by her, I can't blame Sudhir Sir for the anger look he gave me from the very first day I joined NIIT. I decided to stay away from the polities that was going as I didn't want to get into any mess that was already been created. But, when you are already a part of something you cannot run away from it.

A day before the Ganesh Festival I was asked to take an introductory batch of VB.Net and let the students know what they would learn at NIIT. But the thing was I hardly knew anything about this subject. But, being a faculty I had to be prepared for all kinds of situations I was put into. I entered the class which had around 20 girls and 1 single guy. Yet another challenge, I wanted to stay away from girls and was put into such situations again and again. I introduced myself and the asked them to do the same. They began introducing themselves one after another. Through the introduction part I got to know a lot about these girls. Most important I was impressed listening to their career goals and aims for life. After spending about 30 minutes with the introduction I wasn't sure what to do next. So I waited till Sudhir Sir finished his lecture.

"Ok so the good news is I am here only for this lecture. Write your names and phone numbers along a piece of paper and pass it along. Sudhir Sir would be conducting this batch from tomorrow."

"Well that's not good news. We thought you would be teaching us." One of them replied.

"I wish I could. Oh! Sudhir Sir is here." I pointed towards Sir as he peeped inside through the door.

"So, what where you telling them?" Sir asked.

"Nothing. It's your batch, you can take over. I'll leave."

"Where are you leaving, I have just given the other batch a program, so I came to see the new batch. Dhruv Sir you continue. I'll begin this batch tomorrow." He said and left. I asked the batch if they had finished writing their names on the sheet as I had to give it to Sir. Somehow I had developed a lot of respect for this man and would always add a tag Sir whenever I called him, so did he. The girls were done with the details and gave the paper to me.

"Ok then class dismissed. Sir will begin with the lectures from tomorrow so best of luck." I said and stayed back till everyone left the classroom. I entered the staff-room when one girl followed me.

"Sir." She called me.

"Yes." I said as I turned back to her.

"I have a question?"

"Yes, what is it?"

"Are you sure you are a faculty?" She said gathering all her courage. She seemed scared. I smiled back and looked at her.

"Why? Don't I look like one?"

"No. I mean, yes. No."

"What do you mean?"

"Sir I actually thought you are a student. You are very cute." She replied with a smile.

"Good. But I am a faculty. Thanks for the compliment." I said.

"Ok. Bye Sir." She said and left adding a smile to my face. I got back to work and soon Sudhir Sir entered the room.

"What happened Dhruv Sir?" He asked.

"Nothing, this batch. Beware!!!"

"Don't worry I knew what students I have got as I have taught their friends before."

"Good. Enjoy then."

I left early from class as I had to finish the preparations for Ganesh Festival. The decoration was still pending and I was able to recall how 2 years back Radhika and the others had helped to put up the decoration when Diya had left. This time there was nobody to help so I wasn't able to put up a nice decoration. I stayed awake late night to put up the decoration and later was stuck up with cold. Next day I woke up early morning for the Ganesh Puja. Later, mom asked me to join the 2 beds together in the other bedroom. I and Krish did it and after eating breakfast I took medicine for cold. I came upstairs into the bedroom where we had joined the beds. My eyes started getting heavy due to the medicine but I could feel as if Radhika was sleeping besides me. She placed her head across my arm and said, "Mottu phir se sardi?" She then kissed me and then I was not able to recall what happened next. By the time I woke up I found my cousin's daughter sleeping besides me. I was completely fresh and the cold was gone. I got up and went downstairs and found everyone setting up plates for lunch in the kitchen. I came in the living room and looked at the Ganesh idol and thanked him for the wonderful dream and prayed to make it come true someday. I came downstairs and found mom and my cousin's wife washing the plates. They had just finished their lunch. I had my lunch and was still trying to get into my senses after the having the medicine. The cold tablets I took always had some or the other side effect, drowsiness was one of them. I got back into my senses after a while and then spent time with the cousins.

Two days later, Radhika was again in my dreams. This time it was her mom's place that I visited but she wasn't recognizing me. I didn't know why I would get such dreams. Maybe, I was thinking too much. I wanted to get rid of these thoughts and wanted to move on, but it was getting very difficult for me. I continued with my lectures and classes. Soon the five days were over and it was time for the visarjan of Ganesh Idol. During that time dad began to discuss about my wedding. So I was again back into the thoughts of the day when I failed to do anything but cry. That day haunted me every time I wanted to forget it. I called up Parth to discuss the same. I knew Parth never liked to talk about the topic but still he said something that made me fight for myself again. He said that Radhika was not happy with the breakup but will definitely try to forget Dhruv. He asked me enjoy every day and be happy as she was never coming back. 'NEVER COMING BACK...' Those three words would always pull me back from going ahead and I was again trying to find answers to a question, why? Why and why?

Next day I went to MAAC and after the lecture I had breakfast with Anushka and Neha. While coming back home Parth's words kept running in my mind I have to enjoy every day and have to be happy in every possible way. I reached home, there was nobody at home. I began to eat lunch and before I could leave for NIIT many thoughts kept running in my mind. I have to enjoy every moment; I can't live like this I have to be happy. I am happy I will always be happy. I can't be dependent on anyone. I will live an awesome life. I am happy, I will enjoy every moment I will live my life. I kept saying this to myself again and again; while I wiped off the tears that flowed along every bit of food I took.

    Later, I got myself normal and went to NIIT. I had enough time to reach there as I was in no hurry. Although, I was called early to take care of the preparation, we were celebrating the 1st anniversary of NIIT of our branch. I had asked to students to come in a particular dress code. Black was the color decided and while I had completely forgotten. I was stopped by one of the colleagues.

"Where is the dress code sir?" She asked.

"Dress code? Oh I forgot." I replied back immediately. We then moved upstairs as we had to wait for the others to come. Our counselor Neha came in nice red saree, while Sudhir sir and the others were dressed up in their regular outfits. After sometime the owner of the institute arrived and we were introduced to him one after another. He seemed to be a very humble guy but then as I always said looks could be deceiving. He spoke with everyone and then he went to the venue where the event was going to take place. We were asked to be in the class till the other students arrived and guide them the way towards the venue. That time we faculties were chit-chatting on various topics, when a girl entered the premises. Sudhir sir asked me to check who she was. I saw her and was stirred by her beauty. She introduced herself as Gayatri and was here to enroll herself for Java lectures. She was told by few students about the class and wanted to join. I asked her about the timings when she told me that she was told by the students that a faculty in the afternoon teaches java nicely and wanted to be in the same batch. I couldn't hide my excitement and asked her to come for the party. She paid the fees and which I collected and gave her the receipt Neha had already prepared for her. She took the receipt and left with a smile and I moved back to the staff room where our discussion continued.

"Sir if you all are paid so less why can't you start your own institute?" I asked.

"It's not that simple Dhruv sir." He replied back.

"Why not sir? You can teach most of the subjects, whereas madam can teach visual basics, dot net and java nicely. So, where is the problem?" I said and waited for a response. Sudhir sir looked at madam and then turned back to me.

"You are right sir. We can go for it but who will look after the other things?" He asked.

"Things….?" I questioned

"There are many other things Dhruv sir. We have to make sure the admissions are done properly as well as the fees collected, gets deposited properly in the bank. And most important the salaries of the faculties, finding a right location for class." Madam said taking interest in the discussion. Overall I figured out that they were not happy working here but were scared of taking that big step.

"We have to divide the work among each other and have to trust each other if we want to work this out. Actually there are few ideas that came up to me this very moment." I said.

"What are they?" Sir asked.

"First of all if you people agree we can work upon this secretly without letting anybody know, we can make this a big hit. We can start an institute which has almost everything in it, starting from the programing languages to teaching musical instruments. The students who come to learn can get most of the options to select. I also have a name for it. 'MORE DREAMS TO COME (MDTC)' It would be one of its own unique class that would help every guy/girl fulfill his or her dreams."

"Wow that actually sounds nice." Madam said and continued, "You seem to be working upon this for a long time sir."

"No ma'am this just came from within, just like that." I wondered how I could get such ideas. It sounded pretty strange but both sir and madam agreed to work upon it secretly. For some time I forgot everything that ran in my mind. I was in an illusion or rather feeling proud to get such ideas as well as people to appreciate it.

Soon we all left towards the venue as most of the students were gathered. The party hall that was selected by us was nicely decorated with colored balloons. The chairs were arranged in a way that there was place in between to move ahead at the front. It took another hour for all the students to come in order to celebrate the occasion. We had faculties coming from the other branch as well to celebrate. I was clicking pictures of everyone as I was asked to carry a camera. The owner of this institute gave a speech followed by felicitating the old students with gifts as they got placed in few well-known companies. The rest of the staff was also appreciated and gifted for their performance with the students. I ceremony concluded with cutting the cake which was brought right after the ceremony. I continued to click pictures of everyone. It seemed to be a completely different atmosphere. Few students fed me with the piece of cake whereas few thanked me for being their faculty. I was introduced with the other faculties of the various branches. Later, we had the music setup for the students along with dinner at the food counter. The students pulled me and the other faculties as they enjoyed on the beats of the music. I felt happy and enjoyed every moment without feeling a need to enjoy.

While coming back home my mind started again. No matter how happy I was with the students I was still missing Radhika. I had to move on as she had gone. The show must go on it can't stop if the person in your life disappears.

Your role doesn't end here it's much more to come. I said to myself with a smile throughout. I was happy that the day ended with a smile and the hope to fight back as there were people around who were carrying hopes and I was the reason behind it.

*****

Chapter 29

More Dreams to Come...

NIIT anniversary added a smile and a reason to prove that I am the best. Somewhere I was still trying to find that lost Dhruv within me. I was actually trying to be happy although I missed Radhika most of the times. The next day most of the students were eager to see the pictures I clicked. Many of them liked and the fun continued the entire day, after which, I was back into the animation class. During the lecture Sir informed us that he would be teaching us the concept of Conversion. The day to night conversion, which is done in most of the studios through CG composition, but that was not so easy. Sir gave us a task that was to study the light difference. He asked us to click pictures of any scene nearby our homes, maybe streets or any campus. The motto was to make us understand the variation in light at different point of time. He had given us enough time as he wanted us to click pictures for the entire day for an interval of an hour. I actually liked this idea as I would get a chance to hold the camera and click pictures. I had a very nice view from NIIT. So I clicked the pictures from there. I decided to spend an entire night at NIIT along with Sudhir Sir who had some work at night to finish.

So it was two days after the anniversary at NIIT, I began clicking the pictures after every hour. Whereas, the students were lined up to ask me questions one after another out of curiosity, while I finished all my lectures. I went home and informed mom about the work I had to finish at NIIT. I got a movie copied onto the pen drive as Sir asked me to do so. We connected the speakers to the computer which was attached to the projector. As there was nobody else in the class I got a very good time to talk with Sir about setting up the new institute. Sir was pretty impressed by the way I had put the topic in front of everyone as he had been trying to do so for quite a long time. His only fear was that the two madams would inform the Center head and everything would be messed up. I assured that nothing of this would happen. That time I recalled it was his birthday, so I went out to see if I could get something for him. Unfortunately all the shops were closed as it was very late. I somehow managed to get CAD-B (chocolate thick shake) one of the famous things in Pune. I and Radhika had spent quite a time at this shop. Also I couldn't forget her harsh words, how she had spent on me for this thing. I got rid of the thoughts immediately as I took the parcel and came back to NIIT. Somehow I wanted to make Sudhir Sir feel special on his birthday. He almost had tears in his eyes when I gave him the CAD-B and wished him Happy Birthday. He never expected I could do such a thing for him as it had been 3years since he had celebrated his birthday. That moment he shared his entire life, the past events that had changed his life completely. His was a very big family in Orissa. He had four sisters and has lost them one after another. One who was the youngest of all and also the closest to his heart was burnt to death due to dowry. Also he said that this was the one who would always try to make his birthday special and chocolate was one of her favorite things which I had got. Sudhir Sir cried a lot as he was missing his family. I tried to console him but his story had completely shaken me. He studied a lot everyday so that he can forget everything. Also his parents tried to get him married but the worst thing that could happen to him was she dying in a car accident. I was speechless and continued to stare at him. I didn't know what to say.

"Dhruv Sir..." He looked at me and said.

"Yes."

"Go take your picture it has been an hour." I got up from the place and clicked the picture. I came back and looked at the glass of CAD-B. Chocolate- gave rise to so many memories. The first was Radhika's harsh words and then Sir's sad story. I tried to cheer up his mood by saying.

"Sir, come-on, finish the chocolate."

"Dhruv Sir this is horrible and I hate chocolate."

"Come-on Sir it is good. See I finished mine. But even Radhika hated chocolates at start."

"Yes you have told me and I don't want you to start your story. One sad story is more than enough for the night." He said.

"This is not done, I was not going to tell you anything."

"I know I was just kidding. Go start the movie."

He said as he wiped off his tears and we watched two movies one after another. I went off to sleep in between when Sir kept me awake. He assured that he will make our dream come true. He wanted to get out of NIIT and start something new for himself. I finished clicking the pictures by morning. The night had ended into a beautiful Sunday morning. I went back home and went off to sleep and woke up when Sudhir Sir called up. He asked me to get ready and come to Garware College for the Bavish Jyoti Scholarship (BJS) program conducted by NIIT. Faculties from all the centers had arrived at the center. I got ready and went there. Many students had arrived for the scholarship test. I was helping Neha our counselor with the registration process for the students.

Later, Sir asked me to join him in the classroom as an examiner. Something I was completely not prepared for. It was a great experience. I distributed the answer sheets and then the question papers to the students one after another. Later I was watching them while the thoughts began to flow. I could have told this to Radhika. This is one such great feeling that I could never imagine. Being a faculty I had got many experiences this was one of them. We all got free by evening and I went to meet friends. So after a long tired and joyful experience I was back home stuck with fever and cold.

'*If you want something you never had, do something you have never done.*'- Radhika status on Facebook was telling me again and again that I had to work very hard. The things which I am planning are not very easy. Hard work and dedication is very necessary to make things simple. I started searching few advertisements in the newspaper for commercial places in the nearby location which could be suitable for starting an institute. I had taken a leave at work, next day I thought of listening to music, so I gathered few songs and loaded them on a flash drive. I then carried it downstairs and connected it to the mp3 player which Krish had purchased during the Ganesh festival. The moment I turned it on and the song begun my father shouted out loudly and asked me to turn it off. I felt bad, actually very bad at the moment as well as was angry. I kept thinking as what exactly did I do? I only wanted to listen to music for some time. Am I not supposed to do that? But then I controlled my anger and left the living room and came upstairs in my room and kept thinking over it. After some time I got ready and went to NIIT. I began with the first lecture of Java and during this time I was feeling a strange attraction towards Gayatri. I wasn't sure why this was happening. After the lecture I went to ask sir but at the same time I got a call from a person in regards to the commercial space. Sir and I went to see the place as all the other lectures were cancelled. The place was nice and was in a location that had 2-3 colleges around. We opted for the location and began with other plans.

The next day after the lectures were over I had to reach my cousin's place for dinner. As I reached there I saw mom and the others had already finished eating and were about to leave. I asked her to stay till I finish my dinner. She asked me to come alone after I was done rather waiting for me. She had got dinner packed for Krish instead as he was about to come late. I couldn't understand why my parents were behaving like this. I needed them to be with me as I was going through a bad phase. But every time I tried to expect anything from them, my expectations were ruined. I finished off my dinner as the thoughts kept running over my head. I had to stay neutral and carry a smile which I did.

Next day being a Sunday morning we were asked to be at class. Few students who had missed the BJS exams we had to conduct the exams again for them. I reached there early and as the students were seated I distributed the papers and the exam started. As I was monitoring them madam called me outside.

"Dhruv sir, seems like you are taking this job very seriously now a days." She said.

"Seriously…Why? What happened ma'am?" I asked in a confused tone.

"It's just that I haven't seen you so early to work. That too being a Sunday you are here so early."

"I was asked to come early, ma'am."

"Anyways, what is the progress of the institute?"

"Going well ma'am, sir and I saw a place two days back. Let's see how it works. You are with us right ma'am?"

"Yes I am sir. And yes before I forget, you got appreciated by few students."

"Oh! Is that so? Who are they?"

"The girls from the Adv. Java class. Remember?"

"Yes I do, the ones who complained about me not able to teach them."

"Actually it was not your fault; they said you taught all the concepts so clearly that even I have not been able to teach it that way. It was only because they were used to my way of teaching, they found you a bit slow or rather too theoretical."

"How strange are these girls?"

"Yes, let it be sir. Keep up the good work." She said and then went in the lab to continue her lecture.

Those words felt nice and gave me some positive vibes. Later, I collected the papers from the students and then was seated in the staff room. Sudhir sir joined me and we began to talk.

"Sudhir sir something is happening. I know it's wrong, please help me with it." I said.

"What happened sir?" He asked and I told him about Gayatri the girl whom I was getting attracted to.

"Dhruv sir you have an aim in front of you. You are fighting to get back your love. These will be few things that will hold you back from your aim. All you have to do is kick them away from your path or else you would be left alone. You have to help yourself, nobody will stand beside you." He said. His words had a deep impact and maybe that's what I needed I got my confusion cleared and was happy the way sir explained the things to me.

Sometimes when everything is going proper we start to get a feel that now everything will be normal. But actually it's never that way. There is something else that's been planned to set back all that you feel is normal. The same thing was happening with me. 29ᵗʰ September 2010, a day that very few would like to recall here in Pune. I had finished my class and after lunch had reached NIIT. After the continuous lectures I got an off as few students didn't turn up for the lecture. So Neha and I left NIIT to have light evening snacks. One of Sudhir sir's students joined us.

"Sir, Can I ask you something?" She said.

"Yes."

"Sir, it's a little personal but still I want to ask."

"What is it?" I stressed a bit.

"Sir first of all let me tell you, you are very handsome."

"Thanks and what is the question?"

"Do you have a girlfriend?" She asked immediately. I kept quiet as I didn't knew how to respond to her at that moment.

"No, he had a breakup recently." Neha spoke while I kept thinking.

"So sad, I wish I would have been your girlfriend, actually I would like to be. You are not single right sir?" She asked and waited for me reply I smiled at her and didn't say anything and finished eating.

"Come-on let's go your lecture would begin soon." I said and we three came back into NIIT.

I continued with my work as there was no lecture for me in the evening. I was watching through the window the change in the atmosphere. A cool breeze was blowing throughout, as there were signs of rain. Neha told me that she was leaving for the day. I waited for a while and then got back to work. Sudhir sir joined me in the staffroom after finishing the class. The girl gave me a smile and I smiled back, thought I should avoid her. It began to rain as after sometime as I was still watching Sudhir sir. Something was wrong I sensed from sir's behavior. I tried to ignore at first but later I couldn't resist.

"What happened, Sir? Why are you so tensed?" I asked.

"Nothing, everything is fine."

"I don't feel so, look at you it seems something really bad has happened with you today."

"Sir the rain will stop in a while, don't worry I know you don't like rains. I hate rains too."

"It's not about the rains." Sir immediately replied and I made him speak. I was amazing at this.

"So here you go Sir, now please tell me what's wrong. I promise I would not tell anybody."

"You should have done that before Dhruv Sir."

"Means...? I don't understand what you are trying to say."

"I had warned you not to utter a word in front of the ladies."

"Yes, you did but both the madams promised us they won't share it with anybody."

"Do you really trust them? I have been working with them for the past one year."

"I believe in myself Sir. I know they would not tell anybody."

"Good. Then there is nothing I would like to say." He said and left the staffroom. I went behind him as he was trying to switch off the lights of the classroom. The rain had begun to rise gradually. I tried to ask Sir again when he finally came back in the staffroom to finish off the remaining work. I then forced again when he finally said,

"Our Center head knows that we are trying to setup a new institute. She has informed that she would inform Sir directly about this. You very well know that man. He is crazy he could fire us anytime he wants and then we neither have this job nor the new institute. Everything is over." I was quiet after hearing this. I wanted to speak but then hearing this made me numb. I tried to utter a word but then it was difficult for me. Although I gathered my voice and tried to ask him if there is anything else we could do to stop this from happening. Sudhir sir had no answer to this. Now he kept speaking and all I heard was a dead silence. The sound of the thunder lightening had increased so did the rain. I then tried to say that maybe we could hope for the best. The Center head let's assume had not heard anything. But then Sir didn't seem to fool me. He was serious about it. We sat quiet for a while and never noticed it was already 10. The rain didn't seem to stop, the water kept pouring with the same intensity. Sudhir Sir wanted to leave as they would be able to eat if reached late. So we decided to lock the class and leave. The rain didn't stop so we finally left in the rain. Sudhir sir took an auto-rickshaw and left informing that we would try to find a solution upon this.

So it was me, thinking whether to leave or stay back. I thought for a while and left in the rains. My dream was broken again when I was trying to start something new. I was trying to remind myself everything will be fine. But

nothing was fine. I was lost once again. Tears began to roll as I started moving on the bike in the rain. The rains didn't stop rather it kept increasing. I didn't know how to begin but I had questions, questions and never ending questions. *"Why? Why? Why? Why again this thing to me?*
Should I just go and end up my life? Or maybe I really don't deserve anything new. I need something new in my life I need a change I need to setup my life. This is not helping me. I really want to setup this institute I want to become someone in my life. This is not want I want. I am trying to find a new dream and this is not helping me. God you are not helping me. Stop playing with my mind and emotions. I need Radhika back in my life. I need her. I cannot get her until I become someone in life. What are you doing this is not helping me. Please..., please I beg you."

I was completely broken that day. I kept mumbling to myself as I was riding my bike in the rain. I wasn't aware if the rains were hurting more or the broken dream was hurting me more. I really wanted to know what was in for me. Someone to guide me I couldn't keep wondering and let people mess up with my life. I needed that one thing which would let me know that this is what I've always wanted and nothing else. But that night I had no answers to it. Only the thoughts that kept telling me I was lost and I need a way out. I reached home safely completely drenched. No electricity and the heavy rains had made it the worst night for me. I changed my clothes and avoided all moms' questions and hopped in my bed.

*****

Chapter 30

Ray of Hope…

I was broken completely and had almost thought of giving up. I needed a new direction and motivation, but was not able to motivate myself anymore. I slept without eating anything and had decided to give up and call up Radhika to tell her I cannot do anything. I won't be able to become anybody in life. You made a right decision of leaving me forever. Maybe you deserve someone better. I would always be a loser. Thank God, you are not here to see how broken I am with my dreams. Do I really have any dream left? I guess one should never dream, because dreams never come true. I kept mumbling these things again and again till I felt asleep. I found myself sitting alone on a rock watching the waves of the sea flowing back and forth. I kept staring at it continuously when Radhika came and sat beside me. Yes, I was dreaming again.

"What happened Dhruv? Why are you sitting alone?" She asked.

"I am a loser Radhika. I can never win." I replied.

"Who told you this?"

"No one. But I know I can never win. Maybe that's why you left me. You knew this. Don't you?"

"Dhruv, I left you for some other reason. You would certainly find it out for yourself someday. But I know Dhruv what you are capable of. Believe in yourself."

"I do. But then…"

"Do you really believe in yourself Dhruv?" She asked again. I kept silent as I didn't know what to say.

"If you really believe in yourself Dhruv, do something that will make me feel proud, as I know you are much more capable than you think you are not." She said as she hold my hand and took me along with her. We walked for a while and later a bright light flashed in front of me and a name glittered into that light. 'DREAMWORKS'. Something that Radhika tried to tell me once again or maybe it was something else. I didn't realize as I woke up and all I could remember was the bright light and Radhika holding my hand when I woke up. It was 7.30 am; once again Radhika woke me up. I could hardly recall the dream when I woke up. I got ready and went to class. The class was cancelled due to the Ayodha's result that was going to be declared in a fear that some riots could happen. Most of the shops were also closed. As usual most of the students had bunked the class. It was me Anushka and Neha who spent some time together at our favorite restaurant. Yes, I had almost started being with them every day for breakfast. Anushka had begun to share quite a lot with me. I had once asked her whether she would help me to light up a scene of Wall-e and Eva. The same model which I had once created in Autodesk Maya for the exhibition. She agreed to help me with it once she gets to see the file. She also agreed that if at all I setup an institute she will help me with it and so did Neha. That brought a smile on my face and encouraged me to work hard.

Later, I went to NIIT, the parking of the building was flooded with water. Most of the students returned back home as they couldn't cross the parking flooded with water above knee-level. Sir and I managed to get inside from the other side of the building and he asked me to inform everyone to take a day off. I called up everyone and later was reading the newspaper. Around 15 people had died in the heavy rainfall. Like I said such rain I had never seen in Pune before. Sir told me who was responsible for spreading the news till the Center Head. We continued to discuss things as we had given off to the students. I told Sir that if we could work secretly on this nobody would know and maybe we could continue to work. Sir agreed and said that they would check, if their father could help in some way. I started gathering information through newspaper for a location for the institute. Later I called up a person from the advertisement I saw and we both went to see the location. I liked it but thought we could view some more locations before jumping up onto any decision. We then came back to NIIT and later left for home. The day ended when I met Vishal after a very long time. He came to meet me at home along with a girl. He introduced her as his fiancée. I was surprised as well as happy for him and thought how time could fly away. I had once introduced Radhika to him and said will be marrying her soon and here I was listening to their love story. I had nothing much to say just congratulated him.

Next day, the water was cleared from the parking and we were back to taking classes. My busy schedule started again. First lecture began teaching Java; Pragati had joined this class along with two other girls and two boys. Next was the batch for the unique student who tried to copy me a lot. He wanted to have the same hair-style as I did. And yes he was a very good friend of the Center Head Sonal. I had to take this special one hour batch only on her recommendation. Later 4pm to 6pm was C++ batch of Pragati and a newly joined student Yash who was one of the eldest students I had in my class. Well much elder than me. After this batch I would get one hour of free time where I would work on the notes or go out along with Neha or Sudhir Sir for breakfast, as I had the alternate day batch of Java and GNIIT students. That free gap was soon taken when I got free from that one student. Once I was taking the Java lectures in the afternoon I almost forgot it was 3. Students were discussing the topic which I had to cover and also wanted to plan an outing along with me. The plan was made for a movie. I wanted to avoid it but was not able to get any proper reason to say no. We continued with the discussion and later around 3.30 I tried to look for the student I noticed him sitting alone in the lobby. I tried to ask him when he came on which he yelled upon me.

"Sir you know I am here only for an hour. Now half an hour is almost wasted, doing nothing."

"Hey listen, you should have informed me that you were waiting outside. I didn't find you out around 3, so I continued teaching them. I was covering an important topic." I said and tried to keep myself calm and asked him to be in class. He said he was late and had to leave early today and will come tomorrow and will let me know if at all I was in a lecture, before he left. But that was not all, the same evening I was questioned by Sonal. He being her best friend, she was very upset on my behavior.

"You know Dhruv that he only gets 1 hour to learn. Now look what you have done. He is very angry and doesn't want to come back." She said. All I wanted to say was, I don't care. I never wanted to teach that dumb friend of yours. Instead I said sorry. I then tried to defend myself that he should have informed me.

She later told me that he had a lot of ego problems and will never come back. I was happy he wouldn't come back but he convinced her to finish the portion. I wrapped the syllabus in the next 2days for him. Soon I was given a new batch from 3-5. The 4pm batch was shifted to 5pm. So I hardly got any time later for anything. I had to now start teaching C to this new batch of again 7-8 students. I wished I wouldn't have girls in it but there were again 4girls in that batch. It started off good and I was happy that being busy will keep Radhika's thoughts away from my head. But as I was not getting time for anything made me fall ill. I was stuck up with cold. Even after I was happy that being busy all the thoughts of Radhika would be out of my mind for few days. But then she was not a person whom I could forget so easily. I was checking something to eat in the fridge when suddenly her voice echoed into my ears. "Dhruv don't eat anything from the fridge. You will fall ill. You already have cold." I immediately closed the door of the fridge and then I was not able to take her thoughts out of my mind. I always feared this one day after breakup where I am not able to concentrate on anything. But then it happened again and I was not able to teach anything in the afternoon Java batch. I told the students that I would continue the topic next day. The entire class agreed except for one girl who was continuously behind me to finish the syllabus by the end of the month. She had to apply for the Java entrance so I took her to meet Sudhir Sir to guide her for the test. Sir gave her some notes and asked her to study through them. She took my leave with a smile and asked to continue the next day. I could see a lot of hope in her eyes and I was leading nowhere. One by one every batch of mine was facing trouble where I was not able to stand up to the student's expectations. I got back in the class where other students were still chit-chatting with each other. I joined them for a while and got rid of them thoughts and continued with the other batches. That girl never came back for any lectures, when called she informed me that she was preparing through the notes for the entrance. That moment I directly asked her if she was not able to understand anything I taught on which she said that I taught the concepts very nicely. She was able to understand everything properly but the only thing was she didn't have much time. Time…! It was running for me as well. Four months were almost over and I was still doing nothing.

Anushka checked my file and liked the modeling part. She encouraged me to work upon the modeling skills and keep it as a secondary option in terms of specialization. I thought of working upon it. I had started spending most of the mornings with her before and after class as once I took her along with me to buy gift for Diya for her birthday. After two long years I finally wished Diya on her birthday and gave her the gift. The very next day Anushka called up to know if she liked the gift. It was like I had started building a new friendship along with her, although, it had many restrictions that I had built up for me. Breakfast after class actually would lighten up my day as I would meet Anushka and the others. Once after class everyone decided to go for shopping. But that's when the limitations to this friendship came I wasn't earning a lot to spend on shopping. But then Anushka would have contributed for me I thought. Yet another Radhika came in my mind and I straight away said no. I stopped myself from being carried away. I had promised Radhika I would become someone within these 6months and I had to work upon it. But even if I tried avoiding one thing the other was already there to distract me. The girl from Sudhir Sir's batch in NIIT, who would always wave her hand with a smile whenever she saw me. That day she stood in front of me and kept smiling.

"How are you Sir?" She asked.

"I am fine." I replied back and tried to escape.

"Sir." She shouted back which made me wait. "I wanted to tell you something. You are looking nice today."

"Thanks." I said as I once again turned my back to her.

"And how is it that you don't have a girlfriend?" I smiled at her and left without saying anything. Sir had warned me not to be involved in anything that comes into my path towards success. These things could pull me down and I had to get back to work.

Anushka had asked me to be present on the last day before we break for Diwali leaves, so I went class without fail. Anushka was sitting alone listening to music. I pulled off the headphones from her ears.

"What are you listening?" I asked.

"Nothing as such. You want to listen?"

"No I hate music."

"Yes I know breakup and its side effects."

"Shut-up, it's nothing like that."

"Ok, instead of standing over my head sit her." She said and made some place besides her.

"Are you sure I should sit here?"

"Ok don't sit. Anyways I have emailed you the image you need to model. I hope you would be able to do it."

"Do you have any doubts on it.?"

"I know you can do it, but I am sure you will say something after you see the image."

"What's so strange about it?"

"Just check it and call me when you see it."

"Sure." I said and never knew when our conversation had turned up into serious discussion about work until Palak joined us followed by the others. I knew I was going to miss her but was surprised how she had a strong belief in me that I would be able to do anything, just like Sudhir Sir did.

Sudhir Sir was handling a batch of Java. It was a special batch for a couple who were working in a corporate firm. Sir wanted me to take this batch; I was able to skip it as I already had a batch. But 2-3 days ago Sudhir Sir came inside my batch,

"Dhruv Sir." He called out my name.

"Yes." I replied and followed sir outside the classroom.

"Dhruv Sir you need to take this batch for the next few days."

"No sir, I can't"

"Yes sir, you can." He smiled.

"Sir they are very highly qualified than me, within a moment they would understand I know nothing." I said in a confused yet scared tone.

"Trust me. You know a lot of things than you pretend you don't." Sudhir sir always knew how to boost up my confidence with all kind of jazz. But sometime he was right I was underestimating myself at many occasions. He somehow got me convinced and I had to begin teaching Java instead. I entered the other classroom while Sudhir Sir informed my GNIIT batch that it will be again conducted on alternate days starting tomorrow. These three guys were very happy as they got to leave early. I was scared as I didn't know how to begin. I closed my eyes and gathered my confidence. Both the husband and wife were seated on different bench. Close to each other and they were really elder to me. They were around their forties I guessed. I had to do this without being scared, so I started teaching and within an hour I almost finished teaching half of the notes which took me two weeks to complete in the other batches. So my new students were very happy as they were able to understand the concepts very easily. I took their leave and came in the staff room where Sudhir sir kept smiling at me.

"Don't look at me like that sir." I said.

"I told you, you can do it."

"Sir!" I shouted. "You know something; I have finished 2weeks of teaching in just one hour for these two."

"So that's good."

"Nothing is good. Look at me I am shivering." I said and put my hand on sir's arm as it was turned cold.

"Dhruv sir you don't have to be scared of anything. I know you are a multi-talented guy." That compliment I had heard after a very long time. It was Radhika who used to say I have a multi-talented boyfriend. I smiled at sir and yes the fear of teaching someone elder to me as well as highly qualified than me disappeared. I felt more confident after that.

Next day, I was waiting for the married couple to show up when they called up and informed that they would be late from work so I asked them to take a leave. Meanwhile, I tried to check the image and kept staring at it when I called up Anushka.

"What is this Anushka?" I asked.

"What happened?"

"This is such a complicated image."

"I know, but I thought you will be able to do it."

"I have never worked on such difficult concept before."

"Is that so, then let it be, I'll give it to someone else."

"No wait. I will do it." I said immediately."

"Seriously." She replied with a smile.

"Yes."

"I know you can do it. By the way how many days will you need?"

"When do you want?"

"After Diwali..."

"Fine, I will try."

"Thanks Dhruv and best of luck for the image. See you soon." She said and we hung up. I could sense the happiness on her face when I didn't give up.

I studied the image over and over again to decide where to start from. It was a game setup of an old village. I decided to install the Maya software on one of the computers at NIIT and begun working on the image. Don't know why but I never wanted to give up on anything. Even though there were many thoughts running in my head I wanted to work and get back to where I had been thrown away. Anushka had shown me the ray of hope to get back into animation and make my dream come true one day.

*****

Chapter 31

The Interview...

"NO EGO...
ONLY ATTITUDE!!!
But Still,
DOWN TO EARTH..."
"How does this sound?" I asked Sawaari and Anup. We met at the coffee shop after I finished my lectures on Saturday.
"It's awesome. The best t-shirt quote for our group..." Sawaari shouted excitedly whereas Anup wondered how I could get such ideas. We decided that we would get it printed for everyone and when I messaged everyone they all liked the quote. That time I thought of getting one such t-shirt printed for Radhika as well. Never did I think how I would give it to her after getting it printed.

Since the day she left me I had become allergic to every couple who were in love. I could never be around them. Instead being with Anup and Sawaari kept me happy. But just being with them for a while would help me keep all the thoughts away. Sawaari would continue to talk about the fights she had in class or about new crush. But she would never forget to mention that one faculty in their class who taught them one of the subjects of the CA course. Radhika would talk about him a lot. I guess all CA girls I knew were crazy for this faculty. But it was fun to hear how Sawaari would describe it in her own unique style waving her hand and moving her body while talking, she would always forget that her voice would increase to the level audible to every person standing or walking nearby and Anup and I used to hold her and make her talk softly. It was fun and on the other hand Anup would always come up with some or the other business ideas and we would be lost in the discussion for hours.

The idea for the t-shirt quote disappeared within a few days and one day Sam called up as he was nearby. I finished my lecture and came along talking with Sudhir Sir when I saw him at the pizza outlet. After a while I went inside to meet him and wanted to leave immediately as Avni was seated along with him. Not that I didn't want to talk with them but their conversation kept me reminding the days along with Radhika. I left soon and didn't know why this would happen to me. I was waiting for the signal turn green when a bike stood on my right. I turned my head and saw a girl tightly hugging the guy in the front. Immediately I turned my head towards left. Well the same thing happened on the other side. I nodded my head and just thought of looking behind. I turned back and saw another couple, where I saw a girl feeding a chocolate to the guy in front. I stayed calm and thought over and over again why was this happening with me. I was only attracting things around which I never wanted for me. The signal turned green and I drove my bike in full speed to run away from them while I looked up at the sky and shouted loud stop playing mind games with me.

Few days passed, the students at NIIT began to take leaved for Diwali vacations. I already had no lectures in MAAC as sir had given ten days of leaves for Diwali. I wanted to keep myself busy but as the students demanded for leaves there was nothing much I could do. I got leaves in NIIT as well for 3 to 4 days. The days got over soon and I didn't make any plans for movie this year. I just wanted to stay away from anything that would lead me to some thoughts about Radhika. I had to get back to work as I had promised Anushka that I would begin working on the image soon and finish it quickly. I began to work upon it and soon realized it would take a long time to finish. But somehow I had to start with it without any hesitation.

I had another weird dream. Something was telling me that Radhika was not able to concentrate and on the other hand it was Anushka. Anushka had come back from home after the vacations and was very excited to see her image complete. I soon woke up and was confused about the dream. I prayed to God to help Radhika concentrate in her studies and wanted to share this dream with Sudhir Sir. But something else was on Sir's mind. He continued to ignore me throughout the day. I decided to ask him what the matter was.
"Sudhir Sir what happened to you all of sudden?"
"Nothing."
"Sir you are continuously ignoring me."
"No, I am not. I am just busy with work."
"Come on Sir I can see it. You hardly had one or two lectures the entire day and all you did was keep yourself busy in some or the other work. What's the matter Sir?"
"Ok, but first you tell me what's going on with you?"
"Me?"
"Yes, did you propose one of my students?"
"What?" I shouted. "Are you crazy? Why would I do that?"

"I don't know, you tell me."

"Ok Sir. Firstly, I never proposed any girl. Instead she was the one who did try. I am avoiding her. I still am. But how did you come to know this stupid thing?"

"You never told me but still I know it. Your friend Neha told the entire class."

"What the hell? Is she crazy?"

"I don't know. But I want to know it from you sir. Do you really like her?"

"Sir what is wrong with you?" I asked again. "You very well know that I am waiting for Radhika to come back. How can you even think like this about me? Seriously…Not expected from you sir." I was somewhat disappointed as well as angry on Neha as she had screwed up for me. Sir realized his mistake and then said sorry. Our discussion continued as Sudhir sir had his misunderstanding cleared completely. That time a message flashed on my phone… 'JOB REQUIREMENT- Internship for RHYTHM & HUES for Animators.' I immediately called up MAAC and spoke with Smita ma'am. I decided to go for the interview.

My thoughts began to flow in different directions and I wanted to get rid of the thoughts that Sir had put in my mind. I could soon see the dirty politics that had begun in NIIT and I didn't want to be a part of it. Next day I went to MAAC with my showreel and showed it to the faculty in charge for sending people for the interview. He informed me that I can apply with the showreel for the internship as they were only looking for freshers in animation. I was happy and somehow wanted to work hard on this one opportunity that was right in front of me. The interview was on Monday 15th November and I was very excited about it. I wanted this interview to work for me. Rhythm and Hues is one of the reputed studios in the world of animation. This internship program was one such chance for me to get into it. I started gathering all my resources to prepare for the test. Later when I was back in NIIT I messaged Aman best of luck for his CA exams which were about to begin. I had no lectures for the next few hours and that was the time I could prepare myself for the test. But soon Aman's reply got me into a thinking mode. Obviously, I was lost in Radhika's thoughts again. I didn't want myself to be carried away so I called up Diya. Within a moment she understood the reason I called.

"Why is it like this? The people who are always in our mind don't care about us." I said.

"I know Dhruv whom you are referring to." Diya replied immediately.

"I just want to throw her off my mind, if she is never coming back. But it's not happening."

"Why?"

"I mean I have tried everything that is explained in 'THE SECRET'. Everything actually comes true but then. Why not Radhika?"

"Dhruv."

"Yes."

"That simply means you are not trying harder. And did you forget one thing?"

"What?"

"Radhika knows 'THE SECRET'. She was the one who showed me that book and she very well knows how and when to use it."

"Yes, you are right! Sometimes I actually feel like I should never get married. Stay away from everyone all alone just like Salman Khan. That way, I wouldn't have to regret anything."

"Are you sure you can do that?"

"I don't know."

"But then Dhruv did you ever gave a thought. Even Salman Khan had a bad phase in his life. His movies were not successful on the screen. There are many other things that have tried to pull him back. In life nobody can escape a bad phase in their life. So may it be Salman or I or you. Taking some harsh decisions would not make you great or successful; if you keep working hard maybe someday you would be one. Just understand one thing which I always said. Give time some time." Diya said and almost proved her point. I knew my thoughts would lead me nowhere. Diya knew that this was a bad phase for me and she also knew I was working over it. All she wanted me to was work harder and let go off these thoughts. It took me a while but then soon a message helped me forget everything.

"Hey guys I am back meet you tomorrow in class." That was from Anushka she was back from home and that reminded me of one thing. The image was not complete and I didn't know how she would react. It was strange sometimes how our thoughts would fluctuate from one person to other.

Next day I was early to class. I was going through the notes when I saw Anushka enter the class. My face lit up with a smile, she gave me a hi-fi and sat next to me and then we began chit-chatting. She told me about the CDT training that she attended in Mumbai. Her work was appreciated a lot. She informed me that the image shown on the projector screen during the CDT training for reference was the same I was working upon. She felt happy about it and also I could see it in her eyes how happy she felt while her work was appreciated. Anushka asked me to visit her place the next day so that she could plan the work accordingly to help me with modeling and finish up her showreel. She had made up some plan to work upon with me. That sounded great and I was excited about it as it was motivating me to get myself somewhere from where

I had lost track. I told her about the interview for Rhythm and Hues and she wished me luck. In the evening I was handed over with new students for a new batch and my free time was again occupied by a new batch. I informed the center head about taking a day off on Saturday.

It was a pleasant day to begin with, I woke up around 8. The feeling that something new will start again and I would work hard for animation kept a smile on my face. I got ready and had my breakfast and informed mom about visiting Anushka's place. I left home around 10am and for some god reason there were only thoughts about animation in my mind and I was happy about it. It wasn't hard to find her place although she lived at the extreme end of the city. It took me an hour to reach her place. I parked my bike in then walked towards the lift. She stayed in an apartment on the fourth floor along with her brother. By the time I reached her floor she was already waiting for me at the door. I smiled at her and she waved her hand and said hi. I was a bit nervous seeing her. Is she alone at her place? This was a question in my mind. I was relieved when I saw her brother. She was wearing a t-shirt and three-fourth jeans or maybe it was a track pant I didn't pay much attention to it. I was distracted by the t-shirt she was wearing. It was a short t-shirt and every time her hand was lifted up a bit I was able to view her navel. I was dying to tell her please change the top. I didn't want to recall Radhika as she used to wear such t-shirts. Please change it Anushka. But I stayed quiet and tried to look around everywhere in the room. She showed me her bedroom and asked me to wait while she went outside. She came back within a minute.
"Thanks Anushka." I said.
"Thanks for what?" She said immediately.
"Thanks for changing that t-shirt. I really wanted you to change but was not able to say it."
"I wasn't feeling comfortable in it so I changed it. Anyways, it was too short."
"I know. But it was not about how short it was, the problem was something else."
"What was it?"
"Since morning I had no thoughts abo ut Radhika, but the t-shirt you wear wearing kept reminding me that she used to wear the same when she was at home."
"You should have told me, I usually wear it at home but then I thought what you would feel so it's better I wear a long top."
"Seriously Anushka?" I said and looked at her and she had a nice smile on the face, a moment to capture but I didn't do any such thing. "But why do you have to expose so much?" I said and she hit me.

"Kamine chal let's do our work." She said and began to explain me things. She had got some reference images which I could work upon. The images were some interior and exterior of houses. Some old village scenes and few characters. I should say she had done quite a research for me. But she cleared my doubt; she told me that those images were taken from MAAC during the exhibition time. She told me everything about what happened in MAAC during the exhibition days. These guys were in charge of every activity conducted in MAAC. The exhibition got cancelled to some unknown reasons to them as well. Her expressions could tell me every bit of effort these guys had put in to make it a success.

Our talks continued along with the discussion of the work we had to do. After a while she asked me what I would like to eat. I wasn't sure if I would stay at her place that long so I had no answers for it. But my hunger couldn't stop me from answering that question.
"Whatever you would make?" I replied.
"Okay. But, would you like to eat lunch or just normal food would do?" She asked again.
"I don't know whatever is easy for you. But are you sure you know how to cook?" I said, but she completely surprised me with the food she cooked. It was nice and tasty. After lunch we finalized the work and she asked me to complete the image first and then start working on the other files. I told her that the image would take some time as it was getting converted into a heavy file. I then left her place while she wished me luck for the interview. On my way back home I got a call from Anup and he asked to come near guitar class as everyone had planned to meet for some time. While the other arrived I continued to read "Two States", the book I had got from Anushka. I then spent time with the others as they arrived and came back home.

Next day being Sunday, I thought of watching a movie before I begin the preparation for the interview. So it was me and my cousin Shivam watching the animated movie Caroline. Next day, I gathered all my work and got ready for the interview. It was held in the one of the centers of MAAC so I had to reach there by 11am I knew that the interview would begin with the test which would take some time so I messaged the students. I informed them and asked them to come tomorrow for the Java lectures. Also made sure I dropped a message to the center head for not being well. I was busy with the test trying to make sure I crack the interview and give my best. The test was over and I came to know that one of a student received my message late and he informed the center head about my interview. I got tensed and didn't know how I should react. I scolded the student but then it was not his fault. I should have been more careful. I shouldn't have informed them about the interview in the first place I thought. I called up Anushka and told her the same. She asked me to be cool and then said not to worry as I should focus more on animation rather than NIIT.

Next day I went to NIIT and everything seemed normal. I spoke to Sudhir sir about the interview and he informed me that nothing bad would happen as he would help me. He asked me to stay calm and continue with the lectures. I did the same. Yes the lectures went well and then there was no reaction from the center head. Anushka called up to know what happened at NIIT.
"Nothing, I mean nothing happened. I thought she would say something. But she was normal as if that Monday never happened and I was completely present at NIIT. I said
"Oh Dhruv, seriously I was so happy that now you will get time to focus more on animation if you are asked to leave. But seems like teri toh kismat hi kharab hai." She said and we both laughed.

*****

Chapter 32

No more a Faculty...

"You are a part of someone's beautiful life.
You may never know where you fit,
But remember, that one day someone's life...
May never be complete without you...!"

I read this status update on Radhika's Facebook page early morning. The thought inspired me but I couldn't understand whether it was for me or someone else. Radhika would never be out of my mind even though I tried hard. I needed someone who would help me keep her thoughts away so that at least that one day would be saved for me to work. I was a bit concerned for Radhika but then I knew she would study hard this time. But what about me the more I tried not think I kept thinking over and over again about her. I decided to go to class and maybe get some thoughts cleared. So I was saved again. Sir came late that day but the lecture didn't happen. I joined the others for breakfast along with Anushka. So it was me, Anushka, Sid, Neha and Palak. I had a feeling that these guys didn't like me much especially Sid and Neha, but it was for Anushka I tried to stay. Later after breakfast Neha and Palak went along with Sid at his place. This was a common hangout place for all these friends. Anushka stayed as she had a friend coming to meet her, I asked if I could company her until she comes on which she agreed. We both went to MAAC and then later to see the Japanese Doll Exhibition opposite MAAC. We almost spent an hour together looking at the various dolls exhibited there. It was nice and somehow I felt good and it also helped me to get rid of the thoughts. Later her friend arrived and I came back home. I had to reach NIIT so I had lunch and left soon. The day went good and I was happy throughout without any bad thoughts to spoil my day.

Harry Potter and the Deathly Hallows released the other day and I wanted to watch it but I wasn't sure with whom. I went to temple before leaving for class. But again the class was cancelled so I was a bit disappointed as nobody informed me about it. I slept was sometime and as there were no lectures at NIIT I was completely bored. Soon then Aman called and asked me if I would like to come for the movie. I thought for a while and then we both went for the evening show. As usual Aman had brought the last row corner seats. I could understand how he always managed to get the corner seats. But whatever it was

I was happy that I was watching the movie. The movie was an entire roller-coaster ride for me as I could gather all the mixed emotions of being happy, sad, thrilled, excitement and much more. In between I did had a thought in my mind that is it because she was attached too much with Parth or was it only because of me, I not being as smart and caring like Parth. But then Parth had already given me a reason why I should not carry such thoughts. So I avoided the thought and by the end of the movie I was happy and kept talking about the movie with Aman.

"The movie was awesome. I just want to watch it again Aman." I shouted as I was riding his bike.

"This was nothing; wait for the next part it will be super-amazing." He said as he has read the book.

"You know I feeling like I can manage without Radhika. I don't need her. Maybe I should call her and tell her right now."

"Are you sure that you really want to do that?" Aman asked.

"I don't know. But I seriously doubt if I can ever say that."

"I know, just don't think too much let things be as they are. She is busy with her studies, let her clear the exams then you can think about it."

"Yes, her exams are important. She should become a CA, that's her dream, I won't call." I said and we were quiet for some time. I was again in my thinking mode, her exams, her studies, her dreams, her parents, her brother, and her friends everything that's important for her, she should get it. I was or maybe I was never important so me saying anything to her doesn't matter at all.

"I just said don't think too much. What are you thinking?" Aman asked and I replied back.

"Nothing let it be." I replied back. It was late; Aman dropped me home and left. I didn't know what magic that movie had over me, I actually slept peacefully. I believe that was the only time I had no thoughts no dreams just pure sleep. Next day, Diya called and asked to meet. I met her at my aunt's place and then it was me and my three sisters again for the movie. I didn't mind watching the movie again it was fun. After the movie our talks got us into something that was related to Radhika. My cousin agreed that Radhika was nice and a sweet girlfriend I ever had. I smiled and didn't utter a word and never let anybody know my inner feelings. I was missing Radhika badly. That moment if she was in front of me I would have hugged her tight and never let her go. But that wasn't possible as Radhika was there with me only in my thoughts and memories. The day ended and it was almost midnight. I called up Parth and wished him; fortunately I was the first to call on his birthday. I had decided not to talk about Radhika with him, but that didn't last long. I asked him how she was doing and he tried to get me out of it as always.

Monday morning, the new start to the week. If there's anything that you want to work out, this is the day to begin with. I was heading nowhere and seriously wanted a path rather a schedule to follow. I decided to prepare a time-table for myself with the list of activities I would perform in order to excel towards animation. I decided that along with the NIIT job I will continue to work upon animation showreel so that I will be able to go somewhere. The schedule looked pretty simple but a bit difficult to follow. I made up my mind that I would follow it rigorously and never back out. So I planned out accordingly as per how to prioritize the work. After everything was setup properly I went to NIIT. After the first two lectures were done, I was seated in the staff room and Sudhir Sir joined me.

"So Dhruv Sir what's the plan?"

"Nothing, as of now. But I am planning to get this book published soon. I have made up a schedule for myself and it should work for me."

"It will work, just follow your heart." He said and we would be into this discussion but were interrupted by the Center Head. She peeped in and asked me to come out as she wanted to talk.

I followed her out and was not sure what she would say to me. She seemed tensed and as well there had not been a single word she spoke since the day I went for the interview.

"Dhruv, how are the lectures going?" She asked.

"Going good, anything wrong?" I asked.

"When can you finish the syllabus? It's been a very long time that you have been teaching and the syllabus is still not complete." She said. I knew this would come up someday as I went for an interview without informing. I tried to defend myself by saying that students were on leave and many other reasons. But then it didn't work.

"The students have been complaining about you. They don't like the way you teach. First it was the batch of Advanced Java which I had to ask the other faculty to teach. Now it is the regular Java batch which you have been taking from day one."

"The problem is not my teaching; it is the students who have caused trouble. You can ask the others in the afternoon batch for Java. They never have any problem." I defended myself.

"Oh yes I would like to add, there is a student in the same batch who wanted to finish the syllabus quickly but you have still not done it."

"Ok she wanted me to finish the syllabus quickly but I cannot change the pace of my teaching for a single student. Does she ever have any issue with my teaching?" I asked on which she had no answer. I continued to defend myself as I knew I was not wrong. But you can only talk about yourself if the person is ready to listen. The arguments between the two of us continued for more than 15minutes and finally she came up with a solution that I need to find another job. She had already hired a new faculty and now she wanted to leave. I was given one week's time to find another job. I wanted to tell her that she was the one who got me into this situation and now she is to be blamed and not me. But I stayed quiet and came back in the staff room. Sudhir Sir had left the room as one of the students wanted their help in the computer lab. I waited for Sir to finish as the Center head left the premises.

Sir took a while to finish the lecture and in the meanwhile my mind was about to blow with some unexpected thoughts. I had prepared the time-table early morning and had tried to setup my mind to follow a strict schedule. Now with the termination from NIIT I wasn't sure if I will be able to work on it even for a single day.

"Sir I had made up a schedule in such a way that I will learn the new VB language from you and try to improve myself in the areas where I failed to delivery myself as per the standards of NIIT. I can't think of anything else if I lose this job. All my plans would fail the very first day if I have to quiet the job." I kept talking to myself in the room, when Sir joined me. He asked me about the meeting and I told every single word of what actually happened. Sudhir Sir got tensed and assured me that they will do something.

"She can't remove you even if she wants." He said. I didn't know what they actually meant by saying this. I am sure they would have felt that I might break into tears so very cleverly assured me that they will discuss the plan of action the next day. Somehow they had to leave early so didn't discuss much with me. Sir asked me to remain cool and avoid any thoughts. I agreed and left NIIT along with them. On my way back I tried my best not to get any negative thoughts but it didn't help.

The next day I informed all the students in the batches that I was asked to quit the job. The students felt sorry for me but then I told him I had some different plans and NIIT was never in the plan. I was left with only 3batches in which the syllabus was almost over. After I was done with the batches I desperately waited for Sir to finish their lectures. Sir would give the students some problems or maybe a program to work upon and would come out to give me company. I tried my best to keep all the thoughts away and focus on the time-table I had prepared. I stood by the window of the empty classroom after I could find anything to do in the staff-room. I saw the change in the weather while the rush on the road increased. I had been with my batch for coffee along with Sudhir Sir in the afternoon and I kept wondering about the bill I couldn't pay.

"Dhruv Sir what are you doing out here?" Sudhir Sir shouted from the door of the classroom.

"Nothing Sir." I replied back as I turned towards Sir.

"Let's go out and eat something."

"I am not hungry."

"I know, I am hungry Dhruv Sir. Let's go I have a lecture in the next 20minutes." Sir said and we began to walk downstairs in our regular café for breakfast. We sat there for a while and discussed many things. Sir tried to cheer me in many ways. He kept saying that the Center head would not take any action and I will stay with NIIT.

"Sir you are filled with so many talents can you check what it's in me for the coming years? Will I make any progress?"

"Dhruv Sir the only problem with you is your laziness. The day you throw it away nobody can stop you."

"Ok sir one more thing will it rain today?"

"Yes it will and exactly for 10-15mins." He said and we started laughing. We finished our coffee and came upstairs. Sir began with their class and then I was standing in the window watching the streets when it actually started raining. Sir's prediction was right, I checked the time and soon within 15minutes the rain stopped. I gathered few more questions for Sir. I went back to the staffroom and was surfing the net when Sudhir sir joined me for a while.

"Sir exact 15minutes as you said. You are a magician."

"I am just an ordinary man."

"Sir please, let me know. Will Radhika ever come back?" I asked. I waited for a while and then asked me to show her pic. I immediately opened Facebook and searched for her. He saw her profile picture and sat quiet.

"Come-on sir, say something. Don't just sit like that. Will she come back?"

"Hmm, I don't want to comment on this."

"Sir please, I need to know."

"She can come back but only if she wants to. Something is stopping her, maybe it's her studies, her family or it could be you."

"Me?"

"Yes, you have to do something, be someone only then she would think of coming back. Now let me go my batch is not over yet. We will leave after I finish. Your java students the husband wife are not coming even today. So we can leave early."

"I know you finish your batch I'll wait." I said and logged out of Facebook. I wanted to believe he was right that she will never come back but I never wanted the hope to die. I called up Anushka and spoke with her for a while. She boosted my confidence and asked me to meet in class. Next day I was completing the lecture for C programming when the Center head peeped in. She asked the students if I was teaching properly and if they had any doubts. The students replied in a rude way that they have got the best teacher ever. It gave me a proud feeling. I smiled for a while and got the slam-book filled in by few of my favorite students. Some gifted me some handmade gifts and I concluded the last day of this batch.

30ᵗʰ November' 2010, the last day of NIIT. I still had to inform everybody at home. I preferred to stay silent over it. Early morning I reached MAAC for the Fusion lecture where Anushka met me and gave a hi-fi.

"All set for the last day." She asked.

"Yes. Maybe now I will get more time for the showreel."

"It's good you can now focus upon this and try to finish it as soon as possible. Don't worry I am with you." I smiled at this statement and later thanked her for it. The lecture was over and soon I was at NIIT for the last day. I only had this two batches and I knew I would be free from NIIT. I was waiting for the students to arrive. The Center Head called me and I went to meet her.

"Dhruv you were in Convergys and have worked with the networking stuff?" She sounded confused.

"Yes I did. It was almost for a year and half."

"You should have told me before, anyways I have an offer for you." Now she confused me as well.

"NIIT is started a new networking course for some students from the working background in order to support their future."

"That's cool. So what's in for me with this?" I asked.

"We were looking for a faculty and now that we already have you I would like you to start teaching them. The class timings would be morning 7 to 9 and later 5 to 9 in the evening."

"Okay that sounds cool, but you very well know that I have my animation class at 9."

"I know so you could leave early by 8.30 till the time you class continues."

"Okay if I get to leave early I have no issues, but what about the salary."

"Yes I was going to tell you. You will be offered a thousand more than the package which you are on right now."

"That's good."

"So you are happy? You would still be in NIIT for the next one year."

"Yes I am, I still have a job. What else I want? When do we start?" I asked and she told me that the batch would begin from 2nd December. I knew this had something to do with Sudhir sir. As soon as he finished the batch he came and asked me.

"So Dhruv sir got the new job?"

"I knew this has to be because of you."

"I told you she would not remove you."

"Yes Sudhir sir you are a life-saver. Thanks a lot."

I had to again change my plan of action. I called up Anushka and told her that we would have to meet later in order to discuss the show-reel work. She was happy for me as I still had a job and said we will work something else for the show-reel.

*****

Chapter 33

When Dreams come true...

2nd December 2010, the first day of the hardware networking class. I wasn't excited about it. I knew that I will handle the batch properly but what I would teach them I had no clue. The batch timings were from morning 7 to 9 and evening 5 to 8. I had already spoken to the Center head about my animation class in the morning but I didn't tell that it was about to finish in a day or two. I reached NIIT around 7.15 in the morning and saw many students had gathered and were waiting for me to open the class. I asked them to be seated in the classroom and then I took the book I had to distribute along with me and gave a copy to each of them. I noticed that the class benches were completely full and it looked more over-crowded. Once I was done distributing the books I could sense the eagerness in everyone to open them. So talking about the new batch every other person seemed to be elder than me like 5-6 years difference. They were working in some or the other company. I introduced myself to them and told them about my experience with Convergys and also about learning animation. I told them that I will be leaving them early as I had my animation classes every alternate day. Some of them were happy with the thought that they will get to leave class early.

Once I was done introducing myself and giving the required instructions I asked each of them to introduce themselves and later asked them to write their name and phone number on a piece of paper and pass it along. Some of them were working with Tata Motors, Bajaj and many other different companies. I wasn't sure how I would manage teaching these people but one thing was an advantage for me. I knew at-least the basis of networking to begin with. On the other hand they knew nothing.

The first day of the class went well; everybody was impressed by my teaching style. Later I went to MAAC and found that there was no electricity and the class was cancelled. So the final lecture was postponed again for a week. Anushka and I were disappointed as even she was not able to plan anything further. She asked me if I was able to complete the village scene. I told her that it was almost complete but I still needed some time. I told her that Neha had asked me to work upon a small scene and I was completing that scene. I also assured her that it will be complete by the next week. She agreed as she still had some time. Anushka was planning to shift to Bangalore and I so wanted her to stay back in Pune. She was moving to Bangalore to learn some more advanced level texturing and lighting skills from one of her friend. I knew that if she leaves I would not be able to complete the task again. But I tried to focus. The entire week passed by teaching networking concepts at NIIT and working upon the village scene for Anushka and the other scene for Neha. During this I had also started creating a new stage concept for my demoreel. Listening to Anushka and keeping modeling as an option against animation had helped me develop my skills in both.

7th December' 20010, finally it was the last day to end my animation course. Sir decided to teach the day to night conversion which was the only topic remaining. I cursed myself for not carrying the images I had clicked staying away the entire night in NIIT. But then Anushka had few images to show. Sir showed us how the actual color changes in each scene and how we could reference them in order to create the night scene in Fusion software. It was a boring lecture like always but finally it was over. The lecture that was supposed to be finished within a month lasted for almost four months and now that it was over gave us a strange feeling. We won't be meeting each other again. Some were happy that finally the classes were over and they could work upon the showreel to get into the animation studios as soon as possible. On the other hand I was not sure what was planned next for me. We left from the class and Anushka said she would call me and tell me about meeting at her place.

While returning home I was again lost in my thoughts. I had few friends Vishal, Natasha Abhishek and few of my college friends. Life was simple. But then I complicated it by bringing so many people around for who maybe I don't even matter. Riya said she will always be there with me. Mahi said I am the best thing that happened to her. Radhika said she loves me and will never ever leave me. Parth said call me any time dude I'll be there. Where is everybody? I don't see them, I don't find them. It's only me and everyone has gone somewhere forever. Maybe I should have not let anybody be a part of my life. And maybe that's the reason I am alone today.

The breakup with Radhika had changed me; I knew I had to stop thinking so as I reached home I tried to put a stop to these thoughts. In the evening I met Aman and spend time with him. I told him that I would be leaving NIIT as I need to focus more upon the animation. He was not sure that if I was taking the right decision, because I had left jobs before and was not able to make it into animation. But somewhere Anushka had given me a hope that I will make it into animation one day.

A day later, she called and informed me to come to Saket's place. I had not been there before so she guided me the way. I had decided that I will not go to NIIT anymore that only person who was aware of this was Sudhir sir. He valued my decision as her saw me work hard in completing my showreel. I reached Saket's place and finally I met Rahul, whom I had heard a lot about from Anushka. His specialization was modeling and Anushka told me that I could get a lot to learn from him. We talked for a while and I came to know that he was working more in 3Ds Max software than Maya. I saw his work and it was pretty descent. Later I called up Anushka who was busy talking with Palak and Saket in the other room. She came out and we opened the file on Rahul's computer. The village scene left them speechless. She was very happy at the output and thanked me for working so hard. I told her I only tried my best as I could.

"Seriously dude this is far better than my work." Rahul said.

"Has to be he is my friend." Anushka said proudly.

"Shut up Annu, its nothing to do with you he has worked hard." Saket said while he hit her slightly on her back.

"But I was the one who gave him the file." She said.

"Guys, guys let's not debate over this. I would have never been able to do it, if it was not for Anushka. She is the one who motivated me."

"See, I am the one." Anushka said with the smile. She later checked the file and asked me to show what was remaining. I told her that I would still need a couple of days and will give her the final output soon. Later, Palak and Anushka cooked some noodles as there was a little food left for lunch.

They got the cooked noodles and the rest of the food in just two plates and everyone sat in a circle and began to eat. They asked me to join and I was being shy at first. I was not sure how I would eat with them. But what I saw was completely unimaginable. These four were enjoying the food and in between they were also feeding each other. They really shared a true friendship bond and I was happy to be a part of this friendship. After lunch they made up a plan to visit the Panshet dam and asked me to join. We all left on our bikes within the next 15-20minutes and I was not sure why I said yes. Some thoughts started running in my mind on the way.

"Dhruv you have so much of work to do. Why the hell are you going out with these guys? Remember you only have few days left and then the six months will be over." My mind started questioning me. I knew I would have fun with these guys but then I might miss on many things. So I finally decided to tell Anushka about it when we stopped at the petrol pump.

"Hey Anushka listen I have some work at home. You guys carry on I will meet you later."

"Okay and where the hell are you trying to go. You are coming with us, you can do the work later."

"Seriously Annu, I have to finish the work."

"Okay let's do one thing." She said and went to talk with Rahul. I waited for a while and later she came towards me. She sat on my bike and said let's go. *"See what you have done, I never wanted them to think in this manner."* I cursed myself, but then later made up my mind to go along with them. We enjoyed taking pictures and later the boat ride in the river. I kept talking with Anushka on our way and later while returning back we sang songs. She complimented me that I have a nice voice, whereas Radhika would never like me singing. It felt good. We reached Saket's place at around 7 pm. He asked me if I would drop Anushka home on which I agreed. Anushka and I stopped at a coffee shop and then we continued talking about the showreel and other options.

Next day I completed Neha's scene and called her. She told me that there is an animation test at MAAC and she wanted me to enroll myself in it. So I went there and got myself enrolled. I took the test paper for modeling and animation both. We have to submit the test the next day. So many students had started working in the class. I took the test and decided to start working at home. I gave her the file and the other paint room reference which I already had created before. I went home and began working when Anushka called up. She told me to take both the test, she did not take the test as she was not interested in applying to this company. She wished me luck and then I started working. I was half done when I checked the time. It was almost midnight. I was not able to complete the model which I had to submit by 11am in MAAC. I still had to start up with the animation test. But as time passed by I realized that I will not be able to complete the test. So I called up Anushka.

"Hi. How's the test going or are you done already?"

"No Annu I am not able to complete the test. I am totally disappointed, 2 years of animation course and I can't even complete a simple test."

"Come-on Dhruv don't be de-motivated. I know that the test was not at all simple. I didn't apply as I already knew the company doesn't treat the employees properly."

"You should have told me before."

"I wanted you to at-least attempt the test so that you would know where you stand. I am not saying your work is bad or anything like that but at-least you get to know you need speed."

"Yes you are right. So, what should I do now? Should I, try to complete or maybe get rid of it?"

"As of now concentrate upon your showreel. I am sure you would get a good job after that. By the way my Bangalore trip is getting finalized so you don't have much time. Can you do one thing, come to my place tomorrow, and okay wait not tomorrow. Come day after tomorrow on the 13th and then we will plan the sequence of your showreel. I have some work tomorrow."

"Okay." I said and we hung-up.

Later, I called up Diya to check what her plans are. She asked me if I would like to come for a movie. I instantly said yes and the next day we both went for a movie. I seriously needed one. So it was a Bollywood movie, 'Band Baja Baraat'. The movie was nice and it actually cleared my mind and many questions I had about Radhika. Later when I came home I called up Aman and asked him to lend his bike for a day. He said I could take it only have to drop him at office in the morning. I agreed and he was home the next day early morning. I called him upstairs as I was looking for some good movies. Anushka had given me a list of movies she wanted to see so I was searching.

"Take this disc dude it contains the best porn movies you both could enjoy it together."

"Shut-up Aman, as it is she is alone in her house and I am a bit nervous about it."

"So that's an added advantage, go take this along with you. She will be happy and maybe you would have a good time together."

"I'll kill you if you don't stop talking rubbish." I shouted and he started laughing. I took my slam book along with me and he started again.

"Why are you talking this along with you? Listen to me maybe you should take something else."

"Shut-up Aman. Aren't you getting late for office?"

"Oh ho!!! Someone is in such a hurry to meet her."

"I am going there to do some work."

"Yes you can do some work as well. Come directly in the evening and you can take the entire day." Somehow I couldn't stop him so I just pushed him out and asked him to wait and I packed my bag drank a glass of water and came downstairs. He smiled at me and later I dropped him at his office.

"Have fun dude. I am proud of you."

"Get lost." I said and headed towards Anushka's place. When I reached there I saw she was already downstairs. She had come along to buy some eggs. She was planning to cook egg curry for us. We went upstairs and I waited in the living room till she finished her work. We then moved into her bedroom and Aman's word did have a wrong effect on me. My heart started beating faster and I kept myself calm as I knew she was a nice friend and nothing else. Screw you Aman I said to myself and later tried to focus upon what I was here for. She copied the movies and later discussed the plan for the showreel.

I was feeling positive in terms of my career whenever I was with her. I was sure that if I continue to work along with her I might be able to get a nice job for me. She told me that her Bangalore trip might get postponed and I was hoping for the best. She asked me when I will complete the village scene and I told her that it would take another 2-3 days. She was happy that the output was good but wanted me to work fast. Later she cooked the egg curry as I helped her in cooked. Well, I kept watching her while she was cooking. Within some time the food was ready and we ate it watching a movie. After we finished our lunch we were again working upon the showreel. Around 5 in the evening she asked me to drop at Saket's place. We left home and I really enjoyed the time I spent with her. I never thought I would end up with such a nice friend around me. After dropping her I came back to Aman's office who was very concerned to know what I did.
"You are a total waste Dhruv."
"Shut-up Aman, you know that I love Radhika and I will never do any such thing."
"Yes Radhika I know. She must be enjoying now as the exams are over."
"Please check with her Aman if she is coming back to Pune?"
"Hmm I will." He said and we left to meet the guitar class friends. Reaching there I received a call from Sudhir sir. He informed me that two of my C batch students were here to meet me. Both of them got distinction in the subject.
"That's amazing news sir. I wished I would have been able to meet them. Did you congratulate them on my behalf?"
"Yes I did and we should talk later my batch is here." That was good news I told everyone at the guitar class and everyone shouted. "PARTTTYYYYY!!!"

Later at midnight I received a call from Aman it was a conference call. Aman, Sawaari and Anup were on the other side. Anup had conference the call to Aman, then Sawaari and later it was me. It was her birthday. She told me that the cold war between her and Aaliya was finally over and they had started talking with each other.
"Well that's awesome news Sawaari." I said.
"Thank me for it." Aman said.

"What did you do?"

"Nothing."

"So why should people thank you?"

"It's free you can use it anytime."

"Ha… Ha… Ha. Very funny." Sawaari said and we all started laughing.

"So tell me everything that happened." I said Sawaari and on the other end Anup and Aman stayed quiet.

"So are you guys done? I mean Dhruv and Sawaari it's 12 now and I guess we should wish you." Anup said from the other end.

"Yes guys wish me quick."

"Happy Birthday Sawaari!!!" We said in chorus and later individually. We then spoke for some time and then later we got off the phone. I was happy that finally these two girls started talking with each other. Morning I went for an interview. Mom had insisted me to attend this interview in camp for a faculty job. I gave the interview and was sure that I was not selected. So later I went to Saket's place to meet Rahul. He showed me his incomplete model for the test. Seeing this I said maybe I am faster than him and I smiled. Although his model lacked some details but was according to the specifications.

17th December 2010, Anushka called up early morning to inform that she will be leaving the next day for Bangalore. She asked me to come at Saket's place and said she will reach there too. I asked her to get the slam-book along with her. She asked me about the village scene and was upset when I said I will email you the file. Later, I opened the file and check if there was anything missing. The file was almost complete and I wanted to give her a surprise. When I reached his place I found that Rahul was still sleeping. I woke-up when he saw me. I asked if Anushka has arrived. He told me she is on the way and so are the others. He then went to get fresh and I called up Anushka. She asked me to pick her from the bus stop as she didn't want to walk so I went to get her. As we were back at Saket's place she gave me the slam book and told me that I have written something nice for you. I checked the book and found the space was empty.

"Annu are you sure you have actually written something for me?" I asked her.

"Yes I have." She said and showed her the book.

"Oops! I guess I wrote it on the other paper and forgot to copy her." She said and took the book and began writing. I later read it and it got a smile on my face.

"Well I have something for you." I said and gave her the village scene file.

"You completed it?" She screamed in excitement.

"Yes two days back."

"Thank you Dhruv." She said and hugged me.

"Are you guys done?" Palak interrupted as she came in.

"Yes." We both answered together.

"Well Dhruv now that Annu is gone you won't come to meet us. Right?" She said.

"I will come to meet you Palak. Don't worry."

"Yes please come daily Dhruv or else she would cry." Anushka said and we all started laughing. It was her last day with us and so Palak asked me if I could take her out for some time. They were preparing a farewell gift for her. I agreed and later Anushka and I left the place. We went to Dagduseth temple and later some book store where I got a gift for her. I gave it to her there itself. Later I called up Palak to check if they were done on which she said they would need some more time so we sat outside in the society campus.

"Annu I will miss you a lot after this."

"I know Dhruv I will miss you too. And listen please don't come tomorrow. I wanted to meet you today so I had called you. Most of them don't like you they are nice with you only because of me."

"Okay, anyways I was not planning to come. You know I am not good with good-byes." I said and we both laughed.

"Jokes apart, Dhruv I want you to work hard and get a job into animation. If we stay in the same field I am sure we would get to meet much often. Just 3-4 months and I will be back from Bangalore and will being the job search. Complete your showreel so maybe we could search it together."

"Yes I will Radhika." I said and immediately she corrected me.

"It's Anushka."

"I am sorry."

"It's okay. About your book whenever you start writing send me a copy via email so that I could help you edit it and call her now check if we can go or else I might cry here with you. People would take other meaning of it."

"Yes." I said and Palak told me to give her more 5 minutes so we continued our talk. I hold her hand and told her that it will be difficult to work if she is not around. She assured me that she will be in regular touch with me. We then went inside and these guys continued with the regular talks. Neha had come along so they put on some music and danced along with it. We clicked pictures and had a lot of fun. I made cold coffee for everyone. Well, everyone complimented me for an awesome coffee.

Later in the evening Anushka asked if I would drop her home. I immediately agreed and we left the place. It was almost 8 in the evening and I never realized that I had spent the entire day with her. As I reached her place we spoke for some time. She told me not to come tomorrow and also said the same thing to work hard on the showreel and get a nice job. She hugged me before she left and I began to ride back home. I was sad once again, the only friend I made here was leaving me and I couldn't stop her. She was thinking about her career and at the same time she told me that she would help me. But the distance will play a major role I knew. I just wanted this to end somewhere for me. I looked up at the sky and shouted out loud. Please... Please... Please end this for me God. I can't be like this always I need something in my life that would actually make me feel happy from inside.

I didn't cry but when I came home I had nothing to work upon. So I put on the movie Anushka had given me. I didn't watch it complete only kept clicking the right arrow on the keyboard to fast forward the movie. I stopped at a point when a song started playing, it was the 'Warning sign' I couldn't utter a single word. My eyes were filled with tears. I didn't say anything just let them flow. I never knew I could land up like this one day all alone with nothing around. I wiped off my tears and then turn off the computer. I took medicine for cold and went off to sleep.

18th December'2010 Saturday, I woke up late and when I was seated in the living room I got a call from MAAC. The Center head asked me my specialization and confirmed if I could go for an interview immediately. I agreed and decided to go. I informed mom about it and left home within an hour. I had to find a studio named Acme Toons located in Kothrud which I was able to find within some time. I went inside and saw an ex-faculty from MAAC. Okay the studio was owned by him. He asked me to be seated inside the cabin and wait for him. While I was waiting I kept looking at the interiors of the studio it seemed nice. I was overwhelmed with the ambience.

Later sir entered the cabin and asked me if I have worked upon lip-sync into animation. I said I have only that I do not have much of an experience over it. He told me that he has a project that is on hold as an animator left the company and he needs someone to take his place. I agreed and said I could join from Monday. He said Monday will be fine and offered me the job. Within a fraction of seconds everything was discussed and I was out on my way home when I called up Anushka. She cut the phone so I started my bike. I went a little ahead when I received a call from her. I stopped my bike and picked up the call. "Dhruv you called?"

"Yes, I guess you were busy."

"No I was getting into the bus so I cut the phone. Tell me, what happened?"

"I am not sure Annu, I guess I just got a job."

"What?" She said as she sounded confused.

"There is this studio Acme Toons, I received a call from MAAC in the morning for a post of animator. I went in and found that I could apply for it and got selected."

"Acme Toons, I have heard this name. I guess it started by one of the faculty from MAAC."

"Yes, I don't know the name and I just told you that I got the job."

"Seriously, I didn't hear it properly. Well congratulations. See good things started coming your way the moment I left Pune. I am lucky for you."

"Ha… Ha…Ha… I still can't believe I got the job."

"It happens Dhruv, I am very happy for you. See now you will be busier than me."

"I know let's see."

"Anyways I call you once I reach Bangalore and best of luck with you job and congratulations once again."

"Thanks Annu." I said and was back with my thoughts. I guess there were no thoughts for a moment. I was not able to figure out what just happened. So I just tried to keep the handle steady and reach home.

In a while my mind started with me. *"Dhruv do you realize what has happened?"*

"No I don't please help me."

"Dhruv you just got your dream fulfilled. You became an animator." That voice echoed in my ears and I again had my eyes filled with tears. I became an animator my dream came true. I couldn't believe myself so my excitement just double. I started calling everyone from the guitar class but first I went and told Aman. He was very happy for me. So that's it my book ends here. I became and animator what else I could expect. I got wanted I always wanted to be so maybe I should stop writing and you should maybe buy another book and throw this away if you are still reading this. All I wanted to write and end this book here but something else was planned for me.

So here it is, I went to meet Diya immediately and told her about becoming an animator. She congratulated me and was happy I fulfilled my dreams. She also gave me some money so that I could treat my friends. Later, I went home and told my father about getting the job into animation and becoming an animator. Well, I didn't get much of a reaction. Later I told him that I am going out with friends. Mom was out for some work. I called her and told her about getting the job. She congratulated me and asked me to come home early. I was all set to meet my guitar class friends. We had decided to meet near the class; I reached and found that Akshada and Aaliya had already reached.

"Okay Dhruv now quickly tell us what has happened?" Aaliya said.

"Hmm, I became and animator and got my first job into animation." I said being excited about it.

"Awesome!! So finally you achieved what you got. So tell me everything and did you tell this to Radhika?"

"PARTY!!!" Akshada shouted and later I told them everything about how I got the job. Soon Aman and Anup joined us. Aaliya told me to send a message to Radhika and let her know that this was because of her. It would make an effect she thought.

"Okay Dhruv quickly tell us the reason for calling us so urgently." Anup said as he parked his bike and came walking towards us.

"Wait let Sawaari come."

"She is not coming she had some work in office, she will call you later."

"Come-on dude tell us quickly." Aman said.

"What is it Aaliya? This better has to be good." Anup said it again.

"I have no clue I am still waiting for him to tell us."

"Okay now the others are not coming so please tell us." Aman couldn't wait any longer.

"Okay, the thing is…"

"Come straight to the point Dhruv." Anup interrupted again.

"Let him say what he wants to…" Aman said and they laughed.

"Should I say it or not?"

"Yes I guess we should let him talk, after all we are here to know what he has to say. Right Anup."

"Guys!!!! Will you let him talk? Dhruv you continue." Akshada shouted and finally I said it.

"I got a job into animation."

"What?" Anup looked at me with big eyes.

"Yes, I became an animator."

"WOOOHHHHHHHH!!! HHOOOOOOO!!!! PAAAARRTTTYYYY!!!!!!!" Aman and Anup shouted together as they hugged me. We all continued to shout like this for some time when Aaliya shouted.

"Guys what are you doing? We are on the streets."

"This is called excitement. It has to be big." Aman replied.

"You guys are crazy." Akshada said.

"So where's the party dude?" Anup said.

"Once I get my first salary we will go for a party." I said.

"Today at-least we could go for coffee." He said.

"No coffee I have to leave we will meet later; I came to meet Dhruv but can't stay for long. Congratulations Dhruv and wish you all the best." Aaliya said and so did Akshada. So we had to cancel the plan and as they left us, we waited for some time and later went home. As I reached home mom said, "So finally got what you always wanted."

"Yes." I said with a smile. Later logged into Facebook and wrote a message to Radhika and then went off to sleep.

Sunday 19th December' 2010, it was Vishal's birthday so I went to Somwar Peth in the morning after giving bath to my pets. He was out of town so spoke with him over the phone and later I went to meet Natasha. I told her about the job and we spoke for some time. Later, I went to meet Abhishek. He congratulated me for getting the job. I told him maybe if I would have concentrated before I would have been an animator long back. On which he just smiled and said it's better late than never. When I left from his place I again had many thoughts in my mind. It felt like that these thoughts would never end. I had to meet Sudhir sir so I went straight to Kothrud and called him. He was having lunch at his regular place.

"So Dhruv sir you are an animator now. How does it feel?"

"Right now I am feeling awesome sir. There was a time when I was not able to recall my dream and now that it has come true I have no words to express. Well tears rolled out the moment I realized I fulfilled my dream."

"That's good. So when are you joining?"

"I join from tomorrow. I am excited but a little nervous as well."

"You don't have to be nervous sir. I know you will do well just like you did here."

"Hmm, let's see. By the way sir how is everything going in NIIT? How is the new faculty?"

"Well, she is good and the best part is she is from our side. Your students did well in the college exams most of them passed with good marks."

"What about the couple are they still coming?"

"Oh! The husband wife, they have asked for refund as you are no longer teaching. They do not want to learn java from any other faculty."

"Hmm that's strange and well I am sure this has something to do with you." I said and he began to laugh.

"Sir why did you do this?"

"If she does something to you, she has to bear the consequences. They are still trying to find a faculty for networking."

"I guess they won't be able to find anyone so quickly."

"Yes, forget that I want a party and it has to be right now."

"Sudhir sir I don't have any cash."

"I don't know anything I want to eat ice-cream and you are treating me." He said and took me to the nearest ice-cream parlor. I had to pay for the ice-cream but it didn't matter that moment as I knew maybe I would never be able to meet this man again.

Monday 20th December 2010, first day of the job, I woke up early and got ready quickly. Aaliya dropped a message saying all the best for the first day. Whereas Aman called me to tease again.

"Hello Mr. Animator, how are you?"

"I am good, getting ready for office."

"Office!!! Kya baat hai… All the best."

"Thanks Aman."

"Ok listen I am leaving today and will return in a weak."

"Where are you going?"

"I told you, that I will be going home for some time."

"Oh yes, I forgot. So when are you leaving?"

"I will leave directly after office. Are you coming?"

"I am not sure what time I will come back or else I would. I will call you once I am free."

"Okay fine and all the best for the first day."

"Thanks." I said and later left home.

I reached office around 10.30am the time which I was told to come. I saw the office it wasn't big but was nicely setup. So talking about the people working, there were two modeling artist, two texturing and lighting artist, two rigging artist and two animators one of which was me. Everyone welcomed me in the team and later I was briefed about the project. I had to work upon lip-synced scenes which were around 25 and was given references for the same. I felt happy and excited at the same time. They told me about the sequence that needs to be followed. I started working and actually I was working upon lip-sync animation for the first time. I had the knowledge about it but had never implemented or got a chance to do so. But then I began the work and it turned out pretty well. In between I face some issue with the character so I had to ask the rigging artist to work upon it and make some changes. He began to work upon it and it took him almost an hour. That time I yelled upon myself for taking a nap.

We then left for break and later I started working. This time I concentrated and the first scene of 750 frames was complete. This was a real big achievement for me. I showed the work to sir and he liked the speed. He also told me some corrections and told me to work upon them the next day as it was late. I then checked the time, it was almost 8pm. The entire day I didn't look at the watch I was working and was happy with the output I gave. Once I left office Anushka called and said that she was not able to call before. She was all set in Bangalore and was about to begin her work. I told her about the first day in office and she was happy for me. "See now you don't even have to worry about the showreel now. You have job in animation."

Radhika called me and wanted to meet. I wanted to avoid her because I knew if I meet her I would end up spoiling my day. But then the very next thing I see is I am in front of her.

"How are you Dhruv?" She said.

"How would I be without you Radhika?" I said.

"You have to be happy Dhruv; now that you have become an animator I am happy for you."

"I am not happy Radhika even though I have fulfilled my dream. Somewhere in the corner of my heart I still miss you."

"It's of no use Dhruv now. I am getting married. I am engaged to…" She said and I woke up. It was a dream. I was worried what if this comes true I kept thinking when I heard another voice.

"Hello Dhruv…" It was the mirror guy I knew as I was alone in the room and it was again covered with fog.

"So now that Radhika is getting married, how do you feel?" He asked.

"How I feel? Are you crazy? I will go mad if such a thing happens in reality."

"So you do feel bad for not having her in your life."

"Does that even, I mean who are you by the way and why do you have to come up and who gave you the rights to say anything about me and Radhika?" I got angry as although I was not able to see a blurred image of the guy in the mirror of the cupboard.

"Okay let me tell you." He said and without taking any permission was able to convince me as he began to talk.

"I very well know what you state was and what you have been through all this time. But now I would like to talk about Radhika. I am sure you would listen to me."

"What is it?"

"You know just like you Radhika come to Pune with some dreams in her eyes. She never thought she would be living in Somwar Peth and someday will fall for a guy. She was crazy for you. She would do anything to make you happy but then she realized that she was only being treated as an alternative. You were going on with Mahi and when Mahi was around you would ignore Radhika completely. Somewhere that kept hurting her and she was not able to forget it even after you both were in a relation. I don't know whether it was her brother, her friend Adeena and your friend Parth to do anything with it but she found an alternate world with them and tried to be happy. She realized that being with you, she was not able to achieve her dreams and you would never treat her properly."

"But I was ready to change for her."

"I know Dhruv you were ready to do anything to make her smile and be happy. You gave her new friends but the fact of Mahi and the way you treated her she was never able to forget. Maybe, that's why she broke-up with you. So what's now...."

"Yes what now? Is she really getting married?"

"You still don't get it Dhruv. There is a whole new world out there for you to explore. You would be making new friends getting new jobs. You would work hard and sometimes you will be disappointed. But that's the way someday you will move on. I don't know if it will take few days, or months or years. But that day you will realize that this had to happen to make you the man you are." He said and I was not able to recall what he said after this. It sounded as if his voice was fading and something else was coming on my ears. It was a song. Oh yes the song I would always like to and wakeup. He did tell me Dhruv your alarm is ringing you need to wake up and I jumped out of bed.

I was clueless as what happened to me all this time I was dreaming. I was trying to recall everything I saw in the dream. Radhika getting engaged, Oh! That's horrible I can't even imagine this. And I did see someone in the mirror in a suit I guess. Who was that guy? I kept thinking but didn't utter a word. I got ready, took a shower and had breakfast. I turned on the music on my computer the same song I had been listening many time. I didn't pay attention to it until the last words came across my ears.

Ab agar tum milo toh....
Itna yakeen hai.
Has denge hum toh,
ab rona nahi hai...!

I turned off the computer after the song was over and went downstairs. Mom tried to talk with me to check what time I will be back home from office. I had no answer to it. I was only trying to recall the dream. Somehow I got into my senses and told her that I might be late just like today as there's a lot of work. I went downstairs started my bike and so did my thoughts I was able to recall the entire dream and what he said to me.

"Radhika was the best thing that ever happened to you and won't be able to forget her. She will always be in your heart. Make her sweet memories as a weapon for success. Don't let yourself down. She loved you; maybe she still does but had to let you go. Maybe you would need more time. Work upon the showreel, the book you might want to write about Radhika and try to complete it someday."

I was trying to say it to myself, maybe I would need another year and I will forget her. Maybe more I would never be able to forget her. She was there, she is there and maybe she will still be there somewhere in the corner of my heart. I knew I can never forget her. Someday maybe, things will be fine once again. My father would realize that Diya needs to be with her family. She was in love and there was nothing she did wrong. She only followed her heart. I did try the same but maybe it was late.

I was almost there to reach office and wanted to finish what the mirror guy said to me I close my eyes for a moment and tried to listen as I slow downed my bike. He told me to wake up and when I did saw the mirror guy was no one else. It was me, I saw myself in the mirror wearing the tie and in the suit. I guess somewhere some part of me knows I will make it to there. So the things I said to myself will always help me. Thank you God, for giving me that ability to fight back and win all the hearts.

"Life will not always be easy. You will see bad days along with the good ones.

People will come and go. You have to make your heart strong.
Accept what you get and strive to improve every day.
*Life is what you want to see as there are and there will, always be **more dreams**
to come...!*

*****

What they had to say...
Few Friends from Convergys:

- **My Tech Lead -** A cute little boy who has just come out in a city to fulfill his dreams and is full of talent and creativity.
- **Gaurav -** Someone who is very dedicated towards his girlfriends.
- **Vishal -** Needs to concentrate more on work rather than girls, although very talented guy.
- **Abhi -** Chocolate boy of our team
- **Riya –** Dhruv... my sweetheart (Oh! He would be in clouds now). A great friend with lots of innovative ideas. I wish him all the best in life.

My girlfriends:

- **Mahi –** You are nice, lovable, cute, charming, handsome and not least but an idiot friend of mine. You will always be in my heart.
- **Radhika –** The most hard working, down-to-earth person I have ever met.

My NIIT Students:

- The first impression I had about you is that you will be very lively and jolly and it turned out to be quiet correct I guess. You are very creative, have a great sense of humor and are always carrying a smile on your face. And you are a good show I'm sure behind your smile there's lot of hardship and sufferings. Best of luck with your life.
- You are caring; you are a writer that was unexpected (Sorry!!!). I am sure you would be a better friend than just being Sir.
- You are friendly and a great person. I adore you not because of your knowledge but your behavior also. Be successful in life.
- You are friendly and a sweet person. Good looking and handsome. You have a rocking character and the best teacher of my life.

Not to forget her:

Anushka – A very, very, very nice friend and the most important thing which I like about you is your determination towards your work. And you know the most amazing thing about you is the work you do with you full determination results into a perfect output... Keep rocking dude!!!

376

Characters of the book:

Dhruv- Well you would find out for yourself. The one who calls him innocent has a lot to learn.

Dhruv's Family:

- **Diya** – Dhruv's elder sister with whom he shares everything.
- **Krish** – Dhruv's younger brother
- **Sana, Shivam and Pal** – Dhruv's cousins

Dhruv's Friends:

- **Natasha** – Dhruv's childhood friend also his neighbor.
- **Vishal** - Dhruv's childhood friend who stays nearby.
- **Abhishek** – Dhruv's college friend who stays nearby.
- **Suresh, Enosh and Ajit** – College friends
- **Akash** – Dhruv's school friend.

At Convergys:

- **Amar** – A friend at Convergys who helps Dhruv boost up his confidence.
- **Ashwin and Neeraj** – Dhruv's friend he never wants to loose.
- **Riya** – The dream come true girl who means a lot to Dhruv.
- **Abhi** – Riya's friend and Dhruv's team-mate.
- **Nishant** – Dhruv's team leader.
- **Gaurav Dubey**- The most second member of his team.
- **Saurav** – Another team-mate.
- **Parth** – Teammate and later a real good friend.
- **Vishal** – Team-mate.
- **Gaurav Shekhawat**- Operations manager.

Girls from the Hostel:

- **Jiya** – The girl Dhruv gets along easily.
- **Mahi** - Dhruv's first girlfriend.
- **Radhika** – Dhruv's best friend and later his girlfriend.
- **Shreya** – Girl who came along with Radhika.
- **Devika** – A girl who addresses Dhruv as Bhaiya (brother).

- **Mentos** – Devika's room-mate.
- **Pooja** - Mahi's room-mate and later a friend of Dhruv.
- **Mona** – New roommate after Mahi left.

Friends from the Guitar Class:

- **Prasad** – First friend at the guitar class.
- **Preeti** – One who has just cleared her 10th.
- **Harsh** – One who is always behind Preeti.
- **Aman** – Dhruv's friend who is ready to do anything. The next would be CA.
- **Aaliya**- The girl in the team because of Prasad but a good friend.
- **Akshada** - The new girl introduced by Preeti.
- **Sam and Avni** - The one's with whom Dhruv never had any real conversation but were still friends.
- **Anup and Sawaari** – The most talked guys and another CA from the group.
- **Ajunkya** – The new guitarist who owns an electric guitar.
- **Sahil** – Radhika's classmate who is in love with her.
- **Adeena** – Radhika's best friend and the girl Dhruv hates the most.
- **Dhaval** – Radhika's brother in Mumbai.

Friends from Ventura:

- **Ajay** – The first day friend at the new office.
- **Vruhika, Madhavi and Trupti** – A girl who introduces herself to Dhruv and later comes his friend, the other two join her along.
- **Mridula** – The beautiful girl who stays nearby Dhruv's new home.

Friends from MAAC:

- **Pramod** – The only friend when Dhruv is unable to stays for long hours in office.
- **Anuksha** – The most sensible girl and only friend who helps Dhruv to get out of his bad phase.
- **Palak** – The beautiful girl.
- **Neha** – Always a late-comer at class.
- **Saket, Rahul, Ketan** – Friends from MAAC who would be together while having breakfast.

NIIT:

Sudhir Sir- The mentor and a very good friend with a bad past.
Neha – Counselor at NIIT, also a good friend of Krish.
Pragati, Gayatri – Students at NIIT.

Printed in the United States
By Bookmasters